AN
UNFORGIVING
PLACE

Also available by Claire Kells

Girl Underwater

The National Parks Mysteries

Vanishing Edge

AN UNFORGIVING PLACE

A NATIONAL PARKS MYSTERY

CLAIRE KELLS

CROOKED
LANE

NEW YORK

Published in the United States by Crooked Lane Books, an imprint of The Quick Brown Fox & Company LLC.

Crooked Lane Books and its logo are trademarks of The Quick Brown Fox & Company LLC.

Library of Congress Catalog-in-Publication data available upon request.

ISBN (hardcover): 978-1-63910-123-8
ISBN (ebook): 978-1-63910-124-5

Cover design by Nicole Lecht

Printed in the United States.

www.crookedlanebooks.com

Crooked Lane Books
34 West 27th St., 10th Floor
New York, NY 10001

First Edition: November 2022

10 9 8 7 6 5 4 3 2 1

For my parents, who instilled in me a love of mysteries

PROLOGUE

For Kelsey Greer, rock bottom was the day she walked out of the Spruce Street Fertility Clinic with an overdue bill in one hand and a crinkled ultrasound photo in the other. The sobs in her throat were choking her, mocking her. When Tim embraced her, his familiar arms felt like lead on her shoulders. This burden was hers to bear, but maybe it shouldn't have been.

They climbed into the back seat, which smelled faintly of fried food. Kelsey dropped her gaze to the faded gray carpet in the footwell. She felt a tear roll down her cheek. She was so damn tired of crying. More than that, she was tired of feeling like a failure when the doctor had made it clear that, well, she wasn't. Tim was the one with the issue.

He just refused to admit it.

It was selfish, she knew—this stubborn fixation on bearing her own child. But Kelsey had confronted death before, starting at the age of six, when she was diagnosed with a rare form of leukemia. The chemo had banished the cancer, but Kelsey had spent most of her life since then fearing its return. The mental burden of almost dying didn't come until much later.

Her leukemia was almost thirty years behind her now, but as she endured the failures of trying to conceive, she once again felt like she was living on borrowed time. The only way to escape the burden of her own mortality was to have a child of her own, to give life to *someone with a clean slate. In her heart, she really believed this to be true.*

Of course, Tim felt differently. He wanted to be a dad for the same reason most men did, she supposed: to have a playmate, a buddy, a coachable kid. Sometimes Kelsey thought about what would happen if they did have a child—would her husband take on the responsibility of being a single father? Kelsey had entertained adoption more than once, but in her darkest moments, she often wondered if he'd stand by a child that wasn't his. He had told her before they married that he didn't need to be a dad, but if they had a kid, he'd raise it and do his best. He'd do it for her.

Well, those days of "casually trying" had long since passed. At some point, it had to end.

What if that day had come?

The Uber dropped them off at their compact brick house on a tree-lined street in South Jersey. It was drizzling, the remnants of a summer hurricane. To afford the IVF treatments, Kelsey and Tim had taken out a second mortgage on their house, knowing that one day they would be grateful they'd stayed in this perfect little neighborhood. But at that moment, it didn't feel perfect at all. It felt vindictive, as a herd of elementary school–age children tore down the street on their way to the pool.

"What if . . ." Kelsey trailed off as she nibbled on her cuticles. Tim was not going to like having this conversation again.

"What if what?"

"What if we tried a sperm donor—"

"No," he said. "No. You know I draw the line there. It wouldn't be my child, Kelsey. It wouldn't be fair to anyone."

"I know, but—"

"They said IVF can work, Kelsey. We should just stick with what we know."

His face tightened with the muscle memory of a thousand arguments. Kelsey hated talking about his "sperm issue," but she also wished he'd at least come around and acknowledge it existed. Tim was the youngest of eight. Every time she saw his parents, she felt like they were judging her—like they viewed her as a failed biological vessel of their future grandchildren. After all, they knew about her cancer and the fact that the chemotherapy all those years ago could have impacted her fertility. It was easier for them to blame her.

"Blame" was the wrong word, Kelsey knew. Not just the wrong word, but a dangerous one. If she kept blaming Tim for their failure to be parents, those feelings would eventually deteriorate into resentment. She had to let it go.

As they walked inside the house, Kelsey tried her best to look on the bright side. She was a cancer survivor, after all, and like most cancer survivors, she didn't wake up every morning thinking about what she didn't have. On her good days, she saw every day as a gift—something ninety percent of people diagnosed with her type of cancer never got. She had beaten the odds. It was time to be thankful for what she had.

The problem was, becoming a mother was her lifelong dream, and she couldn't just let it go. It was the cancer, the loss of her dad, the deep-seated yearning to be a parent—all of it made her feel like having a child of her own would somehow soften the sharper edges in her past, the sting of grief and loss. It was all she could think about.

While Tim went to hop on a Zoom call—he'd missed so much work for these appointments that his boss was always threatening to fire him—Kelsey went into the bathroom with her computer and sat on the edge of the tub. This tiny little room was the only place she could go to seal herself off from the rest of the world. Tim didn't even use this bathroom. He preferred the one with the updated shower and the faucet that didn't leak.

Although a hot bath probably would have served her better, Kelsey checked all of the websites she went to daily—infertility forums, cancer survivor forums, blogs, social media. She went through her emails, her direct messages . . .

And saw something on Twitter—a direct message from a user she vaguely recognized. Kelsey rarely logged onto Twitter since she didn't tweet and had no followers except a couple of bots. She was a consumer, not a user—or at least, that's how she described herself when Tim caught her online. She lurked on Twitter and a half dozen other social media platforms looking for help, support, a miracle—anything that might help her convince Tim to try sperm donation. Over the years, she couldn't even remember all the leads she'd tracked down, all the quacks she'd interacted with. This message was probably from one of them.

The user's name was @pittailiniq, which she assumed was a random assortment of letters until she typed the word into Google. Pittailiniq was the Inuit word for pregnancy taboos—practices and behaviors meant to inform a healthy pregnancy and birth. Kelsey, heart pounding, opened the message, which read:

67°42'01.1"N 150°56'47.3"W. exp. July 2

It felt like spam, especially since the username had no public tweets associated with its account. But when Kelsey typed the coordinates into Google, she immediately dismissed that possibility. The coordinates took her to a dropped pin in northern Alaska. Her heart fluttered.

According to internet lore, a man named Zane Reynolds was up in the arctic somewhere, recruiting infertile couples to his "retreat" and sending them home pregnant. Some women who shared her predicament were among them. Unfortunately, Reynolds had no online footprint except for his cryptic social media accounts.

Kelsey had tried, of course, to learn everything she could about him. The closest she'd gotten was a Word document containing a collection of old blog posts authored by a woman named Amy Shortbeck, who had chronicled her whole fertility journey before abruptly taking down her website three years ago with no explanation.

Later, though, Amy had turned up on Instagram—same name, different vibe. This time, Amy's focus was on her young daughter. The only reason Kelsey had even heard about Amy's new account was that the online infertility community couldn't stop speculating about one Instagram post in particular. The caption read: My sweet Pinga Koyukuk—light of my life, girl of my dreams. *The accompanying photo was of a cherubic baby girl clutching a stuffed lamb.*

It wasn't long before some of the women on those online forums started talking about going to Alaska, desperate to unravel the truth surrounding Amy Shortbeck's baby and the forces that had made her a reality. One woman—whose husband was a private investigator—actually tracked down Zane Reynolds to an area near the Koyukuk River. The @pittailiniq Twitter user didn't have a photo associated with the account, but the PI had amassed other clues to identify him. He concluded that Reynolds was operating a "fertility group" of some sort in the Gates of the Arctic National Park—and that, yes, he seemed to be targeting couples with "reluctant male infertility," as he called it.

That was two years ago, and now, seeing this message in her inbox, Kelsey's first instinct was to question it. She'd fallen for scams before—herbs and medicinals and creams, the psychics and the naturopaths, the zealots and outright criminals. But Amy Shortbeck was a real person, and so was her baby. Her infertility journey, too, was real—like Kelsey, she was a cancer survivor. It was how Kelsey had found her blog in the first place. So for a woman like Amy Shortbeck to travel to Alaska, delete her blog, and then turn up a year later with a baby in her arms—the whole thing was stranger than fiction. And that's why it had to be true.

There was, of course, one small caveat to this hopeful story. Amy Shortbeck had made no mention of her husband in any of her social media posts since her daughter was born. Had her Alaskan sojourn ended their marriage for good? What, exactly, were Reynolds' "miraculous" methods? Kelsey tried not to think too much about that for the time being.

She went back to the message. What did "exp. July 2" mean? Kelsey figured "exp." was an abbreviation for "expires," which filled her with dread. Today was June 29th. If the coordinates expired on 11:59 PM on July 2nd, that gave her less than three days to get to some remote outpost in Alaska. She'd have to be on a plane tomorrow to have any hope of getting there in time, and that was assuming the weather cooperated.

Tim would never go for it. He was on the verge of losing his job—and besides, he would never go for something that put the onus on him. If she went to him with this Twitter message, he'd resent her for even bringing it up. Because it was crazy; of course it was crazy. To hop on the first plane to Alaska—Alaska, for God's sake!—and run off to some middle-of-nowhere spot in one of the remotest parts of the continent was quite simply the definition of insanity. Forget the expense—they could die. Kelsey had never been outside of the tristate area, had never even seen a real mountain. She didn't know the first thing about camping either.

But her gut told her that this was it—this was her path to motherhood. It would be natural too—an escape from the doctor's offices and procedures and miserable fertility treatments. Maybe Zane Reynolds understood men like Tim in ways Kelsey did not. After all, she was never going to convince him that he had a sperm problem. Even the experts couldn't convince him of that. But maybe Zane Reynolds could.

At the very least, it would be a new beginning for them, a chance to start over. Just her and Tim and the wilderness, and Zane Reynolds too, although Kelsey couldn't prove that these coordinates had come from him. She knew they had, though. She could feel it in her gut.

For the first time in months—years, even—she felt a strange emotion surge inside of her.

Hope.

CHAPTER

1

THE OLIVE GARDEN was a far cry from my current assignment in Denali National Park, but I was trying to make the
best of it. The salad was crisp, the breadsticks fresh. I liked the
cheerful colors of the booths and bicycle-themed wall art.

But for the most part, my sojourn into the Anchorage sub-
urbs had been a disaster. The snot-nosed toddler in the booth
behind me kept tugging on my hair. Our waiter had dropped a
tray of sodas on my lap. And my date—well, what could I say
about Orin? He was a dentist who didn't believe in modern anes-
thesia. I was starting to get a bad vibe.

Then the gods smiled upon me: my cell phone rang.

Orin frowned as he watched me reach into my pocket. "Are
you going to get that?"

"Sorry." I glanced at the screen. On the display was a caller
ID that brought mixed emotions: Ray Eskill. I could have sworn
I'd filled out all the proper paperwork and sent all the necessary emails to confirm that I was, in fact, cleared to take vacation during my current assignment at the Investigative Services
Branch, but my superior wasn't the type to care about that sort
of thing. He didn't really believe in vacation either.

Ever since my return from medical leave, I'd done all I
could to get back into my groove—reviewing case reports, taking online classes, adhering to a physical therapy schedule that

bordered on obsessive—but it still felt like I'd lost a step. My last case in Sequoia had ended with a satisfactory result from an investigative perspective, but from a personal one, not so much. The bullet in my shoulder had thrown me for a loop, to say the least. I was still rattled by that whole debacle. So far, my tenure in Alaska hadn't brought nearly as much drama as Sequoia had, but I kept waiting for the other shoe to drop. Seeing Ray's name on the display now, I wondered if that time had come.

I moved the phone away from my ear and said to Orin, "Do you mind if I take this? It's my boss."

"Right now?"

"He only calls if it's an emergency."

Orin frowned. "Okay, I guess."

I went outside and walked around the corner of the building. Once the coast was clear, I hit the redial button. Ray picked up immediately.

"Harland?" His voice was gruff. "What are you up to?"

"Hello, sir. I'm . . . uh . . ." I looked around the parking lot. "Nothing."

"It's Saturday night. You must be up to *something*."

I cleared my throat. "Is there something I can do for you, sir?"

"Look, I know you're on vacation, but I've got a time-sensitive issue here. The chief ranger in Gates of the Arctic found two bodies on a river up there."

"Gates of the Arctic?" Even after a few months in Alaska, I hadn't yet seen the state's second-largest national park. "Has ISB ever worked a case up there?"

"Not in recent memory. But he says he's got two victims on the Alatna River, and he wants our help—thinks it looks suspicious."

The truth was, I had only a passing knowledge of Gates of the Arctic National Park, which was above the Arctic Circle and, therefore, many miles off the grid. It was the remotest and least-visited national park in the United States, with about ten thousand visitors each year. Yosemite, in contrast, averaged between four and five million. It was hard to imagine a murder in place that saw so little human activity.

"What else did the chief ranger tell you?" I asked.

"Not much. He's got their wildlife biologist up there too. He says there's evidence of some wolf activity at the scene, but he's never had a wolf-on-human attack in the park, that he's aware of. Bears, sure, but not wolves."

"The wildlife biologist should be able to sort that out, though."

Ray grunted. "There's more to it than that—something about where the victims were found, the condition they were in. But, look, his sat phone connection was cutting in and out, and I missed most of what he was telling me. All I can say for sure is that he wanted somebody from ISB to come up and have a look, ASAP."

I couldn't help but think about my older sister, Margo, who was expecting me in Seattle tomorrow night to help with the preparations for her fortieth birthday party next weekend. Our sisters were flying in, too, and I hated letting her down. After all, it was Margo who had put me on a path to becoming a federal investigator.

However, if a seasoned ranger was calling us from a scarcely visited park, it meant he really needed help. The chief rangers in these remote parks saw their fair share of lost hikers and hypothermia, but they didn't call ISB for things like that. It was only in the event of a possible crime that they requested our assistance.

Maybe I could still make this work. Assuming Ray found me a ride up there, I could fly to Gates of the Arctic tomorrow, have a look around, and be in Seattle by next weekend. *Margo will understand,* I reasoned, even though I knew she probably wouldn't.

"Are the rangers up there still on the scene?" I asked.

Ray coughed loudly into the phone; he always seemed to be fighting a cold or an asthma attack of some kind. "Yup. They're waiting on you."

In a way, this was welcome news. I usually arrived on the scene long after Mother Nature had destroyed most of the evidence, which made it that much harder to sort out what had happened. Knowing the bodies were still there gave me hope of cracking this case pretty quickly.

"I'm in Anchorage," I said. "And Hux is still in Denali. I can't get up there till tomorrow at the earliest."

"I figured. If you're picking up Hux first, then the fastest way to get there is a charter from Fairbanks to Bettles. There's an outfitter in Bettles that can get you a bush plane to the Alatna River, or pretty close."

"Hux is on administrative leave this week."

Ray barked a laugh. "Tell him he gets a pass."

"Sir, he needs it for his training—"

"Give him an extension, then," Ray said, a note of sarcasm in his voice.

I looked around, at the pickup trucks and SUVs and mini-vans. Teenagers loitered in intimate groups, entranced by their cell phones. Young moms and dads wrestled their children into strollers. An old guy popped the hood of his truck and unleashed a slew of obscenities that would've made any sailor blush.

I felt a little out of place here, but then again, I felt out of place just about everywhere. I was a thirty-three-year-old, wid-owed, female federal agent specializing in wilderness crimes. There weren't many of me, that was for sure.

"So, I'm canceling my vacation, then," I said, hoping that my resigned tone made him feel a *tiny* bit guilty about it.

"Nah," he said. "I bet you can wrap this up in a couple days."

"Not if it's a double homicide," I said.

"It's probably just the usual—two amateur hikers who got in over their heads and died. Just go up there and see if you can help the chief out."

I peeled my hand away from my face and stole a glance inside the restaurant. Orin was getting antsy, scanning the aisles as he downed another Coke. Our eyes met through the window. He mouthed, "I'm hungry," while rubbing his stomach, which was something Hux never would have done—not in public anyway. When Hux was hungry, he solved the problem by getting him-self something to eat. I wondered if he was eating over a campfire somewhere right now. When I'd left Denali, I hadn't bothered to ask him what his plans were for the weekend.

"I'll need to make sure Hux is on board," I said.

"Of course he's on board—he's your direct report. Just make sure he's at the Fairbanks Airport by seven AM tomorrow."

"That early?"

"Yup. Just got a text confirming it with the pilot. I'll work on the bush plane out of Bettles. In any case, I want an update by tomorrow afternoon."

"Yes, sir."

"There's one more thing."

"What's that?"

"Search and Rescue is actually up in that park right now, looking for two hikers who were reported missing by a family member a week ago. I'm told they got to Alaska on July second, went off somewhere near Boreal Mountain, and haven't been seen since."

I glanced at the date on my cell phone. "That's almost a month ago now. Why did the family member wait so long?"

"Like I said, I don't have a whole lotta details."

"So is it them?"

Ray cleared his throat with a wet cough. "The chief ranger couldn't make the ID—he thinks it might be, though. You want the names of the missing hikers?"

"Sure."

"It's Timothy and Kelsey Greer. I'm waiting on a copy of the missing persons report, but you might get there before I can get my hands on it." He coughed into the phone again. "I've got another call coming in. Send me an update when you're on the ground up there."

He hung up before I could get another word in. Ray always had some other crisis to deal with, or at least he liked me to think he did.

I walked back inside the restaurant. Orin was watching something on his phone—looked like a YouTube video about stamps. The menus were gone, and he'd ditched his Coke for a beer. He caught my eyes when I sat down.

"Hey," I said. "Sorry about that."

He smiled at me, but there was a hint of judgment behind it. "No problem."

"Did you order?" I was a little stumped by the missing menus, since he couldn't possibly have known what I liked. We'd only been on three dates, and none of them had entailed a meal, which gave me the feeling he was a little cheap.

"Just did," he said. "I got you the eggplant parm."

"Oh."

"You're a vegetarian, right?"

"No." I studied his face for a beat. "Are you?"

"Pescatarian."

I sipped the lemonade Orin had ordered for me—an odd choice, but I decided not to ask why he'd gotten me a nonalcoholic beverage while he indulged in a pint of beer.

"I, um . . . I actually have to go," I said.

"Oh." He put his beer down. "A work thing?"

"Yeah," I said. "Feel free to take my eggplant to go. Have it tomorrow for lunch or something." I reached into my pocket for a twenty-dollar bill and put it on the table. "Here. Take this. I really am sorry."

"It's, um, not a problem," he said, pocketing the twenty with such speed it made my head spin. "Can I call you later?"

"No, that's all right," I said. "I don't think it's going to work out."

"Are you serious? Why—?"

"Take care, Orin."

I grabbed my jacket and walked out of the restaurant, regretting the abruptness of the "breakup" but feeling delightfully unencumbered once I was outside. *Christ, that was rude,* I thought to myself. But life was short, and I hated wasting time on relationships that weren't going to pan out anyway. At times like these, I wondered why I bothered at all.

I took out my phone and scanned through my recent calls. On the list were Orin, Ray, a couple calls from my mom, and Hux. In my contact list, he appeared under his real name: Ferdinand Huxley. He despised it, of course, but it made me smile every time I saw his given name in all its formal glory.

I hit the call button and waited for it to go straight to voicemail. None of the parks out here had cell service, so I didn't actually expect his phone to be on. Hux spent all of his free time exploring Denali and nearby areas because he didn't want to miss an opportunity before our assignment ended in October. As for me, well, I didn't mind sleeping in a real bed now and then.

This time, his phone *did* ring. He picked up right away.

"Hey," he said. I could picture his smile. "Aren't you supposed to be in Seattle?"

"Change of plans," I said. "Any chance you're available for a trip to Gates of the Arctic tomorrow?"

"Are you serious?" His excitement came through loud and clear in his voice. Hux wasn't the type to hide his feelings. "Something big happening up there?"

"Could be," I said. "A ranger found two bodies on the Alatna River. The chief thinks something's off and wants our help."

"Just tell me where to be."

"I'll pick you up on my way to Fairbanks. Bring a week's worth of gear and a fully-charged cell phone for taking photos. You've got that add-on for your phone?"

"Yes, ma'am," he said cheerfully. Hux was always happy to indulge in modern technology. In a place like Chicago, you could bring a whole van's worth of forensic technology, but where we were going, the most important thing was packing light.

"Where are you right now?"

"Closest town to me is Cantwell. I can be there in an hour."

"No rush. I've got to pack up and check out of my hotel."

"The Four Seasons?"

I snickered at Hux's familiar joke. "Hampton Inn."

"I don't know why you put yourself through the whole hotel experience," he said. "Is it the free cookies at tea time?"

I laughed. "You take what you can get in this gig."

"I assume this means I get a pass on my online modules?"

I could hear the giddiness in his voice. "We'll talk about it."

After we hung up, I slipped my phone back into my pocket and tilted my face toward the sky. To my surprise, it wasn't disappointment I felt at giving up the first part of my vacation, but excitement. Even my nerves had seemed to settle a little bit. Maybe it was Hux, who was always good-natured and ready for adventure. Or it could have been the change of pace, since I'd spent most of my time in Alaska ensuring that historical artifacts in national parks were treated with the proper care and attention. I missed the thrill of the chase, the allure of the unknown.

With Hux as my partner, anything could happen.

2

AFTER A STOPOVER at my hotel, I hit the road just after ten PM. The blue sky gleamed gold with the setting sun, but it would be another hour before darkness descended. I was a little nervous about the long and torturous drive up Route 3, which cut through the towns on the outskirts of Denali before heading east toward Fairbanks, a city I'd never been to.

I texted Margo to let her know I had to delay my arrival by a few days. After some thought, I added a bit about a "work emergency." I put my phone away before she could respond.

Of my three sisters, Margo was the most like me—a straight shooter to the core, with no time or patience for "feelings." For years, Margo had worked as a county prosecutor in Seattle, but after her third kid was born, she had transitioned to family law. I firmly believed that only a tiny subset of the population had the stomach for that kind of work, but Margo was one of them.

Almost instantaneously, my phone chimed with a new message. Margo was a lightning-fast responder, whereas I was the slow, thoughtful type. Even so, she expected quick answers from everybody. This time, I had no excuse.

They don't pay you enough to cancel your vacation, she had written.

I replied via Siri: *I don't do this for the money.*

I know you don't. You do it for the hot, sweaty park rangers. You still working with that Navy SEAL?

I decided to sit tight for a minute before firing off another reply. The last thing I wanted to do was admit to Margo that I'd recruited Hux to work with me in Alaska. After all, we'd only known each other for a little over a year. He'd joined me on my first big case in Sequoia almost by accident, but he'd proved his worth and then some during those hard miles on mountainous terrain. He had a stellar emotional IQ and good instincts, not to mention otherworldly stamina. And, yes, he was quite handsome and, at times, sweaty. I couldn't deny any of this to Margo.

Margo could sniff a lie from a mile away. In fact, Margo knew Hux was in Alaska because she'd called ISB headquarters herself to inquire about his status. On the one hand, she was curious, since the guy had literally saved my life by administering first aid when our prime suspect, feeling cornered, had shot me in the shoulder. On the other hand, she hadn't believed me when I'd told her earlier that summer that I had no idea what Ferdinand Huxley was up to.

Margo probably assumed that I was weirdly attached to the park ranger, who had all but ensured a positive resolution in the Sequoia case. *Well,* I thought, *I'm* not *attached. I'm grateful, but not attached.*

Margo wasn't entirely wrong to worry about my lifestyle, though. My social circle had shrunk to the size of a pinhead since joining ISB. I kept in touch with a few friends from the bureau, but that was about it. I lived a nomadic lifestyle, renting condos in small wilderness towns, based on whatever geographic region I was assigned to. Could I live that way indefinitely? Better yet, did I *want* to live that way? I'd met loners of all sorts during my Alaska assignment, and in some ways I envied their lack of constraints. In other ways, though—well, it made me feel sad, the prospect of never having a place to call home. Even Hux had that: his cabin in Sequoia.

I drove in a brief, hazy darkness on a road known for its broad shoulders and expansive scenery, not that I could see much of it. Night was a fleeting thing this time of year. The sun set around midnight and rose just a couple of hours later. In another few weeks, however, days and nights would start to feel like separate entities again, which was something I missed about the lower forty-eight. After our assignment ended, I hoped to head south again.

At just past two AM, I pulled into the parking lot of a little sandwich shop in Cantwell called Jam Jam's Spot. It was one of several meet-up places Hux and I had agreed on months ago, back when our assignment in Denali began. But of course it was all closed up at this hour, the lot empty except for the owner's car out back.

Almost as soon as I parked the truck, I watched Hux stride across the lot on foot with my Australian shepherd mix, Ollie, in tow. Hux wore his usual olive-green backpack on his shoulders, a gray beanie on his head. Because he was off-duty, he wasn't wearing his usual Park Service duds, but I knew he'd change into them before we got on the plane to Bettles. For now, though, he was making do with dark hiking pants and a light jacket.

I took a shaky breath. No idea why it shook, but it did. *Dammit.* He looked good—some stubble on his jaw, an easy smile on his face. Even though it had only been a few days since we'd wrapped up our last case in Denali—an aggravated assault charge—I realized, on seeing his familiar grin, that I'd missed him a little bit.

I rolled down the passenger side window.

"Hey," I said.

"Hey, stranger." He put his arms on the doorframe and poked his head inside the window. Ollie pranced around in circles with his tongue lolling. I tried once more to remember why I'd decided that jetting off to Seattle without him was a good idea. Hux was always happy to take him, but I hated leaving my dog behind. It felt like I was abandoning a loyal friend.

I looked around the parking lot. It was still dark out, hardly any lights on in Cantwell, but I was used to working with Hux after hours. Being a federal investigator with ISB wasn't a nine-to-five job, and we both liked it that way. "How'd you get here?" I asked him.

"I had a friend drop me off."

I quirked an eyebrow at him, catching myself before I could ask who this "friend" was. I wasn't about to grill him for details about his personal life. That was a line that we didn't cross.

"You want me to drive?" he asked.

"You don't mind?"

"Nope. Not at all."

A year ago, I would have scoffed at the suggestion, but our relationship had evolved quite a bit since then. I was grateful for the reprieve from driving on such dark, monotonous roads. Hux could go on four hours' sleep like it was no problem at all. I couldn't. My brain turned to mush; my mood tanked. I was miserable company when sleep deprivation set in.

It felt like I'd just nodded off when I woke to a gentle jab from Hux's elbow. It wasn't yet six AM, but dawn was on the horizon, a soft amber light that illuminated Fairbanks's muted skyline.

"We're early," I said.

"Yup," he said. "Hungry?"

"I could eat."

He pointed to a brightly lit café just ahead. "How about that place over there?"

I rubbed my eyes in the hopes of seeing it a little better. An amateur painting of a pancake filled one of the windows, and a greasy burger occupied another. This was definitely Hux's kind of place. He didn't like desserts, but when it came to carbs, the guy was a bottomless pit.

The parking lot was full, which was always a good sign. Ollie stayed in the truck, but I promised him some leftovers. Hux walked with a spring in his step toward the entrance.

We found a booth in the back, right under a faded photograph of a frozen tundra cast in the shadow of a hulking mountain. Hux ordered his usual: a double stack of pancakes. I was hungry after a chaotic night of packing and traveling, so I splurged for the Fairbanks Special: a conglomeration of eggs, sausage, and homemade bread. For a jolt of caffeine, I ordered a hot tea.

"So bring me up to speed." Hux drank from his tall glass of ice water. "What are we dealing with here?"

"I don't know a whole lot," I said, relieved that Hux didn't seem interested in my botched weekend in Anchorage—or at least was just too polite to ask me about it. "Ray got a call from the chief ranger about two bodies that turned up on the Alatna River."

"Huh. Near Arrigetch Peaks?"

I felt my eyebrow go up. "You know the area?"

"I, well—I've never actually been there, but I've seen it on the map."

"Is there anything you *haven't* seen on a map?"

"You know me, Harland," he said. "If I'm not tracking someone, I'm thinking about how I *would* track someone. And Gates is a real ballbuster."

"It does seem that way." I shifted my weight a bit on the booth's stiff cushion. "It's eight million acres with not a road to be found."

"I hear there are some game trails, though."

"Well, I'm hoping we won't have to track anyone through the park. Search and rescue was actually looking for two missing hikers in a different area when these bodies turned up; it's looking like this could be them, unfortunately."

He took another swig of his water. "What else?"

"The two missing hikers are named Tim and Kelsey Greer. They were last seen near Boreal Mountain—"

"Wait, Boreal Mountain?"

"Why? You know that one, too?"

"Not personally, but I do know it's nowhere near the Alatna River."

I rubbed my temples while trying to convince myself that it was no big deal that I didn't already know this. In my frantic rush to get to Fairbanks, I hadn't had time to study a map. Hux didn't have to study a map. He just kind of knew these things.

The waiter came by to top off our drinks, but Hux looked disappointed that the food hadn't yet arrived. I could tell he was ravenous. "What do we know about the Greers?" he asked.

I took out my cell phone, thinking there was no way in hell a place like this would have Wi-Fi or good cell service, but I was wrong on both counts. It only took a few seconds for me to pull up my email and see the latest message from Ray. He had attached a copy of the missing persons report for the Greers that had been filed in New Jersey.

I summarized the details for Hux. "They flew into Fairbanks on the first of July and made a stop at Bettles Outfitters on July second." I opened the attachment. "Here's a photo of the Greers." I clicked on a JPEG and rotated my phone so Hux could see the screen. Kelsey was small-boned and petite, with delicate features and wide-set blue eyes. Her smile was coy, as if she was trying to hide something from the photographer. Tim, on the other hand, was barrel-chested and brash. His gregarious grin outshone Kelsey's by a mile.

Hux remarked, "The husband here—he's a stocky fella."

"He used to play football, apparently. Penn State for two years."

"Huh," he said. "Impressive for a guy his size. He can't be more than five-nine." He scrutinized the photo for a beat. "She looks—hmm, how do I say this? Dainty." Hux glanced at the photo again as he took out his notepad and jotted something down. "How recent is this picture?"

"Hopefully pretty recent. It's the only one we've got."

He stopped writing and looked up. "So, is SAR still searching near Boreal Mountain?"

"I believe so. The chief ranger will give us the full update when we get there."

Hux turned his head as a noisy church group came through the front door. "Has anybody looked into the Greers' email or cell phone records yet?" he asked. "Are the state police involved?"

"I doubt it. It's tough to get a warrant for cell phone records if the person in question might still be alive, which is the case here."

As the church group was getting seated, our waiter returned with two massive plates of food, the pancakes glistening with grease. I dug in, too famished to worry about offending Hux with my appetite. I knew I'd better eat now, while I had the chance.

After Hux had consumed three whole pancakes, he leaned back in his seat and stared out the window with a fork in one hand. He looked deep in thought.

"Look, I know you're supposed to be on administrative leave this week," I said. "I would completely understand if you wanted to bow out of this."

He cut his remaining stack of pancakes right down the middle before drowning them in melted butter. No syrup, though. "So I can work on some online modules about toxic plants?" His lips twitched with a smile. "No, thanks."

"I'm serious. I don't want you to miss out on your training."

Hux started in on another bite. "It almost sounds like you *want* me to bail," he said.

"Not at all," I said. "You're an asset."

"Is it my lousy sense of humor?"

"It's not that bad."

He feigned an *aha* moment by raising an eyebrow and leaning forward. "Was it that joke I made about your Midwestern accent?" He spoke in a hushed voice, an attempt to sound conspiratorial.

It worked. "No," I said, laughing.

"Your obsession with portable campfires?"

"It's not an obsession."

"You carry those little tins everywhere."

"I like to be warm, okay?"

"You mean, like, on-the-go warm?"

I sipped my tea to hide the smile on my face. "Finish off your eighth pancake there," I said. "We're leaving."

I scooted out of the booth, fully aware of the hardened locals staring us down. The cute elderly couple sitting in the adjacent booth smiled serenely at us. The woman lifted her hand and pointed at Hux. "Hottie," she mouthed, then winked at me.

Fortunately, Hux's back was to them, but I smiled back at her, feigning ignorance. I grabbed the bill and hustled over to the register to pay it. Hux said, "Are you sure ISB is covering this—"

"I'm sure," I said as a sweaty cook rang me up. I glanced at my watch, which informed me that it was 6:47 AM and fifty-three degrees outside. For this latitude, the weather conditions were about as good as one could hope for.

But that could change, of course.

It could change on a dime.

3

THE TINY VILLAGE of Bettles, Alaska, had a post office, an airport with one runway, and a seasonal road that serviced the two. I learned from a bit of online research that the current population of the village hovered around ten people.

As we stepped off the plane, the air tasted crisp and cool, the sky a serene blue that belied the ruggedness of the place. I glanced at my watch to see that it was only eight o'clock, which meant we had a couple hours to kill. Ray had found us a bush plane through Bettles Outfitters, which was only about a mile from the airport. *The owner will pick you up,* Ray had texted. *Orange Jeep. Tess Flint. Have her take you to the rangers station. Chief's name is Brinegar.*

Despite the early hour, the day felt fully formed already. The familiar fast trill of an arctic warbler struck an ominous note. Ollie barked at the treetops, answering its call.

I looked out at the gravel parking lot and saw a bright orange Jeep just as Ray had said, its paneling emblazoned with the words "Bettles Outfitters: Your Gate to the Arctic." It looked like the kind of vehicle you'd risk your life to hold on to during the apocalypse.

A lanky woman with long blond hair was leaning on the front bumper. She raised a hand in a wave as she made her way over to us.

"Welcome to the North," she said with a broad, seasoned smile. "I'm Tess Flint." She extended a hand for me and Hux to shake. Her grip was firm, her skin bronzed from the sun. The crow's feet around her brown eyes cut deep, but she only looked to be in her late thirties.

"Good morning," I said. "I'm Special Agent Felicity Harland, and this is my colleague Hux Huxley." Hux reciprocated with a smile that put me at ease a little bit. My nerves were on overdrive, but even more draining was the effort it took to hide them.

Hux and I put our backpacks in the trunk of Tess's Jeep and climbed in the back seat. Ollie hopped in too. I noticed the water bottles in the seat-back pocket and heavy-duty mats on the floor. Maps jutted out of each of the passenger doors.

"How long have you lived up here?" I asked.

Tess glanced in the rearview mirror to meet my gaze. "Oh, jeez. I guess it's coming on eight years now."

"How's business this time of year?"

"Pretty good. July's always busy. It's a great time to explore the park." She gripped the wheel with her left hand and operated the stick shift with the other. *Old school.* "Have either of you been to Gates before?"

"No, ma'am," Hux said. "We've been in Denali the last couple months."

"Denali, eh?" she said. "How's it there this time of year?"

"Busy."

"I bet." She shifted into a lower gear as we climbed a hill. "So, I assume you're here about those folks that went missing up near Boreal Mountain?"

"We've heard about them, yes," I said, deciding to keep the details close to the vest. I figured Tess was entrenched in the search-and-rescue network up here, but I didn't want to speculate about the situation without more information.

"What do you know about them?" Hux asked.

"In my line of work, I hear about everybody that goes missing in the park," Tess said. "I like to warn my customers, too. You'd be amazed how many people come up here thinking Gates of the Arctic is pretty much Yosemite, just with more salmon and grizzly bears."

"What's the SAR outfit like up here?" Hux asked.

"Tough as nails. But Gates is tough too, and folks that go missing tend to stay that way."

"That seems to be the rule in Alaska," I said.

"Well, it's a real epidemic when you think about it. But I actually met the folks that went missing, so it feels different this time."

I wasn't surprised to hear that Tess had a personal connection to the missing hikers. The locals were always a valuable source of information, and they tended to pay attention. "Can you tell us what you remember about them?" I asked.

"I can do even better than that," she said. "I've got surveillance footage from my store. I showed it to Chief Brinegar and the SAR team before they set out."

"We'd love to take a look at it sometime, but we're supposed to meet our pilot at the airstrip at ten."

She flashed us a smile. "That's Bill, my husband. He's flying you up there."

"Oh."

Hux glanced over at me. "We'd love to take a quick look," he said. "Thanks."

"Sure thing."

Tess turned the Jeep down a dirt road that hugged the river, which brought us to a log cabin with a half-dozen kayaks piled on the shore. An employee in a crimson hat and clamdiggers was helping a customer load his gear into one of the kayaks. I couldn't imagine venturing out alone into a wilderness this vast and remote, but the customer looked like he knew what he was doing.

Tess parked out front, leaving the prime spots open for customers. We walked up to the cabin, with its broad, impressive windows that were adorned with retro bumper stickers and signs. One of them said "Dogs welcome!" I breathed a sigh of relief for Ollie's sake.

The cabin's interior was bigger than it looked from the outside. The floor-to-ceiling shelves complemented the rustic hardwood floors. Everywhere you looked were camping supplies, maps, and gadgets. Even the wall art was pleasant and tasteful, and the air smelled like spiced pine.

After saying hello to her employee at the front desk, Tess headed past the framed photos and mounted salmon into a small office in the back. The door was open. She caught my gaze over her shoulder and said, "Careful. There's a very intimidating six-year-old boy back here."

The boy looked up from his iPad with a big grin for Tess, although his smile turned shy when he saw me and Hux. He was blue-eyed and fair, with a few stray freckles dusting his nose and cheeks. His hair was as blond as it could be without being white.

"This is my son, Sean," Tess said. She whispered to him, "These folks are from the Investigative Services Branch—they're like police officers. Can you say hello?"

Sean looked at me. "Hi," he said. He glanced back at Tess, a silent plea in his eyes. I could see that he wasn't quite ready to give up his show.

Tess sighed. "It's fine, you can keep watching." She turned back to me and Hux. "Kids and their screens—it's a losing battle, you know?"

"I'm just surprised you've got high-speed internet up here," I said.

"Oh, I've got no choice. Our business is all electronic these days."

Which seemed to be true, at least based on the appearance of the office. On the small desk in the corner were two laptop computers, several Garmin devices, and a top-of-the-line satellite phone. As far as storage went, there wasn't so much as a filing cabinet. If Tess Flint kept paper files or receipts, they weren't at this location, that was for sure.

Tess gestured to the three empty seats at the table. "Can I get you something?" she asked. "Coffee?"

"No, thanks," I said. "I appreciate it, though."

Hux declined with a smile and a polite, "Ma'am."

Tess walked over to her desk, reached inside the top and only drawer, and pulled out another iPad from its depths. "This is my old one," she said, powering it on. She swiveled the screen in our direction. "This here's from the morning of July second."

The video started playing on-screen: it was Kelsey and Tim Greer, paying for supplies at the register. I recognized their faces right away. My heart sank, a familiar reaction I'd come to recognize as fearing the worst. I didn't know them, but seeing them in the store, preparing for their big adventure, made them real to me.

Tess said, "It's a real shame. They were nice people, from what I remember."

I asked, "Did they say where they were headed?"

"Boreal Mountain. Bill flew them up there."

I created a new file on my phone's note-taking app and titled it "GOTA/Greer" for Gates of the Arctic. "What else do you remember about them?" I asked.

"They were polite. I got the feeling they weren't really cut out for this place, though. Her hiking boots were brand new, and he was wearing a hoodie. Their backpacks weren't the right size. I asked if they had a guide."

"Did they?"

"They said they did, but that they were meeting him in the park. Bill had a bad feeling about it when he dropped them off. He even asked his pilot buddies to see if anyone had flown a guide up there recently. But no one had."

I glanced at Hux, who was already taking copious notes. "So, for the people who want a guide, do they go through you first?"

"For the most part. I give them a list of local guides and tell them to call and inquire if they haven't got somebody lined up yet. I used to be a guide myself, but I'm too busy with the store now to be off-site for long stretches of time."

"How many people go into the park without a guide?"

"Depends," she said. "The off-grid survivalists don't want one. The city people want a whole entourage."

I knew it wasn't Tess Flint's responsibility to remind people of their own limitations, but as an outfitter, she was pretty much the last line of defense between inexperienced tourists and disaster. I supposed it should have reassured me that they had a guide, but the fact that no one could confirm this piece of information made me skeptical.

"Okay," I said. "Anything else you can tell us about them?"

"No, but you're welcome to talk to Bill."

"Will do," I said. "Thanks."

"I hope they turn up. It's always a real shame to lose somebody out there."

I was pushing my chair away from the table when a knock came at the door. A tall redhead poked his head in and offered an apologetic smile. "Sorry to interrupt." He shifted his gaze to Tess. "Can you give me a hand with the canoes for a minute?"

"Sure thing." Tess put her hand on Sean's shoulder as she rose from the table. "Ten more minutes, okay, bud? Jenny should be here any minute."

Sean nodded, but his eyes stayed glued to the iPad. The fire-fighting dogs onscreen were zipping around a zoo. I was glad I didn't have to contend with the complexities of screen time and young children. It was all Margo could talk about these days.

Hux was trying to rub out a finger cramp that tended to develop after aggressive bouts of note-taking. He always took a ton of notes—too many, in my opinion, but I wasn't about to disabuse him of that notion.

As we were waiting for Tess to return, my cell phone chirped with a new message. I figured it must have picked up the Wi-Fi signal in the store.

"Who's harassing you now?" Hux smirked.

I glanced at the display. "Ray," I said with a flutter in my stomach. "He's got an update on the Greers."

CHAPTER

4

ACCORDING TO THE police report that Ray had sent me, the detective back in Kelsey Greer's hometown had managed to recover her email and social media accounts thanks to a lax password strategy. In my experience, most people were pretty careless when it came to passwords. It was bad practice for the individual, but for law enforcement, that kind of oversight could be a gift.

I started with the most recent email in Kelsey Greer's account, dated July 1st. It was the day Kelsey and her husband had arrived in Alaska.

Hi Mom. I'm in Fairbanks (Alaska). We're going to Gates of the Arctic National Park. We needed a vacation—things have been hard. I would have called, but it was a last-minute trip. We'll be back in a couple weeks. I love you.

I saw Hux's expression change from consternation to concern. "A couple weeks? That's a long time to be hanging out in an arctic wilderness."

"Especially for an amateur."

"Yeah," he said. "Smells fishy to me."

After scrolling through the file, I found documentation of Kelsey's recent browsing history. There was the usual stuff—news, celebrity gossip, recipe websites—but the bulk of her interest centered around infertility stories. In the months before her disappearance, she had done a deep dive into social media, blogs,

forles, and even scientific literature updates on the subject. It
seemed to be a secret obsession—no mention of it to her friends,
family, or anyone in her social circle, at least based on her text
messages, social media accounts, and emails.

"They didn't have kids, right?" Hux asked.

"Doesn't look that way," I said. "Wait, take a look at this." I
showed him a direct message in Kelsey's "secret" Twitter account,
which had no tweets and only a couple followers. The message
had arrived in her inbox on June 29th.

67°42'01.1"N 150°56'47.3"W. exp. 2 July

The message had come from a user named @pittailiniq. Hux
did the honors of googling it.

"*Pittailiniq* is an Inuit word," he said, reading off his phone.
"It's a cultural practice that involves refraining from certain
behaviors. Wikipedia has a whole list of them having to do with
pregnancy."

"Can you give me an example?"

He scanned his screen. "Don't walk backward or the baby
will be breech." He knitted his brow. "I wonder if there's some
truth to that one."

"Why? Were you breech?"

"Yeah."

"Did your mom walk backward?"

"Well, she was teaching kindergarten back then, so . . ."

I smiled at the visual of Hux's mom backtracking in a class-
room of five- and six-year-olds to set somebody straight. Hux
talked about his mom often. Even though it had been years since
they'd lived in the same state, his respect for her always came
through.

"We should get a move on," I said. "I'll go find Tess."

Hux stood up. "I might need a couple things if this turns
into a tracking expedition. Mind if I have a look around the store
for a minute?"

"Go for it."

While Hux went back inside, I ventured outside with Ollie,
to find Tess. Technically we were on her pilot husband's time
line, but I didn't want her to think we had hours to spare. For one

thing, three Park Service rangers were waiting on us in inhospitable territory. For another, evidence had a habit of disappearing
when exposed to the elements. I wanted to go get up there as
soon as possible.

I had just spotted Tess talking with a small group down
by the river when I saw a black sports utility vehicle turn into
the parking lot. I'd noticed that most of the vehicles in Bettles
were purely functional—trucks, Jeeps, four-wheelers that could
handle the terrain. Part of the reason for this was that the road
connecting Dalton Highway to Bettles was only accessible two
months out of the year, and that was only because a dozer and a
grader filled in the right-of-way with snowpack. In the summer,
the only way to get to the village was to fly.

But this particular SUV was flashier than most. My guess
was that it belonged to someone in the area and was being loaned
out as a rental. Everyone in these remote villages in the summertime was trying to make a buck. Who could blame them? The
tourists were generally well-off because they had to have means
to come all this way for a vacation.

I walked down the front steps toward the parking lot, with
Ollie in tow. It was curiosity, mostly, that compelled me to
wander a little closer to the SUV, since the occupants in some
ways reminded me of Tim and Kelsey Greer. They were white,
young, and attractive. They appeared to be arguing about
something, their voices barely audible through the passenger
side window.

Suddenly, the driver revved the engine and shifted into
reverse. Ollie's furious barking seemed to catch the man's attention right before he ran over me. He slammed on the brakes.

"Hey!" He jutted his head out the window. "Watch where
you're going!"

"Maybe you should take a second to cool down there, sir," I
called out.

With a nasty look in my direction, he shifted the car into gear.
As the tires crunched the gravel, I glimpsed the heart-shaped face
of the woman. Her cheeks were covered in a thick matte of zinc
sunscreen, which struck an unsettling contrast with her dark

eyes. The topographical map in her lap was splayed out over the dashboard, encroaching on the windows.

They had just disappeared down the dirt drive when I turned to see Hux striding out of the cabin with a handful of new maps. He raised an eyebrow when he saw me standing in the middle of the parking lot. "What happened?" he asked.

"Nothing," I said. "Well, not nothing. I almost got run over."

"Huh. Thank God for your lightning-quick reflexes, eh?" He smirked at me.

I glanced at the paper bag dangling from one of his forearms. Ollie sniffed the bag. "What did you get in there?" I asked.

"Oh, just some snacks, mostly."

I looked out at the road, which was quiet again. The only sign of the SUV that had driven off in a hurry was the faint imprint of its tire tread in the gravel.

"Harland?" Hux asked.

Ollie licked my hand. I reached down and rubbed the scruff between his ears, which gave me a moment to think. Ollie often had that effect on me.

"I was just thinking about that message from *pittailiniq*," I said. "It felt so . . . I don't know . . . methodical. Like it was part of a protocol or something."

"The set of coordinates, you mean?"

I nodded. "That and the expiration date. I mean, to give the recipient seventy-two hours to get to Alaska? That's bold. It almost felt targeted."

Hux bit into a piece of beef jerky. "So, what does that have to do with the SUV that almost mowed you down?"

"They fit the profile, is all. Close to the same age as the Greers, clearly out of their element this far north—I don't know. Just made me wonder."

"You want to follow them?"

"We can't. We've got to get to the airport."

"Bill's delayed. He needs thirty minutes to fix his rudder or something."

"Bill?"

"The pilot."

"You talked to him?"

Hux nodded. "He was in the store, packing up."

"How did you know it was him?"

A sly smile spread on his face. "I've learned a thing or two since I started working with you, Harland."

Delays were inevitable in most ISB investigations, usually due to some combination of weather and scarcity of resources. No matter what the cause, though, they pained me. Deeply. "Then maybe it's worth a stop," I said. "I bet they're staying at the Cabins."

The Cabins was the only bona fide resort in town, with its rustic accommodations and riverside setting on the Koyukuk. I had no plans of staying there, of course—the local motel was more my speed—but the Cabins catered to a certain clientele. I couldn't imagine where else an SUV of that size and expense was headed.

"I'll get us a ride," Hux said. He jogged back into the store, with Ollie at his heels, giving me no chance to argue with him. But that was Hux: a procurer of things.

I took out my cell phone and had a look at all the texts and emails that had come in during the last twenty-four hours. The file on the Greers was the most compelling. A young couple struggling with infertility flies to Alaska on a whim and a prayer. Who was *pittailiniq*? And why had they sent a set of coordinates to Kelsey Greer?

As the group of outdoor enthusiasts talking to Tess set out on the water, Hux emerged from the store with a Bettles Outfitter employee by his side. It was the tall redhead from before, holding a set of car keys. He pointed to a beater in the parking lot—a gas-guzzling Chevy with a rusted muffler. "That's Darla," he said proudly.

"What's your name?" I asked.

"Cody."

"He won't take any payment," Hux said. "I already asked."

Cody said, "I love ISB. You're badasses."

"We appreciate it," I said. "But we're reimbursing you for gas—don't argue with me."

"Whatever you say, ma'am. You guys are staying over at the Cabins?"

"No," I said, a little too quickly. "We just need to talk to someone there."

"Well, I recommend it. For romance, I mean. Me and my girlfriend—"

"We're here strictly on business." I avoided Hux's gaze as an excited Ollie and I climbed into Cody's pickup. A sun-bleached rabbit's foot dangled from the rearview mirror.

After just a couple minutes on the two-lane road, I spotted the sign for the Cabins Resort, with its appealing tea lights and a well-manicured lawn out front. Sure enough, the black SUV from before was in the valet line. Cody parked in a spot near the dumpsters.

It occurred to me in that moment that I hadn't thought this through enough. I could barge into the lobby and use my credentials to demand answers from this pair of complete strangers, but something told me that approach wouldn't get me very far. If the SUV occupants *were* part of some kind of infertility group, I couldn't imagine them being forthcoming about it.

I considered Hux as a viable alternative. He might fare better than me. After all, he was the honest-looking guy with knowledge of the land, whereas I was the random woman with a prickly attitude. They might think I was trying to sue them—or worse, shoot them.

"I'll hang out with your dog," Cody said.

"Thanks," I said. "We'll only be a few minutes."

Hux and I climbed out of the truck and made our way to the lobby. Just as we were about to walk through the doors, I stopped.

"Aren't we going in?" Hux asked.

"I'm not," I said. "If they *are* part of some infertility wilderness expedition—or whatever *pittailiniq* is—I don't think they'll talk to a federal investigator. But a friendly park ranger, who knows . . ."

Hux mused on this for a beat. "What do they look like?"

"They looked fortyish, both Caucasian with dark brown hair. His was curly, hers was up in a messy bun. He was wearing a black jacket and a ski cap. I couldn't see what she was wearing—she was petite, like me. Pretty. Heart-shaped face."

"Okay," he said. "What's my objective here?"

"See if they've heard of *pittailiniq*."

"The concept or the Twitter handle?"

"The Twitter handle."

"Got it. How much time do I have?"

I checked my sat phone for any incoming calls or messages, but there were none. "Ten minutes," I said. "Then we're going to the airstrip."

"Ten? That's way too much. I can blow this wide open in five."

"Have at it, then."

I caught the smile in his eyes as he walked through the doors into the expansive lobby. Hux had a languorous, unhurried stride that I couldn't help but admire—and others did too, judging by the heads that turned as he strode past the registration desk. But even out on the harshest of terrain, Hux seemed to glide while I trudged and labored. Even so, I was looking forward to getting out there with him; embarking on a new case with Hux was the best part of the job.

After four minutes hanging out front, I decided to head inside. The rustic restaurant was off to the left of the lobby, with booths lining the walls and a few tables scattered around the center of the room. From what I could tell on first glance, the clientele included locals, big game hunters, and outdoor adventurers dining on farm-to-table biscuits and eggs. A fireplace burned in the hearth. I determined that the seating area was busy enough to blend in, but not too busy to eavesdrop on a conversation taking place nearby.

I spotted the couple from the SUV huddled together at a table in the back. The woman was talking animatedly to Hux, who had established himself at a two-top table next to theirs. I admired his instincts. He'd chosen a spot close enough to insert himself seamlessly into their conversation without seeming intrusive.

While the woman spoke, the husband shifted in his seat. My first impression was that he seemed irritated by his wife. I noted the flashes of anger in his eyes, the impatient flexing of his fingers. He barely looked in her direction.

I walked over to a plush sofa by the hearth and sat down about six feet from where their conversation was taking place. As luck would have it, there was a giant mirror sitting over the mantle, which let me see the whole exchange.

I caught Hux's eyes for a moment in the mirror, which I hoped conveyed my approval of what he was doing. A day-old newspaper languished on the counter, pinned down by a salt shaker. I opened it up to the second page and pretended to read.

Hux and I had played this game a few times before, where we'd act like strangers so that one of us could ride the momentum of a favorable situation. In this case, the woman was already talking a mile a minute, which meant things were going well.

While Hux listened to her tell a story about their last-minute trip to Alaska, I feigned interest in a local dogsledding story. But I couldn't resist the urge to watch the scene play out.

"Dora," the exasperated husband was saying. "Come on, honey. Please. He really doesn't want to hear all this—"

"But he's a real *outdoorsman*, Greg," she shot back. "And since you're so worried about getting eaten by a bear or falling off a cliff, maybe he could teach you a thing or two about what we're in for." She turned back to Hux. "My husband doesn't even like the outdoors. He just says he does to sound manly."

Greg grunted. "I like the outdoors—"

Dora cut him off before he could finish. "We're from New Jersey," she explained. "North Jersey, actually. We're practically New Yorkers. Our idea of the great outdoors is, you know, going out to get the mail or whatever."

"So what brings you all the way out here?" Hux asked, taking the opening. The way he voiced the question sounded innocent enough, like he was just making small talk.

The man started to say something, but his wife interrupted him again. "We've done four rounds of IVF," she said. "Six rounds of IUI before that. The only option we've got left is surrogacy, but that's complicated . . . and expensive. We've already drained our life savings." Then, she quickly added, "Oh, sorry," maybe in response to a confused expression on Hux's face. "Those are fertility treatments."

I almost smiled. Hux had a talent for playing dumb.

"Gotcha," Hux said.

Greg said, "Look, babe, he really doesn't care—"

"My husband has azoospermia," Dora said.

Greg rattled the table with his fist. "That's none of his goddamn business, Dora."

"It's not a dirty word, Greg," Dora said. "It's really not." She inhaled sharply before turning back to Hux. "He's not making any sperm—well, not enough. The doctors can't explain why they haven't been able to fix the problem and get me pregnant."

Greg was fuming. I understood why, too, since Dora had gone deep into personal territory with another man she'd only just met. I almost felt sorry for her husband, despite the fact that he'd come pretty close to mowing me down in a parking lot.

"All I ever wanted in life was to be a mother," Dora went on. Her voice wavered, which brought her speaking volume to a more normal level. "I know how it looks—here we are, privileged white people, flying across the continent in a last-ditch effort to have a baby. But we're not the first ones to try this—I mean, there are lots of success stories in the Pinga group."

"Dora—"

"It took me eight months to even learn his name," she said.

"Whose name?" Hux asked, feigning ignorance.

"Zane Reynolds," she said. "He's the group leader. He's a fertility *mastermind*."

"Sounds like he's a cultural appropriation mastermind too," Hux said pleasantly. His sarcasm flew right over Dora's head. She just smiled.

Greg had had enough, it seemed. His chair scraped the floor and fell over as he got to his feet. The clattering sound made me turn around.

I saw Greg grab his wife by the arm and tug her sideways out of her chair. Dora wasn't having it. She retaliated with a look that would have melted steel. "Sit down, Greg," she demanded. "You're being such a drama queen."

"We talked about this," he warned her.

"Who's he gonna tell?" she snapped back. "He's just a park ranger."

Hux didn't flinch. One of my partner's most attractive qualities was his ability to let things slide right off him. Now, if someone insulted *me* . . . well, that was a different story.

"You know," Hux said, "I've actually heard the name before."

"You have?" Dora asked. Greg seemed surprised too. What I didn't completely understand, though, was why all this secrecy existed in the first place. Infertility was a sensitive issue for many, yes, and perhaps even embarrassing for men like Greg, but why buy into a guy who seemed to celebrate the cloak-and-dagger approach in an arctic wilderness? There had to be a reason Zane Reynolds was operating out of Alaska's remotest wilderness area and not hosting seminars in downtown Chicago.

"Something about *pittailiniq*," Hux said. "I'm no expert in Inuit traditions, but—"

"Oh yes," Dora said. "That's part of the credo."

"Sorry?"

Greg sighed. "He doesn't know what that means, babe."

"Zane is the leader of a very exclusive group," Dora explained.

"Like a cult?"

"No, no, no," she said with a brittle laugh. "It's not a cult. It's really not like that at all." She took a breath to slow her rambling. "Zane is a wonderful man. He helps people who are desperate— people like us who just want to be parents."

Perhaps realizing that he'd lost control over the situation, Greg sat down again. Dora barely acknowledged him.

"So what have *you* heard about him?" she asked Hux.

"Not a whole lot," Hux said. "Just that he might be based around the Boreal Mountain area." He sipped a glass of water. "Is that where you're headed?"

"No—um, I don't think so," Dora said. "The group moves around a lot. Zane usually sends out secret coordinates to couples he's interested in, but the last set he sent out leaked somehow . . ."

She forced a nervous smile. "Now, I know you must think we're crazy, but—"

"He *does* think we're crazy," Greg interjected.

Dora continued speaking as if her husband hadn't said anything. "The thing about Zane is that he has to come to you—*most* of the time."

I caught Greg rolling his eyes.

"Anyway," Dora went on, "Zane has been known to take people who just show up in Alaska and find him on their own."

"How does that happen?" Hux asked.

"People leak the coordinates on Reddit or whatever."

"Huh," Hux said. "You know that for sure?"

"Oh yes—"

"No," Greg said. "No, she doesn't."

Dora sighed. "Greg is not *completely* on board with this plan, as you can see."

"Of course I'm not completely on board," Greg said, leveling his anger at his wife. "You tricked me. You said we were going on a cruise for my birthday."

"We'll do the cruise afterward."

"I have a job, remember?" He put his head in his hands. "This is insane."

Dora said to Hux, "Here, take a look. These are the coordinates I found online just a couple days ago." I assumed she had them on her phone, but I wasn't going to turn around and look. I didn't want to make them suspicious when we were this close to sealing the deal.

"Do you know where this is?" Dora asked. "Because Greg seems to think Google maps is the answer to everything, but he couldn't find it on our paper map."

"It's called a *topographical* map," Greg clarified unhelpfully.

Dora exhaled. I had to wonder, was there any love there at all? Or had all their struggles to have a child sucked the life out of their marriage? I couldn't relate to what they were going through, but I did understand how one partner's obsession could tarnish the whole relationship. Having been married once, I used to feel like Kevin and I were lucky in that we'd shared an affinity for travel and adventure. But I was the one who had planned all the trips, including the one that had ended in his disappearance. That fact haunted me still.

Hux said, "I'm sorry, ma'am. I could give you my best guess, but once you're out there, anything could happen. I'd recommend hiring a guide if you're serious about this."

"But—but it says you 'can't miss it.' See? Right there in the message."

"That's sarcasm, Dora," Greg said bitingly.

Dora was quiet for a moment, but I sensed that the floodgates were on the verge of bursting open. Greg, too, seemed to pick up on a subtle but important change in his wife's demeanor. He reached across the table and grasped her hand.

"This is nuts, babe. We both know that."

Dora dropped her gaze to the table. Her shoulders trembled. "Any chance you could take us up there?" she asked Hux.

"I can't do it, ma'am," Hux said. "I'm sorry."

She used her fingernails to pick at the frayed edges of the wooden table. Greg moved his chair over to her side. When he put his arm around her, she tensed at his touch before giving in to the human contact. With a pitiful sob, she turned her face into his chest and started to cry.

Hux said, "You know, hearing you talk about this Zane Reynolds guy, I'm wondering if it's worth it to send some rangers up there."

"No, don't—please," Dora said. "You're not supposed to share his location."

"I respect that, ma'am," Hux said. "But it sounds to me like he's making people take risks they're not comfortable with."

"That's exactly what I've been trying to tell her!" Greg said, sounding very animated all of a sudden. "I wish someone would go up there and see if he's the real deal or just a scam artist."

"He's not a scam artist," Dora protested.

"He *is*, babe," Greg said. He turned to Hux. "He charges a fee, you know."

Dora interjected, "We don't know that for sure—"

"Of course we do. That one woman said as much on her TikTok. What was it, twenty-five grand?"

Hux whistled. "That's a lot of money."

"It's worth it, for a baby," Dora said.

Greg blew out a breath. I look over my shoulder to see Dora sliding her phone in Hux's direction. "Here, look—see? These are the coordinates."

Hux glanced at the screen. "Well, I could at least check them against my map," he said. "You mind if I take a photo of that message on your phone there?"

"Sure," Dora said. "I have my map, too, if you need it." She unzipped her backpack and reached deep inside it.

Hux took her crumpled map and laid it out on the table. He was a real wizard with coordinates, and, in fact, I doubted he needed a map at all to know where that location was. But to appease Dora, and maybe to buy a little more time, he went through the motions of pinpointing the location.

"Oh, shoot," Hux said. "These are way off the grid—the Alatna River."

"The where?" Dora asked. Greg sighed.

"The Alatna's about sixty miles west of here, near the geographic center of the park. It's a little more off the beaten path than the Koyukuk."

Greg mangled a laugh. "Is that even possible? Christ."

"I suggest you two get yourself a guide," Hux said.

"No one's available," Dora said. "We tried."

"The best guides book out months in advance," Greg said. "We're not going up there with some amateur."

"Then I wouldn't go at all." Hux spoke in a tone that was both sympathetic and stern. "I got wind of a situation up in that area that could turn out to be dangerous."

"What kind of a situation?"

Another waiter carrying a basket of rolls walked past me and deposited it on Dora and Greg's table. "Two dead bodies," the waiter said, as casually as if he'd been a part of the conversation from the start. Even Hux seemed startled by the waiter's interjection.

Greg threw his hands up. "Well, then that's it. We're not doing this."

The waiter made nice with a smile. "Now, what can I get for you this morning—?"

"*Wait a minute,*" Dora cried. "I . . . I never said . . ." She sniffled. "Are you sure? About the dead people?"

"Yup," the waiter said. "Do you need another minute with the menu?"

Dora grabbed a handful of napkins and stood up, her chair scraping the floor. "No," she sobbed. "Greg, let's go." I watched her reach for her map, but something seemed to give her pause. To Hux, she said, "You should go up there."

"Ma'am?"

"I want to know if he's real—Zane Reynolds. Pinga." She straightened her shoulders a little bit, but I could tell she was trying hard not to break down. "If it is, we'll try again. If it isn't, well . . . someone should put a stop to it. False hope is a dangerous thing."

Hux nodded. "I'll do my best," he said.

"Thanks." Her voice was a whisper.

Greg helped Dora with her coat, a tender gesture that made me reevaluate their relationship a little bit. Maybe he was just relieved to be off the hook for this Alaska excursion. I felt bad for Dora, but the practical side of me believed that Hux might have just saved their lives.

The defeated couple walked out of the restaurant, past more than a few locals who seemed amused by the clueless tourists treading on their territory. It must have been a common sight, this time of year. The locals here had learned to tolerate the outsiders for their monetary value, but they also always seemed happy to see them go.

Hux grabbed his sunglasses off the table, flicked his gaze at me, and headed for the exit. I closed my newspaper and followed him out of the dining room. I had mixed feelings about how things had ended for Dora and Greg—especially Dora, who had come to Alaska on a high and was leaving with broken dreams— but I reminded myself that we weren't here for them. We were here for the two people who had perished in an arctic wilderness. Were they Tim and Kelsey Greer, the hikers who had gone missing near Boreal Mountain? And if they were, what did that tell us about Zane Reynolds, the mystery man in the wilderness?

Was he a miracle worker—or a murderer?

5

WHEN WE WERE all back in Cody's Chevy, Hux pulled up the photo he'd taken of Dora's iPhone screen. "These coordinates aren't actually close to the ones Kelsey Greer got," he said. "They're much farther west, closer to the Arrigetch Peaks area."

"I know," I said. "I heard you talking about it in there."

"I'll have to double-check these on my map," he said. "But if you ask me, it's pretty damn close to where those bodies were found."

"You don't trust GPS, do you?" I asked. "Is it a military thing?"

Hux shrugged. "The threat of someone hacking into the GPS satellite system and learning your location is always in the back of your mind, yeah. But for me, it's more about not relying on technology to save your butt. This far off the grid, anything can happen."

I knew from experience that he was right. For me, directional coordinates were like a language for which I would never achieve complete fluency. In this case, both sets of coordinates were sixty-seven degrees north, but Dora's were one hundred and fifty-four degrees west to Kelsey's one hundred and fifty. The discrepancy suggested that Reynolds's group did indeed move around a lot, which raised some other questions.

The clock on the dash was showing 9:42 AM when Cody turned his Chevy into the airport's parking lot. An American flag stood next to the runway, billowing in the wind. The blue sky had gone overcast with feathery white clouds, and the air smelled of river muck.

Ollie bounded out of the truck, sensing a new adventure. Hux, too, seemed a little more animated than usual as he hoisted his backpack out of the pickup's bed and slung it over his shoulders. I was always the cautious one—skeptical of my own abilities, wary of the unknown. My body had healed from past injuries, and my mind was in the right place. That didn't change the fact that every wilderness was different, which made it hard to completely trust myself.

On our way to the airstrip, I tried calling Chief Brinegar's satellite phone to let him know we were on our way, but no one answered. I hoped he was a patient man. For all sorts of reasons, it couldn't have been easy for him to put everything on hold while he waited for our arrival.

Bill Flint greeted us in front of a white Cessna that glinted in the sunshine. He was a stout fellow with a graying beard and long dark hair tied in a ponytail at the base of his neck. His flannel shirt looked soft and worn from years of use.

"Mornin'," Bill said, extending a hand for each of us to shake. His grip was firm. He glanced at Ollie. "Your pup comin' with us?"

"Is that all right?" I asked.

"Fine by me," he said. "Tess'll be thrilled."

"She's coming too?"

He nodded. "She's got a guide up there that needs a few things. Depending on the client, sometimes it makes sense to get 'em what they need right when they need it."

As if on cue, Tess pulled up in her heavy-duty orange Jeep—a perfect complement to her competent wilderness persona. Her boots reminded me of an old catcher's mitt, weathered and worn and entirely resistant to blisters. Her jacket looked warm but versatile on her six-foot frame. She wore her hair in a casual ponytail that tumbled over her collar.

"Aw, jeez," Tess said as she walked over. "I would've given you a ride. Sorry I got hung up at the store—everybody wants to get going quick in the morning."

"No problem," I said. "We had a stop to make anyway."

After a brief orientation from Bill, we loaded our backpacks into the cargo pod and boarded the plane. Tess sat in the copilot's seat, and Hux and I took two of the four open seats in the back. Ollie lay down on the floor at my feet.

It was a smooth takeoff that did nothing to settle my nerves. It had taken me a couple months to get accustomed to Denali, but Gates was a totally different animal. The valleys were vast and bare, marked by sinuous rivers that made their way through the gravel bars. The arctic horizon seemed to extend to the ends of the Earth.

Our flight path took us west, over the Alatna Hills and Deadman Mountain. I followed our route on the map, unable to reconcile the vast distance between the Greers' coordinates and the location of the two bodies the rangers had found. Boreal Mountain was on the eastern side of the park, but the Arrigetch Peaks were much farther west. They would have had to cross about ten rivers and several mountain passes to get there, a distance of almost eighty miles. It was an almost unfathomable distance in this part of the world.

Bill and Tess were up in the cockpit, their conversation drowned out by the loud engines and the rush of air over the wings. I felt restless as the plane's white noise amplified every thought in my head, while Hux admired the scenery with a placid look on his face.

Alaska was everything I had imagined it to be—majestic and grand, unlike any other place I'd ever been. But it also made me wonder if I'd adequately prepared for what awaited us down on the ground. In a park like Yosemite or Death Valley, you were never that far from a road or trail. People got lost, yes—and even died—but as long as you had a satellite phone, help was never more than an hour away. That wasn't the case out here, not by a long shot.

"You nervous?" Hux asked.

I turned my head toward him. "No," I lied. "You?"

"A little," he said.

"Oh, come on," I said. "You're never nervous."

"This is all new territory for me," he said. "In a lot of ways."

I always appreciated these moments of vulnerability from Hux, but I couldn't help but question them too. The truth was, I had high standards for my partner—maybe impossibly high—but I knew that he expected the same from me.

So far, Hux had been an asset in Alaska. Sure, he'd made some amateur mistakes—digging up a box of artifacts in Denali, in an effort to "be helpful," had drawn the ire of a whole department's worth of archaeologists—but aside from that, he had done well. His interviewing skills were improving every day, and he tolerated the bureaucratic nature of ISB, which I supposed had more to do with his military experience than his personality. When it came to private citizens, Hux had no problem standing up to the assholes and sleaze bags. With me and other official personnel, however, he was always respectful and deferential.

After an uneventful flight, Bill put the plane down on a lake that flanked the Alatna River, just east of the Arrigetch Peaks. We grabbed our gear out of the cargo hold and thanked Bill for the ride. Tess gave us a thumbs-up from her seat in the cockpit.

"You've got my sat phone number," Bill said. "Call me or Tess if you need a ride back down to Bettles."

"Will do." I put my backpack down on the ground to inspect each of its compartments one last time before we set out. "Thanks."

"You got your bear spray?" Tess peered out the window.

"Sure do." Hux held up the small red canister that he carried everywhere he went in these and other national parks. "You think we'll need it?"

"There's a good-sized brown bear population up here," Tess said. "But it's been a weird year. Their environment's changing. We've seen more aggressive behavior than in years past—even a couple stalker bears."

"What do you mean by that?" I put my own bear spray in a side pocket for easy access.

"Just some strange activity—bears following folks out in the wilderness, terrorizing them at night. Heard about a woman who died a few weeks back when a bear broke into her tent and plundered her from her sleeping bag." Tess punctuated this alarming description with a sad shake of her head. "These things happen, unfortunately."

"Good to know," I said. "We'll be on alert."

With that, Bill revved the engine of his Cessna in preparation for the second leg of their flight. Hux and I waved goodbye. The smile I plastered on my face didn't put me at ease about being this far off the grid, but being an ISB agent sometimes required a little acting.

We had three unique sets of coordinates in our possession at this point, but our priority was Chief Brinegar's location. With Hux in the lead, dictating our route, we headed northwest along the river toward the Arrigetch Peaks area.

"Any word from the chief ranger?" Hux asked. "Are they still on the river somewhere?"

"I sure hope so. I haven't heard otherwise."

"We'll just follow the river then." He put his sunglasses on and squinted into the sun. His water bottle dangled from a green strap by his hip, which somehow accentuated the perfect fit of his pants. He looked like a cover model for *Outside* magazine, which used to annoy me, but now I appreciated that his commanding presence upped my street cred.

We didn't talk much. Hux must have sensed the urgency in my stride, the relentless pursuit of an unfamiliar destination, but I trusted Hux. He felt confident that at some point within the next hour, we'd see the rangers on the gravel bar that lined the river. After all, he'd been a park ranger not all that long ago, and he was familiar with their protocols. Visibility was everything out here.

Sure enough, with about four minutes to spare before the hour was up, he stopped and pointed. "I think I see them," he said. Ollie barked his approval.

I looked in the direction he was pointing. About a quarter mile away from where we stood were three hardy-looking individuals. One of them was crouched down, inspecting something on the ground. A blue tarp fluttered in the wind, catching its gusts from below.

I took my binoculars out of my backpack and lifted them to my face. Hux was patient. He must have sensed what was coming.

"Well?" Hux asked.

I released a long exhale.

"It's them," I said.

6

OUR SHORT TREK north along the river to meet the rangers felt like a hundred miles. My feet dragged; my muscles rebelled. I walked in silence, training my gaze on the distant sight of the rangers in front of me. It had been over a year since I'd worked a homicide case as a federal agent with ISB, and I was feeling a little rusty. But first impressions were crucial in this line of work. I straightened my shoulders and walked with a steady, deliberate stride.

The group turned at our approach. It included a young man and a woman, maybe late twenties or so, and an older guy who looked about twice their age. I assumed the salt-and-pepper-haired fellow was Brinegar, the chief.

They were all wearing Alaska's official Park Service uniforms, which in this part of the country was a gray shirt with charcoal-colored pants. The chief sported a dark green jacket, and the woman wore waders over her boots. They certainly gave the impression of being experienced outdoors people, but then again, I hadn't encountered many rookies in Alaska.

The man I assumed was Brinegar raised a hand when he saw us. "Hello there!" he called out. "Are you two ISB?"

"Yes!" I shouted back.

"Come on over, then!"

Hux and I exchanged a glance. Competency was the name of the game in these kinds of investigations, and we were about to learn how much of an asset or liability Chief Brinegar was going to be. His eager reception was a reassuring sign. I had no interest in a turf war with the rangers out here, although, in Alaska, the battle was typically with the state troopers, who handled criminal investigations in the state.

On the other hand, Brinegar had clearly called us for a reason. To me, this meant we weren't dealing with a simple case of exposure, but it wasn't a clear-cut homicide either. Brinegar had called us because he wasn't sure how to proceed.

As I'd expected, the elder ranger introduced himself as Jeremy Brinegar, the chief ranger out of Bettles station. I shook his hand.

"I'm Special Agent Felicity Harland," I said, "and this is my partner, Hux Huxley."

"Pleasure. I'm sorry we couldn't meet under better circumstances." Brinegar offered a perfunctory smile. "My junior ranger here made this discovery on patrol yesterday evening." He jutted his thumb at the woman standing next to him. "This is Ranger Emily Wiseman."

Emily responded with a curt smile. Her short, solid build seemed well suited for the elements. She tucked a strand of strawberry-blond hair under her wide-brimmed hat.

Brinegar gestured to the other Park Service employee among them. "This here is Dave Spector," he said. "He's our wildlife biologist—knows everything there is to know about bears, wolves, moose, reindeer, Dall sheep. You name it, he knows about it."

Dave had quite the beard, such that I couldn't tell if he was smiling at me when he shook my hand. He had some trouble making eye contact, though.

"Nice to meet you all," I said. "Let's have a look, then."

"Yes, ma'am," Brinegar said as he bent down and gripped the corner of the tarp.

I held my breath as the wind caught the tarp and lifted it, revealing the unmistakable sight of two sets of human remains. To my surprise, the bodies were well preserved, although some wildlife had clearly gotten to them. Their parkas were tattered and torn, their exposed flesh scraped and bitten, but overall they were in better shape than I'd expected, which was good news. It meant more opportunities for clues.

I studied them for a beat—the woman, facedown in the river; the man, also prone but with his head turned to the side. The woman's legs were up on the riverbank, and her long blond hair billowed in the current. The man's vacant eyes stared out at the Alatna River.

That sinking feeling I'd had not long ago returned with a vengeance. Having seen the photo of Tim and Kelsey Greer, I knew that we had found them. Even though I couldn't really see the woman's face from this angle, Tim Greer was instantly recognizable. They were also both wearing the same red parka from Tess's surveillance footage.

One thing I could say with certainty was that they hadn't been out here long. There was very little evidence of decomposition, which was unusual for a body exposed to the elements in July. As Brinegar had insinuated in his call to Ray, *something* had gotten to them. *But what?* Tim Greer had been disemboweled, and the woman had puncture wounds on her neck and jaw— inflicted by teeth, most likely. Sharp teeth. I figured Dave would tell us more about that.

On initial inspection, though, I wasn't seeing any evidence of an obvious crime. My first impression was that these two unfortunate visitors to Alaska's remotest area had simply expired on the shores of one of its greatest rivers, and the wolves had done the rest.

Their positioning, though, raised some questions. They were lying side by side in the river muck, as if they'd decided to die there together. They weren't malnourished from what I could tell, and hypothermia seemed unlikely. In the latter case, victims often stripped naked as their internal temperature dropped. They became disoriented, confused. They probably wouldn't have even been aware of one another at that point, much less united in death.

I turned to Emily. "So it was you who found them?" I asked.

"Yes, ma'am." She snagged a piece of gum with her teeth and pushed it back toward her throat. "I was just out here on patrol yesterday afternoon, floating down the Alatna. I got word about a tent in the river—a pilot saw it from above. So I came out to investigate, but then I heard wolves howling and followed 'em here. Lemme just say, I never expected to see this. It's not often you find dead bodies in Alaska."

"What do you mean?"

"Folks go missing a lot," she said, "but for the most part, they don't turn up again."

I shifted my attention to Dave, who had bent down to tie a shoelace. "Tell me about the wolves up here," I said. The puncture wounds on Kelsey Greer's neck certainly looked like bites to me. There was minimal bruising and hardly any blood, which suggested they were postmortem, but I wanted to hear Dave's opinion.

"Um, well." Dave cleared his throat in the dry, arctic air. "The thing is, wolves are effective predators, but they don't tend to attack humans. If I had to guess, I'd say the pack moved in to pick off the remains."

"Is that common?"

"Well, sure, but wolves don't abandon a kill without a good reason. They'll eat everything that's there—tendons, hair. Even bone. Now, sometimes they'll go off for a while and return to the carcass later, but this here's an exposed spot. These, um . . . this meal here, it wouldn't have lasted long on the river."

"So what's an example of a good reason?"

Dave glanced at Emily, but she made no effort to offer a response. Her silence seemed to fluster him a little bit, which I found interesting. Maybe Dave didn't get along with Emily. Or maybe—and I found this more likely, for some reason—they were more than just colleagues.

"Usually a threat of some kind," Dave said. "A hunter. A bear. Wolf packs don't like to ditch a meal, but they won't die for it either."

"So you don't think this was a wolf attack?"

He scratched a spot behind his left ear. "Nah. There are other clues too. Like the way they died—the two of them together, peaceful-like. It doesn't look to me like they put up a fight."

"No," I agreed. "It sure doesn't."

Tim Greer didn't have any defensive wounds on his forearms or hands, and from what I could see, neither did Kelsey Greer. In a true predatorial attack, those kinds of wounds were a given. I hadn't dealt with any animal encounters in Denali, but I'd read enough ranger reports to know what those injuries looked like and which species were responsible for them. Dave was right in that wolf–human encounters were rare. Deaths were virtually unheard of.

It was becoming obvious that I couldn't blame this unfortunate event on the wolves, then. An accident or exposure was possible, but I wasn't ready to land on that conclusion just yet.

"Did you see anything unusual on the river before you found the bodies?" I asked Emily. "Maybe a campsite or something?"

She shook her head. "No, ma'am."

"Any other hikers, fishermen . . . anyone?"

"Nope. I knew about the two hikers who went missing near Boreal Mountain, but that's a long ways from here. It wasn't even on my radar to think it might be them."

"How about after you found them?"

She shook her head. "Truth is, I never saw the photo that's been going around. My sat phone's busted."

Hux looked up from his notepad, seemingly intrigued by this admission. "So how did you get in touch with the rangers station?" His tone was curious rather than accusatory, but I wondered how Emily would take it.

She shrugged. "My Garmin," she said.

Brinegar folded his arms across his chest. "You can't be out here without a functioning sat phone," he said to Emily. "You know that."

"Yes, sir," she muttered.

The Garmin devices used for wilderness excursions like these could send and receive messages, but they couldn't do anything close to what an Iridium or other top-of-the-line satellite phone could do. I didn't know many rangers that carried the smaller handhelds, to be honest. The extra few ounces of pack weight usually wasn't worth it.

All that said, *I* had a Garmin. I'd put it in my backpack at the last minute because I wanted to have multiple backups in a place as remote as this. After getting stranded in the Australian outback with Kevin, I tended to overprepare in that regard.

"Let's have a closer look at the bodies," I said. "I'd like to turn them over."

"Are we allowed to do that?" Dave sounded nervous. He kept fidgeting with the joints on his fingers, but he wasn't wearing a ring. He struck me as a little young to be divorced, but that was just a guess based on my impression of his age. Interestingly, his nerves seemed to irritate Emily. She kept glaring at him, like, *Get a grip.*

Brinegar said, "She can do whatever she wants, Dave. She's the investigator."

Dave's cheeks flamed red. "Right."

Hux had already taken a mountain of photos with his cell phone, so I wasn't too worried about disturbing evidence. I put on a pair of gloves and waited for Hux to do the same. With the rangers' help, we gently rolled both bodies over onto their backs. I held my breath and braced myself for the carnage. It was never easy seeing the faces of the dead.

The man was in worse shape than the woman. The wolves had attacked the most vulnerable part of his body, the soft belly under his ribs. But they hadn't really reaped the benefits of their efforts, maybe on account of the heavy coat he was wearing. This, too, struck me as odd. The last few days had been fairly warm. Also, where was the rest of their gear? There was that report of a tent in the river, but Emily had denied seeing a campsite.

"Did anyone ever find the tent?" I asked, directing my question at no one in particular.

"Not that I heard," Emily said. "The Alatna's been running pretty high right now, so it could be anywhere. The pilot did say it was bright orange, though, the kind you carry around if you want to be seen. Means you're scared of getting lost."

"Did anyone report seeing a campsite?"

Emily and Dave exchanged a glance. "We had a look around," Brinegar said, "but we stayed on this side of the river. Didn't want to wander too far."

I bent down for a closer look at the body of Kelsey Greer. She had the bite marks on her face and neck, but her torso was intact except for the damage to her parka. Interestingly, her lips weren't at all chapped. Her hair had a freshly shampooed sheen. She really did look like she'd spent the last day of her life at a nice outdoor spa, not a rugged wilderness.

Since we knew she'd been out here for several weeks, the best explanation for her cleaned-up appearance was a well-stocked campsite. Way out here, for a couple of amateurs like the Greers, my best guess was a smooth-running operation with a seasoned outdoorsman at the helm. *Someone like Zane Reynolds.*

Hux and I searched the victims' pockets, but we came up empty-handed. "Did you find any ID by chance?" I asked Brinegar.

"No," he said. "In fact, we didn't find a damn thing."

"What about their backpacks?"

He looked out at the trees on the other side of the river. "No, ma'am. But, like I said, our search radius was pretty small. We wanted to stay close till you got here."

In my seven years at the FBI prior to my transfer to ISB, I'd encountered plenty of open-and-shut cases—gunshot wounds, strangulations, overdoses. The cause and manner of death were obvious right from the start. In this case, nothing was clear. Nothing at all.

It wasn't a promising start.

The medical examiner would perform an autopsy, of course, but while we were on the scene, I wanted to document as much as I could. Hux proceeded to take photos, which he would download later to a master file. It was always helpful to have a look at them later, when we were hunkered down in an office somewhere and not fending off the elements.

With the rangers standing by, we removed the Greers' matching red parkas to check for other injuries—anything that might fill in the picture of what had happened to them. The only thing that jumped out at me was some shallow abrasions on the ulnar prominences on their wrists. They both had them.

"These abrasions here," I remarked to Hux. "I wonder what they're about."

Hux leaned in closer to have a look. "You're sure those aren't just collateral damage from the wolves?"

"I don't think so," I said. "They look almost like ligature marks. But they're definitely premortem; you can tell by the scabs."

"You think they were tied up?"

"I don't know." I lifted Kelsey Greer's arm. "Why would you tie someone up all the way out here?"

"Could've been a sexual thing," he said. "Some kinky behavior in the woods?"

"Hmm. Maybe."

I stood up and surveyed the gravel bar that lined the river, a smooth strip of land that almost looked like a road if it weren't laid out next to a wild river and a remote mountain range. "Where is all their stuff, is the question," I mused.

Brinegar hiked up his pants by his belt. "Like Emily said, the river's been running high this year—snowmelt and such. Could be their gear got swept downriver."

The Alatna took a meandering path through the mountain valley, disappearing from view as it went around a bend. In some areas, the river flowed through narrow wooded areas; in others, the gravel bar extended hundreds of feet before turning into wet tussocks.

My hunch was that the Greers' gear was somewhere close by, but that didn't mean it would be easy to find. A bush pilot had reported seeing a tent, but how reliable was that information? It wasn't easy to see small objects from the sky, especially out here, where the dark greens and earth-tone browns made for a bland color palette. Emily's claim that the tent was orange, though, gave me hope.

For me and Hux, the next step in this investigation was clear: We had to find the campsite.

7

Accordingd to ISB protocol, I was supposed to call my superior with an update as soon as we had one. With Hux and
Ollie prowling the riverbank for clues, I took out my sat phone
and placed the call to ISB headquarters. Within ten seconds, I
had Ray on the line.

"Ray, hi— it's me. I'm up here near Arrigetch Peaks." I heard
him clear his throat and noisily drink something. "We found
Tim and Kelsey Greer."

He swallowed loudly. "Confirmed?"

"We didn't find any ID at the scene, but it's them. Brinegar already notified SAR to peel back the search in the Boreal
Mountain area."

I glanced at Hux, who was going through his crime scene
photos on his phone, marking his favorites and taking notes on
his pad. Over by the river, the rangers had put the tarp back on
the bodies to protect them from the flies, but it wasn't doing
much to temper the frenzy.

"Does it look suspicious?" Ray asked. A hard scrape on the
floor, footsteps echoing on the line. Wherever he was going, he
was walking fast.

"Well, it's hard to say without the ME's preliminary report.
But we got wind of an outfit up here that might have something
to do with this. I want to look into it."

"What kind of outfit?"

"An infertility group of some kind—a cult, possibly."

"A *cult*?" He barked a laugh. "Come on, now, Harland."

"We've seen cults operating out of national parks before," I said. "If that's what's going on here, I want to make sure no one else is at risk."

The footsteps in the background suddenly went quiet. I had a hard time picturing Ray in his office, which overlooked a parking lot despite its singular focus on crimes that occurred in national parks. Ray didn't seem to care about the irony of such a setup.

"What other info do you have on this cult?" he asked.

"I've got a name: Zane Reynolds. Can you run it through the system?"

"I'll do my best, Harland," he grunted. "Now, look, those two bodies you found up there, is it homicide or not? You know I don't like wishy-washy answers."

"I need more time to investigate."

"How much time? 'Cause we've got another agent covering for you in Denali, and it's not going well. She's got some feminine issues."

I wasn't about to ask what he meant by "feminine issues," but I could guess. "I'm supposed to be on vacation this week anyway, sir."

"Forget that," he said with a snort. "You can take a vacation in October when you wrap up there in Alaska."

"But I have a family obligation—"

"Then wrap this up quick, so I can send Hux back down to Denali."

I looked back at the tarp, flapping in the wind as the flies fought for purchase on the decomposing bodies underneath. The whole scene felt so desolate, so utterly removed from the world— a terrible place to die, really. I wasn't looking forward to calling Tim and Kelsey Greer's family members, but that was part of my job. And in some respects, it was the first step toward getting them closure. I tried to remember that.

"Yes, sir," I said.

With Ray, negotiating was a pointless exercise. I hung up, noting that my battery life was down to ninety-four percent before I put it back on standby mode. In a wilderness area as remote as this one, every bit of battery life mattered—perhaps more so than any place I'd ever been.

"Well?" Hux had an expectant look on his face.

"He wants us back in Denali ASAP."

Hux laughed. "Of course he does. Well, don't worry—I took no less than five hundred photos. We'll walk the scene a few times and go through everything later. This is how we do."

I managed a smile. "Yup, this is how we do."

Because there was no hope of getting a forensics team to cover our bases, Hux and I had to do it ourselves—establish a perimeter, collect anything that might pass as evidence, document details that could turn into important clues later on. Even though Hux was turning into a capable investigator, I'd still be responsible for any mistakes down the line.

Crime scene barriers didn't really exist in places like this, but that wasn't necessarily a good thing. As a general rule, it was better to err on the side of creating a perimeter that was too large rather than too small, but since it was just me and Hux, we couldn't canvass a few square miles by ourselves. So, I kept the perimeter pretty small: a radius of twenty paces from the remains, which was more like fifteen for Hux. Emily had waders on, so I asked her to search the riverbed. My intention was to put Ollie to work searching for the missing campsite, but we weren't ready for that yet. The crime scene always came first.

For the next couple of hours, we canvassed the area around the Alatna River, searching for clues that might tell us more about how the Greers had come to be here. The gravel bar in this part of the Alatna was an assortment of smooth rocks—most of them smaller than a foot in diameter but clustered close together—and river silt underneath. The silt was impressionable, and it had been marked by the chaotic prints of the wolves that had been here. I made note of the human footprints too, although my suspicion was that they belonged to Brinegar, Emily, or Dave—not that I blamed them for contaminating the scene, since they had little choice making a discovery like this. Hux added them to his photo collection for analysis later.

As the lunch hour came and went, Ollie was getting restless. He sniffed the ground, looked up every time a wolf howled, and paced the gravel bar from one side to the other.

While we searched for clues, Brinegar called a chopper to arrange for extraction of the victims. He had plenty of reasons for the expediency—wildlife, weather, the chance of a tourist or two stumbling on this grisly scene and posting a bad review on social media. Even the wolves were getting impatient. I could hear them howling in the distance.

Hux and I had gone over the perimeter three times when I decided to have one last look at the victims themselves. I knew the medical examiner would do a thorough autopsy, but I liked to go into that conversation with a set of questions prepared.

Hux walked over to me while I was crouched down, inspecting Kelsey Greer's face. There was some subtle white residue around her lips. Chapstick? An energy drink? Something else?

I used a stick and a gloved hand to pry open her mouth. Her mandible had gone stiff with rigor mortis, and I wasn't making much progress.

"You need a hand there?" Hux asked.

"Maybe a little."

With a little muscle, we managed to get her jaw open an inch. I shined my flashlight into the void of her mouth and swept the beam from side to side.

Huh, I thought.

"What is it?"

"The mucosa is pretty ragged; I'm seeing a number of ulcerations."

"Could that happen postmortem? Just from being out here?"

I shook my head. "No, this looks more like a disease state. Hand-foot-and-mouth disease, herpes esophagitis, maybe toxic ingestion . . ."

"Does he have it too?" Hux asked.

"I haven't looked yet."

Our exam of Tim Greer's oropharynx showed the same thing. On a city street, that white residue around their lips would have called to mind any number of illegal substances: cocaine, oxy, heroin. Out here, though, my mind went to the local plant life.

"You didn't bring your plant identification book by chance, did you?" I asked Hux.

"Sure did." He walked a short distance to where his backpack lay on the ground and pulled out a pocket-sized guide. Hux had made it clear that he much preferred the app-based plant identification tools, but those didn't work without a cell signal. "What am I looking for here, boss?" He waved the book at me.

"Berries, possibly. Something with white skin or fruit."

He walked back over to where I was standing. The pages of his pocket guide were tattered and worn, and he flipped through them with a deft hand. "Baneberries," he said. "Can be white or red with a round, glossy shape, so that fits. They're also called 'dolls' eyes' because of the red dot on white berries." He squinted at the page. "All parts of the plant are poisonous—oh."

"What?"

"The first symptoms of toxicity are burning and blistering of mucosal surfaces like the mouth and throat." He looked up and met my gaze. "That tracks too."

"It does, but have you ever heard of someone dying from baneberry poisoning?"

"Hmm." He read down the page some more. "Well, they're apparently supremely toxic, but it says here they have a bitter taste. So, that's a deterrent, for sure."

I thought on this for a moment, considering the possibility that Tim and Kelsey Greer had eaten a dozen horrible-tasting baneberries before prostrating themselves on the river and dying a miserable death. What didn't fit for me was the fact that they didn't look malnourished or even desperate. I was willing to bet that the autopsy report was going to show a recent meal in their stomachs, which meant they'd been camping and eating and doing their normal things until just a few hours before they died. So what had prompted the baneberry ingestion? *Curiosity?*

If so, it sounded like they would have stopped eating them rather quickly because of the taste.

"We'll have to wait on the ME's report," I said. "If it was a toxic plant, they'll try to identify the species. If Tim and Kelsey Greer ate enough to kill themselves, they should be able to determine that too."

"How long do you think that'll take?"

"A day or two, I hope."

Ollie was standing at the river's edge, staring pointedly at the opposite shore. "He thinks they came from across the river," Hux remarked. "He's been whining for the last hour."

"What do *you* think?" I asked.

"I tend to agree."

"They aren't wearing waders." I gestured to the Greers' hiking boots, which were laced up to the top. "And the water looks pretty deep here."

Hux gingerly grasped Kelsey Greer's boot. "It's still wet," he said.

"Have you ever experienced dry boots in Alaska?"

His lips twitched with a smile. "Are you okay with me taking it off?"

"Sure, go ahead. You got a knife?"

"Why?"

"The dead aren't as limber as the living."

Hux nodded, acknowledging the grim truth in that statement, as he proceeded to untie Kelsey Greer's shoelaces. In the end, he had to remove them altogether to get the hiking boot off her foot, which came free with a small gush of water.

Hux was right. The significant volume of water in her hiking boots meant she had waded into the frigid, wild, dangerous river. Had something, or someone, chased them across the Alatna? It was a disturbing thought.

Ollie seemed to read my thoughts as he pawed at the gravel bar where it met the water. Hux tugged at the brim of his baseball cap.

"I think we should at least have a look on the other side," he said. "If a bush pilot saw a tent in the water, it actually makes more sense that they were camping there. I checked the weather reports, and the wind was coming from the east last night."

"Hm," I said. "Good observation."

He turned to face me. "You look perturbed."

"Perturbed is a strong word."

"Flummoxed?"

I smirked at him. "Are you sure you're a math guy?"

"I've been known to flex my robust vocabulary now and then."

"I'm just having trouble putting this all together," I said. "It's one thing to cross the river and then die, but to die *here*? Like this?"

"What are you saying, boss?"

"I'm saying I haven't ruled out a homicide."

The distant sound of a helicopter made me look up at the sky. It was approaching from the southeast, probably from Fairbanks or even Anchorage. The closest major medical center was in Fairbanks, along with the county morgue. I'd worked with several medical examiners in the state so far, and every experience had been positive. Alaska didn't have coroners, who were elected to the position and often lacked relevant training for this kind of work. It wasn't that I hadn't worked with competent coroners before; it was just that I liked knowing that I could rely on someone with specialized training when I was in a different state, in unfamiliar territory.

When the chopper landed, it felt like reality was setting in— these two dead bodies on the Alatna River with their bizarre injuries, the cult we'd been tasked to find in the middle of nowhere, the mystery of a windblown tent spotted on the river. And then, of course, there was the question that had taken root in my mind, planting a seed of unease that had already begun to bloom: *Was there a killer loose in the park?*

Out of the corner of my eye, I saw Brinegar striding toward me. He tucked his chin against his chest to ward off the wind. "This is your chance to get back to Denali right now, Agent Harland," he said. "There's room on the chopper for both of you, if you're interested."

"We're going to hang back a bit," I said. "We're not quite done here."

As if on cue, a lone wolf howled into the void. "Be careful," he said. "Those wolves out there might hold a grudge."

"Don't worry," Hux said. "I sleep with a big stick."

Brinegar looked at Hux like he was trying to decide if he was being serious, but I knew Hux. He *did*, in fact, prefer to sleep with a big stick that he could grab at a moment's notice.

"It's not just the wolves," Brinegar said. "We tend to attract some hardcore survivalist types up here. They don't like company."

Hearing him mention a "survivalist" made me think back to Hux's conversation with Dora and Greg. "Any chance you've heard of one named Zane Reynolds?" I asked.

The lines in Brinegar's leathery brow deepened. "You know about him?"

"*You* know about him?"

"I've never met the man," he said, "but I've heard his name through the grapevine. We hear about guys like him from time to time—fugitives, ex-cons, doomsayers that come up to the arctic wilderness to live out their fantasies or what have you. Some of them are armed." He glanced at the holster on my waistband. "I'm just saying you should keep an eye out."

"Any chance you think one of those types might be responsible for what happened here?"

Brinegar shoved his hands deep in his pockets. "I can't say I'm even sure what you mean by that, Agent Harland. Are you thinking this was murder?"

"No," I said. "I'm not necessarily saying that. I'm just trying to decide if these two ended up here all on their own. Seems unlikely to me."

"I'm in agreement that they weren't out here on their own for nearly a month," Brinegar said. "I saw the report that went out on these two—that they were last seen in Bettles almost a month ago. Could it be they stumbled into a bunker? Or got abducted by some nutjob?" He shook his head. "To tell you the truth, ma'am, that's above my pay grade. But I trust you'll work through it. Just, again, keep an eye out."

"We will," I said, even though I wasn't entirely sure what he meant by "keeping an eye out." In an area that covered eight million acres, it wasn't all that hard to stay under the radar. I was more worried about *not* finding Zane Reynolds than I was about him finding us.

I spotted Emily heading our way, planting her hiking stick in sync with her strides. Even though the wind had picked up and the daytime sunlight had started to wane, she seemed impervious to the cold. I had encountered several people like her in Alaska. And yet, here I was, layering up even on the warmest summer days.

"Um, Chief?" she said to Brinegar.

"What's up?"

"I heard you talking—about this survivalist, I mean. I know a ranger that mighta stumbled on his campsite a couple months back."

I glanced at Hux, giving him the sign that he should go ahead and take it from here. Hux said, "Where? Near here?"

"Not really." She adjusted the straps of her wide-brimmed hat. "You familiar with Mount Chitiok?"

I started to say no, but Hux cut in with, "Sure. It's west of here, over the Divide—right?"

Emily looked impressed. "Yeah."

"So what happened?" he asked. "Did your friend talk to anyone at the campsite?"

"He talked to the main guy—the leader, I guess. My buddy was concerned about the size of the group, which he said was at least twelve, maybe fifteen. The limit in the park is ten."

"Why is that?" I asked.

"To help preserve the ecosystem. The vegetation near the rivers is getting trampled. We try to tell people to camp on the gravel bars, but some people feel like it's not private or scenic enough. Since you don't need a permit here, you can really camp wherever you want. So all we can do is limit group sizes."

Hux and I exchanged a glance. "Any chance we could talk to this ranger?" I asked.

"Um, maybe. But I think he's in Nepal right now."

"Nepal?"

"He's on a mountaineering expedition out there."

"Got it." I couldn't fault a guy for pursuing his passion, but it could be a challenge getting in touch with him. Even so, it was worth trying to track him down.

"Any chance you could send me his contact info?" I reached into my back pocket for the slim stack of business cards I kept there. Every once in a while, they came in handy.

"Uh, sure." She took my card, glanced at the front and back with a slight look of disapproval, and stuffed it in her pocket. I made a mental note to follow up with her later.

Brinegar shuffled his feet a bit. "Well, I'm gonna hitch a ride with the chopper," he said. "You all take care now."

"Safe travels," I said. "We'll give you an update when we have one."

"Appreciate that." Brinegar walked off toward the helicopter, its rotors whirring in the thin air. Emily munched on a granola bar while Dave made his way over to us. He had spent most of the last hour packing up his things.

"Are you and Dave sticking around?" I asked Emily.

"Um, just for a little while," she said. "We were supposed to meet up this week for a wildlife survey."

"Which way are you headed?" Hux asked.

Emily pointed to a collapsible canoe languishing in the water downstream. "That there's our ride," she said. "It's the best way to travel if you ask me." She tightened the straps of her backpack as the gusts of air from the helicopter nearly knocked us off our feet. She caught her hat at the last second.

Dave said, "We got a call about an injured bear not too far from here. Not that there's much we can do about it, but injured bears can turn into aggressive bears, so we like to be proactive."

"I see," I said. "Well, good luck." I handed him one of my cards. "Just in case you need to get in touch about anything."

As they made their way down to Emily's collapsible vessel, I briefly wondered if we were making a mistake letting them go. It wasn't that I suspected Emily or Dave of any nefarious activity, but they both knew the Alatna River basin better than anyone, and it surprised me that Emily hadn't seen a bright orange tent or a random campsite nearby. As for Dave, he looked out of his element, a wilderness biologist who feared the wilderness. I wondered what his backstory was. Even though he had spoken capably about the wolves, something seemed off there.

"What did you make of those two?" I asked Hux.

"I was waiting for you to ask me that," he said with a chuckle.

"Well?"

"Well, they're definitely *together*."

"You think?"

"I do think."

Here we were, bumping up against the whole personal–professional boundary again. It always made me a little uncomfortable to talk about other people's workplace romances because, well, we were at some small risk for one. Margo certainly thought so. She loved to bring it up every time we talked on the phone.

"Beyond that, though," I said. "You didn't think Dave was a little odd?"

"Odd, how?"

"He just seemed nervous."

"Maybe because he was. I saw it all the time when I was interrogating people overseas. You ever hear of white-coat hypertension? It's like that, except the person's wearing military fatigues or a law enforcement badge."

Ollie wandered over, his impatience having given way to resignation. He barked once—weakly, hoarsely. I knew what he wanted: to explore the other side of the river.

"He's about to give up on us," Hux remarked.

"I know, but we should eat first."

"Thank God," Hux said. "I'm in a red zone over here."

Hux took charge of the food prep while I picked a dry spot by the river and studied my map of the park. The next meal would be my turn.

After a couple minutes, Hux walked over with a pair of spinach wraps, apple slices, and a piece of chocolate in the shape of Mt. Denali. "I got the chocolate at the airport," he explained.

"I didn't get you anything," I said, a little sheepishly.

"Eh, you'll make it up to me."

"Don't count on it."

His lips curled up in a smile as he handed me one of the spinach wraps. As soon as I took that first bite, I realized how hungry I was. It had been a grueling day, with more hard hours to come. Now that the rangers had left, I wondered if the wolves were feeling emboldened. I could still hear them howling in the distance, a lonely chatter that rolled through the valley.

When we'd finished our dinner, I looked back at the final resting place of Tim and Kelsey Greer. In some ways, it was a serene setting—the river, the white spruce, the vast Alaska wilderness. The sky was a dazzling blue.

But I'd been doing this job long enough to suspect that they hadn't died peaceful deaths. The toxic berries. The wounds on their wrists. Their bodies prostrated on a riverbed of rock and silt.

Something sinister had happened here.

The question was, *what?*

CHAPTER

8

WITH DUSK RAPIDLY approaching, Hux and I set out across
the wild and scenic Alatna River. My first hard lesson
coming to Alaska was getting used to the fact that my feet were
always wet, no matter the weather or the terrain. Wet sponga,
rivers, and streams were everywhere in the arctic landscape, and
there was no avoiding them.

I gritted my teeth and ventured into the river, bracing myself
for the inevitable chill. *God, this sucks,* I thought. It would take
hours to warm up again.

Ollie was a capable swimmer, but Hux carried him in his
arms most of the way because, well, he didn't like taking chances
with my dog. Hux was rather attached to him, which was cute.
Seeing them navigate the river together took the sting out of the
misery of being cold and wet.

After a smooth crossing without any major disasters, we
made it to the other side. Ollie resumed the hunt almost as soon
as his feet hit the ground, and Hux urged him on, using a glove
from each of the victims that I'd given him permission to use for
tracking purposes. Barely a minute passed before Ollie started
howling.

I cupped a hand over my eyes and scrutinized a potential
path eastward into the wilderness. "It feels like we're in for some
bushwhacking," I said with a groan.

Hux caught my eyes briefly while looking up from his map. "You don't sound super pumped about it," he said with a laugh.

"Well, I'm a foot shorter than you, so your whacked bushes tend to hit me in the face."

"Are you telling me you'd like me to do my bushwhacking from a crouch?"

I couldn't help but briefly imagine what that would look like—essentially an unobstructed view of Hux's muscular backside for hours—and decided to banish the thought from my mind as quickly as possible. "You do you," I said. "I'll survive."

"Whatever you say, boss."

As we walked, I tightened my chest strap a bit, relishing my backpack's familiar shape and weight. I had come a long way since my Sequoia assignment. I now had a backpack that suited me and a weight limit that I could handle. I knew how to pack my things in the most efficient way possible; in a side pocket were extra evidence bags, gloves, and a pair of tweezers. In the other side pocket were a compass and my Garmin inReach device.

Hux and I followed Ollie into the brush, covering mostly flat terrain that was rather inhospitable to trees. The lack of wooded areas made for good visibility but poor shelter in the event of bad weather. I hoped we wouldn't have to deal with the latter on this trip.

We'd been hiking for less than fifteen minutes when Ollie unleashed a high-pitched bark and darted out of sight. I felt my stomach clench. Ollie wasn't one to waste an opportunity or signal a false alarm. I was confident he'd found something.

Hux and I hurried after him, careful to stay within view of each other. Our one rule in the wilderness was to always stay together. Hux treated the buddy system like a religion.

Ollie was pawing at the dirt beneath a tall spruce when we found him, throwing chunks of mud behind him as he stuck his snout in the enlarging hole. What struck me from the outset the most was the disturbance of leaves and dirt in the area. There appeared to be footprints too—or at least fragments of them—but they were human in origin, not from wolves or bears.

It seemed unlikely, then, that Tim and Kelsey Greer had been chased off by a large mammal.

Either way, if this *had* been their campsite, there was no definitive proof of it. Hux and I were operating on the information that their tent had blown into the river, at least according to a bush pilot, but what about the rest of their gear? It almost looked to me as though the campsite had been cleared out. To hide evidence, maybe? But if that was the case, evidence of *what*?

"Over here!" Hux called out.

I went over to a crooked little spruce tree to find Hux rubbing the scruff around Ollie's neck as my dog stood proudly over the discovery he had made.

It was a wool sock.

Not just a sock, but a sock that appeared to have something inside of it. Ollie waited for one of us to reach inside the hole and pluck it out, since he had learned long ago not to tamper with potential evidence.

I said to Hux, "Go ahead. You do the honors."

Even before Hux could reach into the depths of the article of clothing, I could guess what was inside based on its shape: a satellite phone. Hux extracted it with a gloved hand. The phone was a cheap brand, nothing fancy. It looked like it had seen a least few seasons' worth of use.

Hux powered it on, which sent me through a whole spectrum of emotion—hope, anxiety, fear. *Why would anyone have buried a satellite phone in the dirt?*

The screen flickered to life. I realized I was holding my breath.

The sobering punch of reality hit hard: the phone had been wiped clean. There were no messages, texts, call records—nothing. Here I was, thinking we were about to find a full account of the events that had transpired in this isolated corner of the world, but all we had was a cheap, wiped satellite phone with twenty percent of its battery life.

That, and a sticker on the bottom: "Property of Bettles Outfitters. If found, please call 907-692-0001."

"It's a rental," I said.

Hux rubbed his chin. "Yup."

"We'll check with Tess and see if she can match the serial number to whoever who rented it."

"Did she mention anything about the Greers renting a sat phone?"

"Not specifically," I said. "But I'm sure she has a record of it."

Hux put his hands on his hips and gazed into the hole Ollie had dug. "I wonder why they buried it here."

"Assuming Tim and Kelsey Greer were the ones who buried it . . ."

"Well, the sock definitely belonged to one of them—Ollie's not one to get his signals crossed." Hux gave Ollie a piece of beef jerky. "Right, boy?"

Ollie inhaled his reward for a job well done, which made Hux smile. But I couldn't shake the feeling that we were missing something significant. The strange positioning of the bodies, the tent in the water, the buried satellite phone—none of those things on their own pointed to murder, but all three of them added up to something seriously questionable.

"It's getting late," I said, glancing at my watch. "We could camp here for the night and get an early start in the morning."

Hux shook his head. "It's supposed to rain tonight. Usually rain's a good thing for a tracking dog, but there's a lot of slope to the ground here. Ollie could lose the scent from the campsite here pretty quickly."

"So you want to keep going?"

Hux crouched down and scrutinized the dirt. "We've got a good lead here." He pointed at a subtle impression in the earth. "See here? These prints clearly came from downriver." He pushed himself up and followed them about a dozen yards through the wet sponga before the trail petered out. Hux was right; it was clear that whoever had camped here had come from the south, which meant they'd probably stayed close to the Alatna before veering east, up toward the mountains.

We followed the trail all the way back to the river, where the footprints disappeared for good on the gravel bar. Hux was standing near the water's edge, probing at rocks with a stick, when he said, "Wait a minute."

"What?"

"I think there's a third set of prints here."

I walked over to see what he was looking at. "Where?"

"This print here." He pointed at an impression in the river silt, which was partially hidden under a rock. "It's different from the others."

"You're sure?" I could make out the partial outline of a hiking boot, but it wasn't a slam-dunk, that was for sure. I didn't understand how Hux could be so confident that this partial footprint had come from a third party.

He took photos from several different angles with his phone. "You can tell by the impressions here." He now pointed to the pattern of ridges and lines on the sole. "It's similar to the other two we found, but not the same. I'd say it's probably a men's size nine."

"Or a women's eleven."

He furrowed his brow. "It's a men's shoe, Harland."

"Not necessarily. Let's keep an open mind here."

"How many women wear a size eleven?"

"Look, I wear a size five and a half, so I'm not one to dismiss outliers."

Hux glanced down at my boots. "Well, hey, I never noticed your elfin feet before, but now that you mention it . . ."

I rolled my eyes at him, which brought a smile to his face. "Tim Greer wore a size nine, so how can you be sure this isn't his?"

"How do you know what size he wore?"

"Because I checked the sizing on everything he was wearing at the scene."

Hux looked deflated. "Good thinking. I should've done that."

"Don't beat yourself up about it. Just so you know, he was wearing a size nine extra-wide shoe. Hers were size seven. So it sounds like the print isn't hers, but it could have been his."

"It doesn't match the pattern from the hiking boot he was wearing, though," Hux said. "I already checked it against the photos I took at the scene."

"Could be he was wearing different footwear here for some reason."

Hux shook his head. "Nah. Why would anyone carry two sets of hiking boots? That's too much weight to be lugging around up here. It's a third party."

"Let's have another look around, then," I said. "See if we can confirm three unique sets of footprints."

"Good plan."

Mindful of the time and the encroaching darkness, we scoured the dirt and gravel bar for a solid hour. For the most part, though, it was a fruitless search; the shoe impressions were mostly partials, which made them hardly recognizable as footprints at all. But I did have to concede that Hux was right about the mysterious "third-party" impression.

"All right, let's call it a day," I said. "We can camp here."

Hux tilted his head toward the sky. He didn't wear a watch, which mystified me. I was so attached to mine that I almost wished it was sewn into my skin.

"We've got another couple hours of daylight," he said. "And with this rain coming, I say we make the best of it while we can."

I took a breath, frustrated by the constraints of the weather, which always seemed to be working against us. Even so, Hux was right; we had to keep moving before the rain moved in. Thanks to our extreme latitude, we had a few more hours of daylight at our disposal. I did have to admit, however, the thought of being caught unawares after dark made me deeply uneasy.

"Are you feeling okay, boss?" Hux asked.

"Fine. Great," I said as I tightened my shoelaces. "You're right. Let's keep moving."

"Is your back—"

"My back's good. Everything's good." It wasn't often that Hux mentioned the back pain that had sidelined me in Sequoia, the sequelae of the severe injuries that I'd sustained in Australia. Once in a while, though, he liked to check in with me. I had promised him that I'd tell him the truth when he asked, so long as he didn't ask too often.

"Alrighty," Hux said. "Onward, then."

9

Ollie led the charge along the river, but it was Hux who decided our route. He kept his compass and map handy since he checked them both frequently.

Hux, after all, was a master tracker. During his tenure in the Park Service after several tours overseas, he had tracked down missing persons, hikers, tourists, and even a killer. His tracking abilities had predated his time in the military, even, but they'd proved an asset there too. With Hux Huxley by my side, I never had to worry about getting lost. All I really had to worry about was making myself useful.

I suddenly realized that Hux was trying to get my attention from his position out in front. "Sorry," I said. "What was that?"

"Just wondering what you think of the park," he said.

"Oh," I said. "Well, I mean, it definitely puts the 'wild' in 'wilderness.'"

Hux groaned.

"What?" I asked.

"That was pretty cheesy, even for you."

I laughed. "What do *you* think of the park?"

"No complaints," he said. "But I'm more of a Sequoia guy."

"You miss your cabin?"

"Sometimes." He looked over his shoulder at me with a wistful smile. "But it'll still be there when we get back."

Even though I would never admit it, I thought about Hux's cabin from time to time. It was the kind of escape I yearned for in my own life—a place to retreat but also call my own. In the last year of our marriage, Kevin and I had talked a lot about buying a cabin on a lake somewhere, but those aspirations had never come to pass. Now, I wasn't sure how I felt about lakes. They were a little too inert for my taste.

When Ollie suddenly started barking at the river, I reached for my map. Hux didn't have to. He clearly already knew where we were.

Takahula Lake.

"Looks like we're going to have to cross back over," I said, trying and failing to sound upbeat.

Hux laughed. "Let me guess—you're thinking you should've put in for the Great Sand Dunes National Park?" There was a smile in his eyes.

"Or Badlands or Arches or even Death Valley . . ."

"Skin cancer central."

"Better than hypothermia headquarters."

He turned and looked at me. "Your jokes are something to behold, and I mean that in the worst way possible," he said with a straight face. "I'm worried about you."

"Oh, shut up."

He snickered as we waded into the river for yet another water crossing. When we encountered dense brush and alder trees on the other side, Hux pulled out his machete and let it rip. I grimaced every time he swung it. I knew machetes were an invaluable tool when it came to bushwhacking in the backcountry, but I'd seen what they could do to people too. It was one of a few cases from my tenure at the bureau that still haunted me.

My tool of choice was a big stick as we made our way around the oval-shaped Takahula Lake. I used it to push brush and branches out of the way, even though Hux was doing most of the heavy lifting. Every so often, he'd miss a branch or some other prickly piece of brush that would swing back and hit me in the face. My white T-shirt was speckled with blood by the time we emerged from the thick of it.

Hux gasped when he saw me. "Are you okay?"

"Totally fine," I said with a grunt. "Are we close?"

Hux took out his map while I looked at the sky. The smattering of clouds had cleared, revealing the sun's golden orb on a palette of pale but fading blue. It was 8:32 PM. The black and white spruce trees that surrounded us provided hardly any cover at all from the sun, wind, the elements. The mosquitoes feasted on my bare skin every time we stopped. August's rainy season would reduce their numbers, but for now, my neck and arms were covered in welts.

"I feel like we're close," Hux announced. "Ollie's gone quiet."

"He doesn't want to give away our location," I said. "Smart pup."

"How are you holding up?"

"I'm great," I said, determined to keep my complaints to a minimum. Hux quirked an eyebrow, as if he didn't quite believe me. I couldn't see my own face, but I knew it was battered—by brush, bugs, and the sun. I wasn't in pain, so there was that.

"Did you forget your bug spray?" he asked.

"No," I said.

"Sure seems like you did."

"I practically bathed in it before we headed out this morning."

"Then it must be your abundance of sweat."

"Har." I took a swig from my canteen and walked right past him. The density of trees and brush impacted the visibility in this part of the park, which made me uneasy. If Reynolds was camped out here somewhere, we risked surprising him.

Hux suddenly stopped swinging the machete. We stood in silence for a beat, listening for signs of human inhabitation. He pulled the brim of his cap down over his eyes and twisted his hands around the worn handle of the machete. I could tell by the look on his face that he felt conflicted about something.

"What's wrong?" I asked.

"It's getting late. I just don't want to be doing this after dark."

"Me neither," I said. "We can stop whenever you want."

He plucked a new piece of grass and stuck it in his mouth. "Let's give it another hour or so," he said.

"Sounds good to me."

The trail doubled back northward in the direction of the Arrigetch Peaks, which, at an altitude of seven thousand feet, towered over the neighboring mountains. I suspected we had landed on an old game trail, a weathered path cut unnaturally through the brush.

As we ventured farther from the river, a set of human footprints suddenly appeared in the dirt. "Hux," I said. "Are you seeing these?"

"Yup," Hux said excitedly. "Two of the impressions look familiar—Tim and Kelsey Greer, I'd say."

"Are you seeing a third?"

With daylight waning, we shined our flashlights on the ground to get a better look.

"Here," Hux said. He pointed at a spot in the middle of the game trail, where the tread cut fairly deep into the mud. I could see the two sets of footprints clearly here, but a third—to me, at least—wasn't obvious.

"It's overlaying the other print," he said. "See?"

"No," I admitted.

"It's there. Trust me."

I glanced at him, conveying with a look that of course I trusted him. "Size nine again?"

He nodded. "Looks that way."

"Okay, so there was a third person in their party. A guide, maybe?"

Hux shook his head. "The overlay suggests to me that they weren't traveling together. Someone was trying to cover their tracks."

I was starting to realize why Hux was one of the best trackers in the world. "Why?"

Hux was quiet for a moment. "Hard to say. My best guess is that they didn't want Tim and Kelsey to turn around and realize they were being followed."

"Is there any way to know how far behind them this person was?"

Hux frowned. "It's on the order of minutes or hours, but that's as specific as I can get."

It was coming on ten o'clock, with hardly any daylight left. Exhaustion was setting in. I liked to think I could just power through anything, but at some point, Mother Nature claimed victory. A part of me was grateful to see the sun go down, but another part of me hated the prospect of quitting this close to the finish line.

According to my map and heading, we were standing near the source of the Takahula River, which put us about six miles west of the Alatna. The game trail that had taken us here ebbed and flowed, making a series of serpentine turns and unpredictable switchbacks.

Ollie kept his nose to the ground, and Hux used his flashlight to make sure we stayed on course. With a sliver of twilight on the horizon, the narrow trail spilled out into open space, giving us a direct path to the mountains.

I lifted my gaze to the statuesque rise of the Arrigetch Peaks, where, in the fading light of day, I glimpsed something at eye level: a speck of artificial green in a cluster of spruce trees.

It was a tent.

10

I COULD HARDLY BELIEVE my eyes. Aside from the Greers' phantom campsite, this was the first sign of human inhabitation I'd seen since stepping foot in the park. In most national parks, tents were ubiquitous—part of the landscape, even. But that tiny speck of green on a sprawling canvas of wet tussocks felt like a mirage.

Hux took out his binoculars for a better look. We were about a quarter mile out from the campsite, a bit above it in terms of elevation but shielded from view thanks to the spruce trees.

"I see three tents," Hux said as he peered out in their direction. "They look like twofers, so I'm gonna say six people max. Could be fewer than that, though, if people are camping alone. Or more, if somebody's hiding out nearby somewhere."

I frowned, remembering Emily's claim that her ranger friend had associated Reynolds with a much larger group. Maybe this *wasn't* them.

"Do you see anyone hanging around the camp?" I asked.

Hux was quiet for a moment, moving his binoculars ever so slightly from side to side. "No. Just the tents. The color match with the background is impressive. This crew clearly doesn't want to be found."

Over the course of my tenure with ISB, I had started paying more attention to tents—their size, their color, their intended function. For the most part, campers in remote areas of national parks preferred bright colors, mainly because they were easy to find after a long day of hiking. But in recent years, the "low impact" neutral grays and greens had become more popular. I didn't like those tents as much. In my experience, the occupants were less forthcoming. It was a generalization, sure, but for the same reason I'd never relished raids with the FBI, I didn't like walking up to a tent unannounced.

"It's too bad we don't know more about this Reynolds guy." Hux lowered his binoculars. "But if this is him, I'm thinking he's got some military experience."

I had to admit this did not come as welcome news. "What makes you say that?"

"Just the way the tents are arranged. It's expedient and deliberate. That dark green color, too—you can tell this guy is all about camouflage. It could be he's just a hardcore survivalist, but those types don't tend to hang out with other people."

I put my hands on my hips and looked out at the campsite. "Are we in over our heads here?"

Hux looked at me. "Could be."

"You think he's armed?"

"I don't know, to be honest. This whole setup feels a little strange. On the one hand, if this campsite belongs to Reynolds, he's not your garden-variety weekend warrior, but on the other hand, you've got Dora, who seemed ready to nominate him for sainthood." Hux surveyed the campsite again with his binoculars. "Hold up," he said. "I'm seeing some activity."

"What kind of activity?"

"Four people are gathering around the firepit." He handed me the binoculars. "Here, have a look."

I peered through the lenses with a gnawing sense of trepidation. Hux was right; four adults were congregating around a wood piling. One of the four was crouched down and trying to light the kindling with a match. In the dark, it was impossible to make out their faces. That left two people unaccounted for, at least based on Hux's educated guess.

"I'm not seeing any firearms," I said. "They look like civilians to me."

"We haven't seen the whole crew yet," Hux pointed out. He reached back and stretched his arms behind him, which he often did to keep his muscles loose. Hux never seemed comfortable while idle. Ollie was the same way, but for now, he was staying put.

"What's our move here, boss?" Hux asked.

"I'm thinking."

"I know. I can hear the gears grinding in your head."

"Grinding, huh?"

"Oh yeah," he said with a smirk. "Your gears are loud and slow."

I rubbed my knuckles, debating what to do before someone spotted us and made the decision for us. Something told me Zane Reynolds wasn't going to cooperate with a pair of federal agents asking questions. He probably wouldn't even give us his real name. Out here, there was no accountability. Carrying a form of personal identification wasn't required, which made it easy to lie about one's identity. I'd encountered those types before.

I thought back to our interaction with the loner types we'd encountered in Sequoia—the skittishness, the distrust. And then, later, the outright lies. There was no rule in the ISB play-book that said we had to go in there as federal agents; in fact, I'd received plenty of training in undercover operations during my tenure with the FBI. I'd even gone undercover as a minor in a few sex trafficking stings in Chicago. Need a fourteen-year-old to solicit sex from a creepy old guy? Call Felicity Harland; she's five feet tall and looks every bit the part of a doe-eyed high school dropout.

In this case, I was wondering if it made sense to adjust our tactics. Hux had played the "oblivious park ranger" for Dora and Greg so effectively that I had no doubt he could inhabit another fictional role without missing a beat.

"Let's talk logistics first." I rubbed my hands together, to stay warm. "If we get separated for some reason, we need a rendezvous point." I showed him the spot on my map: Takahula Lake. "Here, just west of the Alatna River, that little strip of land between the lake and the river. Right across from Millichetah

Creek. All three are solid landmarks that should be easy to find, even for me."

"I like it," he said. "What about a sign/countersign?"

I responded with a blank stare. Sometimes Hux used military terms that simply weren't a part of my vocabulary. He was always happy to explain them, but admitting my ignorance didn't come naturally to me.

"A code word," he said. "For if things go to shit and only one of us knows it."

"Oh, right," I said. "Yeah. Good idea."

He looked like he was about to say something—make a joke, bust my balls—but he didn't. Instead, he said, "'Sequoia.' That can be the code word for a potential problem. If you mention it in conversation, it means we need to find a place to talk ASAP."

"Okay," I said.

"Now, if either one of us says 'spark,' it means abort mission. We get out of there fast and go straight to the rendezvous point. Use a flare if you have to. You've got one, right?"

"Yes," I said.

"Okay, sorry—just checking."

"Don't be sorry. I'd rather err on the side of caution than make a sloppy mistake."

"I'm right there with you." Smiling, he tucked his rogue blond hair under the brim of his baseball cap. I knew Hux could handle anything that came his way, but still, seeing his youthful face in all its glory gave me pause. Technically, as his superior, I was responsible for him.

As I was tightening my chest strap, debating how to broach the subject of an undercover op with essentially no preparation, I suddenly noticed the FBI insignia on my T-shirt.

"You admiring your shirt there?" Hux asked.

"Um, well . . ."

It was decision time. We were infiltrating this campsite one way or another. The only thing left to decide was whether we would be going in as federal agents or random backpackers. And if we *did* decide to play random backpackers, how could we convince a group as insular and secretive as this one to let us join them for a night or two?

Fear, I thought. *Fear works wonders in these situations.* We could tell them about Tim and Kelsey Greer—about the fact that the rangers were investigating two suspicious deaths only a few miles from here. Even if they told us to take a hike—or said nothing at all—I suspected we'd learn a lot from their reaction to the news.

"Uh-oh," Hux said. "The gears are grinding again . . ."

I slung my backpack off my shoulders and onto the ground. "I'm just wondering if maybe it's worth it to go stealth for this one. You remember what happened with Delia and Spark when we talked to them the first time?" I often thought about the two climbers we'd encountered during the course of our investigation in Sequoia. I couldn't help but feel like I'd put both our lives in danger by misinterpreting that situation. I had underestimated the potential for law enforcement to make certain people skittish and reactive.

"Yup," he said.

"Right. So I think this time, we go in as a pair of civilians—backpackers, outdoor enthusiasts, whatever. We tell whoever's camping here that we heard about the two dead bodies found nearby and that those people might have been murdered."

Hux was quiet for a moment. "It's risky," he said.

"I know. Is it *too* risky?"

He tugged on the brim of his cap with one hand and tightened the back strap with the other. "I agree that if we go in there as federal agents and find this guy Reynolds, he's going to tell us to take a hike—right after he gives us a fake name and tells us he's never heard of Tim or Kelsey Greer. And then he'll vanish into the ether and that'll be that."

Hux was right about something else, though: every undercover operation carried a unique set of risks. One consolation was that we wouldn't be here long, maybe a night or two at most—assuming Reynolds let us camp with his group. In that time, we'd focus on finding a way to talk to the other campers to see if we could establish a connection between Tim and Kelsey

Greer and this campsite. Then we'd head back to civilization to sort through the evidence. I was also planning on taking a close look at everyone's hiking boots to help us solve the mystery of this unidentified third party.

"Here's the thing," I said. "Going undercover has its risks, and I know you haven't been formally trained . . ."

"I've gone undercover before."

I felt my eyebrows go up. "Is there anything you *didn't* do in the Navy?"

"Um, yes, but I'm not allowed to talk about it." He grinned.

I shook my head, although admittedly I liked our repartee. But time was short, and we had to get moving if we were going to do this.

First things first: my wardrobe was a problem. Nearly everything I had in my backpack was standard-issue FBI or ISB, which made me a walking advertisement for federal law enforcement. This undercover operation wasn't going to last long with me dressed like this.

I said to Hux, "You might want to dump your Park Service T-shirts."

"I don't have any."

I looked up at him. "Your Navy stuff, then."

"I left that at home too—can't wear it as a civilian."

With Hux standing by, I unzipped my backpack and removed all my clothes. Among them were a folded stack of FBI T-shirts, an extra pair of sweatpants, my wide-brimmed hat . . .

Hux went through his own backpack in a gesture of solidarity, even though I knew he wasn't going to find anything incriminating inside. "Ooh," he said. "I found a pen." He tossed it in the bag. I glanced at the pen. It was from a Holiday Inn.

"I'm not understanding the issue with it," I said.

"I don't think our undercovers would stay in a Holiday Inn."

"You don't? Why not?"

"I know how loyal you are to Hampton Inn."

I rolled my eyes. "Come on, Hux. Just admit it—you came prepared. I screwed up." I had laid out all my clothes that weren't going to pass muster—the T-shirts, shorts, pants, underwear—when I caught Hux eyeing one of my sweatshirts.

"You've got a lot of FBI gear there," Hux remarked. "Are you still trying to convince me you were a bona fide FBI agent?"

"You're right; it's bad," I said with a sigh. "All I'm missing is the tattoo."

I took stock of my plain white tank tops, which I used for layering. My last trip to the laundromat outside of Denali had shrunk all of my undershirts to miniature proportions. I hoped the weather stayed chilly so Hux didn't notice, but even so, I was going to smell like a high school weight room by tomorrow afternoon.

I glanced over at Hux's stash of shirts. He'd folded them into squares that were slimmer than a sandwich, and they all fit perfectly into his backpack. His talent for the mundane never ceased to amaze me.

After I'd sorted my clothes and other personal effects into distinct piles—"keep" or "toss," the first pile was worrisomely small—I deleted all the calls and messages from my satellite phone. I didn't want it to be an issue if someone asked to borrow it.

The real sticking point was my gun. I was reluctant to leave it behind, even though it didn't fit with our cover at all. Besides, if Reynolds did have military or even law enforcement experience, he'd know it was a service weapon rather than a recreational firearm.

"I can take the Glock," Hux said. "Reynolds probably won't think twice if he sees a guy like me carrying it. It's bear country, after all."

"We can't take the chance," I said. "It's clearly a cop's gun."

"Then what do you want to do?" The intensity of his gaze made me wonder if he was testing my mettle, not that there was anything wrong with that. I knew it was better to test each other now than later, when we were in too deep to turn back.

"I'll put it in my backpack," I said. It was a compromise of sorts—a way to feel safe without sacrificing our cover. I removed the magazine and cycled the action a few times to make sure I hadn't missed a live round. Satisfied the gun wasn't going to fire while I was wearing my backpack, I tucked the Glock inside one of my tank tops and put the magazine in a side pocket. If Reynolds searched my bag and found either one, he'd think I was either an undercover cop or a complete moron. I was hoping it didn't come to that.

The sun's rays had dissolved into a silvery halo that lit the mountaintops, a punctuation mark on a long day. I wrestled my much-lighter pack onto my shoulders, but all I could think about was my gun, haphazardly thrown inside. I didn't like it one bit.

I looked over to see Hux shaking his sat phone.

"What's the problem?" I asked.

"It's not turning on."

"Your Iridium?"

"It's not my Iridium," he said. "The screen on mine cracked, so I had to send it in for repairs. This is a loaner."

"From who?"

"A friend." He didn't elaborate. "Anyway, it's not working at the moment." He tried to power it on again by holding down the button for a good five seconds. "No dice," he said, shaking his head. He sounded despondent, which was unusual for Hux.

"It's okay," I said. "We still have mine. And I've got the Garmin, too."

"Maybe you should leave that here as a backup plan, in case we need to get out of there in a hurry. Kind of like a backup to a backup."

He had a point. I could imagine a scenario where we might have to hightail it out of there without packing our gear or breaking down our tent. In that case, we didn't want to be in the wilderness without any communication devices.

"Sorry." Hux gave his bum sat phone a hard shake. "I don't know what happened."

"We're good. Don't worry about it."

Hux exhaled as he tossed the broken sat phone into the waterproof bag we planned to leave behind. "So what's the deal for this op?" he asked. "Are we friends? Outdoor enthusiasts who share a passion for going off the grid? Fugitives on the run?"

"Outdoor enthusiasts," I said. "Married a few years, no kids. We need to garner sympathy from the group. If the infertility piece is real, it makes sense for us to be a married, childless couple."

"Do we have infertility issues?"

"No," I said. "Too coincidental. I think we just try to fit in as best we can without forcing it. We'll say we're from New Jersey, like Dora and Greg—you're an insurance salesman, I'm a teacher—and we love going off the grid in the summer."

"The same way you did with Kevin," Hux said. There was no judgment in it; he was just stating a fact.

"A little like that," I admitted, even though the truth was that I hadn't been thinking about Kevin until that moment. Now that Hux mentioned my husband, though, I couldn't help but notice the parallels.

"What are our names?" he asked. "Oh, wait—I know."

"What?" I could hear the skepticism in my voice. Hux and I shared a particular aversion to our first names, albeit for different reasons. For a law enforcement officer, "Felicity" had never gone down easy with the old guard. Harland worked better. Hux, though, was open about his hatred for Ferdinand, a family name that he'd inherited and always shunned.

"I'll be Brad," he said cheerfully.

"Brad? Like Brad Pitt?" I held back a laugh. "No way. That's too on the nose."

"What do you mean?"

"It's just . . . it's not you."

"Huh?"

I found myself delighting in Hux's confusion. "You can be Fred. You know, for Ferdinand."

"Harland, I *hate* that name—"

"I know you do. You can pick mine, okay?"

He thought for a moment. "Maybe Carlin. It sounds like Harland—you know, so you won't get confused." He added a little smirk for my amusement.

"Sounds good to me."

Hux held his hand out. "What about our rings?" Hux asked.

"What?"

"Someone's gonna notice we aren't wearing wedding bands."

"We'll just say we left them at home," I mumbled.

"Can't do that. It's too convenient. Gotta sell it if we're gonna do it."

I supposed he had a point. I glanced down at my ring finger, which at the moment was bare. After the debacle in Sequoia, the doctors had cut off my wedding band because of the swelling in my arm and hand. The ring, having been repaired since, was currently sitting in a drawer in my vacant apartment in Reno. Hux had never said anything about it, but now I realized that he'd noticed. He was a budding investigator, after all. I told myself that Hux's observation in this regard had nothing to do with me, but instead was just Hux doing what I had taught him to do.

"Here." Hux handed me a piece of dead grass, which he'd tied into a loop, securing it with two tiny knots. The grass was the color of straw—not quite a glistening gold, but close enough.

"How cute," I quipped. "What are you going to wear?"

Hux reached into a side pocket of his backpack and fished around until at last he pulled out a thick gold band. I knew what it was the moment I laid eyes on it: a service ring from Hux's time in the Navy. It was beautifully crafted, with an eagle clutching a trident in its talons featured on the crown.

"It's lovely," I said. "But do you really want to go in there as a Navy SEAL?"

"I'll turn it around so it's just the band that's showing," he said. I watched him slip the handsome ring over his finger. It looked good on him.

"Why don't you wear this more often?" I asked.

He shrugged. "I'm not really a ring guy, I guess."

Hux didn't often talk about his time in the military, and to respect his privacy, I didn't press the issue. If he ever *wanted* to talk about it, I'd be all ears, but he was so forthcoming about everything else that I felt like this was one line better left uncrossed unless he initiated it.

"So you've got the fourteen-karat gold, and I have a piece of grass," I said. "At least people will know who wears the pants in this relationship."

He laughed, which put me at ease a little bit, even though my anxiety was mounting. With Hux, there was no pressure to be some amped-up law enforcement version of myself, but pretending to be married was a whole different game. I found myself questioning that decision, thinking maybe it would have been better to play it as brother and sister. *It's just for a day or two,* I told myself. *It's not like you're going to have to kiss the guy like they do on* The Bachelor.

"So who are we, then?" Hux asked. "Aside from Carlin and Fred Dinglehopper?"

"Dinglehopper?"

"All right, all right," Hux said. "Just Hopper."

"We can keep the Dingle some other time," I said. "But as for who we are as people, I say we just pick someone in our real lives and be them. You could be your brother, for example."

"Joe?" Hux seemed surprised to hear me mention him.

"Isn't he an insurance salesman?"

"It's just—I mean, I love Joe . . . it's just that I have this strong tendency to fall asleep every time he talks about his job."

"Doesn't he have his face on the side of a van or something? You could talk about that."

"You mean a white-paneled van? No, he'd never do that. No self-respecting insurance agent would ever do that."

"How about you don't have your face on a vehicle, then?"

"Well, I kind of want that, now that you mention it."

"In real life?"

"No, as part of my persona."

I shook my head. "Hux, you do what you need to do to be Fred Hopper."

All joking aside, I knew that Hux appreciated the gravity of the assignment. Though it was true that he wasn't thrilled about his underwhelming undercover, for an ex–Navy SEAL, there weren't a whole lot of options that would have appealed to him.

"What about you?" he asked. "Anything I should know about your approach to Carlin? Is this going to be Academy Award worthy?"

"Hardly," I said. "I'm basically just going to be Ellie."

"Your sister, Ellie?"

"Yeah. Why, is that too unoriginal?"

"Isn't Ellie the kindergarten teacher who bakes eight hundred cookies for Christmas and tells everyone you're in the CIA?"

"Yep."

"So Carlin loves kids?"

"I mean, not particularly. I *like* kids, I guess." I backtracked a bit. "I mean, kids are fine. I'm neutral on them. But, no, I'm not the one kissing babies or dancing with six-year-old boys at a wedding or whatever."

"So then don't play it that way. Be the kindergarten teacher that loves teaching but takes pride in keeping those little monsters in line."

I laughed. "I'm not sure that's going to fly."

"It'll fly. Don't pretend to be someone you're not."

Deep down, I wasn't concerned about blowing my cover in the first five minutes by failing to convey my affection for children. I was still fixated on the prospect of convincing a bunch of strangers that Hux and I were *married*. And not just newlyweds, but a longtime couple that had been through all sorts of ups and downs. Married couples tended to know everything about the other person—what proportion of ice they liked in their soft drinks, what comfort TV shows they watched depending on their mood, whether they believed in sunscreen as a real thing or a marketing ploy. I didn't know those things about Hux. In fact, there was a lot I didn't know about him.

Still, in my mind, it was worth the risk. To figure out what had happened to Tim and Kelsey Greer, we had to inhabit their lives a little bit. If this campsite *did* belong to Zane Reynolds, we'd only have one chance to get on his good side. I knew Hux was up to the task.

Was I, though?

There was no point asking the question.

Failure wasn't an option.

CHAPTER

11

THE FIRST PERSON to notice us making our way toward the campsite was a slender woman in khaki shorts and a white linen shirt. She was hanging a kettle over the fire when I locked eyes with her from about thirty yards away. Her reaction was guarded—no wave, no friendly smile. She put the kettle down and discretely got the attention of the others sitting around the fire.

I slowed my strides while Hux fell into step beside me. He certainly didn't *look* like an insurance salesman from New Jersey—especially in his tightish white T-shirt, which practically made his muscles glisten. His hair was a little too tousled, his stride too relaxed. I was tempted to tell him to slouch or something.

It was different for me. I had no problem projecting the general weariness of someone who wasn't accustomed to the great outdoors. And then there was the fact that I was genuinely exhausted after a long day trekking through the arctic. *So far, so good.*

The woman who had spotted us grasped at something dangling around her neck and brought it to her lips. The sound that followed was a birdcall of some sort—a hawk maybe, or a falcon.

Was she sounding an alarm?

This thought gave me pause. There were very few places in the world where you could kill someone out in the open and not have to worry about witnesses or police or even evidence. Gates of the Arctic National Park was one of them. What if Reynolds *was* a fugitive, who lured couples into the wilderness on a strange pretense of fertility assistance, only to kill them if something went wrong? And what if Tim and Kelsey Greer weren't his first two victims, just the first two that had been found? I tried to remind myself that my training had prepared me for encounters with unpredictable people, but this felt different. My Glock was unreachable in my backpack, and my credentials were in a hole in the ground. It was after dark, and we were outnumbered.

"Hi," Hux said to the group, holding up a hand and flashing a tentative smile at the four people sitting around the fire. "We're, ah—well, I'm Fred, and this is my wife, Carlin." He did his best to sound timid, but Hux didn't have a timid bone in his body.

When no one responded, I thought for a second that Hux had blown it, that everyone somehow knew he was lying. But then one of the two men sitting around the fire said, "Sorry, man, but this is a private party." He was on the shorter side, overweight, with spotty facial hair. His slippers looked like lambswool. *Slippers.* They were also on the smaller size—a size nine, perhaps? It was close.

I also thought about Kelsey Greer with her shiny hair and painted nails. Where she'd been before she died, she hadn't been roughing it. So far, I was feeling confident that we'd found her well-appointed camp in the arctic.

"Oh, well, we know, and we're so sorry," I said, chancing a smile. "But you must've heard about the two dead bodies that turned up just a couple miles from here. It's just us two, and, well, we're a little spooked. We were hoping to maybe join up with you all for the night."

"Wait, what?" The woman who had first noticed us shot a look at the man sitting next to her—a trimmer, leaner one. "Two people died? Where?"

"On the Alatna River," I said. "You haven't heard?"

"No," the man said—dark eyes, disproportionate features. His baseball cap ran low on his forehead. "We didn't hear nothin' about that." He had a southern accent . . . Texas, maybe.

"We were hiking the river when we ran into the rangers," I said. "They told us to steer clear, but we could see the tarps . . ."

"When was this?" the man asked.

"Earlier today."

"So why didn't you head back to the rangers station with them if you were so spooked?"

The man made a good point. I could sense Hux trying to find a way to rescue me from the misstep, but I managed to recover before he could intervene. "Because we just made it up to the park here," I said. "My husband's stubborn. We had an itinerary and a plan, and we haven't been on a real vacation in years. He wanted to stay the course."

"What about you?" the frumpier guy asked. "You tend to do everything your man tells you to do?"

Before I could answer, Hux said, "Most of the folks we've come across out here are friendly. We figured you'd be hospitable, but maybe not."

The men said nothing. The women looked at their hands. I could see, though, that something had rattled them a little bit. Maybe it was Hux, or maybe it was the news of two dead bodies. In some strange way, though, they weren't quite as rattled as I expected them to be.

There were a couple explanations for this. One, they felt safe here. If Zane Reynolds was the hardcore survivalist with a bunch of guns, I could see how that might give them a sense of security, false or earned. Two, they already knew about Tim and Kelsey Greer. Perhaps they even knew what had happened to them.

"So then, is it just you four?" Hux asked.

No one answered.

"We saw three tents," Hux said. "There must be somebody else camping here."

"Nice math there," the heavyset man said, which garnered a scolding look from his wife. "But yeah, there is. He's around."

Hux shifted his weight a bit, a subtle maneuvering into defensive mode. We each had our own flashlights, but now that the sun had set, danger felt more imminent. I couldn't help but think about Tim and Kelsey Greer marooned on the Alatna

River—the blisters in their mouths, the abrasions on their wrists. For all the nature that surrounded them, their deaths struck me as distinctly unnatural.

That said, it was hard to imagine five people conspiring to murder a young couple seeking a miracle from a fertility cult, but I'd been surprised before. I was also tired, which meant my guard was down and my wits were dulled. I stole a glance at Hux that said, *We better figure out what's going on here—fast.*

"Any chance we could talk to him?" Hux asked.

The woman sitting next to the man in a baseball cap stood up. "I'll go get him." Her voice was barely above a whisper. I was struggling to get a read on those two. They sure didn't strike me as gullible hipsters who believed in cults and miracles.

The other man gestured to some prime real estate in front of the fire. "Feel free to take a load off. There's coffee in the kettle there." He studied us for a long moment, like he couldn't quite decide if he wanted to impress us or not. "I'm Vince, by the way."

No one else introduced themselves. It wasn't a cozy gathering, that was for sure—no blankets, chairs, or bottles of beer. Everyone was roughing it, and yet no one seemed thrilled about it. I thought back to Dora's impression of the whole enterprise, which she had gathered from her social media trolling. I wasn't about to judge the validity of their need to have a child, but it helped to keep it in mind as I tried to get my bearings in this group of strangers.

"So, how did you find us?" Vince asked.

I glanced at Hux. "We got lucky, really. After we talked to the rangers, we stumbled on a game trail that pretty much brought us right here."

"Not *right* here," the other man said. "We left that trail at least a mile back."

"My dog helped us out," I said, ruffling Ollie's fur. "Ollie is Fred's hunting partner."

A dismissive snort. "He looks like more than a hunting partner."

Hux said, "He failed out of police K9 training—so, yeah, he *was* more than a hunting partner. He just didn't have the right guarding instinct for that kind of work." Hux spoke with such confidence that even the man in the baseball cap seemed to take him at his word. The man shrugged, sipped his coffee, and probed the fire with a stick. He didn't bother looking up again.

"It's a hell of a hike up here, isn't it?" Vince remarked. "Where'd you fly in? Bettles?"

Hux said, "That's right."

"No guide, though?"

"Nope," Hux said. "We did stop by Bettles Outfitters, though." He looked around the circle, waiting for someone to take the bait. It was a strong tactic, since the outfitter was one definitive link to the Greers. If someone here had been there, that could be a way in to further questions. "Anybody been there?" Hux asked.

Vince nodded. "We stopped in. The owner there helped us with our gear. She tried to convince us to use one of their guides, but we saved a bundle of money doing our own thing."

"We had a guide," the woman next to him, whom I assumed was his wife, cut in. "Please don't get the impression my lawyer husband could ever interpret a set of coordinates. He couldn't find *Alaska* with a set of coordinates."

"Oh, come on, Yi," Vince snapped. "It's not like you've looked at a map since high school."

Before their marital tension could go nuclear in front of our eyes, I cleared my throat. "How long have you been out here?" I asked.

"Sixty-four days," he said. "But we're heading home soon." He pinched his wife's triceps. "Yiyin wants to stay until the bitter end." His tone was sarcastic.

The woman he'd referred to as Yiyin pursed her lips into something that barely passed as a smile. Her unflinching gaze reminded me of the many sociopaths I'd encountered over the years. Now, maybe it wasn't entirely fair to pin her down as such based on a single look, but there was something about her that made me think she'd have no problem at all mixing up a deadly cocktail and serving it up to someone who pissed her off. I made a mental note to ask her about baneberries tomorrow.

As Hux and I were trying to navigate the strange group dynamics, a tall man with close-cropped salt-and-pepper hair approached the campsite. He wore dark pants and a nondescript jacket, but it was the way that he carried himself that caught my attention. Even without saying a word, he exuded the kind of confidence that came with being a natural leader.

Hux, of course, showed no deference to the master. He probably should have, though, simply because Fred Hopper would have. But Ferdinand Huxley never cowed in the presence of a dominant male; it just riled him up.

Vince cleared his throat. "This is, uh, Carlin and Fred," he announced. "They ran into some rangers who said they found two dead people down by the river."

The man standing in front of us stared at me, his glassy blue eyes boring into my skull. As Felicity Harland, I would have met his gaze head-on, but as Carlin Hopper, I looked away. He seemed like the type to stake a lot on first impressions.

"Is that so?" he asked.

"Yessir," Hux said. "We saw the tarps—definitely looked like a couple of dead bodies under there."

The man I believed to be Reynolds asked, "And where exactly was this?"

"Near Takahula Lake," he said. "Less than a half-day's hike from here."

No one spoke—not even Vince, who sat there massaging his pudgy knuckles while Yiyin shivered in a cold wind. The other couple sipped their coffee in silence.

The group leader eyed Hux before shifting his gaze in my direction. "So, why are *you* here?" he asked. "Trying to stir things up with talk of mysterious deaths in the wilderness?"

It was a strange question, but also a valid one. Had he spoken with the park rangers somehow, maybe by satellite phone? What if Brinegar had outed us to him and his fellow campers before we even got here? The Park Service did send out emergency alerts from time to time, using a free subscription service that delivered messages to satellite phones and other devices. There was also the fact that most sat phones, and even some handheld devices, had access to the internet. But out here in the lowlands of the Brooks range, service was spotty, and those park-wide alerts didn't come through that often.

"Not at all," Hux said. "We just wanted to hunker down with a bigger group since the rangers weren't sure what had happened."

Yiyin said, "Maybe it's related to that Fairbanks murder."

"What Fairbanks murder?" The other woman suddenly jerked her head up. Her dark eyes reflected the amber light of the fire.

"Sorry," Yiyin said. "A triple murder. I've been reading about it on my phone."

"You've got Wi-Fi out here?" I asked.

"We have a satellite that works sometimes." She looked at Hux before shifting her gaze to me. "Did the rangers mention that at all? I mean—did they think it was connected?"

"Of course it's not connected," the unnamed leader cut in. "Whoever it was that died on the Alatna got lost and died. It's got nothing to do with the street crime going on in Fairbanks." He glared at Yiyin as he spoke, but to my surprise, she didn't wither under his gaze the same way her husband did.

The truth was, I *had* heard about the Fairbanks murder, being stationed so close to Denali. Hux and I had assisted in the initial APB that went out to the entire county and beyond, but that was well over a month ago now. We had even prepared for a manhunt, right up until the FBI told us to stand down. The trail had gone cold—so cold, in fact, that the murderers had seemingly vanished into thin air.

In those killings, though, the victims were well-known drug offenders who had been shot with a revolver. Here, we were dealing with two suburbanites who had eaten poisonous berries. I planned to revisit the Fairbanks case with the investigators there once we finished up here, but for now, I had a hard time believing the two were connected.

The man who had asserted himself as the camp's leader reached for the kettle and poured himself a cup of coffee.

"I think maybe we should call the rangers," Yiyin said.

"No," the man said. "I already explained why that would be foolish."

Yiyin was quiet for a moment, but she struggled to contain her anger. Failing to garner any support from her husband, she settled her gaze on Hux. I couldn't get a read on her expression, but it felt like trouble.

"I think they should stay," Yiyin finally said with a breathy exhale. "You know, safety in numbers and all."

"What if *they* are the ones who killed those people on the Alatna?" Vince said. "Or Fairbanks? Hell, they could be serial killers." He laughed awkwardly at his own joke while Yiyin glared at him.

I said, "You're welcome to touch base with the chief ranger if you want—Brinegar. He's the one that found the bodies." I sincerely hoped no one took me up on this since I hadn't messaged Brinegar about our undercover plan, but my instincts told me no one would bother.

"I don't think that'll be necessary," the leader said. "I'm sure the Park Service will send out an alert if there's any real danger." He said the word "danger" like it was an ironic joke, which it was, I supposed, in this part of Alaska. Danger was everywhere.

"I still think they should camp here," Yiyin said. "Just in case."

"I leave it to you all to decide."

Despite his words, I suspected that whatever the group decided, he would have the final word.

Yiyin said, "Well, I think—"

"We all know what you think," Vince said with a grunt. He turned to the other couple. "Diego, what do you think? Ana?"

Ana was wringing her hands together, clearly distressed by the news of two mysterious deaths and a potential killer loose in the park. She glanced at her partner, who seemed incapable of showing any real emotion. "I don't know," Ana murmured.

Diego shrugged. "Whatever they wanna do is fine by us."

"I'm not so sure it's a good idea," Vince said, forcing a smile that had that shmaltzy, car salesman veneer. "Look, no offense to you two, but we don't even know you. I don't want to wake up in the morning and all our shit's gone."

"Oh, *please*," Yiyin snarled. "This isn't Port Authority."

"Thanks for the reminder," Vince snapped. Yiyin scooted away from him, like she was repulsed by her own husband.

Yiyin flashed a smile at Hux. "I *really* think you should stay."

"Uh, okay—"

"She just means you, buddy," Vince said. "In case that wasn't obvious."

Yiyin snarled at her husband, but Vince hardly seemed to notice. The leader of the group, who still hadn't volunteered his name, dumped out the grainy remains of his coffee. He turned to me and said, "What's your name again?"

"Carlin," I said. "Carlin Hopper."

He looked at Hux. "And you are . . .?"

"Fred." Hux sounded despondent giving an answer that in any way referenced Ferdinand, which almost made me smile.

"Well, I'm Zane," the man said. "I run this outfit."

Finally. I felt the tension in my back and shoulders suddenly relax, and a new low-level anxiety take its place. We had found Zane Reynolds. But who *was* he, really?

Reynolds had a voice like a bored radio host, hardly any emotion in it at all. "Where are you from, Mr. and Mrs. Hopper?" he asked.

"New Jersey," I said, which was where my sister Ellie lived with her boyfriend. "We're about forty minutes outside New York."

"I remember my last trip to Jersey," Reynolds said. "The smell, that is."

"We like it," Hux said. "New Jersey, that is. The smell too."

Inwardly, I grimaced. Hux just couldn't help himself; it was in his blood to confront people like Zane Reynolds. But I wished he would just shut up and take it.

"Then you'll probably hate it out here," Reynolds said. He tilted his head toward the sky. "I love Alaska. If it were up to me, I'd never leave."

"So why do you?" Hux asked. "Winter?" There was a hint of derision in his voice.

Reynolds wiped out his coffee mug with a rag while he spoke. "Winter isn't survivable out here, my friend. You're welcome to try, though." He looked at Hux. "So what do you do for a living, Fred?"

Hux reached for the kettle hanging over the fire and poured two cups of coffee. He handed one to me, even though we both knew I wasn't going to drink any at this late hour. "I'm an insurance salesman," he said with as big a smile as he could muster.

"Living the dream, I see," Reynolds said wryly.

I nearly choked on my coffee, but Hux just nodded. "Pays the bills."

"I suppose so," Reynolds said. "But you don't strike me as a nine-to-five type." He put his clean coffee mug back on the stack. In fact, everything about the campsite had an extreme orderliness to it. Reynolds clearly liked to do things a certain way. Maybe Hux was right; maybe he was ex-military. It made sense.

"I like it well enough," Hux said with a shrug. "Can't say I'd want to live up here full time."

"Oh no? Why not?"

"I like a hot shower now and then."

Reynolds smiled placidly, which was pretty much where he maxed out on the emotional spectrum. "Ah, well, the modern conveniences of life are overrated, in my opinion. We do just fine without them."

"For the whole summer?" Hux made no effort to hide his skepticism.

When Reynolds didn't respond, Vince cut in with, "Pretty much. However long it takes."

Yiyin looked like she wanted to strangle her dowdy husband right then and there, but Reynolds didn't flinch. Still, the fact that Vince had given such a specific answer had clearly miffed some other people in the group. I caught Diego muttering under his breath as he toed the dirt with his boot.

"How long it takes to do what?" Hux asked.

Reynolds eyed Hux with a sardonic smile. "Are you sure you're an insurance salesman?"

"I'm just curious is all," Hux said. "I can't imagine surviving out here long term. Do you guys have a bunker somewhere?"

Reynolds's smile faded. "We make our way out here the same way people have done for thousands of years. We hunt, we fish, we support one another. It works for us."

Hux sipped his coffee while I pretended to do the same. The goal was to normalize this encounter to elicit information the way people did—over food, drink, and easy conversation. "So how do you know each other?" Hux asked.

Reynolds was quiet for a moment. "We share a common interest," he said.

"Which is?"

I nudged Hux in the ribs. "Don't pry, Fred," I said with a stilted laugh. "It's really none of our business."

"Sorry." Hux spread his palms in a conciliatory gesture and flashed one of his best smiles, which seemed to soften Ana a bit. Yiyin was basically putty at this point.

When no one spoke, Hux went on, "Well, as for me and Carlin, we've been married five years. We met in high school, dated off and on in our twenties. We tied the knot right before her dad died of cancer so he could be there for the wedding. We love the national parks, being out in nature. We try to go once a year in the summer, but this year . . . well, Carlin had some health issues. It was tough."

"Do you have kids?" Yiyin asked.

"No," Hux said, and left it at that.

God, he's good, I thought. He had both women's full attention, although that might have had more to do with his looks than his personal story. But even Vince was leaning forward a little bit, like he couldn't help but be intrigued by Hux's heartfelt account of our relationship. Diego was disengaged and disconnected; I couldn't even begin to guess what he was thinking.

As for Zane Reynolds, he was the loner in a group of couples, the man whose reputation preceded him. His snow-blue eyes reflected the flames from the campfire with a mesmerizing power that reminded me of a bewitched crystal ball. He had compelled people to travel across the continent in pursuit of something that could cost them their sanity, if not their lives.

But was he a killer?

I vowed to find out—before he found out about us.

12

Reynolds assigned Ana and Diego the task of choosing our campsite. They picked a spot that was close to the others, but not too close. Hux and I hadn't even discussed the tent situation since we each had our own, and neither one of ours was big enough to comfortably fit two people. Before we could have a conversation about it, Hux went ahead and pitched his tent as Ana and Diego looked on. When that was done, he ushered me inside.

As Hux was unzipping the flap, Diego remarked, "That's a one-person tent, isn't it? Gonna be a tight squeeze."

"Depends on how you look at it," Hux said with a smirk. Fortunately, it was well after dark, and he couldn't see me blush.

After we had gotten our things situated in the tent, we went down to the creek to store our things in our bear locker, which was part of our routine in this part of the country. Sometimes Hux brought along a bear fence too, but not this time. We were traveling light.

Back in the tent, we spoke in low voices, just in case anyone was standing right outside, hoping for an earful. I couldn't shake the feeling that Reynolds wasn't completely on board with our story, if for no other reason that he hadn't really tested us. But Zane Reynolds also didn't strike me as the careless type, which made me wonder why he'd been so quick to receive us. Did he not see us as a threat? I couldn't imagine Hux *not* intimidating a group of strangers, but maybe Reynolds knew we had nothing to do with the Greers' deaths because *he* was the one responsible for them.

"So what's your take on Reynolds?" Hux asked me.

I kneaded my sore back with my knuckles and took a breath. "He seems like he knows what he's doing," I said. "But beyond that, I really don't know. He must be quite the salesman to get these people to come all the way out here. I can see a guy like Vince or even Yiyin drinking the Kool-Aid, but Diego? He's a little rough around the edges."

Hux nodded. "Yeah, that was my take too. But maybe it's simpler than that—maybe Reynolds's tough-guy persona works on guys like Vince and Diego."

"The male infertility piece, you mean?"

Hux shrugged. "I'm no expert in any of this, but Dora made it sound like they'd gone as far as they could with modern medicine. So, I don't know—could be Reynolds's role here is to convince the guy in the equation to try other methods."

"He doesn't strike me as the therapist type."

"Well, he's no Inuit shaman either," Hux said. "He looks more like a Peloton spokesman."

A rustling outside the tent made us both go quiet. Hux turned his head toward the sound. "It's just the wind," he said.

"That's good," I said, shaking off a chill.

"So," Hux said, "are you thinking we name-drop the Greers, or no?"

"I feel like everyone here must know about the fact that they're missing, don't you? No chance Yiyin doesn't have the best sat phone on the market in that thousand-dollar backpack of hers. I'm surprised she didn't have a padlock on it."

Hux laughed. "Well, who knows. I'm thinking Reynolds controls the narrative around here." He dug into his backpack for his toothbrush. "Any word from the medical examiner?"

"Not yet." I covered a yawn with my forearm.

"Tired?"

"A little."

Hux fidgeted with the cap on his toothpaste before look-ing up. "Harland, I know you wanted to talk about this tent situation—"

"We don't need to talk about it," I said. "You sleep over there, and I'll sleep over here. It shouldn't be hard."

Hux reached over me and grabbed his backpack from the corner as I laid out my sleeping bag. I could smell a hint of his aftershave, familiar and pleasant. He always had good breath too—spearmint, this time. Hux never went anywhere without a stash of mints.

While he organized his things, I pulled a small toiletry kit out of my own backpack. Hux had seen me brush my teeth many times over the course of our field investigations, but he'd never seen my personal effects up close. It made me self-conscious.

"I'm going to, uh, wash up down by the creek." I tugged my sleeping mat up against the edge of the tent and tossed a pillow in the corner.

"You can't do that," he said.

I stopped what I was doing and looked at him. "Do what?"

"Sleep way over there. Bear safety. It's best to sleep at least a foot away from the edge of the tent. You know that."

"I'll take my chances," I said.

"Harland, I'm serious. This is bear country." He let out a breath that rattled a bit, betraying what sounded like nerves. "How about I just pitch your tent and sleep in it? If anybody asks, we'll say I'm a snorer."

I side-eyed him. "After what you said to Diego?" I snorted. "Look, if a bear starts sniffing around, I'm sure you'll hear him long before he gets the chance to eat me."

I grabbed my toiletry kit and yanked on the door flap before he could argue. As I went to pull on the zipper, the same bird-song from before rang out in the stillness. Ollie lifted his head. Hux reached for the big stick lying next to his sleeping bag. We exchanged a glance.

"Hello?" I called out into the void.

Silence. I unzipped the flap a few inches.

"Hello?"

Then, an intake of breath. Footsteps treading lightly on the earth. "It's Ana," came the reply—a soft, timid voice. "Can we talk for a minute?"

I glanced at Hux, whose confusion seemed to mirror my own. I never would have expected someone to walk right up to our tent after dark, especially in a group that went to such extreme lengths to protect its privacy. I was tempted to reach for my Glock, only to remember that it wasn't here. All I had was a pocketknife and some bear spray.

"I'll go," Hux said.

"No, it's okay. It's just Ana."

After a quick scan of the interior to make sure my satellite phone and other essentials were stored away, I unzipped the flap and stepped outside. The inertia of an arctic night was almost surreal, the darkness otherworldly. I wielded my flashlight in my hand and shined it at her feet. Under the right circumstances, my heavy-duty flashlight could work as a defensive weapon.

Ana was in a heavy parka, a hat, and gloves despite the mild weather. She seemed woefully out of her element. "I'm sorry to bother you like this," she said, "but I need to know more about those people who died." She took a ragged breath. "What happened? Did you see them? Look, I'm sorry, I just . . . I need to know."

I glanced at Hux, who was eyeing Ana closely. Like me, he was probably trying to decide if she was telling the truth or putting on a performance. Had Diego sent her out here to gather information? Or was she legitimately terrified?

Hux was waiting for me to answer her. I decided to tread carefully. "We don't know much," I said. "Just that the rangers found two bodies by the Alatna River."

"Were they, like, bodies or skeletons?"

"Bodies," I said. "It sounded like they hadn't been there long, maybe only a day or two."

"*Oh, god,*" she sobbed.

"What's wrong?"

She looked up, her eyes wet with tears. I had my flashlight out, which seemed to make her uncomfortable, but there was no way I was going to have this conversation with her in the dark. "Did the rangers know who they were?" she asked.

"No," I said. "Sorry. Why? Do you know who they might be?"

She glanced back at her tent, which was nestled between two leaning spruce trees. The shape of it was a bulky black mass, no light coming from within. "There was a couple here who left just a few days ago," she said. "Tim and Kelsey Greer."

"When did you last see them?" I asked, doing my best to keep my tone conversational.

"It's been a few days now," she said. "Thursday morning, I think it was. I remembered because they argued that night and left early that morning, before any of us were up. It was so sudden, the way they just packed their things and left."

"Argued with who? Each other?" I knew I was pushing it, but Ana seemed scared to me. I doubted she was thinking about the pitfalls of talking to undercover federal agents. Her husband was a different story, but he wasn't here now.

"With Zane," she said. "I saw him out there too."

"What were they fighting about?"

She dropped her gaze to the ground. "I don't know. I didn't hear."

I could see the change in Hux's expression as he digested this new information about Reynolds. Since Ana was an unknown too, I wasn't quite ready to take her at her word.

Before I could ask her any more questions, a light came on in one of the green tents hidden in the brush. Ana initiated a quick retreat toward it. "Sorry," she said. "I'll . . . um . . . maybe we can talk more tomorrow."

"Wait a second—"

It was no use. She ran back to her tent and disappeared inside.

"So much for that," I said. "Anyway, I'm cold."

We climbed into the tiny tent together, and for the next few minutes, I listened to Hux getting situated—rolling out his sleeping bag, gulping down some water, taking off his jacket. He climbed into his sleeping bag without changing into pajamas.

I did the same, since the alternative was too awkward to even think about.

For a little while, it was quiet. Then he said, "Are you sure you're okay with this?"

"With what?"

"With all of it. We could be the sheep among wolves here."

"I know," I said. "But Ana seemed willing to talk. Maybe this won't take long."

"Are you turning into an optimist?"

"Nope." I pulled my eye shield over my face—a necessity in Alaska if I wanted to get more than four hours sleep—and tried to get comfortable. "Good night, Hux."

"G'night," he said.

It didn't take. Sometime later, I heard him whisper, "Are you awake?"

"Yup," I muttered.

"I really don't mind sleeping in the other tent," he said. "Just say the word."

I knew what he really meant: *"I want to sleep in the other tent."* I couldn't blame him. Neither of us seemed comfortable with this arrangement.

I rolled over in my sleeping bag and turned on my flashlight, which was enough to illuminate everything in the intimate space we shared, Hux's face included. He looked different without a baseball cap on—his hair all tousled, his eyes stunningly bright. He usually kept his hair pretty short, but this summer he'd let it grow out a bit, and the wavy blond strands around his face made him look like a college coed.

Our age differential was something I thought about a lot, even though he was probably only four years younger than me. I had plenty of female friends who treated thirty as some kind of deadline, but I had long since passed that milestone. There were times when Hux's youthfulness made me feel like I was in a different phase of life—one I didn't yet belong in.

"You're right," I said. "This isn't working." I sat up in my sleeping bag and looked at him. He sat up too, which made the cozy space feel even more cramped.

"I know," he said.

"What time is it?" I reached for my satellite phone under my pillow and powered it on. There was one new message waiting for me in my inbox.

"What is it?" Hux asked.

I didn't recognize the sender, but the contents of the email were immediately identifiable. It was from the medical examiner in Fairbanks: the preliminary autopsy report. "We're in luck," I said. I squinted to read the attachment, not because I couldn't see up close, but because my eyes were watering from fatigue.

"You're killin' me here, boss," Hux said.

It was a summary of the findings, not a full report. The ME started off by saying that he was aware of ISB's involvement in the case and had wanted to get in touch with me sooner rather than later because of the time-sensitive nature of the case. I appreciated his thoughtfulness, but the report itself was a bit of a letdown.

I powered down my sat phone with a sigh. "The medical examiner is calling it indeterminate," I said. "For both victims."

Hux muttered something under his breath. "On what grounds? What was the cause of death?"

"Cardiac arrest secondary to toxic ingestion."

His eyebrows went up. "Sounds like the poisonous plant theory checks out."

"He has to send samples over to the university to confirm the species, but he did say there was considerable blistering in the oral mucosa and esophagus caused by an exogenous source. The bite wounds were indeed consistent with carnivore activity, and they were postmortem."

"Hm," he said. "Isn't that what we thought?"

"Pretty much."

A part of me wished I hadn't checked my phone right before bed; it was a terrible habit, one that had cost me many hours of sleep. The truth was, this report wasn't doing anything to put my mind at ease. Maybe the "killer on the loose" theory was looking less likely, but there were still so many unanswered questions: the wrist abrasions, the strange positioning of the bodies, the "argument" that had prompted Tim and Kelsey Greer's departure.

The ME's report made no mention of the wrist abrasions. I vowed to call him first thing in the morning, before all my potential witnesses scattered into the ether. I also had to consider the possibility that the abrasions on Kelsey and Tim's wrists had nothing to do with their deaths.

Even if that were the case, the ME couldn't comment on the circumstances surrounding the ingestion. Was it possible that someone had *forced* Tim and Kelsey Greer to consume bane-berries? I decided to send one last message before bed: a text to Dave, the wildlife biologist. He might know something about baneberries in the area.

"What are you doing there?" Hux asked.

"Asking Dave about the baneberries in this part of the park," I said.

"Dave the wildlife guy?"

I gave Hux a pointed look. "Yes. Why?"

"I dunno," Hux said. "Did you notice what he was doing when Emily was telling you about the weirdo survivalist in the park somewhere?"

"No. What?"

"He looked—I dunno—confused. Like he didn't believe what she was saying."

"Huh." I tried to remember that brief exchange, but fatigue was clouding my memory. "Well, he's all we've got in the wildlife department." I typed out a quick message and pressed "Send." Almost before my head hit the pillow, sleep came over me.

It didn't last. Sometime later, I heard the quiet trill of the zipper as Hux opened the door flap. He barely made a sound as he crept out into the night.

I went into my backpack for my Glock and grabbed the magazine. Hux had his big stick, but that wasn't going to do me any good.

Now that I was alone, I wasn't taking any chances.

13

THE NEXT MORNING started not with a sinister birdcall, but with the tantalizing aroma of fresh coffee. I rolled over to see the sleeping mat that Hux had vacated the night before.

I dressed quickly, wishing for the thousandth time that I had a spare T-shirt or two. My tank top was already smelling a little ripe. I hated myself for caring so much, but I didn't want Hux to decide that I had a stench. And, yes, there were women like that at the bureau—at ISB too. I didn't mind them. I just wanted to keep things professional, and part of being a professional was smelling like a self-respecting human being in the company of my colleague.

I unzipped the tent and headed down to the creek to get some things from my bear locker. The creek ran pretty low this time of year, but I could still hear the water trickling over polished stone, finding its way toward lower ground. I brushed my teeth and splashed some cold water on my face. It was a few minutes after six AM. The sun had risen hours earlier, and the day felt well trodden already. I remembered with a pang of longing the leisurely pace I used to enjoy as an outdoor enthusiast camping in the wilderness. With ISB, it was a whole different animal.

Reynolds and the others were gathered around the burnt embers of the fire when I got there. Hux was over by the supply tent, helping Ana clean the cookware. They weren't talking, but that didn't surprise me. Diego was nearby, stealing glances in Ana's direction as he washed his shirts in the creek. I stood by the fire and braced myself for an awkward encounter with Vince, who was rubbing two sticks together for no real purpose that I could see.

"Morning," he said as I walked up to him, but his smile was a perfunctory one. He pointed to two empty mugs. "Help yourself. I don't know about you, but coffee's the only thing that tells me it's morning around here."

I stole a glance at the seedy brown liquid in the kettle. *Is this how it happens?* I wondered. *Are we about to be poisoned too?*

"It's not the best coffee you'll ever have," Vince said, "but it's drinkable." He plucked the kettle off the fire and filled the two empty blue mugs to the brim.

"Thanks." I lifted the cup to my lips, allowing the tiniest bit of liquid to land on my tongue. It was quite simply the worst coffee I'd ever tasted—definitely worse than nothing, but it wasn't bitter, which I would have expected from a baneberry concoction.

Hux walked over and said to Vince, "Hey, man. How's it going?"

"Oh, you know," Vince said. "Just another day away from the grind. Can't complain."

I caught Yiyin's gaze from across the fire. Yesterday she'd been wearing linen; today she looked like a model for Lululemon. She excused herself from her conversation with Ana and Diego and made her way over to Vince's side. "Hi, honey," she said, and rubbed his elbow.

He withdrew his arm. "What's, uh—is something wrong?"

"Nothing's wrong," she said before turning her attention to me and Hux—Hux, in particular. "How was your night?"

"Fine," I said. "No complaints."

"Hey, uh, I got a question," Hux said, which I took as an attempt to dispel the tension brewing between me and Yiyin. "How do you guys replenish your supplies? Does somebody come up here on a schedule or something?"

Vince and Yiyin exchanged a glance. Reynolds had made his way down to the creek, out of earshot. With Yiyin staying mum,

Vince said with a stilted laugh, "Oh, we're real survivors—you know, the hunting and gathering thing, living off the land."

"That's not actually true," Yiyin said in a hushed whisper. "Every few weeks, Zane goes off to get us some essentials."

"He goes where?" I asked.

"Not sure. He just leaves for a day or two."

"He goes off on foot? By himself?"

Vince said, "Yeah."

"Sometimes he floats down the river," Yiyin interjected, as if she couldn't help herself from one-upping her husband. "I've seen his canoe."

Hearing this, I couldn't help but think about the fact that Tim and Kelsey Greer had been found on the river. If Reynolds liked to float the Alatna, that could potentially put him at the scene.

As I considered this new information, Reynolds made his way over to the campfire. "Good morning," he said to no one in particular. Yiyin smiled coyly at him. Vince grunted a greeting of sorts but didn't make eye contact.

"Mornin'," Hux said.

Reynolds helped himself to some coffee, cussing as he sniffed it. Vince slouched a bit.

Reynolds looked at Hux over the brim of his mug. "I assume you and Carlin are headed out?" he asked.

"Oh, uh—possibly."

Reynolds's question had caught me off-guard too. I said, "I think we may have underestimated what we're in for out here—you know, trying to get by without the usual essentials. It feels like you really have it down pat."

"That's what Alaska's all about," Reynolds said. "Surviving."

"Is foraging part of what you do here?" Hux asked.

"Of course. Hunting. Foraging. We do what needs to be done."

"Well, we both know how to hunt," Hux said, stealing a glance in my direction. He seemed to have something in mind. I liked that he was taking initiative. "We didn't bring any rifles or anything, but if you've got some handy, we could help you out."

Reynolds responded with a cryptic smile. "Aren't you from New Jersey?"

"Not originally," I said. "We were actually born and raised in Montana."

"Whereabouts?"

Oh, shoot. My mind blanked. I suddenly remembered that my other sister, Teresa, lived in Montana, just south of Missoula in a small town called Hamilton. "Near Hamilton," I said.

To my relief, Reynolds seemed to accept this answer as he walked over to a dark duffle bag by the cookware. The bag had escaped my notice at first, but now I could see by its size and shape that it was his weapons cache.

Sure enough, he pulled out a rifle. Hux muttered under his breath, "What the hell . . ."

It was a hunting rifle—and not a run-of-the-mill one for hunting rabbits or deer, but a rifle designed for taking down big game. It wasn't the only one either. With a gleeful look, Reynolds proceeded to extract five more rifles from the bag, each one more impressive than the last. Three of them looked like Remingtons—namely, the .30/06 700 BDL, which I vaguely remembered from one of my firearms classes at the FBI. Based on my recollection, the .30/06 was introduced by the Army in the early 1900s as a service weapon, but it hadn't been used by law enforcement in decades.

"These are my .30/06s," Reynolds said. "It's considered by many to be the best all-around big-game hunting rifle." He held one out for Diego, who seemed completely at ease as he took it into his hands. Vince, in contrast, flinched as Reynolds thrust the big gun in his direction. He received it like he was being asked to hold a newborn baby that didn't belong to him.

Diego asked Reynolds, "Is it loaded?"

"No." Reynolds sounded mildly annoyed by the question, but for me, it was a telling one. It meant Diego knew his way around guns.

I watched Diego pass the rifle from his right hand to his left, another indication that he had weapons experience. I remembered thinking that he was from Texas, where familiarity with firearms was perhaps more accepted than in other parts of the country. It didn't, however, explain his cold, calculated nature, nor the fact that he didn't seem the "cult type" at all. I stole a glance at his feet. Size nine felt about right for him too.

Hmm.

Reynolds had big feet, though, at least a size twelve. I wondered if Hux had noticed the same thing. He simply didn't fit as the third party we were looking for; there was no way around it.

I also didn't think he was working alone, though. Too many moving parts—the social media accounts, the coordinates, the supplies, the food. It was too much for one man to handle.

Reynolds reached for another rifle in his cache. I recognized it as a .375 H&H, or what big game enthusiasts might refer to as "a lot of gun." He cradled it in his arms like a coveted pet and smiled. He was looking right at me.

"What have you hunted, Carlin?" Reynolds asked me. His tone was deceptively saccharine, bordering on condescending. "Squirrels? Rabbits?"

"She can do a lot better than that," Hux said.

I mangled a smile. It wasn't that I hated hunters—in fact, I had no problem with people who liked to go out and shoot things they planned to consume, so long as they did it legally— I just didn't much like the thought of shooting something for Reynolds's entertainment. Yet, I wasn't sure how else we were going to justify our continued presence here.

Hux gestured for the rifle. "I can take it, Carlin," he said, which reminded me this was all just a big ruse—the cult, our marriage, this ridiculous gun. But holding the long-barreled firearm in my hands, I couldn't help but think that Reynolds was more than just a conniving cult leader. Then again, the Greers hadn't been shot; they'd been poisoned.

"That's okay," I said to Hux. "I've got it."

Hux gave me a look that said, *"I know you do."* He turned to Reynolds. "What's the objective?" he asked. "What kind of meat were you hoping to eat tonight?"

While Reynolds checked his ammunition, I caught myself holding my breath. *This can't end well,* I thought. Then Reynolds looked up, spread his hands wide, and smiled. "Moose, bear, caribou—the bigger the better." He ignored the look of disgust on Yiyin's face. "You asked how you could contribute," Reynolds said. "Well, this is your opportunity. Or feel free to call the rangers to escort you back to Jersey, if you want."

Before Hux could respond to Reynolds's veiled insult, the group leader pulled out another Remington 700. This one, though, wasn't designed for hunting game. It was designed for hunting people—a sniper rifle. Hux had come to the same conclusion, judging by the look on his face.

"Is that—is that your gun?" Yiyin asked.

"It's just a backup," Reynolds said. "In case any of you gets into trouble out there." He grabbed a different duffel, this one loaded with supplies: food, maps, compasses, bushwhacking gear. He inspected each of the items briefly before handing them out. I watched Diego appraise a machete with its carved wooden handle and a stainless-steel blade.

"Now listen," Reynolds said. "The best part of the day is already gone. As you know, there are a number of game trails in this part of the park, and I did you all a favor by marking them on your topo maps. Make sure you stay out of each other's way. I don't want anybody getting shot."

Vince cleared his throat, which caught everyone's attention. Reynolds frowned.

"What is it, Vince?"

Vince gestured to the rifle leaning against his thigh. "Here's the thing. I think we, ah . . . we learned our lesson last time. I'd like to sit this one out—"

"We're not sitting out," Yiyin snapped at him, but I couldn't tell if she was making a genuine argument or trying to stop him from finishing that sentence. "We'll figure it out."

"Figure *what* out?" Vince said, spittle flying from his mouth. "Do you even know where the trigger is on this thing?"

"Oh, please," she retorted. "It's just a gun. They're all the same."

Reynolds said impatiently, "Why don't you pair up with Carlin? She has some experience, apparently."

"Yes, let's do that," Yiyin said before I could offer my opinion on the matter. Hux stole a glance at me, perhaps in some way asking for my permission. From an investigator's perspective, splitting up was a good idea; it would give us a chance to ask questions of two people who clearly resented each other's presence. Yiyin, for one, seemed ready and willing to open up to Hux—in more ways than one. *Ugh.*

"Carlin?" Hux asked me. "Are you okay with this?"

I nodded. "Just be careful."

"You best get going," Reynolds said.

Separating from Hux made me deeply uneasy. One option was to bow out, but that would mean giving up on five potential witnesses. Momentum was a critical component of any ISB investigation; witnesses could scatter back to where they came from, never to be seen again. Other cases could come up, relegating this one to the bottom of the pile. Ray could decide that "indeterminate" really meant "accidental," effectively ending ISB's involvement in the case.

We had to press on. I knew Hux could handle himself, and Vince didn't strike me as a threat. He could barely get from the campfire to his tent on that bum knee of his, much less traipse through miles of arctic wilderness. I knew we wouldn't be going far.

Diego, though, was more of a wild card. He reorganized his backpack with a sure hand, like he'd done this not once, but many times before. I thought about sending Ray a message to see if there were any APBs out on Diego or Ana, but I didn't even know their last names. For now, I decided to focus on Vince.

I picked up the Remington along with the carry strap that Reynolds had kept in his cache. My Glock was back in my tent, where it would remain—no use hauling the extra weight around when I already had plenty of firepower.

Hux nudged my elbow. "Hey," he said, flicking his gaze at the rifle poking over my shoulder. "You up for this?"

"I guess I have to be," I said, keeping my voice down.

"Are you worried about Reynolds going AWOL while we're gone?"

"No," I said. "He's got too much at stake." I stole a look over Hux's shoulder at the closest green tent, the one that belonged to Vince and Yiyin. "Are they getting ready?"

The door flap to the tent was open, but I couldn't see inside. Two backpacks were sitting on the ground outside, next to a pair of hiking boots. Everything looked a little too clean, like they hadn't gotten much use recently. Or at all.

"I helped them pack," Hux said. "They're in the woods having a private moment."

I felt my eyebrows go up. "Sexual?"

"Pretty sure it's more of the gastrointestinal variety."

"Oh," I said, feeling my cheeks flush. "Well, that's reasonable."

I thought I caught a smile on Hux's face as he hoisted his pack onto his shoulders. As usual, Hux looked ready to rumble. Ollie was scampering around in circles, excited for a new adventure. Hux had insisted that I take him; he thought it was safer that way.

We both had our jackets on, but in a couple of hours, Hux would be down to a T-shirt. My favorite shirt of his was a faded red one from his grandfather's auto body business, but he rarely wore that one out on the trail. It was more of a sleep shirt—not that I felt entirely comfortable knowing that.

"There they are," Hux said.

I looked up to see Vince and Yiyin making their way toward us. Yiyin was dressed like an Instagram star, while Vince had on Costco's best sweatpants. *How in the world had they made it all the way out here in the first place?* I wondered. Even Alaska's most capable guide would have struggled to motivate this guy.

My plan was to stay close to the campsite despite Reynolds's insistence on a big-game hunting expedition. I wasn't taking any chances being out there on my own. It wouldn't be hard to fake fatigue or injury if I had to—I had ample experience with both—but Vince had that covered.

"This is gonna suck," Hux said as we watched Yiyin keel over while trying to adjust a strap on her backpack. "You sure you don't want to switch hiking partners?"

"I'm sure," I said. "You'd probably end up shooting Vince."

"It's possible," he said with a laugh. "Just don't let him touch that rifle; if he doesn't blow off his own foot, he could take you out instead."

I was more worried about Yiyin, who was chomping at the bit to get out on the trail with Hux. Weeks of self-imposed isolation could put a tremendous strain on couples who weren't rock solid to begin with. Desperation set in too. After all, Yiyin and Vince had come out here for a reason. Since they were still here, I had to assume they'd fallen short of their goals.

"What's your sat phone situation?" I asked him.

"Yiyin has one. It works—I already tried it."

"Okay, good. If there's a problem, text me the sign/countersign."

"We've been over this, boss," he said, his voice softening. "But, listen, if you're not feeling comfortable with the plan—"

"I'm comfortable," I said. "It's just that I'm technically responsible for you."

"You've got enough to worry about with that goon," he said, referring to Vince. I looked over to see my hunting partner rubbing some Bengay on his kneecap. "Don't worry about me. I've got Yiyin's sat phone if we need it. You're good with a map—"

"I'm not *that* good."

"Good enough. Just stay close to a body of water."

"I will," I said.

I tightened the straps on my backpack and checked the laces on my hiking boots. When Hux wasn't looking, I sniffed my armpits. It wasn't a bed of roses, but not godawful either. Vince probably wouldn't notice, not that I was all that worried about what Vince thought of me.

"If you aren't back by nightfall tomorrow, I'm going to the rendezvous point," I said. "And I'm calling the rangers to mobilize a team to find you."

"How about you try calling Yiyin's phone first?"

"I will. But I'm not messing around."

I watched Yiyin ditch her backpack—and her husband—as she skipped across the campsite toward us. She flashed a flirty smile at Hux. *Oh God,* I thought. *Here we go.* As she sidled up to him, she reached up and squeezed his bicep. I gritted my teeth.

"Are you *sure* you're not an ex–Navy SEAL or something?" Yiyin cooed at Hux. "Because you look so damn fit."

"Nah," he said. "Just an Eagle Scout."

Vince limped into our circle. "Hey, sorry," he said. "I've got this old knee injury—"

"Just take some more ibuprofen," Yiyin snapped at him. "It's not that bad."

"It's bad," Vince countered. To me and Hux, he said, "I played football in college—"

"Sprint football," Yiyin corrected him.

"Yeah, well, Princeton had a hell of a team back then—"

"They discontinued it in 2016," Yiyin said, quick to cut him off as she focused her attention back on Hux. "The sport, I mean. They'd lost a hundred and five games in a row. There were safety concerns."

"That's not true—"

"It's absolutely true," Yiyin said.

"Yeah, well, you were into it at the time. You thought I was this 'hot jock'—"

Hux cleared his throat. "We really should get going," he said. "We're already getting a late start." He glanced at me, his eyes kind and almost comforting. *"Don't worry,"* the look on his face seemed to say. *"She's a pain in the ass, and I'm just doing this because I have to."*

I breathed a little easier, even though every bone in my body was dreading this excursion with Vince. The Bengay odor was making me nauseous.

"You're right," Yiyin said. "We should go."

"Bye," Vince snapped at her.

I didn't know what to say to my partner—*Good luck? Bye? Have fun?* In the end, I patted his arm and mumbled, "Be safe out there."

"You too," he said just as awkwardly. Vince and Yiyin were studying our interaction, no doubt confused by our stilted good-byes. *Was this how a couple who'd been together for years parted before a dangerous wilderness adventure?* I wondered. The answer was obvious: *Of course not.* But I wasn't about to make out with Hux for their benefit.

Hux forged ahead with long strides that made Yiyin break into a trot to keep up with him. I heard Hux ask her about her backpack, which prompted her to run back and grab it. I caught his eyes for a moment, but neither of us spoke. The time for goodbyes had passed.

Now it was down to business.

CHAPTER

14

VINCE LASTED AN hour before he threw in the towel. It was
the varied terrain that did him in; he couldn't handle the
gravel, the tussocks, the many water crossings. Much of the game
trail that Reynolds had marked on the map took us through
thick brush, which was taxing in its own right, even though
some other hunting party had long ago bushwhacked their
way through it. But when Vince went down on all fours, there
was no doubt he was done. He was sitting on the hard earth
with his legs splayed out, massaging his bum knee and cussing like a sailor. Even Ollie seemed underwhelmed by Vince's
performance.

Hux and Yiyin had gone off in a different direction, which
meant Vince and I were alone. So far, Vince had struggled might-
ily to keep up the pace. No surprise there. I should have had
more sympathy for him given my experience in Sequoia, where
the worst back pain imaginable had plagued me for the dura-
tion of the assignment, but I couldn't. Vince was a wet blanket.
He couldn't even seem to appreciate the scenic landscape of the
Takahula River.

In another way, though, I felt a little sorry for him: the tough
guy who was constantly falling short in his wife's eyes. I wondered about his marriage to Yiyin and their failed journey to
become parents. To me, it felt like they had forgotten about each

other in service of an objective that required the utmost intimacy. I couldn't quite get my head around it.

"Did you want to turn around, then?" I asked.

"I don't see how I could possibly go on," he said flatly. "My knee's busted."

I was about to suggest putting one foot in front of the other, but I held my tongue. Ollie sat on his haunches. He seemed to sense we were in for a long wait.

"It wasn't like this a few days ago, you know—my knee, I mean," Vince said. "I aggravated it during one of our 'relocations.'"

"Sorry?"

"Every few weeks, we relocate," he said. "One minute you're asleep, the next thing you know you're crossing a river in your socks."

"Zane makes you do this?"

"Oh yeah. It's his operation, his rules."

"Does he ever give a reason?"

Vince peeled a piece of duct tape off his blistered heel. "Nah. You want my own theory, though? I think he's meeting up with his supply person."

"Which is who?"

"Look, you've seen what kind of people Zane recruits—other than Diego, nobody here knows their way around a huckleberry patch. He has to replenish supplies every week to keep his clients happy." He expressed his disdain with a snort. "This hunting trip is just a way to make us dudes feel 'manly.'"

"Huh. Is it working?"

"Nope."

I wanted to keep him talking without sounding overly curious, but it was hard to keep the investigator out of my voice. "Yiyin mentioned the shipments that come in—don't those come to him?" I asked.

He shrugged. "I don't know. Zane doesn't talk about logistics."

"Does he ever fly back down to Bettles? Or is he always here?"

"He'll disappear for a day or two, but I don't know where he goes."

Of course you don't, I thought. Vince wasn't exactly the most observant guy in the wilderness. "So who's meeting him up there?"

He took a swig from his canteen. "I don't even know. I get the feeling he's got all kinds of people working for him behind the scenes—rangers, locals, probably some natives."

"Alaska Natives?"

"Yeah. Indigenous people." He winced in pain as he shifted position. "Look, I don't know what's PC around here. I haven't seen any Eskimos if that's what you're asking."

As much as Vince would have benefited from some stiff correction on his cultural knowledge of the local area, I decided to let it go for now. He was, after all, dealing with someone who epitomized the practice of cultural appropriation. "Have you *seen* this supply person?"

"Nope," he said. "But I heard him on his sat phone with somebody once—Emily, sounded like."

"Emily Wiseman?"

"You think I'm sitting there listening for a last name?" He made no effort to hide his irritation.

"Sorry." I decided to play dumb with a smile. "I just—well, one of the rangers we ran into on our way up here was named Emily."

"Then it's probably her."

The NPS presence in Region 11—Alaska and its parks—was fairly small. I sincerely doubted there was more than one Emily working with Brinegar's team. But I also wondered why a young ranger like Emily would act as a mule for a guy like Reynolds. Extra cash on the side? It seemed unlikely, but not out of the question. I'd encountered opportunists before, and experience told me they came in all stripes and colors.

"So, whose idea was it to come to Alaska?" I asked. "Yiyin's?"

He shrugged. "I guess."

Vince was proving himself an easy target as an inadvertently helpful witness. He had a number of weaknesses—his wife's withering opinion of him, his physical shortcomings, his disdain for nature. All I had to do was exploit the right one.

"What does that mean?" I asked.

"You've met my wife. Yiyin always gets her way. Whatever it is she wants, she gets. If you're in her way, watch out. She'll trample you, humiliate you, defeat you. Whatever it takes. That's how she made her millions."

Her *millions*? I had to admit that Vince had caught me off-guard. "Pardon?"

"She sold her first company for two hundred and eighty million dollars, her second for four hundred million. After that she became a venture capitalist, got bored, started another company. She works hundred-hour weeks and loves every second of it."

"And you're, what—along for the ride, as you say?"

He snickered. "We met at Princeton. I went to law school, she went to Silicon Valley. For a while, we were happy—just two normal twenty-somethings going to bars, renting a cheap apartment, living it up in the city. And then the money hit—a windfall of it. Yiyin convinced me to quit my job. I took up golf. Pickleball. We traveled. She worked every second of every day no matter where we were. But it wasn't so bad, I guess—living that life, I mean. I got up every day at noon and went to bed whenever I felt like it."

"You don't sound thrilled about it," I remarked.

"Yeah, well, it was all about me, you know? I was the 'supportive spouse,' the stay-at-home-dad that didn't have kids. Then one day she decided she wanted to have a baby, which, well, okay, sure. Because when you're used to getting whatever you want, whenever you want it, it's supposed to happen instantaneously. This time it didn't. Months became years. We saw a reproductive endo in San Francisco who told us exactly what the problem was, and things went downhill from there."

I supposed that a proper suburban housewife by the name of Carlin Hopper never would have pursued this line of thought. It was too intrusive, the kind of thing most women kept quiet about out of courtesy. On the other hand, as a federal investigator, I had little time for courtesy.

"What was the problem?" I asked.

"What do *you* think?" His tone was bitter. I understood, though, what he was telling me—that *he* was the problem. It certainly fit with what we already knew about Zane Reynolds and the operation he was running up here.

"I'm sorry," I said.

"Sorry about what? That I've got a plumbing problem? I'll tell you what, though: for me, it was a relief. I never wanted kids."

"So then why are you still here?"

He palmed the gravel and tried to get up, wincing as he put weight on his knee. Ollie watched him with disinterest. Vince hobbled a few steps, stopped, and bent forward to catch his breath. He looked out at the glassy surface of Takahula Lake, glistening in the distance.

"Yiyin doesn't want to deal with the optics of a messy divorce," he said. "And I don't want to go back to my law firm with my tail between my legs."

"But if she made millions, you'd get a nice chunk of that in the divorce—right?"

He shook his head. "We signed a prenup. Being the lawyer and all, I insisted on it." He barked a laugh. "Can you believe that? I was such a moron."

I watched him trip on a rock and pitch forward. He landed on his hands with a grunt. "This sucks," he muttered. "Alaska sucks."

I offered a hand, which he took without looking at me. He didn't thank me, nor did I expect him to. "Why don't you just go home?" I asked.

He scrutinized my face, searching for an answer to a question he hadn't yet voiced, perhaps. I felt myself squirm under his gaze. Maybe I'd taken this line of questioning too far.

"You ask a lot of questions," he said.

"I . . . well, that's just kind of who I am." I forced a laugh. "Fred says I'm nosy."

"Nosy people ask stupid questions. Your questions aren't stupid."

I gripped the straps on my backpack and tried to turn his attention back to the trail. A part of me was hoping that

Vince would focus on keeping up with me and forget about my questions—for now, anyway. He was a lawyer, after all. He might start to wonder about my real intentions if I asked *too* many questions.

"I've seen two women leave here pregnant—or at least they claimed they were pregnant," he said. "It's how Yiyin keeps convincing me to stay."

"How many couples have there been since you got here?" I asked.

He thought for a moment. "There've been a few. I don't know. Some didn't stay long—only a day or two. Maybe they realized being out in this arctic wasteland wasn't for them."

Arctic wasteland? God, this guy was a real downer. "Did they leave angry?" I asked. "I mean, it's a big investment to come all the way to Alaska."

"He'll refund the fee if you don't get pregnant."

This was a surprise, hearing that Zane Reynolds had a charitable side. It didn't quite compute with the hardcore survivalist persona, but maybe Vince had his facts wrong.

"So you said he's had some success, though? How do you explain that?"

He looked at me for a long moment, almost like he was trying to dissect something in my expression. I realized I needed to change my tone—be more casually curious, less impatiently direct. He was a lawyer, after all. He knew what an interrogation was.

"Vince?"

He shrugged. "Can't say."

"What about Tim and Kelsey Greer?" I asked. "Did *they* have success?" I knew for a fact that Kelsey wasn't pregnant when she left here because her autopsy failed to indicate any evidence of such, but I wanted to hear his answer just the same.

It didn't come quickly. I shifted my feet, waiting for him to respond.

He licked his chapped lips. A stiff wind rattled the low-lying brush until at last he pointed a finger at me. He was smiling. "You're good."

My mouth went dry. "Sorry?"

"The two of you—I almost bought it." He shook his head, like he was entertained by his own musings. "I mean, I *did* buy it for a while there."

"I don't know what you mean—"

"You're not married," he said. "No chance. You like him too much."

I swallowed hard, willing myself not to panic. Even though Vince outweighed me by over a hundred pounds, he was out of shape, unarmed, and injured. If he wanted to hurt me, he wouldn't have the easiest time of it.

As expected, though, he made no move in my direction. He tightened the straps of his backpack, which always keeled to the left, no matter what he did. As I stood with my hand poised on Ollie's head, waiting for Vince to make a move, I could feel the arctic sun beating down on my neck. The collar of my jacket felt damp with sweat.

"Look, I'm not gonna say anything to Zane," he said. "I can't stand that guy. But at least tell me who you really are."

I blew out a breath, remembering one of my earliest lessons as an undercover agent, back when I was dealing with pimps and drug dealers on the street: *When it's over, it's over. Cut the cord.* I could interview Vince back in Bettles, or even down at the field office in Anchorage. It didn't have to be here—and maybe it was best if it *wasn't* here.

"My real name is Felicity Harland, and I'm a special agent with the Investigative Services Branch," I said. "We're a federal agency that investigates crimes in National Parks."

He narrowed his gaze at me. "What kind of crimes?"

"Homicide, for one," I said. "We weren't lying about those two bodies found on the Alatna River—it's why we're up here."

"*We?*" He snorted. "So you and your beefy partner are both federal agents?"

"We're a team, yes," I said.

"The dog too?" He glanced at Ollie.

"No. He's just a damn good hiking partner."

He was quiet for a moment. "I'm not sure I should be talking to you."

"Why not?"

"I don't want to get caught up in anything illegal."

"Why? Were you a witness to a crime?"

He mumbled, "No." A pause. "I don't know."

"Come on, Vince. You went to law school. Be straight with me."

He tilted his sunburned face toward the sky. The sun was nearly at its peak, casting a tepid glow on the valley. The air had turned cool, with a brisk wind coming off the mountains. I zipped up my jacket until the collar touched my chin, as I waited patiently for him to look back at me. When he did, I could sense that something had shifted. He looked weary and defeated.

"I figured Zane was gonna get us all the way up here and lay into me about sperm donation after some serious 'bro-bonding' or whatever," Vince said. "That was my take on the whole thing, anyway. I'll admit I never wanted to go that route with Yiyin. I figured she'd divorce me and take the kid. She's got money, remember. She knows how to find a good lawyer if she needs one. I didn't want to stand there in court and hear about how the kid's not biologically mine."

"So did that happen?" I asked.

"No, not really. Zane and I never clicked. Big surprise, eh?" He rubbed his knuckles. "Anyway, we're still here."

"Tell me about Tim and Kelsey Greer. I heard there was an argument the night before they left."

He seemed surprised that I knew this. "Who told you that?"

"It doesn't matter. Did you witness it?"

"I heard yelling, yeah. I got out of my tent and looked around, thinking maybe there was a bear in the camp or something. We've had some issues with bears."

I couldn't picture Vince abandoning the cover of his tent if he believed there was a bear in the vicinity, but I decided to let it go. "And what did you see?"

"I saw Kelsey crying outside her tent. Zane and Kelsey's husband were having it out right there in front of her."

"What were they fighting about?"

"No idea. It was late, and I was kinda drunk."

I frowned. The supply runs Vince had mentioned explained the alcohol, but the drunkenness was a whole other story. I didn't drink much in the wilderness. It felt like too much of a risk, this far off the grid. At campsites close to civilization, sure, but the rules were different out here. I supposed Vince felt safe and secure in his little bubble, especially with all those guns around.

"Look, I wasn't gonna stick my nose in their business," Vince said, but at the look on my face, all that defiance seemed to go out of him. He let out a breath. "It's them, isn't it?" he said. "Tim and Kelsey."

"Yes."

"You're sure?"

"We haven't had a family member ID them yet, but yes."

Vince returned my stare without blinking. "And you didn't *tell* us?"

I decided not to tell him about Ana just then. He had a reason to be angry, just like I had my reasons for not telling him the whole truth. Since the medical examiner had ruled the deaths indeterminate, the Park Service wasn't in the position to send out an alert. This was peak season: murder was bad for business. I didn't blame Brinegar for that decision.

How I handled Vince in this moment was going to dictate how things went from here. I needed his cooperation, which meant telling him what he wanted to know.

"The medical examiner concluded that they died from cardiac arrest," I said. "There was evidence of toxic ingestion— poisonous berries, most likely."

Vince looked at me like I had three heads. "Seriously?"

"I could go into the details of the autopsy report if you want."

"No, thanks," he said.

"Has Zane ever talked about poisonous berries or plants? Maybe in a fertility context?"

Vince snorted. "He's not that stupid."

"What do you mean?"

"Come on. This isn't a suicide cult—or, sorry, *credo*. He won't get anybody to come here if people get a whiff of this being the next Jonestown."

I had thought about this too, but people made mistakes. Maybe Reynolds had prepared a cocktail of sorts as part of a ritual, only to realize later that it was poisonous.

"When did Tim and Kelsey arrive here?"

"Around the Fourth of July. Kelsey was the quiet type—hardly said anything to anyone. But she did talk to Yiyin. They were kind of friends, I guess."

"'Kind of' friends?"

"They would go on short little hikes together. Yiyin's ability to network with people is her defining characteristic in life. She needs that social capital to feel important."

I was starting to get a sharper picture of Yiyin, but Vince was clearly holding something back. He drank more from his canteen and stared out at the creek. I glanced at my watch, which I hoped would signal to him that he didn't have all day to sit out here.

"Has anyone else at camp been ill recently?"

"Yiyin's convinced she's got chronic hypothermia, but other than that, no."

I wasn't about to dig into the nuances of what that meant. "When did Tim and Kelsey Greer leave?" I asked.

"I dunno—a week ago, maybe? I don't really keep track of that stuff."

"Was it five days, seven, eight? It would help to be specific."

Vince thought for a moment. "What day is it today?"

"It's Monday, August first."

He ticked off his fingers. "I'm gonna say they probably left four days ago. But it could've been three or five."

So much for being specific, I thought. "Okay," I said. "What was the weather like when they left? Was it morning or—"

"Oh, definitely morning. They were gone by sunup." He squeezed his calf muscles with his fingers. "Just so you know, I knew your beefcake partner wasn't an insurance salesman. I'm guessing he's, what, ex-military? CIA?"

I didn't answer.

"Oh, come on. I'll find out eventually."

"He's ex-military."

"There ya go. He looks like Jack Ryan." He shook his head, muttering something under his breath. "Anyway, Zane knows what he's doing. I don't know what he did before this, but I'll bet he was in the intelligence community. Black ops, maybe. He takes 'leave no trace' to a whole new level."

"Has he ever talked about why he's now a fertility guru?"

Vince snickered. "Oh, sure. He's got a whole spiel about what it means to be a man and everything. He's smart, though. I mean, he got our money, and Yiyin's cheap as shit, so there you go."

There was something moving in the brush. I whirled around, reaching for my rifle with one hand while slinging off my backpack with the other. "Hello?" I called out.

There was no answer, just the lonesome howl of the wind through the valley's sparse vegetation. I wished we had stopped somewhere a little closer to the creek, where the visibility was better. Here, I couldn't help but feel a little closed in.

"Let's get going," I said.

"I can't." His whining tone reminded me of Margo's three-year-old twins. "I can't walk."

"You're gonna have to try." I tried to hoist him up, but all I could think about was the vast wilderness at my back, rife with secrets and danger. A thick layer of clouds cast a shadow on the valley, which made the morning seem darker somehow, and more ominous. I thought about the rifle slung on my back, unwieldy and inaccessible. Vince had refused to carry it, which was probably for the best, but it made me slow on my feet.

"You need to get up," I said, tugging at his arm. "Walk on your good leg if you have to."

"My feet hurt," he said. "They're so friggin' wet. I hate this place. My shoes, my socks, my pants—everything's wet all the time."

"Stop whining. We can't just sit out here all day."

"Of course we can," he said. "Hell, I'd rather sit out here than go back *there*."

I briefly debated just leaving him behind and coming back for him later, but I couldn't risk it. For one thing, he could wander off and die, the same way Kevin had done after he insisted on going off on his own to get help. The safer bet was to stick together, even if it meant calling Hux on Yiyin's sat phone to come get us.

"Look," I scolded him, "we've got two people confirmed dead in the wilderness—people you knew personally. Don't you want to know what happened to them?"

He muttered something under his breath as he hopped on his good leg. "I just want out of here. Yiyin controls the sat phone. I can't even call for a plane."

I wondered if Vince was telling the truth about his sat phone. If he was, it wasn't a good look for Yiyin, that was for sure. "We're planning on flying back to Bettles as soon as we talk to everyone here," I said. "You can hitch a ride back with us if you want."

"I can't go without Yiyin." He avoided my gaze, which made me think he was a little embarrassed to admit this. "It'll look bad. And she won't go with me—not until she got what she came for."

"You're worried about the *optics* here?"

He snorted. "Not really."

"We can tell Zane you had a medical emergency."

The skeptical look on his face seemed to say, *Yiyin will never go for that.* But I could tell that the fight had gone out of him—physically, mentally, emotionally. He gritted his teeth and made his way forward, limp-crawling on the wet earth, spewing obscenities as he went.

Ollie and I trudged beside him. "I don't want Yiyin to get hurt," he said. "I don't love her anymore, but I don't want her to die out here. There's something off about this whole setup. I'm not even that surprised that Tim and Kelsey are dead."

I stopped. "What makes you say that?"

"Just the vibe here." He pushed himself to his feet, wincing as he put weight on his bad leg. "Oh, and the bears. Did you hear about Kiga?"

"Who?"

"*Kigatilik* is the Inuit word for demon bear. Let's just say we met him."

"You've met a demon bear?"

"A full-on sociopathic bear, yeah. He got into one of our tents a couple weeks ago and hasn't left us alone since. Kiga thinks bear fences are for his entertainment."

Tess and Dave had talked about the bears too. If I tried hard enough, I could envision a scenario where Tim and Kelsey Greer had abandoned their campsite trying to escape a rogue bear, but Hux and I hadn't found any paw prints to suggest that a bear had ever been there. At the very least, I wasn't prepared to chase a "demon bear" lead just yet.

"Look, I can get you out of here," I said. "I just need a day or two."

He muttered something under his breath.

"What?"

"That's too long."

Too long for what? I wondered.

Before I could ask him, a call came in on my satellite phone.

15

THE NUMBER THAT appeared on my display was local to Alaska, but not one I recognized. Vince was side-eying me, waiting for me to pick it up. There was nothing I could do about the fact that he was about to overhear this conversation.

"Hello?" I answered.

There was a brief pause. "Is this Felicity Harland?"

"Yes," I said. "Who's this?"

Ollie started whining as I strained to hear the voice on the other end of the line. The connection was going in and out, which was typical for this part of the park. Service was much more reliable at altitude than it was in the valley.

"Can you hear me now? It's Tess—Tess Flint."

"Oh . . . hi, Tess."

Vince looked up and said, "The lady from the outfitter? Tell her we need a ride out of here ASAP."

I shushed him with my hand. "What's up?" I asked her.

"Just wanted to see if there'd been any update on that whole situation going on up there. Word on the ground in Bettles here is that the two people found on the Alatna are the ones that went missing near Boreal Mountain. Is that true?"

"I can't confirm or deny that, Tess. I'm sorry. The family hasn't even been notified."

"Huh. Okay. Dave said something about wolves."

I sighed, dismayed by the fact that word was already out about the Greers, which meant the rumor mill was flying. As for Tess Flint, she wanted information, and I understood why. This was her park, her livelihood. If there was a killer on the loose, she had every right to know about it—as did her customers.

I wandered away from Vince, just out of earshot. I couldn't afford to lose sight of him until we were all on a plane back to civilization, not that I was too worried about him wandering off.

"It's still very early in the investigation," I said.

"But there *is* an investigation?"

"If I get called to a scene, then, yes, there's always an investigation. Sometimes it's open and shut, sometimes it takes quite a while." I rubbed my temples. "Tess, I'm sorry, but my battery life is pretty limited. If I hear anything that could impact you or your business, I'll let you know immediately."

"I'm just hearing things down here, is all. Once the rumor mill heats up, it's hard to stop. There's also talk of that fugitive from Fairbanks." The connection cut out before coming back in with a burst of static. "The police might release a sketch soon—" It went out again.

"I know," I said. "I heard about that."

"Well, whoever did it is still out there. The state police told me to keep an eye out, since we've had some criminal types hide out up here before. Anyway, you might wanna touch base with the Staties about it."

I understood her sense of urgency, but the Fairbanks triple murder wasn't highest on my priority list. For one thing, it wasn't in my jurisdiction. For another, that homicide involved firearms and drug dealers. I was dealing with two suburbanites and poison berries. I couldn't get involved in every violent crime in Alaska just because I wore a badge that identified me as a member of law enforcement.

That said, if there *was* a fugitive hiding out in the park, I needed to know about it. Hux would want to know about it too. Hell, he'd want to track them down.

"I appreciate that information," I said. "I'll look into it." Ollie started barking, which meant something must have gotten his attention. I thought about Kiga, the rogue bear. It was time to get off the sat phone and hoof it back to camp.

"Alrighty," Tess said. "Anything else I can do for ya while you're off the grid?"

"No, I think we're good." I caught myself. "Actually, maybe there is. I might need to arrange a last-minute ride out of here in the next couple days. Any chance Bill could come get us on short notice?"

"Shouldn't be a problem," she said. "As long as the weather holds. End of the week's looking nasty."

Oof. This was more bad news. I tried not to let it show in my voice. "I'll keep that in mind," I said. "Thanks."

"Just give a holler when you need him."

"Will do. Thanks." As I ended the call, I turned around to see the startling sight of Zane Reynolds standing next to Vince. It was almost as though he'd materialized out of thin air. I shoved my sat phone in my backpack and made my way over to them as fast as I could.

How long has he been there? I wondered, furious with myself for letting my guard down. Ollie had tried to warn me, but I hadn't listened.

A chilly smile spread on Reynolds's face when he saw me. "You didn't get far," he said. "What happened?"

"Vince was having some knee trouble."

"Oh, come on," Vince said, grumbling. "I was doing just fine. It's Carlin here who wanted to bail."

I wondered if Vince had already blown my cover to Reynolds—something about the way he said my fake name so derisively—but it didn't feel like it. It was also hard to imagine these two in cahoots. Reynolds's disdain for Vince was obvious.

Reynolds said to me, "I'm surprised. You seemed so . . . capable."

"Well, um—I have a bad back, actually," I said, swallowing my pride so Vince could feel better about himself. The truth was, "bad back" was an understatement. I had a titanium rod keeping my spine in place.

"How'd that happen?"

"A hiking accident."

Reynolds's patronizing smile boiled my blood. "Don't beat yourself up about it," he said. "It's a shock for everyone, coming here."

I gritted my teeth. Maybe it was my memory of Kevin when he realized I was too injured to hike out of the wilderness on my own—the panic in his eyes, the desperation in his voice—or maybe it was something else, but I resented Reynolds's assumption that I couldn't handle the elements. I supposed it hit me especially hard because a part of me wondered if it was true.

"Not sure if you heard," Vince said to Reynolds, inserting himself into the conversation, "but Tim and Kelsey are dead."

Reynolds's jaw twitched. "They were the ones on the Alatna?"

"Yup," Vince said.

"Who told you?"

Vince flicked his gaze in my direction. "She did."

"I . . . I don't know for sure," I stammered. "But when we talked to the rangers, they gave us a description of the bodies— a man and a woman, maybe early thirties, wearing red parkas. Vince said it sounded like two people who had been camping with you recently."

Reynolds frowned. "That's a pretty vague description."

"Sure sounded like them to me." Vince was suddenly animated, his knee forgotten. "Tim and Kelsey wore those matching red parkas, remember? We all made fun of them for it."

Reynolds folded his hands together as he stole a glance at Ollie. My dog didn't seem to like Reynolds very much. "Do the others know?" Reynolds directed his question to both of us—but more to Vince.

Vince said, "I don't have a sat phone, so no."

"Then I'll call them," Reynolds said. "We'll postpone this expedition for now." He looked at me. "Can I borrow your phone?"

The last thing I wanted to do was hand over my ISB-issued satellite phone to someone like Zane Reynolds. If he so much as scanned the contact list, it could put my cover at risk. I tried to play dumb. "Don't you have one?" I asked.

"Not on me, no."

Reluctantly, I handed it over. He might see Tess's number among the incoming calls, but aside from that, he'd have to do a deep dive into my messages and emails to see the correspondence from Ray. I doubted he'd do something so brazen with me standing right there.

Reynolds put in a number and waited for the call to go through. Someone on the other end answered. His tone was no-nonsense—sounded like one tough guy talking to another. I couldn't picture him talking to Ana or Yiyin in such a curt, stern style, so I figured it had to be Diego. *Could Diego be his partner in all this?* I wondered.

"Yup, head back now," Reynolds said. "We're about a klick north of camp."

After he ended the call, I wrangled up my gear and called to Ollie to fall into step beside me. Eventually, Reynolds and Vince followed suit. With my rifle resting snugly on my back and Ollie at my side, we set a course along the Takahula River, back toward the campsite. Vince took up the rear, muttering to himself as we went. Ollie barked at him every time he slowed down, which was pretty much constantly.

We'd been walking for about twenty minutes when I heard a stray noise in the distance—a twig snapping, maybe, or an animal bone. When I turned around, all I saw was Vince, limping and grunting as he rummaged through his backpack for something. I scanned the squat bushes scattered around the creek bed, the spruce trees hovering above the earth.

And then I saw it—a hulking beast of a thing, hiding in the shadows. It was a brown bear, a thousand pounds, the stuff of Alaskan lore.

"Oh shit," Vince squealed. "It's Kiga!"

The bear was at least fifty feet away, but I reached for my bear spray anyway, knowing how fast things could change in encounters like these. *Stay calm,* I told myself, which was more than I could say for Vince. If the bear charged, I would play dead.

Almost as soon as I got a grip on my bear spray, Reynolds reached for the rifle in his sling. In one swift motion, he got it into position out in front of him. His movements were smooth and practiced, his finger grazing the trigger with a feather touch.

"No!" I shouted. "Don't shoot. He's not charging."

"This one's trouble," Reynolds said. "I'm taking the shot."

"It's not legal to shoot under these circumstances. The bear hasn't charged."

He turned his head toward me. "And how the hell would you know that, Carlin?"

"I just—I read about it online. That if you shoot a bear with a firearm, you have to take the skull and hide to the State of Alaska office." I sighed. "Look, I'm no bear hunter, okay? I never told you I was."

Reynolds's gaze lingered on my face, his eyes narrowed into slits. "I never took you for a PETA enthusiast," he said as he relaxed his hold on his rifle. "Christ."

Seeing that the threat had ebbed, the bear headed upstream with slow, loping strides, a solitary beast prowling its own territory. We were the intruders here, no matter how much we tried to pretend otherwise. This bear, if it had the mind to, could stalk us for days or even weeks. It could come into our tents at night and plunder our sleeping bags. In this part of the world, bears could—and did—kill.

"That was a mistake," Reynolds said to me. "You'll see."

I didn't have to wonder what he meant by that; I already knew.

It was a threat.

16

WHEN WE FINALLY got back to camp, the green tents stood out like Martians on a lunar landscape. There was no sign of the others, not that I expected there to be. I checked my satellite phone for messages, only to remember that Hux didn't have his phone with him. He was using Yiyin's phone, and I didn't like the idea of sending a message that she might read first.

Thanks to Vince's snail's pace, it was already late afternoon, the day pretty much gone. I recruited Vince to help me with the meal prep so that he wouldn't have an opportunity to talk to Reynolds without my being there. I just didn't trust him.

As daylight waned, I was starting to worry about Hux. I regretted the decision to ditch my Garmin at the rendezvous point, but there was nothing to be done about it now.

Vince was sitting on a rock, peeling an onion. His pant legs were rolled up, revealing a battered pair of sandals. His yellow toenails looked like curdled fossils.

"I'm not seeing that bush plane you promised me," he said, making no effort to keep his voice down. "When's he coming?"

"Who?"

"Bill. Did you ask if he was free?"

"It'll be a little while," I said. "You've got to sit tight."

"Then at least let me borrow your sat phone. I'll call him myself."

As a federal agent sworn to fulfill the ISB's mission and serve the public, I couldn't easily deny Vince's request. And so, with some serious reservations, I handed over my sat phone to a man I didn't trust and watched him fumble with the buttons. "This is a nice one," he said. "Not as nice as Yiyin's, but still . . ." He squinted at the screen. "What's the number for the outfitter?"

"It's the most recent incoming call on the log there." I kept a handwritten list of important phone numbers in case technology failed me, but I was tired of expending energy making Vince's life easier. He'd have to figure it out.

Eventually he managed to place the call. It didn't take long for someone to answer—sounded like Cody—and that poor guy got an earful. Vince kept throwing around big numbers for "VIP service," as if that were a thing in Alaska. But in the end, it seemed to work, because after a brief exchange with whomever he was talking to, Vince hung up with a big grin on his face.

"We're good," he said.

"Bill's coming?"

"I don't know who's coming. But the guy I talked to said somebody's already on their way up here, and I can just hitch a ride with them."

"Good for you," I said. "Did you give them your location?"

"Yup."

I was skeptical, but Vince's departure plans weren't at the top of my priority list. Vince put my sat phone in my hand before going back to his meal prep. "Look, I'll give you my cell number so you can call me later if you need to. Like I said, I don't want to be involved in a federal investigation."

"You're a witness to a potential crime," I said. "Whether you like it or not, you're involved."

He tossed a handful of onion peels over his shoulder. "Has there been a crime? 'Cause what it sounds like to me, Tim and Kelsey ate some bad berries and that was that."

"I'm not sure 'that was that.'"

"I'd take a closer look at Kiga," he said snidely.

I stood up and brushed off my hands, tiny pebbles and dirt landing at my feet. Vince had outlasted his usefulness. I folded up the map and put it in my pocket.

Out of the corner of my eye, I caught sight of a group of hikers making their way toward the campsite by way of the Takahula River. I took out my binoculars and spotted Hux, forging a path slightly ahead of Diego, Ana, and Yiyin.

By the time I lowered my binoculars, Vince's mood had soured. He planted his feet on the ground and got up with a grunt.

"What's wrong?" I asked.

"Nothing."

Hux was closing in on the campsite, his athleticism on full display. When our eyes met, he smiled at me the way a doting husband might smile at his wife. A pang of longing hit me in a strange, unexpected way. But in spite of his warm reception, I could see the subtle tightness in his expression—a clear indication that he was worried about something.

Reynolds made a quick announcement. "Take a minute to rest, get changed—whatever you need to do. I'd like us all to gather around the campfire in twenty minutes."

I had a choice to make—babysit Vince for twenty more miserable minutes, or debrief with Hux back in our tent. At this point, though, I felt like I was on safer ground with Vince, especially now that he thought he was getting out of here. He wasn't going to risk pissing off a federal investigator at this late stage.

"I'm going back to my tent," I said to Vince, but almost as soon as the words were out of my mouth, I spotted a white Cessna coming in for landing on Takahula Lake. It descended quickly, finding purchase on the smooth surface before gliding to a stop somewhere just out of sight. Vince was entranced.

"My prayers have been answered," he said. "Hallelujah!"

I wasn't sure what to expect as the roar of the Cessna's engine faded in the distance, but I had a sinking feeling Bill Flint was about to appear.

Sure enough, to my horror, some thirty minutes after the plane landed, Tess and Bill Flint emerged from the brush.

Seeing them out there was an oversight on my part, no doubt about it. I should have told Tess that Hux and I were going undercover, but it was too late now. Even worse, there was nowhere to hide to buy ourselves time. The spruce trees were about as bulky as flag poles and as numerous as shrubs in a desert.

I tried not to panic. First off, I'd dealt with a situation like this before. Back when I was working as an undercover "teenager," I ran into someone I'd arrested for drug-related crimes a couple years earlier. It was a near miss that could have ended badly, but at the last minute, another agent managed to get me out safely. This time around, though, I couldn't depend on that person to be Hux. We had to figure our way out of this one together.

I signaled to Hux, who was also looking in Tess and Bill's direction. When he started toward our tent, he picked up a tail—Yiyin.

Yiyin grasped Hux's arm just as he was about to step inside our tent. "Where are *you* going so fast?" she asked with a pert little giggle.

Before Hux could answer, I said in a withering tone, "Could you give us a minute, Yiyin?"

"I was just saying bye—"

"Bye," I snapped. Yiyin was still talking, not that I paid any attention to the actual words coming out of her mouth.

As I zipped up the tent flap behind us, I caught a small smile on Hux's face. Embarrassingly, I felt myself blush. Hux wasn't my husband; he wasn't mine to possess. But I was playing a part, and that part called for a little jealousy.

"Sorry," I muttered. "That was rude, I guess."

"Nah. She deserved it."

Doing my best to hold back a smile, I sat on my sleeping mat and stretched out my legs. I'd had some time to change into fresh clothes since coming back to camp with Vince, but being in such close quarters with my colleague was still an adjustment.

"We need to talk," I said.

"You got that right," he said with a weary smile.

"Well, first things first—you saw Tess and Bill."

He nodded. "What are you thinking? Should we just blow our covers and hope for the best? Or try and give them the heads-up somehow?" He reached into his backpack for some trail mix, while I decided how best to tell him that our covers were already blown.

"Vince knows," I said, avoiding Hux's gaze. It felt like an important decision that we should have made together, and I felt guilty about it. "I'm sorry. I should have talked to you first."

"I'm sure you did what you thought was best," he said. "Is he cooperating?"

"Yes," I said. "He saw Tim Greer arguing with Reynolds the night before he left camp with Kelsey Greer. So that could point to motive."

"What were they fighting about?"

"He says he doesn't know. He was drunk."

"People drink around here?"

"I know—seemed weird to me too. I think the guy's full of shit most of the time."

Hux offered me a handful of trail mix, which I accepted. "What do we do about Tess and Bill?" Hux asked.

"I think I should try and talk to Tess before they out us to the group."

Hux munched on a handful of cashews. "I bet they'll help us keep our cover going if that's what we decide to do," he said. "They've been a big help so far."

I peered through the crack in the tent flap to see Yiyin and Vince having some words outside their tent. Bill was talking to Reynolds while Tess stood next to two large duffle bags. I didn't think either of them had seen me or Hux yet, but I wanted to clear the air with them as soon as possible. There was also the question of *why*—namely, why were they both here?

"I'll talk to Tess now," I said. "Bill's occupied at the moment."

"You want me to talk to him?"

I shook my head. "Not yet. What did Yiyin say, by the way?"

"What *didn't* she say?" he said with a sigh. "Once she got going, she never stopped. And, you know, kind of amazingly, she didn't ask me a single question about myself, even after six hours on the trail. I kept waiting for one to pop out, but it never did."

I had to laugh a little bit. "So, what did you find out?"

"Vince has substance abuse issues." He reached into the pouch for another handful. "Painkillers, mostly. But he's a drinker too—which I guess corroborates what you said."

"Huh," I said. "I never saw him pop a pill."

"Do you think she's lying?"

I wasn't sure what to think, honestly. Yiyin didn't strike me as a rule follower—or a truth teller, for that matter. Usually when people lied, though, they had a reason. Then again, sociopaths were an entirely different breed. "What else did she say?"

"That's she's been trying to get pregnant for eight years, but Vince is 'sterile.' I mean, that's the word she used." He stole a glance in my direction, maybe to make sure that he hadn't offended me—which, of course, he hadn't. "Anyway, this is it for them—baby or bust. And by 'bust,' I mean the marriage is over."

"Vince said pretty much the same thing," I said.

I couldn't help but think about Kevin, about our marriage. Our relationship hadn't been tested until the bitter end, but even then, it wasn't like we'd parted on bad terms. Kevin had insisted on going for help when I fell and clearly could not go on; I'd agreed to stay behind and wait for him to return. I sometimes wondered how we would have fared if we *had* been tested—by infertility, illness, or something else. Maybe we would have made a better decision that day.

"Anyway," Hux went on, "after all that beating up on her husband, she did offer some other quick takes. Ana's got mental health issues, apparently. Yiyin found some Xanax lying around with her name on it. And she thinks Diego is an ex-con."

"Any spousal abuse there?"

"Not that she's seen," he said. "I asked her about it too. She actually said Diego is super protective of Ana—almost *too* protective. He never lets anyone get too close to their tent. They participate in all the rituals and whatnot, but they keep everybody at a distance."

"Huh. Interesting."

"And I couldn't get her to clarify what she meant by 'mental health issues.' I get the feeling Yiyin has a tendency to exaggerate."

"Yup," I said dryly. "What about Tim and Kelsey Greer? Did they come up at all?"

Hux nodded. "I never had to come out and say their names; Yiyin got there on her own. Like I said, she talks a mile a minute. Anyway, Yiyin and Kelsey were pretty close, but it sounds like the friendship soured toward the end, there."

"Soured how?"

"I got the feeling that Tim and Kelsey's marriage was rock solid—high school sweethearts, totally into each other, all in on the idea to come here. Yiyin sounded jealous, to be honest. I could hear it in her voice. She resented Kelsey for being married to the love of her life." He crinkled the bag in his hands. "But she never came right out and said it—that was just the feeling I got."

"How strong was that resentment?"

He met my eyes again. "Pretty strong."

"Enough to kill?"

Hux thought for a moment. "I think Yiyin's got it in her, sure . . . and I wouldn't say that about just anyone. She's ruthless, Harland. The way she talked about her companies, her employees, all that money—*yikes*. There were times I felt like I was talking to an alien species . . . like, an enemy alien species. You know, the kind you hope never invades Earth."

"That's a pretty damning assessment."

He popped a few more nuts in his mouth. "I wasn't a fan, is all. But I'm not ready to say that she killed Tim and Kelsey Greer."

"What did she think about the bodies? Did it occur to her that it might be them?"

"No," he said. "She never made that connection. I asked her if she'd tried to contact Kelsey since she left, but she said she hadn't."

"That's kind of odd. I thought they were friends."

"I guess not."

I peeked outside the tent again, to see Tess coming back into camp with another load of supplies. "I better go. Tess is back."

"I'll wait here," he said.

"Just one more thing."

He quirked an eyebrow at me.

"You seemed worried about something earlier—back when you were coming into camp."

"Oh." He rolled up his snack pouch and stuck it in his back pocket for the time being. "It was just something Diego said."

"Diego?" I had assumed Hux hadn't crossed paths with anyone out on the trail, and it surprised me to hear that maybe he had.

"Yeah. I almost forgot about it, to be honest. He said it right before I saw you."

"What was it?"

I zipped my jacket up to my ears, which did nothing to temper the chill that suddenly gripped me. "He said Reynolds is hostile to strangers," he said.

"In what way?"

"Didn't say. That's when we saw you guys."

He handed me my Glock. "Here, take this."

"I can't, Hux. Reynolds will see it."

"Then wear my coat to hide it." He shed his dark green jacket and handed it to me. "Tell him your parka got wet."

I took them both: the coat and the gun. I holstered the Glock on my hip, which made me feel like a federal agent again. I was glad to let go of Carlin, if only for a few minutes; her reticence and fear were starting to wear on me.

"Thanks," I said.

I wanted to say more, but right then, in the tent's intimate interior with a man I trusted more than anyone on the planet, I couldn't find the words.

17

I GAVE THE CAMPSITE a wide berth in an effort to avoid being seen as I went off to intercept Tess. I spotted her at a distance, lugging two large duffle bags on a cart with all-terrain wheels. She wore a harness strapped to her chest to support the load.

"Tess!" I called out.

She stopped and looked up, meeting my gaze across the sprawling river valley. A fatigued smile spread across her face as she lifted a hand in greeting.

Ollie and I jogged over to her, partly to show her that I still had plenty of hustle left in my legs after a few hard days in the Gates of the Arctic, but mostly to make sure we didn't run into someone else from the campsite before we could have this conversation.

"Here," I said, extending a hand as she brought the cart to a stop. "Let me take the load for a while."

"It weighs a ton." Tess winced as she tried to get one of the wheels on her cart out of the mud. I bent down and gave it a heave. "The harness helps quite a bit," she said. "Don't worry about it."

"You need a pack mule," I said with a smile.

"Tell me about it. We actually tried to get that going a couple years back, but we couldn't find any ranchers to take 'em for the summer. So here we are with a harness, a cart, and these Black

Hole duffels. They keep me looking trim, at least." The crow's feet around her eyes deepened, hinting at a smile. To my eye, though, she looked tired.

"So, you're delivering supplies to the campsite here?"

"Yup. We've got a couple longer-term outfits we work with over the summer—groups that tend to stay awhile. This one here, I don't even know the client's name. He pays Bill in cash."

"How often do you come up this way?" I appraised her Black Hole duffel, a deceptively massive bag with a thick strap and all kinds of versatility. Tess was the opposite of most hardened rangers I met out in the field, in that she seemed to relish technology, especially the kinds of things that could help her do her job better and faster. In this case, though, I couldn't help but think that a four-legged animal might have worked better.

"Oh, it really varies. Maybe every couple weeks or so." She put her hands on her knees and sucked in a breath. "Anyway, Cody told me there was a guy here that needed a ride back to Bettles—figured that might be you."

"Actually, about that." I glanced back in the direction of the campsite and was relieved to see no activity whatsoever. Everything was quiet. "We have reason to believe that the victims found on the Alatna were last seen at this campsite only a day or two before they died."

"Is that right?" The smile on her face faded. "Damn."

It was hard to imagine anyone eavesdropping on our conversation way out in the open like this, but I dropped my voice to a whisper anyway. "Tess, we may need your help with something."

"What's that?"

"Hux and I never disclosed our identity as federal agents to the group here. We're flying under the radar a bit so we don't spook the group."

Her eyebrows went up. "Is that legal? Going undercover, I mean?"

"ISB does undercover work from time to time, yes. It's warranted in certain situations."

"Well, you don't have to worry about me," she said cheerfully. "Mum's the word."

"What about Bill?"

She glanced over her shoulder in the direction of Takahula Lake. "I'll talk to him."

"Great, thank you." In a perfect world, I would have talked to Bill myself, but I decided to let Tess handle her own husband. "In any case, we'd like to stay another day or two. The person who called Cody about the ride was Vince, one of the people camping here."

She shuffled forward with the duffels. "Got it," she said. "Well, we can always come back and get you later—just call and let me know."

One of the duffel bags toppled off her cart. I hurried over to fix it before she could unstrap herself from the harness. "If you don't mind my asking, what kind of supplies are you handing off here?" I asked.

She scrunched her forehead in thought. "You know, I didn't pack the duffels. My guys back at the store did. So I can't really say, but it's usually bulk food—rice, beans, things like that. Sometimes beer and wine. Occasionally a client will put in for a more specialized item, like a sat phone or a tent, but I'd know about it in that case."

I was tempted to ask her about baneberries, but I couldn't imagine any legitimate outfitter stocking toxic plants. Then again, I didn't see the downside in asking the question. Maybe Tess knew a plant enthusiast back in Bettles.

"Any chance this client here put in a request for berries?" I asked.

"Oh, you know, I really can't say. Literally. Cody does all the inventory."

"So who packs the duffels?"

"Whoever's available back at the store. I just haul 'em up here."

I cinched the belt around the duffel that had fallen off the cart. "Why?" I asked, realizing a little late that she might interpret this question the wrong way. To be honest, I was curious: why did the owner and proprietor of Bettles Outfitters have a side gig as a pack mule?

She scrutinized my face for a beat, but then the taut lines around her face relaxed. "Bill," she said, by way of explanation. "He's got a bad heart. He really shouldn't be flying alone these days, but copilots aren't required in bush planes." She looked like she was about to say more, but her sat phone started ringing. As a seasoned outdoorsman, Tess didn't have to go digging for it. She extracted it from an accessible pocket and frowned at the screen. "That's him now. I better call him back."

"Sure thing."

I offered again to lighten her load, but Tess insisted she had it covered. Ollie sidled up against my pant leg. He wanted to get going.

I said a quick goodbye to Tess as she waited for a signal on her sat phone, and made my way back to the campsite. Hux was sitting inside our tent, with the door flap open to catch the breeze. He had his phone out, along with a small pad of paper covered in handwritten notes.

"Hey," I said.

He looked up, his brow knitted from what had to be some intense concentration. "Oh, hey," he said. "It's you again." There was a smile in his eyes. "What's new with Tess?"

"All good. She's going to talk to Bill."

He put his aviators on to fend off the sun's glare while talking to me. "So, wait a minute. Does she *know* Zane Reynolds?"

"Not exactly." I decided to stand outside the tent and talk to him rather than join him inside. "He's a cash-only client. She doesn't even know his real name."

A birdcall echoed in the silence, this one followed by three short bursts. "Reynolds must be getting antsy," I said. "This could be our last chance to talk to him."

Hux squinted at Ana and Diego's tent in the distance. "Something seems off there," he said.

"I agree," I said. "Diego seems buddy-buddy with Reynolds."

"Yiyin talked a little about the Fairbanks triple murder while we were out there. She said the victims were shot execution style, like a professional hit." He lifted his sunglasses onto his forehead. "Did you hear anything about that? Is the FBI on that case?"

"FBI and the Staties, yeah. I offered to assist back when it happened, but they had no reason to believe the suspects went anywhere near Denali."

"So they're not looking for a fugitive?"

"Not that I've heard, no," I said. "But I'll check in with Ray about it."

"Hmm."

"What?"

Hux stuck his notepad in an old T-shirt and rolled it up. He buried it way down into the depths of his backpack. "Yiyin said on our little walkabout that the local media just released a report about two possible suspects—a man and a woman."

Hearing this, I felt those familiar pangs of insecurity creeping in. It had taken months to convince myself that I could handle all the moving parts that came with this job—dealing with Ray, managing Hux, solving crimes on a tight time line—but then things like *this* happened. If the media had information about the Fairbanks murderers, why didn't *I* have that information? Tess had mentioned a sketch, but I hadn't received anything from the Fairbanks FBI.

"When was this?" I asked.

"Right before we left. She's got that Wi-Fi satellite." His tone made clear his feelings on the matter. Hux didn't have much time for people out in nature who couldn't be bothered to, well, appreciate nature.

"Did you see Ana and Diego out on your hunting expedition?"

"From a distance, yeah. I didn't want to get too close given that Diego was out there trying to shoot something."

"He really seems to know his way around guns."

Hux nodded. "Yup."

I grabbed my backpack and reached down into the main compartment for my satellite phone. "I'm going to call Ray."

The Iridium battery life was at fifty-five percent, which was a good reminder that we were always on the clock. Hux and I couldn't afford to waste time out here, especially with bad weather coming.

I went inside the tent to place the call, as I didn't want the wind carrying my voice to unwanted places. Despite my best efforts, the call refused to go through. Even with these top-of-the-line satellite phones, there was no guarantee of a reliable connection. Sometimes it had to do with mountains blocking the signal; other times it was the position of the satellite in space.

Hux poked his head inside. "Nothing?" he asked.

"Nope."

"Okay. I need to make a run down to the BearVault."

"Sounds good. I'll be out in a few minutes."

Almost as soon as Hux went back outside, I heard a strange noise in the brush—footsteps, the rustling of fabric. I stuffed my things into my backpack and tossed everything in the corner. I put my sat phone in the bottom of my sleeping bag and rolled it up tight, the same way Hux had done with his notepad.

The footsteps grew quiet. I could see the outline of a tall, broad-shouldered figure just outside our tent: Reynolds.

"Come on out, Mrs. Hopper," he said. "We need to talk."

18

As Hux and I made our way over to the campsite, with Ollie close at our heels, we saw Ana and Diego sitting around the fire. To my surprise, there was now another tent set up at the fringes of the campsite. It wasn't that forest green, but a bright, impossible-to-miss orange-red. The logo for Bettles Outfitters covered the door flap.

Why are Tess and Bill still here? I wondered. I assumed the tent was theirs, since I hadn't seen anyone else disembark the plane. Tess had made it sound like she and Bill were only here to drop off the supplies and pick up a passenger, but Vince and Yiyin's tent was still here too. I hadn't heard any emotional good-byes to suggest he might have left.

As I sat down in front of the campfire, Hux settled in next to me—close, but not too close. Ollie lay at my feet. The ground was damp despite the heat from the fire, but at least the mosquitoes were elsewhere, torturing some other creature. I some-times wondered if Reynolds had sprayed the campsite with some kind of chemical while we weren't watching. For the most part, it struck me that he seemed more concerned with preserving the "credo experience" than protecting Alaska's natural resources.

Hux smiled across the fire at Diego, trying to establish a con-nection that we all knew wasn't going to pan out. Ana studied her hands. I couldn't help but notice their evasive vibe.

"I wonder what this is about," I mused aloud, but again—no response. Diego threw another stick on the fire, which crackled on contact. Ana looked up, managed a tiny smile, and went back to twirling the ring on her finger.

When Reynolds finally decided to grace us with his presence, he wasn't alone. Yiyin and Vince were behind him, both of them bundled up in parkas and boots.

Vince glared at me as he sat in front of the fire. I couldn't imagine how he could possibly blame me for the fact that he was still here, but that's exactly what it felt like.

Once everyone had settled in, Reynolds said, "I have news— sad news." He bowed his head. "Tim and Kelsey are dead."

Yiyin made a sound like a squeak, and Ana and Diego exchanged a look that hinted at some strange mixture of surprise and doubt. *Was this news to them?* I wondered. Ana's lack of emotion at the news also took me aback. Just a day ago, she had seemed so . . . different.

While I tried to make sense of Diego and Ana's muted reactions, Yiyin's emotions took on a life of their own right before our eyes. She looked over at Vince for solidarity, or maybe even support, but he just kind of lifted his shoulders in an air of indifference. Then he went back to lathering up his knee with more Bengay. Its overwhelming stench made me gag.

After realizing that her husband had nothing to say on the matter, Yiyin unleashed a rampage. "So *they're* the ones the rangers found on the river?" She was directing most of her ire at Reynolds. "Are you sure?"

"Yes," he said. "I'm told their families have been notified."

"But what happened?" Yiyin pressed.

"Well, I don't exactly have all the details, Yiyin," Reynolds said, his patience wearing thin. "But it looked like an accident."

I felt my body stiffen. Hux kept his expression neutral, but I could tell by the slight hitch in his breathing that Reynolds's words had taken him by surprise too. There was no chance that Reynolds *knew* the Greers' deaths were accidental. Even I didn't know that for sure, and I was the medical examiner's first call.

"An accident?" Yiyin asked. "Like they froze to death or something?"

"Look, I don't know," Reynolds said. "I called down to the rangers station, but all they said was that ISB was looking into it."

"What's ISB?" Yiyin asked.

"The Investigative Services Branch. It's like the FBI for the National Park System."

"The FBI?" Yiyin shrieked. "What the hell—"

Reynolds splayed his hands to placate the group. "Now, listen. No one is in danger. I want to make that clear."

Diego glanced at Ana, who barely looked at him out of the corner of her eye. Trying to interpret that look was an act of futility, but I tried, nonetheless. They weren't talking to each other, but they sure as hell were *communicating* with each other.

"Now," Reynolds said, "if anyone needs time to process this—"

"Wait a minute," Hux said. "You said it was an accident. How did they die?"

Reynolds's blue eyes glinted in the fire's embers. "Does it really matter, Fred? We've lost two of our friends. I'm not sure we need to discuss the details."

"I know," Hux said, "and I'm really sorry for your loss. But it's just—we got different information from the rangers, so if something's changed, that could be helpful for us to know."

Reynolds folded his hands together like a patient preacher. "Are you familiar with the Alaska Triangle?" he asked.

"I—uh, no," Hux said, which was a lie, not one that came easily to my partner. Hux loved learning about the places we went—to him, knowing the land was a sign of respect for it. In fact, he was the one who was always sharing stories of Alaska's darker side.

Reynolds said, "The points of the triangle are the cities of Juneau, Anchorage, and Utqiagvik, so if you look at a map, we're right in the middle. Sixteen thousand people have disappeared in the triangle since 1988. So to hear about two more people who lost their way in this wilderness and perished as a result—it's tragic, but it's not at all uncommon."

It was hard to argue with Reynolds on this point. Alaska's spectacle and danger were deeply intertwined, and most locals I'd encountered had a story about a friend or family member who had disappeared in the backcountry.

Tim and Kelsey Greer, though, had not disappeared. They had died—under very suspicious circumstances. I wondered why Reynolds was digging his heels in the theory that the Greers had suffered a tragic accident.

"But weren't they here with you right before they 'got lost'?" I asked.

Reynolds looked me in the eye, a seemingly direct rebuke to my question. "Frankly, Carlin, I'm starting to wonder why you two are still here. I just told you their deaths were an accident—there's nothing to worry about. Nothing of the *human* variety, that is."

"What about the two fugitives from Fairbanks?"

A shadow fell over Reynolds's face. "What about them?"

"Is it possible—I mean, could it be that they ran across a bad actor?"

Reynolds barked a laugh. "Out here? This isn't New Jersey, Carlin. You don't just walk out your door and get mugged because you weren't paying attention."

Reynolds put his hands on his knees and stood up. "You want to stay?" he asked me—or rather, forced on me.

"I . . . well . . ." I glanced at Hux, who seemed just as flustered by Reynolds's sudden change in tone.

"You don't feel safe out there?" he pressed.

"We feel safe enough."

He took stock of the makeshift ring on my finger. "You've been married how long?"

"Five years," Hux cut in. "No kids, though."

Strangely, Reynolds's expression seemed to morph into something that almost resembled sympathy. It was an unexpected transformation. "Is that by choice?"

Sensing the shift in tone, Hux fumbled for my hand, but once he had it, there was nothing awkward or fumbling about it. It felt right. "No, but we've thought about it."

Reynolds's gaze flicked to our entwined fingers. "Well, there is good news. Tonight's new moon marks the start of a new lunar cycle. *Tatkik* is the Inuit word for moon. Perhaps your cycles are in sync with *Tatkik*, which would make for a favorable encounter with your mate." He scanned the other faces sitting around the campfire. "Now, I know you're all thinking about the friends we've lost, but this is our opportunity to move forward." He added somberly, "This is what Tim and Kelsey would have wanted."

No one spoke, which seemed to suggest that everyone here but me and Hux knew what he was talking about. Sensing that we were partaking in some sort of test, I asked, "Which is what?"

"Sex," Yiyin said. Her voice had a tantalizing lilt. "Ever heard of it?"

I could feel my cheeks flush. Reynolds folded his hands together and assumed the position of a serene shaman. Talk of murder and mystery had given way to the scandalous appeal of sex in the woods. I was still trying to get my head around it.

To show any signs of affection with Hux now would cross a boundary that we could never uncross. It wasn't professional—hell, it wasn't even allowed. That wasn't to say that dating your fellow agent wasn't permitted, but this wasn't that kind of thing. We *weren't* dating. In fact, I was pretty sure Hux was dating an archaeologist from Anchorage.

Before I could overthink this thing into oblivion, Hux leaned over and whispered something into my ear. It wasn't a kiss; it wasn't even close. But his voice, husky and raw, had the same effect—it made the arctic chill suddenly recede, replaced by a surging, stupefying warmth. I felt my cheeks flush. It was unlike anything I'd experienced before—with Hux, or anyone.

Yiyin's giggling expression had turned surly. *She's jealous*, I realized. *Good.*

Hux pulled away. I couldn't even bring myself to look at him.

Reynolds seemed pleased—like the two of us had accomplished something sexually deviant right in front of his eyes. He turned to Yiyin and Vince with a smile in his voice. "Yiyin, the new moon has come. It is time."

Yiyin stole a glance at her husband, who was so immersed in his Bengay application he might as well have been working out its molecular structure. But he was doing a lousy job pretending Yiyin wasn't sitting right beside him.

"Tonight you may choose a copartner," Reynolds said to Yiyin.

Before I could work out what the hell he meant by "copartner," Yiyin said breathlessly, "Fred. I choose Fred."

Wait, what? I couldn't tell who I hated more in that moment: the man who'd given Yiyin the power to choose, or Yiyin herself. Either way, Reynolds's "credo" was starting to take shape right before my eyes, even as the mystery of Tim and Kelsey Greer's deaths deepened. I was starting to suspect that this ritual of sorts was all for show—that he was testing our cover because he knew who we were and what we wanted out of him.

It was time to escalate our exit plan.

"Very well," Reynolds said, smiling placidly at Yiyin. "Tonight you will engage in the ritual with your husband, Vince, and your witness, Fred."

Yiyin's smug smile showed a sliver of her dazzling white teeth while Hux sat there like a deer in the headlights. I wasn't sure what to do. Could I object? Because every bone in my body *wanted* to object.

I blurted out, "Actually, can you pick someone else?"

All eyes settled on me. Reynolds's blue eyes flickered with mischief.

"Fred is my husband," I said, maybe a little too defensively. "I didn't come here to share him." I didn't dare look in Hux's direction.

Reynolds said, "Now, 'sharing' is not the right way to look at what we do here—"

"I'm not comfortable with this," I said. Reynolds didn't flinch. It suddenly occurred to me that maybe *this* was the subject of the argument that had spurred Tim and Kelsey Greer to leave. It wasn't a stretch to think that one of them had objected to sharing their spouse.

Either way, I wasn't about to send Hux off to some sexual escapade. For one thing, it was against federal law for an undercover agent to be coerced into a sexual act. For another, I was responsible for my younger, greener partner, and this was not part of the job description.

Vince put his hands on his knees and grunted his way to his feet. "Let's get this over with," he muttered to Yiyin, before glaring at me. "'Cause it looks like our ride didn't pan out."

"Isn't your ride right over there?" I saw that the movement inside Tess and Bill's tent had ceased, and the lights were off. Maybe they'd already called it a night.

"Nope," Vince said. "Something's wrong with their plane."

"Don't worry about them," Reynolds said. "They're only here for the night. As soon as they can get a repair person up here, they'll be on their way."

I was struggling to process this strange turn of events. "Their plane broke down?"

Reynolds sighed, his frustration mounting. "I'm sure it'll be fixed by morning. They can fly you back to Bettles then if you want."

It was clear by the scowl on Reynolds's face that he was losing patience, but I suspected that something other than Vince's attitude was bothering him.

I turned to Hux and said, "We're not doing this." In that moment, I wasn't just playing the role of Carlin Hopper; I was acting as Hux's superior.

Yiyin's smile turned snide. "Yeah, well, I don't see *Fred* objecting," she said.

Hux grabbed my hand and hoisted me to my feet. "We'll just be a minute," he announced to the group. Yiyin frowned, clearly displeased with Hux's lack of bounding enthusiasm. Vince muttered something under his breath. Reynolds said nothing.

Hux led me down to the creek, out of earshot from the others. "I think Reynolds is onto us," he said. "Maybe it's time to bail."

I pushed a strand of hair behind my ear. The wind had picked up, heralding a cold night ahead. "We could just tell everyone who we are and hope for their cooperation."

Hux shook his head. "I don't think that'll play. Reynolds has, what, six guns in this camp? I don't want to risk pissing him off."

The campfire's golden aura was already fading into wisps of smoke. Reynolds stood facing our direction, but I couldn't tell if he was looking at me or past me.

"Vince was dreading tonight's ritual," I said. "He knew it was coming. I'm guessing Reynolds himself is impregnating these women—with or without their consent, I don't know. But if he's targeting couples with male infertility, then his methods make sense." I spotted Reynolds putting a pot of coffee on the fire. "I mean, they don't 'make sense,' but it explains what he's doing here."

Hux was quiet for a moment. "That could be," he said. "I'm just not sure we should stick around and find out. Worst case, I'll track him down later."

"He's a survivalist and a con man, Hux. We'll never find him."

"Ye of little faith," Hux said with a teasing smile.

"You know what I mean. It's not easy tracking someone down in a wilderness this size. Plus, we've got a million other things on our plate. You won't have time."

Hux hung his head, but I could see in his eyes that he agreed with me. Out of the corner of my eye, I saw Reynolds was now talking to Ana and Diego by their tent. From a distance, it looked like the three of them were conspiring in some way, but that might have been my imagination. Whatever it was, Yiyin and Vince weren't involved in it.

"Let's see how the next hour goes," I said. "It's not like we can hike all the way back to Bettles, anyway. We have to wait for Tess and Bill."

He nodded. "Fair enough." He looked down at his shoes, which were muddy from the day's activities. "So, you want me to do this thing with Yiyin and Vince?"

"Of course not." My tone was indignant. I was horrified that Hux had even suggested it.

"Not the actual *thing*," he said. "But it could be a good opportunity to ask more questions."

I sighed. "Okay. I'll see if I can crack Ana and Diego."

While I tried to convince myself that we weren't making a huge mistake, I heard Yiyin calling out for Hux. "Fred!" she shouted. "Fred, come on! We're waiting, and it's *cold*!"

"Don't do anything even remotely, uh, sexual," I said, clearing my throat on the last word. "It's prohibited in ISB—for your protection."

"I got it, boss. Don't worry."

As Hux made his way toward Vince and Yiyin's tent, I had to force myself not to go after him. Reynolds caught my gaze, a smile curling on his lips, almost like he knew what I was thinking. Then again, I *had* made it clear what I was thinking: that I didn't like sharing my husband. Hux wasn't my husband, but I still felt possessive of him.

With nothing left to do but stew on my feelings for Yiyin, I decided to go back to my tent and contact Ray. My sat phone was still at the bottom of my sleeping bag, stuffed in a tank top and rolled up tight. I knew it was probably overkill, but I didn't care. My satellite phone was our lifeline, especially since Hux didn't have his.

It was late, just after midnight. At this hour, I wasn't expecting much correspondence from anyone. Sure enough, there was nothing from Ray, but there *was* one incoming message from the Park Service. It was an emergency alert about the fugitives.

I clicked on the link accompanying the alert. It took me to a police sketch of the individuals linked to the triple murder in Fairbanks. *Finally.* Thanks to a spotty satellite connection, the sketch took a minute to load. The resolution wasn't great on my Iridium either, but I felt fortunate to have access to a photo at all. Hell, it was better than the dusty old desktop computers back at the Chicago FBI field office.

Almost as soon as the pixels started coming together on my screen, I recognized the faces staring back at me—the small, asymmetric features on him, the deep-set, dark eyes on her. There was no mistaking it.

It was Ana and Diego.

19

T HE NIGHT HAD gone cold and damp, a harbinger of autumn and its monthslong descent into darkness. I studied the sketch for a long time, scrutinizing every detail of the two faces staring back at me. A sketch was a far cry from the crisp resolution of a photograph, but there was no denying that the faces strongly resembled those of the couple camping next to us.

There was also a description of the suspects—their heights, weights, racial background. Those details fit Ana and Diego too. There was even mention of the suspects' familiarity with firearms, as the three people found on the Tanana River had indeed been shot execution style: three shots to their center mass. I couldn't shake the image of Diego's capable handling of Reynolds's rifles. It sure seemed to fit.

But Tim and Kelsey Greer had been poisoned, not shot. And although the Fairbanks victims had been found near a river, that didn't mean they'd necessarily been killed there. According to the brief report accompanying the National Park System alert, the motive for the killing was unclear. The three victims were low-level criminals with a history of drug possession and distribution, but they weren't big players in the Fairbanks drug market.

I debated calling Ray to find out more, but a shriek in the night gave me pause.

It sounded like Yiyin.

Ollie was outside my tent, howling at the source of the noise. The urgent bleat of a birdcall sent everyone scurrying out of their tents—me, included. Hux, to my great relief, still had all his clothes on. Yiyin was hysterical, walking in circles as she paraded her satellite phone around the campsite. Reynolds was trying to calm her down, while Bill and Tess gathered around the charred remains of the campfire, wearing their coats, hats, and pajama bottoms. But there was no activity at all around Ana and Diego's tent. The interior was dark.

I went out to see what all the ruckus was about, even though I was pretty sure I already knew. The answer was right there on my satellite phone.

"It's them!" Yiyin screamed. "It's definitely them!"

"Just—hold up there," Reynolds said calmly. "Take a breath, please."

"I'm not 'taking a breath.' It's literally *right here*." She shoved her sat phone in his face. Hux intervened—in his usual gentle, diplomatic way—and got her to put the phone down.

Reynolds squinted at the grainy image. "I have no idea what that is."

"It's a *Wanted* poster—with Ana and Diego! They killed three people in Fairbanks!" Hux somehow managed to coax her to sit down. Vince, on the other hand, was clumsily trying to extricate himself from his tent. He spotted Bill standing at the fringes of the campsite and limped over to him and Tess. I saw Bill tense as soon as he saw him coming.

My focus, though, was on Ana and Diego, who had yet to respond to the melee. I was beginning to think they'd disappeared into the wilderness, when Diego suddenly emerged from his tent, dressed in jeans and a loose cotton shirt. Unlike Ana, he seemed immune to the cold, like he was made for this place. Yiyin met his gaze with a seething disgust tinged with fear, but Diego didn't flinch. He just stood there, silently observing her tantrum. He didn't seem offended. If anything, he looked mildly entertained.

"You!" Yiyin screamed. "You're a murderer!"

At this point, Hux gave up on Yiyin and started walking in my direction. Ollie ran over to greet him, but it wasn't their usual carefree reunion. I wondered what had happened in that tent.

Diego put his hands in his pockets while holding Yiyin's gaze. "Say that again?"

"Check your sat phone. The Park Service sent out an alert about the three druggies you killed in Fairbanks."

"Sorry," he said. "I've got no effin' clue what you're talkin' about."

Yiyin marched over to him and again wielded her sat phone like a weapon. "There!" she said. "That's you."

"That screen there's pretty tiny," he said. "I can tell that's a dude, but that's about it."

"That dude is *you*."

"No, it's not," he said flatly. He squinted one eye at the screen. "This here says these lowlifes were killed back in June. We weren't even here in June."

"Prove it."

Vince was standing a few feet away from Tess and Bill, staying quiet while Yiyin went on her rampage. To my surprise, his usual air of disgust around her had morphed into something else entirely. The little smirk on his face was smug—like he was enjoying this.

"I'm not gonna do that," Diego said. "'Cause that's not me."

"Let's have a seat and talk this out for a minute," Reynolds said. "Here." He gestured to the well-trod ground around the firepit. "I'll make a fire."

"I'm not gonna stand here and be interrogated," Diego said. "And neither's my wife. She's in there cryin' her eyes out right now."

"Oh, *sure*," Yiyin said. "I've heard that before."

"You have?" Diego confronted her. "You think you *know* us, huh?"

Despite the argument taking place right in front of him—or maybe *because* of it—Reynolds went ahead and got the fire going. Everyone reluctantly gathered around.

"I think we should call the police," Yiyin said.

Reynolds laughed, but there was nothing good-natured about it. "That's not how it works out here, sweetheart."

I thought for sure Vince was going to blow our cover to the group right then and there, but he didn't. He caught my eyes for a brief moment as he offered Bill and Tess his usual spot around the campfire. Bill didn't seem happy about this impromptu gathering. He said something to Tess, who managed to placate him while the rest of the group assembled at Reynolds's urging.

I sat down next to Hux, who acted as a buffer between me and Diego. Ana was wearing so many layers that I wondered how she could possibly move her limbs. She sure didn't fit the profile of a killer, but she may have just been an innocent bystander. Just because a witness had seen both of them at the scene didn't mean they had both participated in it.

Yiyin had calmed down a bit, but she didn't seem happy to see me, that was for sure. With a withering glance in my direction, she settled in next to Hux. I could see Vince cajoling Bill and Tess to get warm by the fire, but they seemed hesitant. I wondered if it was because Reynolds was giving off a distinctly cold vibe.

Eventually, though, they came a little closer. Reynolds took the kettle off the fire but didn't offer them coffee.

"Is everything okay?" Tess asked as she rubbed her arms to keep warm. "Are we good to go back to our tent?"

"Oh, you don't want to do that," Vince said. "You'd be sleeping within fifty feet of the Fairbanks serial killer."

An inscrutable half smile colored Diego's face. "I see you're real set on that story there," he said. "Could be you think all us Mexicans look the same."

"I never said I thought that was you in the sketch," Vince said. "That was my lovely wife, Yiyin."

Tess stayed quiet, but I saw her sidle up to Bill, almost like she was trying to diffuse some of the tension rolling off him in waves. I figured he was also worried about his plane.

"Why are they even here?" Yiyin asked, casting an irritated look at Tess and Bill. "This is a private campsite."

"Tell that to Carlin and Fred over here," Vince said.

Reynolds patted the air with his hands. "Can we all calm down, please?" He turned to Yiyin. "Yiyin, I saw the sketch just now, and I don't think it looks like Diego and Ana at all."

"Then you're blind," Yiyin said.

Ana, who until now had managed to steer clear of the chaos, leaned forward and leveled her gaze at Yiyin. "We weren't even in Fairbanks last month except for a two-hour layover," she said. "We flew straight from Anchorage to Fairbanks, to here. We never left the airport."

"I don't believe you."

Ana rocked back on her heels. "I don't know what to tell you," she said. "You think we don't all remember how clingy you were with Kelsey? How obsessed you were with her relationship with Tim? You said it was 'sickening' how much they loved each other."

Yiyin's expression tightened. "What are you saying, Ana?"

"I'm saying it's a pretty big coincidence that Tim and Kelsey are dead, and here you are throwing a fit about me and Diego being two wanted fugitives. It's a great way to take all the heat off yourself, if you ask me."

Yiyin snorted. "That's ridiculous."

"It's ridiculous that you think we're these two fugitives from Fairbanks."

"Is it, though?" Yiyin aired her question to the group. "I googled you, you know, way back when we first got here. Couldn't find you anywhere. You're a ghost."

Ana buried her hands in her parka's deep pockets. "That's not a crime."

You're right, I thought. *It's not.* But it was definitely a little bit odd. For Ana and Diego to have found their way here, they must have come from *somewhere*. Somewhere where they had jobs, or at least some savings. It wasn't easy for an outsider to get to this part of the arctic circle.

Which raised another important question: Had they received an invitation from Reynolds to come here? Or had they stumbled on the campsite the same way we had and stayed because Reynolds invited them to stay? Diego, after all, was an asset to the group. He could hunt, handle a gun, and sustain himself. He didn't need the constant handholding like Vince did. It had become clear to me that Diego was useful to Reynolds. Maybe *that* explained his presence here, and the fertility angle was just a ruse.

Yiyin turned to Reynolds. "Did you even invite them to come here?"

Reynolds stiffened. "I keep that information confidential, Yiyin. You know that."

"This is about our *safety*, Zane."

Vince muttered, "If only we had a couple of cops to straighten this out for us . . ." He was looking directly at me, which seemed to catch Tess and Bill's attention too. I thought about my Glock, tucked away in my backpack, and my sat phone, stuffed inside Hux's sleeping bag. I thought about how deep we'd gotten into this thing—and how hard it could be to get out.

"What's going on?" Reynolds asked. He had started by addressing the group, but his gaze landed on me. "Am I missing something here?"

"You sure are," Vince said. "Our friends from Jersey are actually federal agents."

Yiyin's jaw literally dropped open. I felt my stomach flip-flop. Even Hux took a sharp breath that seemed to reverberate in the stillness.

"Is that true?" Reynolds directed his question at me.

It was tempting to deny everything, but I knew the game was up. Tess and Bill knew who we were, and I didn't want to put them at risk.

"Yes," I said. "I'm Felicity Harland, and this is my partner, Hux Huxley. We both work for the Investigative Services Branch."

Reynolds put his head in his hands. He released a loud exhale that seemed to echo through the campsite. He muttered something that sounded like a colorful expletive.

At last, he looked up. "There was no need to lie," he said to me. "I would have cooperated fully. We all would have."

I didn't believe that for a second, but I wasn't going to argue with him right then. "We're investigating the deaths of Tim and Kelsey Greer," I said. "We heard you and your group had evaded rangers before, and we didn't want to lose access to potential witnesses."

"'Evade' is a strong word," he said.

"We just wanted information, is all."

"Then I hope you got what you came for." He brushed his hands on his pants and stood up. "I'm turning in for the night—unless, of course, you're dead set on arresting me for something." The sharpness in his glare made me flinch.

"No," I said. "Not yet."

Reynolds walked back to his tent and disappeared inside. That left eight of us gathered around the fire, navigating a strange, unfamiliar tension. Tess and Bill stood awkwardly off to the side, but it was a cold night, so they stayed close to the fire. I saw Bill turn and say something to Tess. She hiked her collar up around her neck but didn't respond to him.

Bill said, "Tess is gonna call my repair guy again—see if we can get him up here first thing in the morning." Tess turned and walked back in the direction of their tent. As she went, Bill added, "I can take four on the first run back to Bettles, assuming we're good to fly."

Vince shook his head. "And what are we supposed to do until then? Sleep with a big stick and hope for the best?"

"Y'all can go off and camp wherever you want," Diego said. "Be our guest."

"I'm not sleeping outside the bear fence," Vince said. "Not with Kiga around."

Diego shrugged. "Then I guess you're stuck with us."

Yiyin was pacing the campsite, muttering to herself. She stopped in front of me and waved a finger at my face. "If you're a cop, then can't you just arrest them?" She glared at Diego and Ana. "Or at least use some rope to tie them up or something?"

Vince snorted. "They can't just arrest someone because you tell 'em to, Yi."

"Their faces are right there on the sketch. Of course they can arrest them."

She was technically correct, but that didn't mean I had any intention of arresting two potential murder suspects in a remote campsite stocked to the hilt with rifles. As for Reynolds, I didn't know how he would react—possibly violently, especially if he had some connection to Ana and Diego that I didn't know about.

But with Yiyin in hysterics, I had to do *something*. I also knew this might be our last chance to ask Ana and Diego some questions. First, though, I had to make sure they weren't in the position to do anything rash or violent. All the weapons were stored away in Reynolds's cache, and neither of them appeared to be armed. If one of them made a run for it, we could be in trouble. Ollie was quite the runner, though. I was confident the three of us could take them down if they ran for their tent.

"I know you've seen the sketch," I said to Ana, who had come to us earlier and therefore felt like the more receptive subject. "Do *you* think it looks like you?"

"Well, of course," she said. "But it's *not* us—"

"I know," I said. "You said that. Can you help us all understand why it *can't* be you? When did you arrive in Alaska?"

When Ana balked, Diego leaned forward with his elbows on his knees. "We left Texas on June twenty-eighth," he said. "Got here on the twenty-ninth. Like Ana said, we were at the Fairbanks Airport for a couple hours, but that's about it. Never even stepped outside."

"Do you have a copy of your boarding passes, by chance? Some record of those flights?"

Diego snickered. "You tell us where the hell we're supposed to charge our cell phones, and I'll show you our boarding passes."

Yiyin said, "You could use your sat phone—"

"Don't have a sat phone," Diego said. "We've got a radio, that's it."

"How convenient," Yiyin muttered.

"We can table that for now," I said, keeping my attention focused on Diego. It sounded like Yiyin had access to satellite Wi-Fi, but I wasn't ready to demand access to it quite yet. "Did you interact much with Tim and Kelsey Greer?"

"No, ma'am," he said. "Hardly talked to 'em."

"Why?"

"Because everybody's got their own stuff going on. We're not here to make friends."

"So why *are* you here?" He had given me an opening that felt right, so I took it. The campsite fell silent.

Tess suddenly emerged from her tent with her sat phone in hand. "That's our mechanic," she called out, which got Bill's attention. "He can be here tomorrow around ten, but it'll take him some time to fix it."

Vince turned to Bill. "What the hell's wrong with your plane?"

"The tire axle's busted," Bill said.

"Yeah, but we don't need tires to fly, right? Can't we just make do?"

The expression on Bill's face made Vince recoil a bit. "You're a real twit, aren't ya?"

Vince frowned, his cheeks gone red with Bill's condemnation. "It's a fair question, man."

"It's a stupid question."

Vince coughed into his hand. "Would you do it for ten grand?" He ignored the gasp from Ana. "Twenty?" He got up in Bill's face. "Fifty?"

Bill said nothing.

"A hundred?"

Yiyin snorted. "He can't do it, Vince. He already said it's not safe."

"Yeah, well, it's not safe being here either, is it?"

From my perspective, Vince and Yiyin's relentless back-and-forth was exhausting, but it almost seemed to function as fuel for their relationship—the bickering, the arguing, the insulting. They were both getting off on it in a weird, twisted way, not that I hadn't seen that kind of thing before. I saw it quite a lot, in fact.

"Well?" Yiyin said to Bill. "A hundred grand to fly us out of here tonight?"

Bill glanced over his shoulder, perhaps searching for Tess's reaction, but she had disappeared inside their tent. It seemed to me he was considering their offer, if only for a moment. Not seeing Tess to rebuke him, though, had given him pause.

"No," he finally said. "My life's worth more than that."

Vince sighed. "Fine," he said. "I'm going to bed." He shot a glance in Yiyin's direction. "You coming?"

"I want someone guarding our tent." She blinked at Hux, fanning her eyelashes at him. "Any chance you'd be up for that, Mr. Huxley?"

Ana and Diego suddenly stood up. "You know what, we're headin' out right now," Diego said. "Best of luck to y'all."

Yiyin froze. "Wait . . . you can't do that. You're wanted for murder—"

"We aren't wanted for anything," Diego said. "But we're done hangin' around this crew, that's for damn sure." He grasped Ana's hand and hoisted her to her feet. I watched Ana fumble with her flashlight as they made their way to their tent."

"Do they have guns?" I asked.

Yiyin's eyes widened. "Oh God. *Do* they?"

"No," Reynolds said quickly. "I keep all the weapons in a locked crate."

Bill, having had enough of this drama, turned and walked back to his tent. Reynolds got up and did the same, which made me uneasy, but there was nothing I could do about it. At least the weapons cache was over by the food supply tent, which was in clear view of where I was sitting.

"I still think we could use a bodyguard," Yiyin said.

Hux smiled diplomatically, but before he could give Yiyin any more false hope, I said to him, "Can we talk for a minute?"

"Sure thing."

I powered on my Fenix flashlight to its full brightness, which cast a searing beam of light on our tent. A creature of some sort—a small bear, maybe a wolf—scurried out of its arc. I shook off a chill.

Once we were back inside the tent, I adjusted my Fenix to its lowest setting. I kept the door flap open a crack to keep an eye on the campsite. The interior felt intimate in a way, almost cozy. For a few seconds, at least, I could almost convince myself that we weren't in a precarious situation.

"I know that look," Hux said.

"What look?"

"It's kind of a combination of stubbornness and irritation."

"Well, I'm still trying to process what just went down." I shivered in the damp air. "If Ana and Diego are responsible for the Fairbanks murders, I'm not sure how I feel about letting them out of our sight." A gust of wind rattled the tent, but I was still careful to keep my voice down. "I wonder if I should go out and follow them."

"In the dark?" Hux shook his head. "No way, boss."

"I won't be completely in the dark. I've got my Fenix."

"It's a hard no." Hux looked at his hands before drawing his gaze back up to my face. He sighed. "*I'll* do it."

"Hux, no—"

"You're right. They could be armed and dangerous, which puts us all at risk. If I leave now, I can at least get a beat on where they might be going." He reached into his backpack and pulled out his essentials: a flashlight, map, and a compass. After transferring them to his pocket, he zipped up his jacket and tied his shoelaces.

"Are you sure about this?"

He nodded. "I've tracked violent people before. I know how to stay hidden."

I handed him his hat—a black beanie that would help him stay invisible at night. He pulled his gloves on, tucking them under the cuffs of his jacket.

"Take my sat phone," I said. "And Ollie."

Hux rubbed the scruff under Ollie's neck. "Okay," he said. Ollie wagged his tail. I hated to send them both out there alone, but at least they had each other.

When Hux was halfway out of the tent, I called after him in a hushed voice, "Hux, wait."

He turned around.

"If you can't track them down, just go to the rendezvous point. I'll meet you there."

He nodded, something almost tender in his gaze. "Will do."

"Be careful."

"You too."

And then he was gone.

20

THE CAMP HAD gone eerily quiet, except for the soft crackle of the dying flames. It was bad practice to leave a campfire unattended, but the night's events had sent everyone scattering. I understood why. Talk of murder in a wilderness as remote as this put people on edge.

Reynolds's tent was dark—unlike Vince and Yiyin's, which was brightly lit. A desperate attempt to ward off bad things, maybe. Tess and Bill must have moved their tent elsewhere, because I didn't see it at its old site. I wondered if maybe they had made their way back to Bill's plane while awaiting the mechanic's arrival.

One upside to being outed as a federal agent was that I could behave like one again, which meant carrying a firearm. I reached for my backpack, which was sitting on my sleeping bag. It felt lighter for some reason—a lot lighter. A pang of unease swam through me.

I dumped it out, searching every inch of the thing for the Glock's cold, hard metal. But there was no disputing the facts: it was gone.

"That's impossible," I murmured.

I searched again, just in case—our sleeping bags, backpacks, extra clothes. I remembered putting the Glock in there, which meant there was only one explanation for its absence: someone had come into our tent and taken it.

That wasn't the worst of it. Other things were missing, too—my cell phone, my bear spray, the Swiss Army knife my dad had given me when ISB offered me a job.

I scrambled out into the open air. The night sky was peppered with stars, and when the wind blew, it seemed to penetrate the marrow of my bones. *"August can be a wicked, wild month,"* I recalled one of the rangers in Denali saying. *"It's heaven, but it can also be hell."*

"What's wrong?" came a voice from behind me. It was Reynolds.

"I—nothing." All I could think about was that someone had been in my tent—someone who didn't belong there. "What are you doing here?"

"I wanted to clear up a few things before you go and get the wrong idea about me."

"I don't think I have the wrong idea about you," I said.

He frowned. "No?"

"I know you choose couples with male infertility," I said, which seemed to take him aback. "I know what you do here—you impregnate these women yourself."

"Hold up right there," he said. "You saw Yiyin. She chose her partner—and in her case, it wasn't even me."

He was right on that count, but what about Kelsey Greer? Had she chosen someone other than her husband? And was that the argument that had prompted their departure? Even if it had, I couldn't prove that any of those events had led to murder.

I still felt like Zane Reynolds knew more than he was letting on. This was his camp, after all. His food, his tents, his rules. Those baneberries had to have come from somewhere, and he was a man of means.

"Tim and Kelsey Greer were poisoned," I said. "Do you know anything about that?"

He looked off into the darkness.

"Mr. Reynolds?"

"No," he said, turning his head to face me. "I don't."

"I heard they argued the night before they left."

"Did they? I wasn't aware."

"Vince said you were there."

"Well, I wasn't."

I could tell he was lying. Reynolds was a good liar, but he wasn't the best I'd ever encountered. In fact, he wasn't even the best liar at this campsite.

"You must have at least heard them fighting," I said. "Vince said it woke him up."

Reynolds shrugged. "No," he said. "Sorry."

I wasn't getting anywhere with him, which didn't surprise me, but it did frustrate me. Zane Reynolds was clearly no stranger to law enforcement. Any second now, he was going to tell me he wanted a lawyer. He might even settle for Vince if he had to.

"Who told you their deaths were accidental?" I asked.

"One of the rangers," he said. "Emily Wiseman. I talked to her on the phone."

His reference to the ranger that had discovered the bodies on the Alatna River took me by surprise. How many rangers did Reynolds know by name? Was it a coincidence that he knew Emily's first and last name, or was it something more than that?

"When's the last time you saw her?" I asked.

"Who? Emily?"

"Yes."

He thought for a moment. A wolf howled, its lonesome wail echoing in the stillness. "A little over a week ago. She and her boyfriend were passing through."

"Did you get his name?"

"Dave—the wildlife biologist. They were doing a survey."

"What kind of survey?"

He was getting flustered, but I didn't care. "I don't know the details, Agent Harland. They were interested in poisonous plant species—hemlock, sumac, jimsonweed."

I fought to keep my tone event. "Baneberries?"

"I don't know." He sighed. "You came in here and made a mess of things, ma'am," he said. "I've lost all my clients, as you can see. You ruined my livelihood." Anger flared in his eyes.

Before I could respond to what he was saying, he turned on his heel and strode in the direction of his tent. The campsite was pitch-black, the fire long extinguished. I heard something buckle in the darkness—his tent, coming down.

He's leaving.

"Where are you going?" I called out.

Only the wind whistled its low, ominous answer.

21

IN ALASKA, NIGHTFALL was more medieval than modern. To venture into it without the marvels of modern technology was to risk death with every step. The predators who called this territory their own—the bears, the wolves—were just another hazard in a landscape rife with them.

I considered it, nonetheless—hiking out to the lake to find Tess and Bill, or trying to get to the rendezvous point to call for help. I'd already searched the campsite and determined that Tess and Bill had indeed relocated, since there was no sign of their tent anywhere.

Yiyin had a satellite phone, but she claimed the battery had died. Vince zipped up his tent, closing me off to any more questions or requests. It didn't seem to matter to them that I was a federal agent—or maybe it did, and they didn't want to talk to me without their lawyer present. Vince had effectively said as much. Right here, right now, they were a dead end.

I looked at my watch. It was just past midnight, which meant I'd have to survive at least four hours of darkness on the trail. There was my past too, to consider. During that fateful trip to Australia with Kevin, one small misstep had doomed us both—and that was in broad daylight. The terrain here was so uneven and unpredictable that twisting an ankle was almost a guarantee.

And then what? I didn't even have a satellite phone to call for help.

I went back into my ransacked tent and looked for something that could help me get to the rendezvous point, which was four miles away. The weather had already started to turn from cold and clear to wet and ominous. A light but frigid rain pattered the canvas. I knew I could hunker down here and make my way to the lake at first light, but I didn't like the thought of camping here with two fugitives and a vengeful survivalist knowing my exact location.

In the depths of my backpack, I reached in and pulled out a crumpled map of the park and a compass. I pocketed both of them along with my Fenix. In the end, I decided to leave my backpack and tent behind. The extra weight was just going to slow me down.

The Fenix was my best hope at success. It had been one of my few splurges when it came to backpacking gear, retailing for a couple hundred dollars. In my mind, it was worth every penny. It could shine a light up to ten thousand lumens, with a beam that could reach five hundred meters. In some respects, it wasn't just a flashlight, but a personal locator beacon and a powerful spotlight all in one. Even in summertime, when darkness was a rare thing in Alaska, I made sure to take it along with me every time I stepped foot on a trail.

With everything I needed tucked away in my jacket pockets, I abandoned my tent for the wild openness of an Alaskan night. The first thing I noticed was Yiyin and Vince's tent, its dark green canvas illuminated from the inside. I could hear their voices, the staccato exchange of a couple engaged in a heated argument. They sounded like they wanted to throttle each other, which came as no real surprise.

I surveyed the campsite and decided to take the long away around. I couldn't afford to shine my flashlight in such close proximity to Yiyin and Vince, so I made slow progress, testing each step before I placed my foot. The last thing I needed was a broken ankle.

Brrrzzzzz.

I heard it before I felt it—a surge of electricity that sent a full-body shudder from my fingertips to my toes. The bear fence.

I knew bear fences weren't fatal to humans—in fact, the amperage was so low on these things they were essentially incapable of killing anything—but damn, it hurt. I couldn't help the choked yelp that escaped my mouth, the aborted slew of choice words.

Within seconds, I was struck head-on by the beam of someone's flashlight. Squinting into the glare, I made out Yiyin's face in the darkness. She looked pissed.

"You!" she called out. "Where do you think *you're* going?"

Her aggressive tone made me reach for my hip, only to remember that my holster was empty.

"I'm going to make sure we get a ride out of here," I said through gritted teeth, which were still rattling from the shock.

"We *have* a ride," she said. "Their tent is right over there." She pointed in a direction away from Takahula Creek, in an area hidden by thick brush. Somehow, I'd missed it: Tess and Bill's orange tent, just in a new spot. It reinforced for me how easy it was to disappear out here.

"Okay, great," I said. It took some serious effort just to muster a coherent response. "Then it sounds like you're all set."

She snorted. "We *were* all set until you came along."

"What?"

"Zane left—for good." Her scathing glare told me exactly who she intended to blame for this development.

"I'm sorry, but—"

"He's the real deal, you know. You might not think so, but I did plenty of background on him before we came out here, just like I do for all my employees. Background checks, private investigators, reference checks—the whole thing. I researched him for a year . . . well, my team did." She saw the look on my face and said, "That's right. I've got a team, and my teams have teams. They get me what I need, when I need it."

"I thought he was known for his mysterious ways," I said, making little effort to mask my opinion on the matter.

"That's part of his allure, sure. But every secret has a price."

"Uh-huh." I was really getting tired of dealing with this woman. "And your team convinced you that coming here was worth the trip?"

"Look, I know what goes on here, but it wasn't about it. It all came down to Vince, trying to get him to be a team player—and now you've ruined it." She practically hissed at me. "Zane was getting through to him, and now he's gone."

"He left on his own accord."

She clucked her tongue. "Uh-huh."

"Listen, Yiyin, I'm sorry for ruining your plans here. As I explained earlier, my partner and I are conducting a federal investigation—"

Vince poked his head out of his tent. "Don't talk to her," he barked at his wife. "Not until we can get Sam here."

I had a strong suspicion on who Sam was: their lawyer. With one last parting glance, Yiyin retreated to her tent. Once she was inside, Vince zipped up the flap to simulate slamming a door in my face.

It didn't matter. My mind was already on something else: Tess's satellite phone. I could use it to contact Hux and call Ray for backup. At this point, it felt like the better play than venturing out into the wilderness on my own.

I didn't like disturbing someone at this late hour, but Tess and Bill's light was on, which made the intrusion feel a little less personal. I cast the beam of my Fenix flashlight on the door flap and called out, "Tess?"

There was no answer.

"Bill?"

I waited, feeling the oppressive weight of every passing second. The rain had stopped, but I knew it would be starting up again any second now. I hated standing still in the chilly air, waiting for something to happen.

"Tess?"

I tugged a bit on the door flap, but there was still no response. The last thing I wanted to do was go inside someone else's tent, but after several minutes standing outside, I started to wonder if something had happened to them.

"I'm coming in," I said.

I yanked on the zipper. Everything was quiet—too quiet.

The interior was lit by the faint light of an LED lantern, but the sleeping bags were rolled up.

Tess and Bill were gone.

22

*T*HEY WENT TO *the plane,* I thought. *Maybe they felt safer there.*

There were other possible explanations too—the cold rain, the tension with Reynolds and the others, the storm coming in. Maybe they were more concerned about the possibility of Ana and Diego being the fugitives from Fairbanks than they'd let on.

Without a satellite phone, I had no way of contacting them to find out. But I knew their plane was parked somewhere near Takahula Lake, on the way to our rendezvous point. It was either stick to the plan and head out now, or stay behind and babysit Vince and Yiyin.

The decision wasn't as easy as I thought it would be. I didn't trust Vince *or* Yiyin, and though I worried about their ability to survive in the wilderness on their own, it was only for one night. They had shelter, food, and the accoutrements of modern technology. They could make it.

As for Reynolds, I wasn't sure what I was dealing with now that he was gone. Of course it was possible that Yiyin had performed an extensive background check on him—hell, she probably had—but she'd also gone into that exercise with a certain bias. Even if there *was* something shady in Reynolds's background, she would have had every reason to overlook it.

In the end, I decided to make a go for the rendezvous point. Hux would be headed there too. Worst case, at least I'd be able to use my Garmin to contact him.

Almost as soon as I set out, though, I felt like Reynolds's campsite was trying to suck me back in. The air was still, the sky overcast. The creatures of the night were uncharacteristically silent, which exacerbated my own isolation. Something felt off.

Even though it had been some time ago, my FBI surveillance training came back to me in an instant—the tactics, the instincts. What to do you if you think someone might be following you. The problem was that most of the lessons I'd learned didn't apply out in the wilderness. Using reflective windows, for example, not an option. Putting on a hat or a jacket to disguise your appearance—nope. Stay in public and crowded areas. Try to use public transit.

None of those tricks worked in a place with no buildings, streets, or people. If I *was* being followed, all I could do was keep moving and hope my pursuer lost track of me. Keeping those tactics in mind, I varied my speed and direction, even though I was terrified of losing my bearings. Although Hux could get away with the barest of necessities, I relied on landmarks to orient myself. At night, all I had were my wits and the ground under my feet. It wasn't long before I was questioning every step. That was the thing about doubt: it quickly spiraled into fear.

I caught myself looking over my shoulder every few minutes, searching for the beam of a flashlight, the glint of someone's eyes. Had I underestimated Zane Reynolds—or at least misjudged him? Was someone really following me, or was my mind playing tricks on me? After all, I hadn't slept well in days.

I stopped for a moment to look at my compass. I was heading east, in the direction of Takahula Lake and the Alatna River, but what if leaving the campsite had been a mistake? I thought about putting my Fenix on its maximum setting to signal to Hux that I was in trouble—*three quick flashes, three long flashes, three quick ones.* That was the international sign for distress, and Hux would recognize it immediately. The problem was that whoever else was out there would see it too, and I didn't want to give away my location.

Keep going, I told myself. *Use your ten thousand lumens to see what's in front of you and keep moving forward. You can do this.*

Before I could adjust the setting on my Fenix, I heard a series of sounds behind me—quick thumping strides in the mud, a rustling of fabric, a sharp intake of breath. These were human movements, human sounds of exertion. The whoosh of a stick or some other heavy object filled the air. I tried to move out of the way, but I wasn't fast enough. The thing bearing down on me connected with my hip. My left knee buckled.

Then I felt a pair of hands wrap around my throat.

23

ONE OF THE gloved hands was holding a knife. I felt the icy metal against my skin; the sharpness of its blade. It twitched a little bit, drawing blood.

I remembered my training: *De-escalate. Cooperate. Keep your eyes on the weapon.* I forced myself to breathe normally, to suppress the flight-or-flight response.

"I'm unarmed," I said. "Just let me go."

My assailant didn't respond, which was smart. They had no reason to. I was in capable hands, it seemed. Experienced hands.

A grunt. A heave. I was being pushed down a small embankment toward the Takahula River. The trickling sound of water filled the silence.

Then, I saw it—hidden in thick brush:

A tent.

It was too dark to make out any details, but I could hear the flies swarming. *Was there a dead person in that tent?* I wondered. My muscles stiffened, and my momentum slowed. My survival instincts were telling me to go no further.

The arms around my neck tightened, giving me no choice but to move forward. The knife digging into my skin shifted. I felt a trickle of blood course down my neck, a warm wetness in the cold, dry air. The rain had abated, if only for a time.

I understood that at some point, I would have to strong-arm my way out of this. Despite being so damn short, I wasn't a terrible fighter. I wasn't Hux-quality, but I wasn't a total amateur either. Being at such a disadvantage because of my size, I had taken my self-defense training seriously.

The real challenge was finding the right opportunity. If I picked the wrong one, I could be seriously injured or even killed. But there was no way in hell I was letting this person force me into that tent. My best chance of survival was staying out in the open.

I tried to slow things down by dragging my feet, but that plan went to hell as soon as a heavy boot connected with the back of my knee, which sent me flying. I went down hard, hitting the dirt face-first. My forehead hit a rock, and I was so distracted by the ensuing gush of blood that I almost didn't notice that the hands around my neck had moved to my wrists.

Then I felt the rough slide of rope.

The wrist abrasions.

It was a fleeting thought, one that I would come back to later. For now, there were other matters at hand. I couldn't rely on Hux to rescue me from every scrape I got myself into, even the ones that came with the job. Because the cold truth was, I'd let someone get a jump on me. It was on me to get myself out of this.

I tried to get my knees under my body despite the unrelenting pressure coming from above. My attacker had wedged their knee in the small of my back, right where my titanium rod was. It was both excruciating and effective. I could barely move. A wave of nausea rolled through me, made worse by the gag being stuffed in my mouth. I thought I was going to be sick.

Using my lats to mobilize my shoulder muscles, I tried with one gasping effort to wrench my arms apart. A searing pain in my left neck area made me cry out; it was the surgical plate from my clavicle surgery last year, rubbing against bone. I'd felt that pain many times before, but at least I knew my bones weren't breaking. I gritted my teeth and tried again, grunting with the effort as I twisted one arm around and used it to push myself off the ground.

Somehow, I managed to get hold of my flashlight. As a weapon, it wasn't much—but it would have to do. It was better than my knuckles anyhow.

Pivoting hard, I swung my whole body around and made contact with bone. Someone's skull, was my guess.

A dull moan. Then—silence.

I tried to get up—

A cloud of fire hit me square in the face. No, not fire. Chemicals that felt like fire.

Bear spray.

I screamed, but the foul taste of the aerosol particles made me gag. Once again I was shoved to the ground. The slender rope fibers encircling my wrists were pulled tight—tight enough to cut off the blood supply to my hands. A pair of gloved hands pushed my head into the wet sponga, and for a moment all I could taste and smell was mud.

At least whoever had done it was struggling; I could tell by their breaths, quick and ragged. Their gloves were wet—not with mud or rain, but with blood. I could taste it.

Whoever it was stood up, coughed twice, and stumbled away from me.

It was quiet again.

Too quiet.

I knew I wouldn't be alone for long. The cold, wet earth soothed my burning eyes a little bit, but mostly, I was angry— angry at myself for miscalculating the risks of my situation, angry at the mess I'd gotten myself into. The bear spray added insult to injury.

For a while, I just lay there—listening, waiting. The mosquitoes were in a frenzy, landing on my face, feasting on my exposed skin. I tried to roll onto my back, but everything hurt, worst of all my face and hands. The titanium rods in my spine felt like shards of glass. I couldn't see anyway thanks to the gnarly combination of blood and bear spray soaking my eyes.

For not the first time in my career as a federal investigator, I wanted to cry. My transfer to ISB was supposed to restore my confidence, but instead it had merely reinforced my worst self-doubts. A part of me—a growing part—no longer believed that I had what it took to excel at this line of work. Even if I *did* get out of this somehow, how was I going to explain myself to Ray? *To Hux?* I couldn't help but think that I had let Yiyin convince me that Reynolds wasn't a threat.

The mere thought of my partner finding me here facedown in the mud—I couldn't bear it. It would color our working relationship for years to come, and I couldn't have that. Because I *liked* working with Hux. I wanted to have those years.

I tried to focus on one thing at a time. My ankles were tied up too, which was going to make things even harder, but not impossible. I had to get onto my stomach first. Gravity would do the rest. With a grunt, I maneuvered my body into position. The ground beneath me didn't have much of a slope, but it was enough to get me going.

As I rolled onto my side, I heard voices in the distance. *Forget the pain,* I told myself. *Just get up and go.*

A kick with my legs here, a jerk there, and suddenly I was on my stomach. I hiked my knees up to my chest and tried to thrust myself to a standing position. The first attempt failed. The second was an embarrassment, not that anyone had seen it, but I was humiliated just the same. The sloped terrain combined with my hands being tied behind my back threw me off balance. The voices in the darkness were getting louder.

But I was stubborn. At one point, I felt my shoulder pop— the bad one, the one with all the surgical hardware in it. The plate seemed to shift a bit so that its hard edge was driving into bone even worse than before. *Well, this is bad,* I thought, and almost laughed. It was something Hux would have said. He was the opposite of a catastrophizer.

I tried to channel his unflappable nature as I got to my feet and hopped sideways a little bit, inch by inch. Even though Hux was the expert tracker, I'd learned a thing or two from him over the last few months. Human beings lost in the wilderness tended to travel downhill, for one. So I went uphill, thinking my attacker would be less likely to go that way.

I had to hop, which made progress slow and painful. I fell more times than I could count. After one disaster in Australia and another in Sequoia, grit was something I had in spades. I kept going, too stubborn to quit.

I squinted into the darkness, trying to make out a spruce tree or some other landmark. In a stroke of luck, the clouds had parted, and I could see the moon—round, white, and full, shining on the creek. There, in the distance, I spotted a few trees hugging the hillside.

My quads were burning as I hopped and fell, hopped and fell. It seemed to take forever. Finally, I made contact with a tree. I sidled up to it like the bears out here were wont to do and rubbed my wrists against the rough bark. The roped frayed a bit, but my skin came along with it. I ignored the pain.

The voices again—they were back. Closer than before.

Hux wasn't among them. His voice was as identifiable as Ollie's bark, which I also would have heard if he were nearby.

Since it wasn't them, I had to assume those voices belonged to the enemy. Time was of the essence. Every scrape of my wrists against the tree sounded deafening to my ears. I knew my pursuers were listening for clues to my location. At least it was dark—pitch-black, really, thanks to the overcast skies and this fickle storm. The rain had started up again too.

Finally, the rope frayed enough for me to snap it apart. I used a sharp rock nearby to cut the ankle restraints as well.

It occurred to me that cable ties would have worked better, but those weren't easy to come by out here. Was this unplanned, then? Or was my attacker just not accustomed to taking people hostage? On the other hand, whoever had done this had shown some real nerve, coming after me in the night. Diego was certainly capable. Reynolds too. I wasn't so sure about Vince. As for Ana and Yiyin, I just didn't think they had it in them, physically, to subdue me. But maybe that was my hubris talking.

Whoever it was, they'd gone and found help—an accomplice, as it were. I decided to run. The darkness was my best cover and my only hope for escape.

Footsteps pounding the wet earth echoed in the night. The rain was coming down harder now, drowning out the sounds of my breathless gasps. I ran on blindly into the dark.

Is this how Kevin felt? I wondered. *Did the thought of rescue buoy him as he made his way through the outback for help—only to realize that rescue was an illusion?*

I tried not to think about it, about how hope could quickly turn to fear and then to despair. Just because Kevin hadn't made it out alive didn't mean I was going to suffer the same fate.

But, the arctic wasn't anything like the Australian outback, and Kevin had had other advantages—he wasn't being chased, for one thing. He'd set out in daylight. And he'd had a map and a plan, although neither one had delivered him to safety.

It was different for me. I wasn't just trying to survive the elements.

Someone was trying to kill me.

CHAPTER

24

ONE THING I had never needed during my time at the FBI was a compass. There were guys in the Chicago field office who had never even seen one except on the internet—which was ironic, in a way, given how old-school they were. Technology and apps were too futuristic, but compasses were too primitive. That pretty much left dusty desktop computers.

But I had come around on the usefulness of compasses, if only to confirm that I was headed in the right direction. My objective was to get to the rendezvous point, so I could call for help using the Garmin. But my most pressing worry at the moment was Hux. Was he still out there, tracking Ana and Diego?

Was he alive?

I kept resisting the tendency to go back to the river because it was the obvious path to take. So I took a more circuitous route—east, in the direction of the Alatna. I would head south from there to Takahula Lake.

My vision, though, was a problem. My eyes felt like they were on fire. It was agonizing to open them for longer than a second at a time. I was scared to use my flashlight, which would give my enemy a beat on my location. All I had was the intermittent moonlight.

The rain was a comfort in a way, muffling the sounds of the night. I thought about Vince's demon bear—Kiga, stalking me in the dark. I flashed back to the puncture wounds on Kelsey's neck, the feathery remains of Tim's parka—all markers of a coordinated wolf pack. I'd learned to live with the wildlife, but I also understood my place in the food chain. Encountering a grizzly in my current state could end badly for me.

I thought back to Hux's tracking lessons. He had warned me about paying attention to potential distractors. *"Don't be fooled by footprints,"* he'd said. *"They're probably yours."* And another one: *"Don't take any shortcuts."* At one point, I thought I found a game trail that cut north; it was flat, wide, and easy to walk on. After I'd followed it for a short time, I realized it wasn't a direct path—in fact, it was taking me west, back toward the campsite.

As the first streaks of dawn appeared on the horizon, I stopped briefly to tighten my shoelaces. I was cold and wet, and to stop too long would bring on hypothermia.

An animal shrieked—a bird, something else. A wolf answered with a lonely, distant howl.

Keep going.

I was in pain—my back, my shoulder. But these were small, manageable problems. None of my bones were broken. I squinted at the ground before planting my foot with each step.

At one point, though, my toe caught on something, probably a rock. No, a tree branch. I bit back a slew of colorful words as I hopped on one foot and tried to regain my footing. Panic gripped me as I realized what I'd done.

You're almost to the river, I told myself. *Ray will send someone up here when he doesn't hear from you. Hux knows how to protect himself.*

But someone had picked up my trail; I could feel it. I lifted the compass to my face until it was mere inches from my eyes. Even then, I could barely make out what it was telling me. North. South. East. West. They all looked the same in the dark.

Panic was a dangerous thing. Lethal, even. I had always suspected that it was panic that had killed Kevin. He was among thousands of people who had vanished in nature, never to be seen again. *"Presumed dead,"* the Australian investigators had told me. That didn't make it any easier to process what had happened to him, nor had it given me any closure. Closure was being able to bury the man you loved. That said, Kevin was a capable hiker, but he wasn't a professional. *I* was a professional. I tried to remind myself of that.

Then I heard it—a snort. Behind me.

It wasn't human. It was ursine.

Kiga.

25

I COULDN'T EVEN SEE him—not really, in the rainy darkness of dawn, but I knew it was him. Kiga had followed me all this way. A stalker bear.

Or as Vince put it, a demon bear.

He was less than thirty feet away from me, standing on his two hind legs. Snorts and grunts filled the silence. He bent over and pawed the ground, keeping his snout high as he looked at me, *right* at me. I tried to see his ears. In bluff charges, bears keep their ears up, but in aggressive charges, they tend to be pointed back.

In that moment, I knew with every bone in my body that this wasn't a bluff charge. The massive animal pawed the ground once more, head down. Another snort.

Then he started to run.

The National Park Service website made it very clear what to do in this situation—so clear, in fact, that they put it in all caps.

PLAY DEAD.

I got down on my stomach and splayed my legs apart. I covered my head and neck with my hands and arms. The rain had done me another favor here by washing off most of the blood matted to my face and hair.

Seconds passed, but it felt like years—the bear's giant paws pounding the earth, its snorts getting louder with each stride. I held my breath, bracing myself for the inevitable contact. Would it run right on top of me? Swipe at my head? What if it didn't fall for my ruse?

Its first contact came from its snout, as it butted my head and clacked its jaws. The sound was deafening. It used one of its paws to tear at my jacket, another to try and flip me over.

Don't move.

Playing dead as this thing tried to tear me apart was a real exercise in mental fortitude. I kept waiting for the attack to stop, for the bear to move on, to give up, to decide it could go off and have a tastier meal somewhere else.

But the blows kept coming.

Sometimes, playing dead didn't work. I remembered a wildlife biologist telling me what to do next in that scenario:

"Fight for your life."

I thought about Kevin, fighting for our lives. He had failed. Even worse, I had failed *him*. I knew a battle with this bear wasn't winnable. Some battles weren't.

Just go, I tried to tell the bear—an internal chant that helped keep me calm. *Just go away.*

But he ignored me. He was trying to flip me over.

I kept fighting him in ways he couldn't see.

A loud, angry snort. He thrummed the ground with his paws.

I'm dead, I thought. *This is it.*

But then, as suddenly as he'd appeared, he left.

I waited for a long time. Five, ten, fifteen minutes. I knew bears liked to hang around to make sure they hadn't been fooled.

I sensed, though, that this bear had moved on. The air was still, the early morning transformed. The birds' chirping reassured me somehow.

I got to my feet, shaky as they were, and inspected the damage the bear had done. I was lucky. The worst injuries were to my hands and forearms—defensive wounds. Once again I thought about Tim and Kelsey Greer. They *hadn't* put up a fight.

Why not?

That question reverberated in my brain as I grabbed my flashlight off the ground and tried to run. My joints were stiff, my nerves shredded. I needed dry clothes and shelter. I tried not to think about who—or what—might be following me and where they were. I tried not to think about everything that could go wrong between here and Takahula Lake.

At last, with feeble daylight illuminating the gloom of an endless night, I saw the region's proudest river. The impressive girth of the Alatna was unmistakable, its clear water meandering through the highs and lows of the gravel bar. I wanted to fall to my knees and weep.

But my journey wasn't over. I needed to get to Takahula Lake, which was at least an hour's hike south. The river's visibility was both an asset and a detriment, in that a passersby or ranger could spot me easily, but so could anyone else. I considered taking a less direct route, but that would require more time—time I didn't have.

My only option was to push forward.

It was all I knew how to do.

*   *   *

It was just past seven AM when I recognized the familiar landmarks of the rendezvous site: the two leaning spruce trees atop a small ridge, with Takahula Lake in the background. I was too exhausted to celebrate, not that getting here was much cause of celebration anyway. I canvassed the area twice, searching for footprints or some other sign that Hux had been here.

There was nothing.

The only good news was that everything I'd buried in that hole just a couple days ago was still there. The Garmin's battery life was at fifty-six percent, which was more than enough to send for help. I typed my message out to Ray as fast as I could, careful to give an accurate location.

Encountered armed & dangerous attacker. Need backup.

To my surprise, I saw the Garmin light up with a new message almost immediately.

It was from Ray.

Are you safe?

I texted back:

Yes, but need support from rangers and state troopers. Hux's location unknown.

Is he safe?

I wasn't sure what to say to that. *I don't know*, I wrote.

It pained me to send that message, but it was the truth.

Ray wrote, *Sending a team in now. Can rally state troopers and Fairbanks* FBI.

I responded, ETA?

Approx 09:00.

I checked the time on the Garmin. It was a little after seven thirty AM. The last thing I wanted to do was sit and wait around for help, but what choice did I have? What if Hux was on his way here? I couldn't abandon the location we had mutually agreed on.

OK, I wrote, and powered down the Garmin. I wanted to conserve battery until I had confirmation that backup was on its way. By my estimation, it would take at least twenty minutes for Ray to wrangle up a chopper. Until then, I had to get warm.

Thankfully, there were dry clothes and a tarp in the waterproof bag. I changed quickly and made myself a tarp burrito, a low drag shelter with one side folded over. Keeping low to the ground was a good way to minimize the wind's effects on body temperature. The rain rolled off the tarp onto the ground, where it was quickly absorbed by the vegetation. I could probably last a few hours like this, at least.

I tried to remind myself that people went missing in Alaska all the time—that this was one of the best places in the world to disappear. Whoever was out there looking for me would have a hard time of it. Even so, lying there in my tarp burrito, I didn't feel hidden at all. I felt exposed.

Feeling restless, I powered my Garmin back on. It chimed with a new message, but the number was one I didn't recognize.

8:14 a.m.: It's Hux. Weird stuff happening here. Are you OK?

I sat up in my burrito, too stunned to respond. My fingers were numb and clumsy, but I managed to fire off a reply.

I'm at the rendezvous point.

His reply came at 8:22 AM: *On my way. Are you OK?*

Of course I owed him the truth, but I didn't want to tell him under these circumstances. I decided to keep my answer brief.

Yes. Backup on the way.

I hit "Send" and held my breath as I waited for it to go through. The Garmin was like any other piece of technology; it could work flawlessly, or it could fail.

This time, the gods were against me. It didn't send.

I tried syncing the device.

There.

It worked. I got a confirmation of receipt, which made me feel a little better.

I wiped my eyes with my fists, smearing a salty wetness on my cheeks. The residual bear spray chemicals were making my eyes water. I just hoped there wasn't permanent damage.

The thought of sunning myself in a tarp burrito for one more minute made me squirm, but Hux had said he was on his way. I had to wait for him. To leave now would be to put us both at risk, especially if my attacker was still out there.

I kept replaying the events of our encounter in my mind, hoping to hit on a detail I might have missed. But the biggest question in my mind was, *Who?*

And why?

CHAPTER

26

AT 9:04 AM, I heard the whir of a helicopter's rotors overhead, coming in fast. The new day had dawned wet and gray, faintly illuminated by a hidden sun. My core body temperature felt like it had dropped a few degrees when I emerged from the burrito.

I'd never been so relieved to see an aircraft. The chopper hovered directly over me as it searched for a place to land. I got to my feet and watched it maneuver over the river.

After the helicopter landed, the first person out was Brinegar. The man behind him was a stranger, but he looked every bit like a seasoned FBI agent. He was sturdily built and dressed for the elements, with a dark green jacket and hiking boots. He was accompanied by a giant of a man with a shaved head and army boots.

I straightened my shoulders, fighting off a wave of fatigue and soreness that brought me back to the struggles of the previous night. With stiff strides, I approached the three men, who noticed me right away.

"Are you Special Agent Felicity Harland?" the FBI agent asked.

"Yes," I said. "Thanks for coming up here on short notice."

"I'm Calvin James, FBI. I'm working out of the Fairbanks satellite office." He looked me over, a frown darkening his expression. "What the hell happened to your face—"

"I'm fine," I said, which was a far cry from the truth. I hadn't looked at a mirror in days, but between the bear spray and bear attack, it couldn't have been pretty. I didn't like to admit as much, though, fearing these encounters would make me look weak—or worse, unprepared.

Brinegar whistled. "Did you have a run-in with a bear?" he asked.

There it was. He could probably smell it on me. "I had an encounter with some bear spray, yes," I said. "And a bear."

Brinegar's expression turned serious. "What happened?" he asked.

"I'll fill you in later."

"It looks like you could use some medical attention—"

"I'm waiting for my partner, Ranger Huxley." I pulled my ravaged hood over my head, hoping it might cast a bit of a shadow over my face. "I'm not leaving until he gets here."

Brinegar exchanged a glance with the other two men. "What's his status?"

"He went after two people who may have fit the profile for the Fairbanks fugitives."

Calvin James raised an eyebrow. "Who?"

"Ana and Diego were their first names. Both late-thirties, Mexican descent; he had an accent that sounded more like Texas than Mexico, but I never learned where they were actually from. She was about my height, with long dark hair."

Calvin James shot a look at the guy standing to his right— beefy, white, with a thick, squat neck. On these kinds of assignments, the FBI always sent somebody who could play the role of the muscle. I figured this was him.

"What is it?" I asked.

"I'm assuming you saw the Park Service alert with the sketch?"

I felt the pit in my stomach bloom into something truly vile. "Yes, I saw it."

"Well, we can do better than that now. We've got a photo."

Calvin James pulled his cell phone out of his pocket. In the few seconds it took for him to pull up the photo that he must have downloaded onto his phone, I held my breath. Deep down, I knew it was going to be bad news—for Hux, especially. He was still out there.

With *them*.

Sure enough, the photo confirmed it: the Fairbanks fugitives were Ana and Diego.

In a still from the surveillance footage, they were standing in an alleyway, ensconced in darkness. He was wearing a dark hoodie that almost covered his face, but not quite. A small, dark revolver occupied his left hand.

Ana was almost unrecognizable as the meek, frightened woman at the campsite. She stood with her back ramrod straight, a powerful-appearing woman. Her eyes were wide and alert as she stared directly at the camera, but it was unclear if she could see it or was just searching for it.

"Is this them?" James asked.

"Yes," I said, but the word caught in my throat. "It's them."

"Their real names are Rico and Morena del Carmen. They're part of a smuggling ring that operates up here. Honestly, the triple murder was a clean hit, no witnesses. No surveillance footage at the scene either. The only reason we got ahold of that sketch is that someone turned on them." He rubbed his hands together in the cold air. "Anyway, sounds like you ran into the del Carmens?"

"We did," I said. "Hux went after them, like I said."

"Well, that was dumb," Calvin James said dismissively. "These two are armed and very dangerous. Sounds like your park ranger buddy thinks he's a Navy SEAL."

"He *is* a Navy SEAL."

James barked a laugh, which quickly died in his throat when he saw the look on my face. He coughed into his hand.

Out of the corner of my eye, I caught a glimpse of something moving—an animal, smaller than a bear.

A dog.

Ollie.

And there, just behind him, a formidable man in a black beanie, walking along the edge of Takahula Lake.

"Hux!" I shouted. I couldn't help but grin. Relief and gratitude swept through me as I jogged across the gravel bar to greet him. I heard James muttering something about "SEAL material."

In the physical sense, Hux and I were so different that I could barely get my arms around him—he was too tall, too broad—but he had no problem at all giving me a proper hug. I liked the feel of him—his warmth, his strength. It reminded me of our time in Sequoia.

I pulled away first, if for no other reason than to seem less needy than I felt. When Hux stepped back and saw my face, he gasped. "Holy hell, Harland. What happened?"

"Nothing," I said.

He frowned. "*Something* happened."

"I'll tell you all about it later. Did you find Ana and Diego?"

He took a breath. "I did and I didn't. Truth is, I saw something out there that gave me pause—it was her, really. I knew Diego was good with a gun, but Ana clearly had some special training. Being unarmed in the dark, two against one, I didn't like my odds."

"You were right to back off," I said. "I saw a photo. It's them—they're wanted for the Fairbanks murders."

Hux shook his head. "Damn," he said. "I wonder why they stuck it out here for so long."

"A reciprocal relationship is my guess. They needed time and money; Reynolds needed people who could protect his assets."

Hux nodded. "Makes sense. Are you okay, by the way?"

As I pondered how best to answer that question, I spotted Agent James coming toward us. He rubbed his hands together and blew out a breath into his clenched fists. His collar was hiked up to his earlobes, his hood cinched around his chin.

"We heard there are at least two people back at that campsite you vacated," he said. "Are you up for a quick jaunt over there?"

"Of course," I said. "But one of them is a pilot; he's been waiting on a repair person to fix his bush plane."

"Where's the plane?"

"He said it was close to the lake."

James looked around, but there was no doubting the skepticism on his face. "I'm not seeing a plane," he said. "You sure you got your lakes straight?"

I clenched my jaw and said, "Yes, sir."

"Then we'll take another look from the air." He looked at Hux, who said nothing. At times like these, Hux deferred to me, which I appreciated, but I wasn't sure it changed James's opinion of me. Sometimes it was just impossible to overcome the fact that I was female.

With Ollie in tow, we followed the FBI guys back onto the chopper. It didn't seem they had taken my call for backup all that seriously, given that there were only two of them. Then again, I hadn't given Ray any details about the attack. Maybe they deserved the benefit of the doubt.

Before we lifted off, I told the pilot to follow the small river that flowed west from Takahula Lake. Even though visibility was poor due to the weather, I was confident that we'd be able to see the tents from the air.

Ten minutes into the flight, it was Brinegar who spotted the first green tent. But as we flew over the familiar landscape, I saw that it was the *only* tent down there on the ground. Bill and Tess's orange twofer was gone.

Our helicopter pilot put the chopper down on a flat strip of land not far from Vince and Yiyin's tent. Before we all climbed out of the bird, James turned to me and said, "Why don't you two hang back a bit?"

"Sorry?" I felt my haunches go up.

"Just stay clear for now, okay? We're gonna take the lead on this scene."

It wasn't up for debate. Calvin James and his partner checked their weapons and charged out of the helicopter. Hux and I took our time getting out, since we clearly weren't welcome to join them on their raid—or whatever this was.

"Don't take it personally, boss," Hux said once we were outside.

"How can I *not* take it personally?"

"We're here for the Greers, remember? Let them handle Ana and Diego."

He was right, of course. I just hated these turf wars. They reminded me of my tenure in Chicago, battling with the brass, perpetually trying to overcome the FBI's bro culture.

"All right," I said.

Over by the creek a good distance from the chopper, James suddenly called out, "FBI! Come on out!" He was standing outside Yiyin and Vince's tent.

Nothing happened. There was no response, no reply, no movement from within.

I heard the muscle say, "Should we knock? Is that a thing with a tent?"

"No." James sounded irritated. "Keep your distance."

The tension was palpable. Nothing happened.

"Mr. Reynolds, we have a federal warrant to search this property," James said in a loud, stern voice. "Come on out with your hands up."

"Wait," I said, turning to Hux. "Isn't that Vince and Yiyin's tent?"

Hux nodded. "Yup."

"Should we tell them—"

I heard a soft rustling coming from inside the tent. After a tense few seconds, Yiyin emerged—her hands above her head, black rope dangling from her wrists. I thought my eyes were playing tricks on me, but no. It was the same nylon rope my attacker had used on *me*.

Vince came next—also holding frayed strands of nylon dangling from his wrists. He emerged with his shoulders hunched, his hands palming the top of his balding head.

His face was covered in dirt. I immediately thought back to Tim and Kelsey Greer—both of them found facedown in the gravel bar of the Alatna River, like they'd bent over to taste the earth. But unlike the Greers, Vince and Yiyin were still alive.

So what had happened to *them*?

*   *   *

"Well, he's not talking," James said, jutting a thumb at Vince, who was standing over by his tent. He looked at me with a distant coldness in his eyes. "Not a word."

"Sorry to hear it," I said flatly.

"They're both a little nuts if you ask me," James said. "The woman's been singing Reynolds's praises like he's some kind of miracle worker. She said she would've paid a lot more than twenty-five grand to get someone to talk her husband into sperm donation." James shook his head. "I don't understand these people. I really don't."

"The couples we spoke to had struggled with infertility for years," I said. "Vince and Yiyin, for example—Vince is biologically incapable of fathering a child. Reynolds seemed to be targeting couples in their situation."

James made a dismissive gesture. "Look, I'm not interested in the sob stories—"

"We have reason to believe that Reynolds was impregnating some of these women himself," I said. "From what we've gathered so far, it was consensual. For Tim and Kelsey Greer, we don't know for sure. It's a lead we're working on."

"You're talking about the two people that OD'd on berries?"

I was dismayed that he knew about the case, but not at all surprised. It was his snickering tone that irked me. "Toxic ingestion, yes," I said.

"Sounds accidental," he said.

"The ME said the cause was 'indeterminate.'"

"Not anymore." He looked over his shoulder at the chopper, and beyond that, at his muscleman, who was snacking on a sandwich. "The deputy ME kicked it up to his boss, and Jerry ruled it accidental. So that case is closed."

I willed myself to show no reaction, but acting wasn't my strong suit. On the bright side, Calvin James and his Fairbanks field office weren't going to interfere with the Greer case now that they were convinced it wasn't foul play. The state troopers would probably lay off too. After all, they had two murderers at large to deal with.

"Look, I know it's been a rough ride for you," James said. He flicked his gaze at my face and made a quick appraisal of the damage. "We'll take it from here."

I felt Hux shift his feet beside me, a sure sign that he was getting antsy listening to this guy tear me down. I stole a glance in his direction. *Don't,* I warned him with my eyes. Hux understood the importance of maintaining a working relationship with the local FBI field offices when we were on assignment, but that didn't mean he liked every agent we'd ever encountered. I didn't either, but it was important to avoid petty conflicts.

"Can we talk to Vince and Yiyin, at least?" I asked.

"Those two?" James snorted. He turned and looked over his shoulder at the couple in question. "Like I said, they aren't talking."

Not to you, I thought. *But they said plenty to us.*

"I'd like to try."

James shrugged. "Have at it, then. We're heading back down to Fairbanks in an hour once we've wrapped this up. The weather's about to go bad."

I watched him walk off into a driving rain, holding his sat phone against one ear. Guys like him always seemed mildly irritated by whatever was going on. I hoped our paths didn't cross again anytime soon, but Hux was their best lead on the whereabouts of Ana and Diego. I had a feeling we'd be hearing from him within twenty-four hours once he decided we weren't just a couple of neophyte FBI wannabes.

By the time Hux and I made it over to Vince and Yiyin, they were getting ready to board the chopper. Yiyin was sipping a hot drink out of her own insulated canteen while barking orders at Vince. I was astounded by the volume of gear they'd brought this far out into the wilderness. It must have cost them thousands to transport it all.

"Are you two okay?" I asked.

Yiyin nodded. "Fine."

Vince said, "We're not talking to you."

"I heard." I glanced at Hux. "Can you at least tell me about the rope?"

Vince smirked. "How much detail are you after, Agent Harland?"

I felt my cheeks get hot. "That's not what I was talking about."

Yiyin said, "Well, that's too bad, because you've got quite the partner there." She gave Hux a little wave. He didn't wave back. Ollie let his feelings be known with a displeased little growl.

"So that's it?" I asked. "The rope was for a sex game?"

"It was for our personal enjoyment, yes," Vince said. "Okay, seriously now—we're done talking. We're done with this whole experience, actually."

"We just had a couple more questions about the Greers—"

"Nah, nah, nah," Vince said. "Call our attorney."

"You had plenty to say just a day ago."

He shrugged. "Things change."

"Our investigation isn't over."

"That FBI guy seems to think it is."

I wasn't going to get anywhere with these two pit bulls. It was time to move on. I said a curt goodbye and walked over to a temporary shelter Brinegar had erected by suspending a tarp between two spruce trees. I wished I had a hot drink, but I wasn't about to ask Yiyin for some hospitality. Hux stood next to me— quiet, deferential. He never minded extended silences.

"Not exactly a satisfying end to this case," I finally said.

"*Is* it the end?" Hux asked, turning toward me.

I thought for a moment. "I'll need to talk to the medical examiner. If he decided the Greers' deaths were accidental and put it in his report, that's kind of it. I don't have the resources or the evidence to justify a second opinion."

"Then let's talk to him."

I nodded. "Thanks."

Hux said, "Look, you should at least think about seeing a doctor when we get back to Fairbanks. You're painful to look at."

"Well, you've coped with that reality up to this point, so you should be fine." I whistled at Ollie, who had wandered down to the creek. "So," I said, "are you going back to Denali to finish your online training modules?"

He smiled. "Hell no. That was torture."

"I bet I could get you a few more days up here if you wanted to explore the park."

"Nah," he said. "I'm with you all the way, Harland. If this case isn't closed, then I'm here to work it with you."

I looked out at the drenched ruins of Reynolds's campsite, restored to its former natural glory. By tomorrow, it would look as if no one had ever been here at all. For Tim and Kelsey Greer, Mother Nature would look on them the same way—as a passing presence; a brief intrusion on a pristine landscape that had ended in tragedy.

In my mind, Tim and Kelsey Greer deserved more than a sense of quiet resignation. Someone had tied them up, left them to die by the river, and gone back later to remove the evidence of human interference. Someone had sent them there, never to return.

The same had almost happened to me.

Almost.

And that person was still out there.

27

ONE THING I didn't miss about the FBI was the territorialism. After James and his partner had trampled all over the campsite, he let me know that the scene was clear. I was just waiting for him to leave so Hux and I could process it ourselves.

At last, James's little display of dominance ended. We made nice with some curt goodbyes, and then he was gone. After the chopper left for Fairbanks, I finally felt like I could relax a little bit. The rain had started to wane, leaving in its wake a damp and insidious chill. Hux and I stood under the tarp that Brinegar had kindly left behind for us to use if we needed it.

"Well, they're gone," Hux said.

"Finally."

Hux turned and looked at me. "What happened last night, Harland?"

I couldn't avoid him forever. Hux was my partner; he deserved to know what happened. Still, I couldn't help but feel a little embarrassed by the way things had played out.

"The way I see it, someone was either trying to kill me or silence me," I said. "As for motive—it's hard to say. The attack was a little sloppy. Emotional, maybe."

"Hmm," Hux said. "Yiyin?"

"I don't know. She's a powerful woman who's used to getting what she wants."

"More powerful than you?"

"I don't mean physically," I said. "I'll admit that whoever got the jump on me was capable, but not *that* capable. The restrains, the bear spray, the knife—it felt a little amateurish."

"Well, it couldn't have been Diego or Ana. I tracked them until sunup. They were moving east at a good clip."

"Canada?"

"Felt like it."

I didn't think Ana or Diego made sense, anyway. We weren't a threat to them anymore—not in these circumstances. Their photos were already out in the world, and our involvement didn't change that. Perhaps if they'd had access to Reynolds's weapons, it would have been a different story. I wasn't sure we would ever know.

"You've been through a lot these last couple days," Hux said. "Don't beat yourself up about it."

"I can't help it," I said. "It's part of my shtick."

"It sure is," he said with a laugh. "Shall we have another look at the campsite?"

The answer to that question was always yes. Hux started at the charred remains of the fire and built a perimeter from there. The rain had washed away all the footprints, even the ones belonging to James and his FBI buddy. Ollie sniffed the entire campsite, searching from the creek to the hillside and back again.

As Hux and Ollie went down to the creek in search of foot-prints, my mind drifted to the events of the previous night. A part of me wondered if I was misremembering the attack—*had it even happened at all?* Sleep deprivation could do crazy things to a person's memory. For me, though, all the proof I needed was on my face, neck, and hands.

The knife injury, for instance. The bear hadn't managed to get its jaws on my neck, but the nicks from the knife were still there. I had reviewed the Greers' autopsy reports a few times, but there was no mention of any superficial wounds on their necks consistent with a knife—just teeth. The only other skin injury documented in that preliminary report was the wrist abrasions, which the deputy ME had amended only after I inquired about it. I still needed to talk to the chief medical examiner about his findings.

Exhaustion was setting in. I glanced at my watch but could barely see the numbers on the screen. It was time to wrap this up.

I decided to do one last search of the area Reynolds had used for food prep. Hux was over by Yiyin and Vince's former campsite, which was the only one that hadn't been completely cleared. They had left behind bits of food that probably had all the bears in the vicinity on high alert. Bill and Tess's former campsite, on the other hand, had been cleared so effectively that it was impossible to tell if anyone had been there at all.

I had decided that Yiyin's story about Bill was suspect for several reasons, but I did want to talk to him again. I had already gotten in touch with Tess on my satellite phone, confirming that Bill had gotten his plane fixed. They were back in Bettles now.

"Harland?" Hux's voice sounded miles away. "I'm not seeing anything. Should I keep looking?"

I gazed out at the lake and the vastness beyond it.

"No," I said. "Let's head back to Bettles."

*   *   *

Bill's repaired white Cessna arrived to pick us up within the hour, only a half-mile hike from the campsite. I was relieved to see the familiar aircraft. It made me feel a little closer to home—or at least somewhere less rugged and wild than this.

Bill was by himself this time, bundled up in a thick flannel jacket and workman's gloves. When he saw me, he made a sound somewhere between a laugh and a gasp. "Good Lord, woman," he said. "Did you run into the Abominable Snowman?"

I responded with a half-hearted laugh. "Something like that."

"I could fly you all the way down to Fairbanks to see a doc there, if you like. I've got plenty of fuel."

"That won't be necessary," I said. "We have a few things to do in Bettles anyway."

"Well, let me know if I can take you when you're ready. I'm pretty booked up for the next week or so, but ISB takes priority."

If that's the case, then why didn't you send me a message when you got your plane fixed? I thought, even though I knew it wasn't a fair question. Arranging for a bush plane in this part of Alaska wasn't like calling an Uber. It took time, logistics, fuel, and good weather. Last-minute trips were risky—for both the pilot and the passengers. And it wasn't like Bill and Tess hadn't tried to help; he was here now, wasn't he?

"We appreciate that," I said. "Thanks."

He tipped his hat at me as we climbed onboard—me first, then Hux, and finally Ollie. Hux and I buckled our belts and settled in for the ride. Ollie, at least, was getting used to the frequent air transport. He lay on the floor and let his eyelids droop.

I turned to Hux. "Lunch is on me," I said. "The hotel room is on the federal dime."

"I could just camp somewhere, you know."

"I know, but I need you well rested. We've got a lot of work to do."

He glanced out the window. "What's our game plan?"

I joined him in admiring the majestic Alatna winding through the vast and sprawling valley. "Let's go through the photos first and see if there's anything we might have missed at the scene. I'll try to get the chief ME on the phone."

"What about *you*, Harland?" he asked. "Assault is still a crime, you know."

For some reason, I wasn't ready to talk about it with him. My fumbling response to a violent encounter made me look weak, for one thing. And I hated appearing weak in front of Hux.

My pride had its limits, however. Knowing there was a person capable of abduction—and possibly even murder—at large in my jurisdiction made me uneasy . . . and angry. I couldn't just pretend it hadn't happened.

"All right," I said. "Here's how I remember it."

Hux took out his notepad, which he did for every investigation, large and small. I appreciated his formal approach; it made me feel less like a victim and more like a witness to a crime. I was about two sentences in when I realized how hard it was to accurately recount the events in my sleep-deprived state, but Hux was patient.

"Okay," Hux said. "First off, I want to kill this person."

I laughed. "Don't do that."

"I'm just stating the facts. When we find out who did this, it's probably best if I stay out of the interview room."

I appreciated Hux's protective streak, even though I knew it would never happen. Too much paperwork. "Looking back, I don't think whoever did this wanted to kill me."

"I'm not sure I'd agree with that assessment."

"Well, let's assume the same person who attacked me killed Tim and Kelsey Greer. In some ways, I can see the parallels. Theirs wasn't necessarily a violent or even an effective murder. It was messy. Some of it was left to chance—the poisoning aspect, the wolves. Even the restraints—I mean, I didn't have much trouble getting them off. Why not use cable ties or something more durable?"

Hux looked up from his notepad. "What about the way they were positioned? How does that fit in?"

"I've thought about that," I said. "For them to just prostrate themselves on the river like that doesn't make any sense—unless they literally *couldn't* move."

"They were tied up, you mean?"

I nodded. "I'm fairly certain that's what happened. The killer tied them up and waited for them to expire before removing the restraints."

"Why?"

"You know, that's a good question. It could be that the killer was waiting to see what would happen—would the Greers recover enough to remove them themselves? Or was it clear the berries had made them ill enough to die? Since they *did* die, my guess is that at that point, the killer realized they had a couple choices: leave the bodies there and hope for the best, dispose of them somehow, or remove the restraints and make it look like an accident."

The plane banked hard to the left, which Hux hardly noticed, but I grabbed the armrests to steady myself.

"Sorry 'bout that," Bill said.

Always impervious to turbulence, Hux said, "Well, we'll have to work through that a little more, but I'd love to track down Reynolds at some point—even if it's just to get an alibi out of him. He had access to the rope, the river—and you."

"Forget about me," I said. "I think Reynolds is a fairly despicable human being for exploiting couples like this, using himself to impregnate women whose husbands couldn't cope with their role in not being able to have children. But that doesn't make him a murderer."

Hux frowned. "Could we get him on sexual assault?"

"Doubtful," I said. "None of the witnesses we have are willing to testify to that."

Hux seemed like he was preparing to argue with me when Bill said, "Prepare for landing. I'm putting her down in about five minutes."

The Bettles airstrip was easy to spot from the air, a dusty column of gray in a sea of green. As much as I liked being in nature, I wasn't someone who could live off the grid for an extended period. I was looking forward to catching a nap, a shower, and a hearty meal—maybe even some Netflix if the hotel had decent Wi-Fi. Ray had offered to put us up in the Cabins resort, not because he was generous but because everywhere else was booked.

Tess and her young son met us on the tarmac. The tall, slender boy shouted gleefully at Bill as he climbed down out of the cockpit. "Hi, Daddy!"

Bill ran over and swept the boy into his arms, eliciting a gaggle of laughter from his son. I couldn't help but think that Bill reminded me of my own father—older, but engaged as a dad, even though parenthood had come to him later in life.

"Have fun with your mom?" Bill asked.

"Yeah!"

Bill smiled at Tess—a warm but weary smile. I could understand why. Peak season was behind them, but the busy weeks weren't quite over. Their livelihood depended on these summer months, and there was no letting up until September.

The boy high-fived Hux as we climbed into the back of Tess's Jeep. "Hey, buddy," Hux said.

"Are you a park ranger?" the boy asked him.

Hux smiled. "Sort of," he said. "I *was* a park ranger, but now I'm more of a detective."

Sean turned to me. "What happened to your face?"

I didn't like to lie, especially to children. "I ran into some bear spray."

Tess glanced in the rearview mirror as she shifted into gear. With her arm draped around the headrest, she glanced back at me and Hux. Sean was sitting in the seat between us.

"We've got a doctor in town," Tess said. "He's retired now, and he's technically an obstetrician, but he could take a look—"

"I'm fine," I said. "Really." I shifted in my seat as Tess rolled down the window, ushering in a blast of cold air. It was starting to feel like summer had ended overnight.

"So what happened up there?" Tess asked. "I know we high-tailed it out of there in a hurry, but with the rain and all, we decided to wait it out in the plane."

"That's what I figured," I said. "We met up with the FBI agents from Fairbanks."

"FBI?" Tess's eyes widened. "What were they up there for?"

"I called in for some backup," I said.

Tess was quiet for a moment. "Did those folks from New York get a ride out of there?"

"Yes," I said. "The chopper took them out."

"You know, we offered to let 'em sleep in our plane, but they said no."

Hux and I exchanged a glance. "Really?"

"Yup. It struck me as real odd. The weather was bad, and with those fugitives roaming around out there . . ."

"Did they give a reason?"

"Nope. They just said they'd call us for a ride in a day or two."

Yiyin and Vince's dynamic continued to elude me, but I didn't have to understand it. After all, I couldn't picture Vince coming after me in the wilderness. The guy could barely walk on that knee of his. And Yiyin, for all her talk, wasn't strong enough to take me down, despite her obvious strengths in other domains.

"Anyway, what did the FBI say?" Tess asked. "Did they get those fugitives from Fairbanks?"

"No," I said. "But they've got a solid lead."

The radio crackled to life, but Tess picked it up before I could hear what it was about. For the next few minutes, I checked my Garmin messages. There were a few emails from Ray, telling me that I needed to be in Denali by nine AM Saturday morning. The agent covering for me down there was still in a bad state and wasn't going to last through the weekend. *So much for an extended vacation,* I thought. I would have to call Margo to let her know.

After a short ride, Tess dropped us off at the Cabins resort. Despite its proud rustic nature, the Cabins felt like the Four Seasons compared to what I'd been dealing with in the last forty-eight hours. To avoid any awkwardness with Hux, I walked up to the front desk and made sure we each had our own rooms.

"Cabins 106 and 107," the white-haired manager said. "How does that sound?"

"Just fine," I said. "Thanks."

"Those cabins share a hot tub," he said. "It's real nice this time of year—"

"We won't be needing that."

"Oh, everybody says that, this being Alaska and all. But it's a real treat." He smiled pleasantly at me. "The restaurant opens for dinner at five. It's our grilled salmon special tonight—best in town by a long shot."

I managed a thin smile, but all I could think about was Hux standing next to me. He was probably noodling on my response to the whole hot tub thing.

I glanced at my watch. "It's one forty-five now," I said to Hux. "Let's plan on dinner at six."

"It's a date," he said, before promptly clearing his throat. "I mean, yeah . . . eighteen hundred works for me. I'll see you then."

I turned and walked away before he could see me blushing. Ollie kept close to my heels, trotting happily behind me as I meandered around the property, avoiding Room 106 for now.

For not the first time since our arrival in Bettles, I missed my truck. Tess had offered her services as chauffeur while we were here, but I liked the freedom of having my own vehicle at my disposal. At least the place allowed dogs, but Ollie was honestly happier sleeping outside in a tent.

After killing time for fifteen minutes, I made my way to my room. It was clear from the tea lights and hot tubs that the Cabins emphasized romance more than the cheap motels and dingy Airbnbs I was used to. But at least Hux knew that the Cabins wasn't *my* choice. I had made a point of letting him know that Ray had booked it for us.

I got to 106 without any sightings of Hux, which was a small blessing. His light was on, but the shades were drawn. I wondered what my partner liked to do when he returned to civilization after days off the grid. Did he check his emails? Call his mom? Maybe he was on the phone right now with that anthropologist from Denali—Megan, was it? I couldn't remember her name, but I definitely remembered her prominent cheekbones and pretty smile.

You need sleep, I reminded myself. *Don't go down that rabbit hole.*

I unlocked the door and went inside, surprised to see a plush king-sized bed and a fire going in the hearth. It had been years since I'd stayed at a place like this—since Australia, really. Kevin and I had splurged on a fancy hotel before venturing into the wilderness for that last fateful trip. At the time, I remembered commenting on the extravagance of it all, the fake-looking fire and the staged bottle of champagne. It wasn't the kind of place I ever liked to spend money on, especially since we could just pitch a tent and camp somewhere for free.

But seeing it now, I realized I didn't feel that way anymore.

All I felt was a hollow, pressing loneliness.

* * *

I woke with a start at four forty-five PM, not because my alarm was blaring but because Ollie was barking. Someone was at my door.

I knew it wasn't Hux. He'd never disturb me by ramming his knuckles on my door, especially if he thought I was trying to catch up on sleep.

The knocking continued. I threw on a decent outfit and climbed out of bed. When I opened the door, I found myself face to face with Brinegar.

I had to squint to see him through the window next to my bed. The fiery stinging in my eyes had gone away, but light sensitivity was still an issue. I had read on Google that the aftereffects of a corneal injury secondary to bear spray might last for a couple days, but it didn't necessarily indicate permanent damage. So that was good.

"Chief," I said with as much warmth as I could muster, "what brings you to my door?"

"Good afternoon, Agent Harland. Um—sorry to disturb you like this, but I wanted to touch base before you headed back to Denali."

I stole a glance at Hux's cabin just a stone's throw away. The shades were open now, the windows cracked open. I had no way of knowing if he was awake. I thought about calling him, but sleep for Hux was sacred too, and I didn't want to disturb him—not yet.

"About what?" I asked.

Brinegar shifted his weight from one foot to the other. He was wearing his Park Service uniform, pressed to perfection. "I got a copy of the autopsy report from the medical examiner down in Fairbanks."

"Oh yes—the Greers' deaths were ruled accidental. I'm going to call down there today to clarify that."

"Well, no comment there, but I did see that baneberries were mentioned."

I shivered in the doorway. "Do you know something about that?" I asked.

"I talked to Dave some more. This baneberry thing—he said that this far north, baneberries aren't exactly thriving. He's convinced the victims must've gotten the berries from a botanist or a hobbyist—somebody who collects them."

"Interesting," I said. "But even if that were the case, I can't prove the ingestion wasn't accidental."

He lifted his wide-brimmed hat off his forehead. "That's where I think I can help."

Hearing this, I stepped out onto the porch and closed the door behind me. My two-hour nap had barely made a dent in a few days' worth of sleep deprivation, and I knew I'd pay for it later. But for right now, I was focused on the man standing in front of me.

"Why?" I asked.

"Well, it's got to do with our rangers station. I came in one day a couple weeks ago, and there were jars of berries all over the place. It looked like a science project of some sort."

"So what was going on?"

"Emily said they were *her* berries—she had 'em out as part of a public service project. I asked Dave to come by and help me move everything outside, since I really didn't want some kid coming in and eating poisonous berries."

I made a face. "So you're saying Emily might have had something to do with the deaths of Tim and Kelsey Greer?"

"No," he said. "But here's the thing—when I asked her about it yesterday, she admitted she knows Zane Reynolds." He rubbed his freshly shaven chin with his thumb. "She knows him well, in fact. She's his niece."

"Wait, *what*?" I couldn't quite figure out what else to say.

As I tried to process this deluge of new information, I stole another glance at Hux's cabin. "Would you excuse me for a minute? I want my partner to hear this."

Brinegar nodded. He stood and waited while I strode over to Hux's cabin in my sweatpants. I hadn't even had a chance to knock before the door swung open.

"Hey," I said, a little breathless. Hux was in a T-shirt and shorts, his hair all askew. He was rubbing his eyes. "Did I wake you?"

"Uh—nah," he said.

"That's a yes," I said. "I'm so sorry, but Brinegar's here. He's got some new information that could be useful to us."

"Let me get dressed," he said. "Hold on."

I caught a glimpse of his room—the well-made bed, the backpack on the floor, his dog-eared book on the bedside table.

Hux was organized, but he wasn't obsessive. The windows were open a crack, the blinds slightly crooked. There was a towel hung haphazardly over the bathroom door. I liked his style—imperfect but tidy.

After he'd thrown a wet hand through his hair and put a hat on, he came back out, trying to stuff his arms through the sleeves of his jacket as we made our way back to my cabin. Now that Hux was here, I felt better about inviting Brinegar inside to talk more.

We gathered in the little seating area next to the bed, but no one sat on it. I leaned on the windowsill, and Hux sat in one of the accent chairs by the window. Brinegar stood next to the door, where Ollie sniffed his hiking boots.

I asked him to repeat what he'd told me about Emily's connection to Zane Reynolds, which prompted a few clarifying questions from Hux. "But you never met him?" Hux asked.

"No," Brinegar said. "But I may know where he lives."

Hux and I exchanged a glance. "Where?"

"Emily lives in a nice cabin a couple miles outside the village," Brinegar said. "West of the airport, across the river, up in the hills there. Not easy to get to. But they've got a big satellite dish out there, which she said he needed to get work done."

Could Emily be the wizard behind the curtain? I wondered. It was clear that Reynolds needed someone with reliable internet to recruit couples to the wilderness, and a Gen Z-er made sense. Hearing about this high-tech compound, it was starting to sound like Emily could be it.

"Is Emily still out in the field?" I asked.

"No, ma'am. She's on a short leave—heads out again on Friday."

"Do you think she's home?"

"I assume so. Not much to do in Bettles in the evening time, that's for sure."

I looked at Hux, who had already closed his notebook. Judging by the expression on his face, he was thinking the same thing I was.

I turned back to Brinegar. "Any chance you could give us a ride to that cabin?"

28

J UST AS BRINEGAR had described it, Zane Reynolds's cabin sat
in a mythical setting atop a hill that overlooked the sprawling
Koyukuk River valley. It was surrounded by spruce and alder
trees, the land throttled by thick brush.

I spotted the cabin through the trees—a two-story dwelling
with a slant roof and brown logs woven together at the corners.
The door was a bright red, which struck me as somewhat ironic,
since red doors used to be a signal to weary travelers that this
home was hospitable to outsiders. But based on what I knew
about Reynolds, I wasn't expecting that kind of reception here.

Hux and I climbed out of Brinegar's Park Service vehicle and made our way to the cabin's door. I felt like I was on
more solid footing as an investigator here—my uniform on, my
badge around my neck, my Glock on my belt. Hux, too, struck
an intimidating figure in his uniform. Even though he towered
over me, I felt like his equal when we were standing side by side
like this, ready to confront an unsuspecting person with a few
questions.

Hux knocked.

Brinegar, who had accompanied us to the door, wandered
over to the edge of the stoop and peered through the window.

After another minute of knocking, the door creaked open.
Emily Wiseman stood before us, barefoot in a T-shirt and

lounge pants, with her hair pulled back in a lazy ponytail. She was holding a carton of ice cream in one hand and a spoon in the other.

Her expression was more confused than worried. "Um, hi," she said. "Is something wrong?" For the most part, she was talking to Brinegar.

"These investigators have got some questions about your baneberries," Brinegar said. "And your uncle."

Emily frowned. "Can't help you on the second part. Haven't seen him in a while, don't know what he's up to."

"Why didn't you mention him when we first met up on the Alatna?" I asked.

"I should have," she admitted. "I just didn't think he'd be the type to get involved in any of this. He's kind of a loner."

"Any idea why he might be in the fertility business?"

"I mean, maybe," she said. "He was married to my mom's sister for ten years. She died in childbirth—the baby too. It's a real sad story."

Hux and I exchanged a glance. "I'm sorry to hear it," I said.

"Anyway, I don't ask about his business," Emily said. "Like I said, I haven't seen him in a while."

"Listen, Emily." I tried to adopt a sympathetic tone. "We're not the FBI. We're ISB. The thing we're really interested in is figuring out what happened to Tim and Kelsey Greer. We know they had spent some time at your uncle's campsite—"

"Like I said, he had nothing to do with that."

"Then help us clear his name," I said.

Emily leaned back and put her ice cream on the bannister. "Look, I don't know what you want me to say. I don't have much contact with him."

"Can I ask you a different kind of question?" I asked. "It's going to seem random."

Emily said, "Yup."

"What can you tell us about the berries?"

I expected a flash of defensiveness, but instead, her expression seemed to soften a bit. "Yeah, that was a public service project.

We've seen some folks poison themselves out in the backcountry. It's bad when it happens."

"Was Dave involved in the project?"

"Yup. He's the expert. We tried to collect as many species of toxic plants as we could. The berries were an obvious one. I had twinberry, devil's club, queen's cup, and baneberry. I was still on the hunt for wild calla, skunk cabbage, death camas . . . anyway, it was a pretty big deal. Dave wanted to send them down to the microbiology lab in Anchorage for testing."

After a slow start, this interview was taking a strange turn. None of the promising leads we'd uncovered over the course of our investigation seemed in any way connected to one another.

I decided to back up a bit. "Who had access to your berries?" I asked.

"Um, what do you mean?"

"You said you had them on display at the rangers station, so who saw them? How many visitors a day, do you think?"

"Not that many." Emily glanced at Brinegar. "I couldn't just leave the jars out there unattended. They'd attract bears. So when I was working at the station, I put them out at lunchtime."

"So who saw the exhibit?"

I waited patiently while Emily tried to drum up some names. "Um, a couple people. Cody, Dave, Harry . . . some out-of-towners . . . there was that one weird guy from Hawaii . . ." She counted the names off on her fingers. "Oh, and Bill and his kid . . . and George."

"George?"

"He's our maintenance person," Brinegar explained.

"Got it," I said. *So pretty much everyone in town.* "Did anyone take anything, by chance? Any samples, maybe?"

"Well . . ." She kneaded her knuckles.

"What is it?"

"When I wasn't around, I kept the berries in jars in a BearVault—you know, so the wildlife wouldn't eat them. But one day last week, I went out back behind the rangers station to get things ready for one last exhibit before my field survey on the Alatna and noticed that one of the jars was missing."

I looked at Hux, whose hand suddenly stilled over the pages of his notebook. He lifted his hand and stole a glance in my direction. We waited for Emily to continue, but I wasn't the most patient person in the world.

"Which jar?" I asked.

"*L. Actaea*," she said. "Baneberries."

CHAPTER

29

In Chicago, I would have inquired about the area's CCTV footage, which had a ubiquitous presence on every block of the city. But the Bettles Rangers Station only had one security camera, and it was positioned *inside* the building. I wasn't feeling optimistic.

Emily offered to go with us to show us the exhibit and the missing jar, so we all piled into Brinegar's vehicle and headed back there.

Once we arrived at the rangers station, I asked Brinegar to pull up the security tapes so we could view them. The ones I was interested in were from the previous Tuesday night into Wednesday morning, when Emily had noticed the baneberries were gone.

We were in the office in the back, going through the footage, when Brinegar went to take a call. The video quality was even worse than I had anticipated, capturing a completely dark, motionless interior. We watched it max speed with the audio turned up high, but it was a bust. All we heard was some distant howling of wolves.

"Do you want to see the berries?" Emily asked.

I nodded. "Lead the way."

She took us to the picnic table out back, which was covered in a red-checkered cloth. An assortment of glass jars adorned the table. Each jar had an identifying placard, with the species name and some pertinent information about the berry and its dangers. The placard for *L. Actaea* was still on the table, but the jar that was supposed to be behind it was gone.

"This is a nice collection," I said, admiring the two-dozen jars along with their printed placards. "How long did it take you to assemble these?"

Emily shrugged. "All summer."

Brinegar came striding out the back door of the rangers station with a look of consternation on his face. He joined us at the picnic table.

"Everything okay?" I asked him.

"Yes, ma'am. They got that bear that was causing trouble up near Arrigetch, is all."

Kiga? I thought, but Brinegar wasn't going to know what that meant.

I turned back to Emily. "Is Dave around?" I asked.

She didn't answer right away. It seemed my question had thrown her for a loop. "Uh, not sure." She averted her gaze as she spoke.

"Dave is in the village here," Brinegar said. "We had an issue with some rabid foxes in one of the campgrounds on the Koyukuk River. He's been dealing with that."

"Where does he live?"

"A ways out of town," Brinegar said. "I could pull up his address if you need it."

"We might ask you to do that—thanks." I had a feeling it wouldn't be necessary, though; Dave was clearly living in Emily's cabin. My suspicion was that Brinegar had a policy against romantic relationships among rangers—or at the very least, he discouraged it. Emily was probably reluctant to get into that with him now. "How many other rangers do you have working out of your station?" I asked Brinegar.

He thought for a moment. "We've got two mountaineering rangers that are gone on a thirty-day patrol right now," he said. "But as for park rangers, it's me, Emily, and three fellas who mainly cover the western portion of the park."

"What about Search and Rescue?"

"They're locals, mostly. It's a small group. I can track them down if you need me to."

"We're good for now," I said, acutely aware of our own deadline. I tried to stay focused on the basics—motive, for one. If Tim and Kelsey had been murdered—poisoned, as it were, with baneberries—then who wanted them dead? The missing jar pointed to intent, and if some random SAR volunteer wanted Tim and Kelsey dead, would they really have used baneberries? *No, not a chance,* I decided.

Emily's placard pointed to one other crimp in this narrative— the baneberries' taste. Ingesting them would have been a miserable exercise in perseverance. Although Tim and Kelsey Greer *might* have eaten them if they were on the verge of starvation, that didn't appear to be the case here. The more likely scenario was that someone had forced them to ingest a toxic amount. *Six,* I recalled. As few as six baneberries could be fatal to a human.

I glanced at my watch. It was almost eight thirty, which meant the restaurant at the Cabins resort was closing in thirty minutes. As much as I craved sleep, I needed a decent meal to fuel my brain so I could think through this case. Judging by the menacing growls coming from Hux's stomach, he was probably on the same page there.

"Anything else I can do for you?" Brinegar asked.

"Actually, there is one thing. Any chance you could give us a lift back to our hotel?"

"Of course," he said. "I'd be happy to."

Emily tightened the lids on the last of her jars. "I hope you find out what happened to those folks," she said. "But like I said, my uncle had nothing to do with it."

I thanked Emily for her trouble, but I could tell she had soured on me for ruining her uncle's livelihood. For now, though, I wasn't worried about Reynolds's fertility enterprise. I was still trying to decide if there was a killer loose in the park.

When we got back to the Cabins, I thanked Brinegar for his assistance and walked up to the restaurant. The hostess—young, attractive, in a slim-fitting cocktail dress—frowned when she saw us coming. But all Hux had to do was smile at her, and we were in. She led us to a table in the back, next to the fireplace.

The table was a four-top, which posed a bit of a problem as I tried to figure out where to sit. A couple would have sat next to each other, especially since the table was rather large, but Hux and I weren't a couple. In the end, we sat on opposite sides, despite the centerpiece blocking my view of him. We weren't going to be able to compare notes like this very easily either. But it was better than having to deal with the awkwardness of being on a "date."

We looked over our menus in silence. As soon as the waiter came by, we placed our orders—tomato soup to start, grilled salmon as our entrée. No questions, no clarifications, no special requests. To order anything else was practically sacrilege. I was famished.

"I had a thought," I said, once the waiter had left.

"Uh-oh," Hux said with a smirk.

"I think we should make one more trip back up there."

"To the campsite, you mean?"

"I bet Reynolds is still in the area, figuring out his next move."

Hux reached for his glass of water and lifted it to his lips. The ice clinked in the glass as he drank. "I'm not sure he's gonna talk to *us*, boss—and that's *if* we find him. Which is a big if. I'm not saying I couldn't track him down eventually, but it won't be easy."

"I know. I just feel like we're missing something."

"That's because we are," he said. "We haven't found the person that attacked you."

"That's lower on the priority list—"

"No, it's not."

"Thanks," I mumbled as I looked down at my plate. Our waiter came by with a pair of hot teas with a sliver of lemon perched on the rims. I needed some caffeine to get me through dinner, but not so much that I couldn't sleep at night.

"So you really think Reynolds will talk to us?" Hux asked.

"I do," I said. "Tim and Kelsey Greer are a problem for him—no one will ever go out into a remote wilderness with the guy who *may* have killed them. If he thinks we're trying to clear his name, he might talk."

"*Are* we trying to clear his name?"

I buttered a warm roll. "I'm not a fan of what he's doing out there, but I don't think he killed anyone."

"Huh," he said. "That's a bit of a turn."

"It's just . . . I don't know. It's clear to me he wasn't running a one-man operation. And I don't think he knew about the berries. I really don't."

Hux plucked a roll out of the basket and took a bite. We chewed in silence for a beat, each of us waiting for the other to talk.

"So, then who attacked you up there?" Hux asked.

I forced myself to meet Hux's gaze. "Well, we know it wasn't Ana or Diego because you were tracking them, which gives them an alibi. I also can't figure why they'd go from shooting three drug smugglers to poisoning a couple from New Jersey."

"I'm with you," Hux said. "It doesn't fit. The Greers felt more personal."

"And sloppy."

He nodded. "Yup."

"Then there's the baneberries. Assuming they came from Emily's exhibit, that rules out Vince and Yiyin because they've been up at Reynolds's campsite since May."

"Maybe that's a flawed assumption to make, though." Hux sorted through the breadbasket for another roll. "We can't say for sure how the killer might have gotten the berries."

"True."

He held up his roll, almost like a lecturer holding his pointer. "So, to put it all together, we're thinking your attacker also killed Tim and Kelsey Greer . . . and they probably had an accomplice because you heard two voices that night . . . and they can handle themselves outdoors . . . and they had access to baneberries . . ."

I enjoyed hearing Hux ruminate while he buttered his roll.

"What about Emily?" he posited.

I thought back to Emily's face when she saw us standing on her front stoop at the cabin. I couldn't say she had the look of a guilty person. "It's an interesting thought," I said. "She had means and opportunity, but I can't figure a motive."

"Defending her uncle? Money? Maybe she relies on him for financial support."

"It feels like a stretch."

"Yeah, but you never know," Hux said. "The Park Service doesn't pay much." He finished off his roll and reached for another. "So what's the play?"

"I think we try to see if we can get Emily to meet us *with* Reynolds. She's probably our best chance of finding him."

Hux downed another glass of water before our waiter could come by to top it off. He'd already demolished the breadbasket. "Do you think they're working together on this?" he asked. "The Twitter messages and all?"

I thought for a moment. "It makes sense that he would have had a use for her—she knows the terrain, the popular tourist routes, the game trails. She could even help him avoid other rangers on patrol. I think it's worth exploring their connection a little further."

A waiter came by with two bowls of steaming hot tomato soup and a fresh basket of rolls. Hux grasped his spoon and dug in. "I'm on board with whatever you want to do," he said as he reached for another roll. "You know that."

"I don't want to call all the shots here, Hux," I said. "What do *you* think?"

He downed half his soup before answering. "I think it makes sense to talk to Emily again. We could fly up there tomorrow or the next day, if you want."

"I'd like to take one day to go through all our evidence first. That way we'll know what to look for when we go back to the scene." As I tasted the soup, I thought back to my last pitiful date with Orin. Hux's company was so much more pleasant in every way, but it wasn't a fair comparison. With Hux, there was none of the pressure that came with a romantic encounter— *Does he like me? Where is this going? What are we doing after this?* Then there was the whole "ghosting" thing. I hated men that did that. *Just man up and tell me you're not into me,* was how I felt about it.

Hux put his spoon down while I finished my soup. Eventually, his gaze drifted back to me, and our eyes met briefly over the floral bonanza in the middle of the table.

Sensing my annoyance with the centerpiece, Hux grabbed it and moved it out of the way. His smile widened into a grin. I couldn't help but smile back. "Thanks for doing that," I said. "I never understood the point of a centerpiece."

"Well, it was either that or ask the waiter if they've got some extra phone books back there," he said.

I laughed. "It's unfortunate we can't all be giants like yourself."

"Isn't everyone kind of a giant to you?"

"More or less," I said.

"Are your parents . . . hmm, how do I say this—"

"Short?" I shook my head. "Nope. My sisters are all five seven or taller. My dad's six one; my mom's five six. Apparently, I took after my great-aunt Mary, who was, I'm told, 'a tiny sparkplug.'"

Hux laughed. "I feel like I know this person."

I glanced out the window. The sun was starting to go down, the orange glow of twilight filtering between the trees. I watched a couple walk hand in hand toward their cabin.

I looked back at Hux. "I'm glad you're here," I said.

He was quiet for a moment.

"I am too," he said.

30

THE NEXT MORNING, I woke to the blinking red light of my room phone and Ollie's soft, hungry whimpers. The Cabins were nicely updated, but some of the accoutrements were from another era. The room phones were one example. The blinking red light meant that someone had left me a good old-fashioned voicemail.

I rolled over and checked the time. It was just after nine o'clock, which meant I'd slept for a good ten hours. In Alaska, curtains were a must, and the ones in my room were fastened to the wall, which made it feel like you were sleeping in a sealed chamber. I hopped out of bed and threw them wide. Ollie was already at the door, ready to go out.

I threw on a coat and opened the door. Ollie bounded over to Hux's cabin and barked at me to follow him. "No," I said, shaking my head at him. "*No*, Ollie."

I wasn't dressed for a morning encounter with my partner, who'd probably been up for hours. Hux was one of those rare humans who could function on about four hours of sleep.

But Ollie's barking had let him know we were both awake, and sure enough, Hux came out onto the patio, dressed and ready for the day. He caught sight of me and waved. I waved back.

"Mornin'," he called out to me as he filled Ollie's bowl with some food.

"Good morning."

"I think you missed breakfast."

Ugh, I thought. "I'm going to head over there in a minute to talk to the guy at the front desk about something. Maybe they have some fruit out or something."

"I'll take Ollie. Take your time."

"Thanks."

I hurried back into my cabin to shower, dress, and make myself look presentable. I wasn't sure yet where Hux and I were going to tackle all the evidence we'd accumulated in the Greer case, but in case it was in my hotel room, I wanted to be prepared.

When I was satisfied with the way the room looked, I laced up my hiking boots and made my way over to the lobby of the main cabin. The sun was out, the rain a distant memory. The sign outside the restaurant read, "Join us at 11 for lunch."

Settling for a banana and some tea, I approached the front desk. "Good morning," I said. "I'm in Room 106—is there a message for me by chance? I saw a flashing light, but no voicemail."

"Ah, yes," the man said. "Ms. Harland, correct?"

"Yep, that's me."

He glanced at his computer screen. "Chief Brinegar came by this morning. He left a message for you." He handed me a green Post-it Note from inside a drawer.

I read the note carefully. It was Emily's sat phone number, along with her intended destination. She was heading back up to the Alatna River today.

"Why didn't he just call me?" I wondered aloud.

"He didn't want to disturb you, ma'am. He mentioned you'd been out in the park, investigating the deaths of those poor folks from New Jersey."

"That's true," I said.

The man offered a sympathetic smile. "It's partly out of habit, ma'am. No one up here relies on phones very much—always better to deliver a message in person, if you can."

I understood that. In a place without cell phone service or reliable internet, in-person contact was the only fail-safe method of communication. A radio was a close second, but I didn't have one of those.

"Thank you." I took the note and stepped outside. My temporary satellite phone—a rental from Bettles Outfitters—was in my pocket. I dialed the number on Brinegar's Post-it and waited for the call to go through.

To my surprise, the call went through without a hitch, and someone on the other end answered right away. "Hello?" It was a young woman's voice. "Who's this?"

"Hi . . . Emily?"

"Yep."

"This is Felicity Harland again. Hux and I—we were hoping to see if you'd be willing to help us track down your uncle—"

"I'm heading out with the mountaineering rangers this morning," she said. "I'll be gone for a month, then it's back to Oregon for the winter."

I felt my chest tighten. "This morning, you said?"

"Yeah."

"Whereabouts?"

She sighed. "Arrigetch Peaks area. But I'm on a tight schedule."

"Can we meet you there?"

She sighed. "I guess. Maybe just send me your coordinates."

"Thanks," I said. "I appreciate it."

I hung up, debating my next call. Although I didn't have Reynolds's sat phone number, I did have the email address linked to his Twitter handle. It was a risk contacting him directly, sure, but in this case, it felt like one worth taking. I wasn't sure I wanted to put pressure on Emily to summon her uncle—not yet, anyway. For one thing, Emily was a good ranger. I didn't want to burn a bridge with Brinegar if she had nothing to do with Reynolds's activities in the park.

Next, I thought carefully about what I wanted to say. I'd only get one chance.

We talked to Emily, I wrote. *We're headed to these coordinates this afternoon. If you're anywhere close by, please come meet us. We're hoping to rule you out as a suspect.* I double-checked the coordinates at the bottom of the message and hit "Send."

My next call was to Tess Flint. This whole plan hinged on her and her husband because they were our best hope of getting a last-minute flight up to the park. If Bill couldn't do it, this whole plan could fall apart before it even kicked into gear.

When Tess answered, she seemed uncharacteristically frazzled. The store sounded busy, with a number of customers talking in the background. I got right to the point. "Hi, Tess? It's Felicity Harland. I know this is last minute, but any chance Bill could fly us back up to the Arrigetch Peaks area?"

"When?"

"Today, if possible."

"Today?" She said something to a customer before coming back on the line. "Bill and I were about to head out now to meet some clients, but we can take you up with us if you can be at the airport in . . . fifteen minutes."

"No problem," I said. "Thank you—we appreciate it."

"See you then."

In fact, it *was* a bit of a problem, since I wasn't at all prepared for another wilderness excursion. As I went down to the river to search for Hux, I calculated how long it would take me to pack a few essentials and get to the airstrip. It was going to be tight.

I found Hux playing a tracking game with Ollie in the shallows of the Koyukuk. "We gotta go," I called out. "Pack your gear—we need to be at the airstrip in fifteen minutes."

He looked at me with an air of complete calm. "I'm ready now," he said. "Are we walking there?"

"I, um . . ." I hadn't even thought about our transportation issues, but the airstrip was just a mile down the road. If we set off on foot down the road, someone would probably pick us up and take us the rest of the way.

Or we could just hustle, as Hux liked to say.

"Yes, we are," I said. "I'll meet you in the parking lot in four minutes."

*　*　*

The walk to the airstrip turned into a full-on sprint before we even left the Cabins' parking lot, but somehow we got there in time. Tess's Jeep was parked just outside the chain-link fence. I found it a little odd she hadn't offered us a ride, but then again, she was busy. Maybe she figured we had scrounged up a vehicle, which we hadn't, but that was a different story.

Bill helped us put our backpacks and gear in the Cessna's cargo pod, which functioned as an accessory trunk of sorts and was common in this part of the country. I decided to hold onto my cell phone for the time being. I didn't have any service, of course, but the short flight up there was a good opportunity to read over my case notes and look back at some photos. Everything else went into the pod at Bill's insistence.

"Howdy and welcome aboard," Bill said over his shoulder as he put his headset on. Tess, sitting in the copilot's seat, did the same. I knew she liked to put in some face time with her higher-end clients; a business like hers was built on those relationships.

The storm had moved on, and the skies were clear—for now, at least. Another squall was due to arrive that evening, but I hoped we'd be out of there by then.

Once we were in the air, I turned to Hux and said, "Can I see your phone for a second?"

"Sure." He took it out of his pocket. "Just, uh . . . I saved the crime scene photos to the "GOTA" file. If you just click on the file name there . . ."

I reddened. "Oh, of course—that's what I meant." Avoiding his gaze, I took the phone from his hand. Hux's "GOTA" file had over five hundred photos, as well as his meticulous notes and audio files.

The earliest photos weren't from the scene at the Alatna, but from our brief stop at the restaurant in Bettles. Hux had taken a photo of Dora's phone with the leaked Twitter message containing the coordinates for Reynolds's location, plus the expiration date. But this one had a little something extra too—a personal message to the recipient: *Can't miss it.*

I thought this was a strange detail, in part because of the irony in it. Of *course* you could miss it—nothing was easy to find in Alaska's wilderness. Any park ranger worth his salt could tell you that, along with the thousands of family members who'd lost loved ones to the state's unforgiving landscape over the years. So what did it mean, then? Was it a form of encouragement? Mockery?

More than that, though, those three little words seemed familiar somehow. I looked over at Hux, who was massaging Ollie's scruff as he gazed out the window. I tapped his elbow.

He swiveled his head toward me. "Sorry," he said. "I get lost in it sometimes. This place, I mean—it takes your breath away."

"Have a look at this." I handed his phone back to him. "Did Dora or Greg comment on this message at all? The 'you can't miss it' part?"

Hux scrunched his brow. "I don't think so," he said. "It's a weird little add-on, though. Because, well—I don't agree. Of course you can miss it. It would be weird if you *didn't* miss it."

"Yup," I said. "It also doesn't seem like something Reynolds would bother with, which pretty much confirms for me that he wasn't working alone."

Bill and Tess were up in the cockpit, having a conversation we weren't privy to. I could tell by their facial expressions, though, that something was on their minds. The conversation wasn't flowing well. Tess was doing most of the talking while Bill kept his eyes on the open skies.

Their dynamic reminded me of my old conversations with Kevin—the occasional pokes and prods that came with being married, the stings and the barbs that used to color our disagreements. But the longer I watched Tess and Bill, the more I began to suspect that this was something more than that. Was it about their business? The next bout of bad weather forecasted for the weekend? Their son?

I found myself thinking about the boy they shared. Sean was tall for his age, with white- blond hair and pale blue eyes that reminded me of polar ice. Bill was a leather-tanned lumberjack type, with brown eyes and a stout build. It wasn't that I had always, as a rule, paid attention to eye color—but in my line of work, I'd grown accustomed to paying attention to the details, because details were facts, and facts were invaluable in an investigation.

As I was sitting there pondering the nuances of eye color and the labyrinth of genetics, I thought back to Reynolds with his memorable blue eyes, as pale and stark as the sky on a sun-swept afternoon.

Tess and Bill's son had his eyes.

I became suddenly aware of the knot in my stomach, which had formed the moment we'd boarded the plane for reasons that, at the time, I'd chalked up to nerves. I had gotten used to traveling by small passenger planes, and had even adjusted to the bumpy rides and unpredictable weather. But now that I thought about it—really, truly thought about it—I realized that my unease had nothing to do with the plane, but with the people on it.

Bill and Tess.

Tess and . . . *Zane Reynolds?*

I grasped the armrests and stared at the seat in front of me. Hux was looking out the window. I wanted to get his attention, but I worried about saying the wrong thing ten thousand feet above the ground, with nothing but a curved sheet of metal separating us from the air.

I adjusted my headset, which was currently set to "pilot isolate." This meant that I couldn't hear their conversations, and they couldn't hear mine.

"Tess?" I called out.

She turned around with a start. "Everything okay back there?"

"Yup. I just wanted to make sure Bill is okay with taking us down as close to those coordinates as possible." I gestured to the green Post-it Note stuck on the instrument panel, the one from Brinegar. Bill had put it there after programming the coordinates into his heading.

"Oh, we got 'em." She smiled at me—the irony in it manifesting as a gleam in her eyes. "Can't miss it."

31

H UX HAD HEARD it, too.

"Can't miss it."

There was no doubt in my mind now that Tess Flint was the one sending out coordinates from Reynolds's mysterious Twitter handle. That "can't miss it" was her signature.

That said, her involvement in his scheme wasn't a crime, at least not yet. But I wasn't thinking about Reynolds's operation in Gates of the Arctic National Park; I was thinking about the two people who had died just hours after leaving it. What if it wasn't their argument with Reynolds that had compelled them to leave? What if it was something else?

Tess Flint had motive and opportunity. First off, the timing fit. Vince had seen Tim and Kelsey arguing the night before the Greers left, but what if they hadn't just stormed off in anger? What if Tess had given them no choice?

But why?

That was the question, and our best chance at an answer was Zane Reynolds himself.

With a warrant, it wouldn't be hard to mine Tess's emails for evidence connecting her to his Alaskan fertility enterprise, but murder was a different story. I needed evidence of a crime. I needed the baneberries, to start.

Emily had said that Bill had seen the baneberry exhibit, which implied that Tess knew it was there too. The problem was, I couldn't *put* Tess at the exhibit. The security footage was a mess of static and nothingness. It wasn't going to help us at all.

I heard Bill's voice through the speakers on my headset. He must have changed the setting, tuning us in to his conversation. "Everything okay back there?" he asked.

"Fine," I said, doing my best to sound casual.

Bill banked the plane left, turning at a steep angle. I felt my stomach lift into my throat. *Are we going the right way?* I thought—irrationally, maybe. I had no piloting experience whatsoever. Hux, though, looked a little bit uneasy, and he had far more flying experience than I did.

I thought about calling Ray on my sat phone, only to remember that everything was in the cargo pod—my phone, my gun, my gear. *Everything.*

As we flew over the Alatna River, tracing its twisting route through a valley that seemed to stretch on forever, I tried to stay calm. Bill and Tess didn't know that I was onto them. All I had to do was act like everything was fine.

After fifteen excruciating minutes in the air, Bill put the plane down on the shimmering surface of Takahula Lake. A flock of birds lifted off in a cacophony of wings and shrieks as we skittered past them. I envied them in that moment, their ability to escape.

As the plane's rotors sputtered to a stop, Tess poked her head inside the cabin. Bill unbuckled his safety harness and climbed out the cockpit door.

"This is it," she said. "Takahula Lake."

I forced a smile. "It's spectacular."

As I watched Tess put on a pair of gloves, I thought back to those fraught few minutes in the wilderness at night. My attacker had been wearing gloves—a thin fabric, almost feminine in its construction, just like the ones Tess was wearing now.

On top of that, Tess was a statuesque woman, nearly six feet tall, with wiry arms and a capable build. It all made sense now. She'd had all the advantages in that encounter—knowledge of the terrain, a coordinated plan of attack, superior size and strength.

I gritted my teeth. When it came to dealing with potential suspects, I prided myself in keeping a level head, but right then, all I could think about was confronting this woman who'd had the gall to attack me. It pissed me off.

And what about Tim and Kelsey Greer, the gullible young couple who'd traveled across the continent on a whim and a prayer. How and why had Tess lured them away from the safety of Reynolds's campsite, all the way to the Alatna River? Was it just the sight of a knife that had done it? Or were they too sick from the baneberries to put up a fight?

Hux and I got off the plane to find Bill standing in front of the cargo hold. His keys were in his hand, but something was wrong with the lock. He couldn't get it open.

Tess said to me, "Not sure where you're going exactly, but you might want to move fast. There's a storm coming."

She's telling me to leave, I thought.

The darkening sky to the west was encroaching on the bland cumulous clouds to the north and east. I didn't like playing chicken with the weather, but this was my only chance to get a confession out of Bill and Tess. The problem, of course, was the unfavorable circumstances—the fact that my gun was in a locked pod, for example. Hux and I were defenseless. She could shoot us right here, right now, and no one except her husband would ever know she'd done it.

Before that could happen, Tess's sat phone chimed with a message. As she glanced down at the screen, the crease in her brow deepened. Bill said her name a few times to get her attention, but he was unsuccessful.

When she finally looked up, the expression on her face said it all. Something beyond the ridge had caught her eye—and mine too.

I turned around.

Zane Reynolds was coming over the hill.

32

REYNOLDS WAS ALONE, wearing a light jacket and no back-pack. He looked like a phantom on the ridge, as if Mother Nature herself had borne him on the arctic plains. But I knew he was real. I could tell by the steeliness in his expression, the anger brimming in his eyes.

Bill had backed away from the plane, but both he and Tess were watching Reynolds come down the ridge. I could tell they were both shocked to see him. Ollie's reception was loud and urgent, the kind of barking he did when he wanted to warn me of encroaching danger.

Reynolds walked at a deliberate pace that seemed to under-score the urgency of the situation. He wasn't armed, but nei-ther was I. Bill was still holding the keys to the cargo pod. Hux backed up a few steps and tried to yank open the pod with his bare hands. It wouldn't budge.

"*Hey,*" Bill said. "Careful there—"

"We need our gear, man," Hux said. "Hand over the keys, would you?"

Tess shot Bill a look that changed the tone of the conversation—of everything, really. By then, Reynolds was standing within spitting distance of the plane.

"What's going on here?" Reynolds asked.

Bill tried to channel his even-keeled nature by spreading his palms wide in a gesture of peace. "Nothing's going on here. We're just havin' a conversation."

"Zane," Tess said, almost like she was breathing his name. There was recognition and sadness and something almost like embarrassment. It was clear she hadn't expected to see him, and now that he was here, she was struggling to process it.

Bill put his hands in his pockets and muttered something under his breath. For the first time, the seasoned bush pilot looked his age. His jovial nature eroded into something small and timid right before our eyes. Tess shifted her feet.

"We talked to Emily," I said to Reynolds. "Your niece."

Reynolds's expression hardened. "She's got nothing to do with what I do here."

Hux said, "She had a whole stockpile of baneberries, as it turns out."

"I don't know what you're suggesting, but like I said, Emily's got nothing to do with this. She never even met Tim and Kelsey."

"But *you* did," I said. "You were the last person to see them alive."

He snorted. "The last person to see them alive was this woman right here." He pointed at Tess. "Maybe you ought to leave my niece alone and talk to her instead."

Bill stepped in front of Tess. "Wait a minute here. We've got nothin' to do with this fella here—"

"How dare you," Tess said to Reynolds, her voice a curdled whisper. It made a raspy sound in her throat that reminded me of an animal in distress.

Bill grabbed Tess by the elbow. "Stop talking, Tess."

Undeterred, she shook off his hand and marched over to Reynolds. "I made this all possible for you." Her voice wavered, even as her volume escalated. "All of it—the supplies, the food, the clients. I created the social media accounts, the wire transfers—"

Rather than go after her, Bill backtracked toward the cargo hold with his keys in hand. This seemed to get Tess's attention. She whirled around to face him.

"I'm gettin' their gear," Bill explained. "And we're heading home."

Reynolds said, "No, you're not." He glared at Tess, his anger boiling over. "Not until you tell these federal agents here what you did."

"We're going back," Bill said, more to himself than to anyone else. He managed to get his key into the pod's lock when Tess grabbed the pistol from Bill's cowboy-style holster.

"Tess!" Bill yelled, his scolding voice echoing through the valley. He fumbled in the air for his pistol but came up empty. "Have you lost your mind, woman?"

She aimed it at him. "Don't push me," she said. "I need a second to think." Ollie, seeing the gun, barked furiously, shattering the stillness. His frantic barking made the situation feel almost surreal, a beat of chaos in the stillness.

"Think about *what*?"

Her lips parted, followed by a gasping breath. "Sean."

Hux glanced at me, a darkening storm of emotion and instinct in his eyes. I knew that look. When Hux or anyone close to him was threatened, he shifted into predatory mode. For me, it was all about defense, but Hux had other assets. He could afford to risk going on the offensive.

At the moment, though, Tess had the gun. I tried to focus my attention on her. Was she a good shot? Did she even have it in her to shoot a human being? And if she did, what were the chances that a bullet fired from that gun would be enough to kill a man like Hux Huxley?

Not very good, I thought. *But not zero.*

I inched a little closer to Hux and brushed his elbow. *Don't*, the gesture said. *Not yet.*

Tess turned toward me and Hux. "We'll get somebody else to pick you up before the storm moves in," she said. This was a lie. I could feel it.

The *why*, though, was becoming clearer: her family. Her *son*. If Reynolds was Sean's father, it made sense that she had risked her marriage, her livelihood, and her reputation to protect his business interests and keep him in Alaska. I wasn't sure yet how

Bill felt about this complex relationship, but he surely knew Sean wasn't his. Despite that, he had raised him as his own, which spoke to his character in my book. I wasn't ready to give up on him quite yet.

That wasn't to say that good character counted for much in emotional situations like this. Tess perceived me and Hux as a threat to her family; it was why she wasn't giving us access to that cargo pod. It was why she'd attacked me in the brush. She didn't want us here. But did she want us dead? I hadn't decided yet. *She* hadn't decided yet.

Reynolds must have sensed her ambivalence too. He took a breath and released it, perhaps as a strategy to diffuse some of the tension. He kept his eyes on Tess.

Reynolds's subtle maneuver seemed to work. Tess lowered her arms a little bit. As Reynolds took a step toward her, the expression in Tess's eyes changed—from denial and defiance to admiration and affection. It occurred to me that she would do anything to protect him, the same way she'd do anything to protect her son.

Reynolds said to her, "Tell me what happened to Tim and Kelsey Greer."

Tess shook her head. "I don't know—"

"I put you on shadow coverage to make sure they got to the rendezvous point safely." His voice was menacingly quiet. "So what happened between the campsite and the river?"

Tess's arm seemed to be buckling under the weight of the gun. She steadied it with her other hand. "Nothing," she said.

"They were poisoned, Tess. We both know folks don't just die of baneberry poisoning. We know they don't lie down next to a river and wait for the wolves to get them either." He was standing inches away from her. "So what happened?"

Tess wrung her hands together as she struggled to meet his gaze. "She threatened you," she said. "She threatened all of us."

He sighed. "Tess—"

"That night—the night before they left . . . Tim accused you of raping her." Her voice faltered, almost as if saying such a thing made her physically ill. "I heard him. He threatened to go to the police, send you to jail."

"It was all consensual, Tess."

"*I* know that." Tess straightened her shoulders, her toughness creeping back in. "I know you were just trying to help people. I understood that. That man and his wife—they didn't understand. They were trying to blackmail you."

"They were just bluffing."

"No, they weren't. I could hear it in his voice."

Reynolds shook his head. He stepped so close to her that the barrel of Tess's gun grazed his shirt. She looked down at her trembling hands and caught a sob in her throat. Her finger tightened on the trigger.

"Did you poison them?" Reynolds asked.

Tess looked at the ground. "No."

"I found the berries in with the supplies you delivered the day before they left. The next day, after the Greers had cleared out, they were gone." He lowered his voice. "So what happened, Tess? Tell me now, or we're all going to prison for this. Sean will be an orphan."

Tess covered her face with one hand and sucked in a breath. "I made tea out of it—not much, just a little. I put it in their water bottles. I figured I'd follow them for a while, see how far they got. Well, they got pretty far. I heard the man talking about what he planned to do to you. At that point, I took matters into my own hands."

"Where did you get the berries?"

"In Bettles." She hung her head. "At the rangers station."

It wasn't looking good for Tess. Her actions so far suggested premeditation: going to the rangers station in Bettles, stealing the berries, flying them all the way up to the campsite so she could brew a poisonous tea for two people she blamed for exploiting Reynolds. It also suggested that she'd held a grudge against the Greers for quite a bit longer than she was letting on.

It didn't look good at all.

"You meant to kill them?" Reynolds asked.

"No! I just—it wasn't supposed to happen that fast. They panicked. I saw them leave their campsite in the middle of the night, maybe to try and get help or whatever. They even crossed the river. I think at that point they were disoriented."

Reynolds tilted his head toward the darkening sky. He muttered something under his breath.

"Then what?"

Tess exhaled. "They . . . they just gave up."

Was this part true? I didn't know—I couldn't know. But Tess's role in their deaths was clear. She'd given them the berries, and then, armed with a sat phone, she'd done nothing to help them.

"You've made a terrible mistake," Reynolds said, his voice a guttural whisper.

In the tense silence that followed, I cleared my throat. Tess suddenly seemed to remember I was there. "Why the restraints, then?" I asked her. "Why tie them up?"

Tess stole a glance at Reynolds. "The restraints were part of the credo."

I wasn't sure I understood. "So they had used them voluntarily the night before they left?"

Reynolds said, "I have no idea what people do in the privacy of their own tent. But I would never tie anyone up. That's ridiculous."

Tess seemed to shrink into herself as Reynolds spoke. His hold over her was as intense as it was absolute. I thought she was going to drop the gun, when, suddenly, she turned it on me. "I'm sorry, Agent Harland," she said. "I made some mistakes. I'll admit that. But I can't go to prison—I can't do that to Sean."

Reynolds's eyes widened as Tess's finger tightened on the trigger, but it was Ollie who saw her intent to shoot me—and Hux, a split second later. Ollie snagged Tess's pant leg in his teeth as Hux lunged forward, grabbing the gun just in time to throw it off its trajectory by a millimeter or two—

Pop.

Horror swept through me. I thought Hux had been hit at first—Hux, who had put himself in the line of fire yet again to save me. Hux, who was seemingly indestructible. Then I saw him reach for Ollie with one arm and roll out of the way. He wasn't paralyzed. He wasn't bleeding. He wasn't dead.

He's okay, I thought. *He's okay.*

I had almost convinced myself the bullet had simply found its way into a harmless nothingness when I noticed Reynolds staggering, his blue eyes processing the shock of what had happened to him. The next words out of his mouth succumbed to a deep, rattling wheeze. Hux maneuvered across the ground to put pressure on the entry wound, but a gush of dark red blood found its way to the earth anyway. Reynolds choked and gasped.

Out of nowhere, a searing cloud of bear spray filled the air. Ollie whimpered and whined as he backpedaled out of the way. Somehow, I managed to close my eyes in time to fend off the assault. I squinted one eye to see that Tess's gun had made it into Bill's hands. He fired a shot in the air, eliciting a squawk from the birds that had been watching our human drama play out from their perch on the treetops. Then everything went quiet.

Bill grabbed Tess roughly by the elbow. "Come on," he grunted. "We're leaving."

"But what if—"

"All the pilots I know are grounded on account of the weather—nobody's comin' out here till next week at the earliest. You saw the report." He avoided eye contact with me and Hux, perhaps to convince himself that we didn't exist and that our lives didn't matter.

"It'd be cleaner to just shoot them," she said.

"I'm not doin' that." I wasn't so sure how I felt about Bill's good character anymore, but his stand here gave me hope. Tess wanted to shoot us dead and leave the wolves to do the rest, ensuring that no one ever found any trace of us. With our satellite phones and the rest of our gear in the cargo pod, I couldn't message Ray or anyone else. No one would ever even know our exact location once Tess had wiped the phones. I knew she could do it too, judging by the technological marvel of her store and its business operations.

To leave us alive, though, was to give us a chance. I wonder if Bill understood this—or, if like most human beings, he believed that abandoning two people in the wilderness was somehow less

damning than shooting them. If we survived, the law would dis-
agree with him.

Seeing that she had no choice in the matter, Tess grasped the
stairway rails and climbed onboard the plane. Bill was getting
into the cockpit when Hux yelled, "At least call a chopper for
help, would you? Or give us a sat phone so we can do it." He met
Bill's gaze over Reynolds's body. "Come on, man. Please."

Bill hesitated for a moment as he processed the carnage. I
could see the conflict in the older man's eyes, the knowledge that
if he called Brinegar with our location, Hux and I would return
to Bettles armed with the evidence we needed to convict Tess of
murder.

And if he didn't, we would die.

Well, the average person would die. Without a map, compass, locator beacon, or other GPS device, we were worse than
average. We had Ollie, but other than that, we were completely
unprepared. We were also dressed for mild daytime temperatures, not a volatile arctic storm that was due to arrive in just a
few hours. We were miles off the grid, with no roads or trails to
guide us. Leaving us in a place as remote as this wasn't just cruel;
it was a death sentence.

In the end, Bill's loyalty to his family won out; he closed the
cockpit door behind him. Moments later the propellers kicked
into gear, humming and whirring. In the span of just a few minutes, the plane took off from Takahula Lake, and then it was
gone.

With one last blurry-eyed glance at the plane as it disappeared
into the clouds, I made my way over to Hux's side. Reynolds was
dead, having bled out on the land that had sustained him for the
last several years. He was not the first, nor would he be the last.

There was no time to mourn him. Hux and I had to get back
to civilization somehow, and our time was short. The weather
was about to go to hell.

We were on our own.

33

Hux LOOKED UP at the sky, his frown deepening as the clouds moved overhead.

"We need a plan," I said.

"At least we're out here on the river." He scooped up another handful of the fresh water and used it to flush out Ollie's eyes. He had taken a solid hit from the bear spray. "Someone could come by and see us."

"In this weather?"

He sighed. "I've got to admit this is new territory for me, Harland. Being out here without a map or a compass? It's not ideal."

"We've got our cell phones."

"Yeah, but I'm not really in the mood to take a selfie, are you?" His smile lacked its usual good humor, which scared me more than the encroaching storm or the vast miles of wilderness.

"Let's find shelter," I said, pointing to a felled spruce tree. "We'll hash out a plan there."

He nodded, understanding as well as I did that the priority was to stay warm and dry for as long as possible. We trudged across the gravel bar, the wind lashing our faces as we went. Ollie whimpered as he walked alongside us. The birds that had scattered earlier circled overhead.

Hux and I both knew that a spruce tree with its sparse, skinny branches wasn't going to get us through the night, but that was the dominant species out here. As temperatures dropped, the rain would turn to ice, and then to snow. The gusting wind would make things unbearable.

Our situation reminded me of those harrowing ten days in Australia, but back then, the biggest threats had been the heat and wildfire. Freezing to death seemed worse.

I had to remind myself that I'd been in ISB for a little over a year now, and in that time, I had learned a thing or two about how to survive in the wild. *First things first, make a plan, even if things look dire.* Especially *if things look dire.*

"At least we know where we are," I said.

Hux was quiet.

"You seem skeptical," I said.

He couldn't even meet my eyes. "We're in bad shape here, boss. Ollie took a wallop of that bear spray. I don't know how much tracking he'll be able to do."

A conversation between wolves echoed in the distance. Hux cupped the brim of his hat and wrenched it in his hands, one of his few nervous habits. I was scared too, but I hoped it didn't show. Without my gear, I didn't feel like a federal agent; I felt like an irresponsible day hiker.

By abandoning us in the wilderness, Bill and Tess had imposed on us the ultimate test. It was up to us to survive. The odds were against us, but we weren't dead. That meant we had a chance.

"Reynolds wasn't carrying a backpack," I said. "His campsite must be close by—maybe even in the same spot as before."

"He was good at covering his tracks, Harland. The wind and rain are going to hurt us."

"You don't think Ollie could pick up his scent? I've got Reynolds's glove right here to use as a scent article." I had picked it up in the hopes Ollie might be able to use it.

My devoted canine companion lifted his head at the sound of his name. His eyes were bloodshot and rheumy. I knew exactly how he felt and wished I could take his pain away.

"There's a lot of wind," Hux said. "These conditions aren't ideal."

I tilted my face toward the sky. The cloud cover made it impossible to use the sun as a navigational tool, which meant we were as blind as one could be without a map or GPS.

"Well, we know what direction he was coming from," I said. "Don't you think it's at least worth scoping it out?"

Hux said, "Sure, but if we go the wrong way . . ." He put his hands in his pockets and looked at the ground. I'd seen that look before. I had *lived* it.

"We can't just stay here," I said.

"Why not?" he countered. "We'll conserve energy. Keep warm. Hope for a stroke of luck from a passing plane." He attempted a smile. "Stranger things have happened."

I thought about Kevin, the last time I saw him in the Australian outback. In the early hours after my back injury, Kevin had argued for staying put and waiting for rescue. He knew I couldn't walk, and he didn't want to leave me alone in the wilderness. But as the days passed, his optimism started to wane, and so did his strength. By the time he set out, the odds were against him. I often wondered how far he got before he succumbed to the elements.

"Because that kind of thinking got my husband killed," I said.

He was quiet—solemn, even. "You're not giving me a choice here, are you?"

"No."

Hux never asked about those fateful ten days in the wilderness with Kevin, but I knew he more or less understood what I'd been through. One day, I might ask him about his time in the military, and he might ask me about losing my husband in Australia. But that day wasn't today. As dire as our situation was, I drew strength from it—because I knew what we were facing.

I pointed to a line of spruce trees that stood proudly on the ridge. "Reynolds came from there. Otherwise we would have seen him from further out."

Lightning flashed in the sky, illuminating the tapered tops of the trees. It was impossible to see much beyond their featureless shadows, but I could almost picture the endless miles of arctic wilderness that lay in wait for us. A good pace for hikers in this part of the park was six miles a day, and that was in perfect conditions. But we didn't even have a map, much less a destination. Even if we managed to cover six miles in the rain, we might end up somewhere even farther off the grid. There was some comfort in being close to the river.

As lightning streaked through the sky, I decided we had no choice. "I've been in this situation before, you know," I told him.

"I know." His voice was a tender whisper.

"It's going to end better this time." I cinched the hood of my windbreaker around my neck. "But I need you with me."

Hux's green eyes shone under the brim of his baseball cap. I gave myself permission to relish in them a little bit.

"I'm with you, Harland," he said. "You know that."

* * *

It was Ollie who picked up Reynolds's trail despite the driving rain and his compromised state. For tracking purposes, rain was actually a good thing, as the moisture gave scents something to cling to. Wind, however, was a different story. I was skeptical that Ollie would be able to take us all the way to Reynolds's campsite, but he had surprised me before. For the next hour, as Ollie marched on with his nose to the ground, spirits were higher than they'd been at the start.

It didn't last.

We were going at a good pace when Hux, who had been walking a half step behind me, went down with a grunt. It surprised me, seeing him lose his footing like that. He was a big guy with a lot of mass, and he landed hard. I thought for sure he'd broken something.

"Dammit," he said. "I stepped in a hole."

"It's about time—I was starting to think you weren't human." I loaned him my arm. "Are you okay?"

He muttered something under his breath as he hopped up— or at least pretended to hop up. I could see he was favoring one leg. "I twisted an ankle," he said as he bent down to loosen his laces. "No big deal."

I peered at the hole Hux had fallen into. It was deep and round, the perfect home for an arctic ground squirrel. I had stepped in my fair share of them, but being as short as I was, the forces of gravity had spared me for the most part.

"It's a pretty deep hole," I said. "Are you sure your leg isn't broken?"

"Nah." His voice was firm. "Let's keep going."

I didn't question him. After all, I'd given him the same response countless times. If he said he was good, I wasn't going to push him on it.

After forty more minutes hiking in the rain, we came on a stream, which in the driving downpour looked like a raging river. Ollie started barking. He had finally lost the trail.

Hux limped over to a rock and sat down. I could tell he wanted to take off his boot and inspect the damage, but his impulse not to worry me won out.

"Reynolds must have been walking in the stream bed," he said, doing his best to sound jovial. "The question is, which direction."

Ollie searched in every direction while Hux and I looked for footprints. Despite our best efforts, we all came up empty.

I stole a glance at Hux's bum ankle. His pant leg was covering the top of his hiking boot, which meant I couldn't see the damage. I had a feeling it was bad. It wasn't like Hux to sit down for longer than a minute at a time.

"Maybe we should try and find shelter," I said.

Hux sighed. "Just for a little bit."

Anything would do—a tree, a rock, a cabin. The terrain in this part of the wilderness was practically arctic desert, hardly any topography to it at all. It made for fast travel but abysmal shelter. The rain and fog were added challenges. Soon, it would be impossible to see more than a few feet in front of us. As for someone spotting us from above, I had long since given up on that possibility; no bush plane or helicopter would risk flying in these conditions.

Reality was setting in fast. Suddenly I found myself questioning my bravado—questioning everything, really. Kevin had set out that day feeling confident in his abilities to get help.

"I bet we're only a mile or two from the road," he'd said. *"If the weather holds, I can get there in an hour."* Instead, he'd simply disappeared. Not a day went by that I didn't wonder what had happened to him.

It was the wondering that was the worst part. Had he gotten lost? Injured? What were his final moments like? If I didn't make it out of this, my family would suffer the same fate—that awful, relentless not knowing. Hux's family too. Even though *he* was the Navy SEAL, his loved ones would blame me for making irresponsible choices. No one was above Mother Nature. In the end, she always won.

Preparation was a powerful defense, though. Reynolds had operated a thriving campsite for at least six summers out here, which counted for something. He hadn't just survived, but thrived. I tried to think like him—where he would have camped, which direction he would have gone. Alaska was rife with streams, but this was the first one I'd seen since leaving the river. My best guess was that Reynolds's campsite was next to it, giving him easy access to water.

But which direction?

I rubbed the scruff behind Ollie's ears. I was used to being wrong—hell, I'd been wrong so many times throughout my life that it felt like an act of God every time I was right. Hux was different. The military had trained him to be right all the time. But in my line of work, there was always some room for error—a lot of it, some seasoned investigators would say. In certain situations, I wasn't afraid to be wrong. Failure was part of the process.

I thought back to the coordinates that mapped to Reynolds's various locations. Hux and I had taken the time to mark them on our topo maps to get a feel for his preferences in backcountry camping. I recalled that those three campsites had several things in common: adjacent to a stream or lake, on flat ground, and embedded in some kind of tree cover.

There were trees everywhere at our current juncture, so that didn't help, but the area upstream had something the downstream direction did not: a view. A couple dozen feet upstream, the earth sloped upward toward a narrow ridge that would have offered a clear view to the east and west—important daylight cues in Alaska, given how short the days were in the winter. Reynolds had been a survivalist and a fanatic, but he was also an entrepreneur. He would have wanted his clients to admire and indulge in the setting he'd chosen for them.

"This way," I said, pointing upstream. Hux was bent over, inspecting something in the shallows. He poked at it with a stick.

"Did you find something?" I asked.

He picked up what looked like a bear claw. "Nah," he said. "Just this."

He dried his hands on his pants before dropping the claw in his pocket. Hux's uncharacteristic inwardness was unnerving me. He was usually gregarious, no holds barred, always with a let's-do-this attitude. But every time he looked up at the sky, it seemed to trouble him, putting him into a state of mind I had never seen in him before.

"Hux?"

He met my gaze over the roiling rush of the stream. The rain was coming down hard. At this point, we didn't have time to build a shelter. It was too damp for a fire, which meant our best hope for warmth was to huddle together all night. Even then, it probably wouldn't be enough.

"We're going this way," I said. "Come on."

We stayed close to the stream because it was the most direct route. A sobering truth had crept into my consciousness—that if we didn't find Reynolds's campsite within the hour, we were going to die of hypothermia. In another life, at another time, I would have let panic take over—dulling my instincts, threatening to consume me. It would have won.

Not this time.

Hux was limp-hopping over the rough terrain, but he never complained. I kept my eyes on the tree line, desperate to see something—a tent hidden in the trees, the charred remains of a campfire. Even Ollie looked defeated. He plodded through the water at a snail's pace.

My teeth were chattering. The cold hadn't had a chance to settle in my bones yet, but it was getting there. As soon as we stopped, the raw chill would take over—with a vengeance. Hypothermia would kill us quickly if we didn't stay dry.

Twice, Hux yelled out at me to stop. And both times, I pretended not to hear him. His voice sounded like defeat. "We've got to stop, Harland," he yelled, his voice barely rising over the roar of the flooded stream. "We have to find shelter *now*."

I turned around to face him. "If we stop, we'll die."

He couldn't seem to find a response to that, so he didn't say anything at all. He was soaked to the bone, just like me. His baseball cap did little to hide the fear in his eyes.

"You work on finding shelter, then," I said. "I'm going to look a little farther upstream."

"No way," he said. "I'm going where you go. I just think you're nuts."

I planted one foot between two rocks in the stream, but the water was deeper than I had anticipated. I plunged into the water, my feet flying up behind me. I went in neck-deep.

"Harland!" Hux's voice was pleading. Even Ollie looked like he wanted to stop.

But I got myself up again and kept going—one foot in front of the other. Kevin's final words drifted back to me: *"I'll see you soon."* Even then, I'd known it was a lie. But had *he* known? I supposed he didn't. He wouldn't have left if he thought we were both going to die.

This isn't the end, I told myself. *Reynolds wouldn't have camped far from this stream. Keep your eyes open. Look for high ground.*

We had come to the ridge I'd seen a couple hundred yards back, but to my dismay, there was nothing on it—no tent, no campfire. I squinted into the driving rain and willed a tent to be there. But the storm's gloom seemed to mock me.

In my mind, there was only one other possibility—that Reynolds's tent was on the other side of the ridge, beyond the view of the stream. For his purposes, it made sense. He would have wanted to be close to the water, but not too close. I started walking in that direction—east, was my best guess, but at this point, I honestly had no idea.

"Where are you going?" Hux asked.

"Up on that ridge there," I said, pointing.

"Did you see something?"

"No," I said. "It's just a feeling." I turned and looked back at him, the invincible Hux wincing every time he put weight on his bad ankle.

"Okay," he said wearily. "Let's go then."

With Ollie at our heels, we climbed up onto swollen marsh-land. The rain was coming down sideways, whipping against our bodies as we held up our arms to block the assault. Hux's lips were purple. I couldn't feel my hands. But I told myself that Reynolds's tent had to be there, and that if it wasn't, I'd accept our fate as an ironic act of divine intervention. I wasn't a religious person, but I appreciated the stranger mysteries of life. I knew for a fact that the millions of tiny decisions I'd made in my life had brought me to this moment, which was either going to end very soon or lead me somewhere entirely new.

Driven by pure adrenaline, I crested the ridge. I didn't trust my eyes at first. I thought maybe the bear spray had damaged my vision beyond repair, and now I was seeing things that weren't there.

But I knew Hux's eyes were just fine. When he called out, "There!" I knew I wasn't imagining it.

It was a green tent, nestled in the shadows of the spruce.

34

THE TENT WAS empty, but Reynolds had left behind a stash of invaluable items: two satellite phones, a Mountain Hardware Phantom sleeping bag rated to minus forty degrees, several changes of clothes, and a decent amount of foodstuffs. We knew the campsite was his because his name was on the sleeping bag.

The tent had taken a beating from the rain, but Reynolds had erected his own shelter from spruce branches and brush, which meant the interior was dry. After I had performed a perfunctory safety check of the scene, we climbed in together—me first, at Hux's insistence, because the guy just couldn't let go of the chivalry thing.

Reynolds's personal tent was smaller than the ones he'd used for the couples at his campsite, and I was acutely aware of the tight squeeze. I kept bumping into Hux's back as we stripped off our wet clothes and changed into something dry. Hux's new pants barely reached past his calves, while I felt like a little girl playing dress-up with my dad's oversized flannel. But the clothes were dry, and that was all that mattered.

"You take the sleeping bag," Hux said.

I shook my head. "You're at higher risk for hypothermia," I said.

"According to who?"

"Um, a dozen peer-reviewed scientific studies . . ."

"Not according to the US Army data."

I rolled my eyes. "Are we seriously about to get into the weeds on hypothermia outcomes for men versus women right now? Just take the sleeping bag. Your lips are blue, and your ankle's probably broken." I pulled on another pair of socks. "Plus, I'm the one who got us into this mess, so it's only fair that you should enjoy our plush accommodations."

"Nah," he said good-naturedly. "You're the one who found the tent. That's all that matters in my book." He passed me Reynolds's satellite phone. *Please work,* I thought. My prayers were answered: it powered on. It still had a good amount of battery left.

I caught Hux's gaze in the yellow glow of the tent's interior, lit by Reynolds's lantern. The rain was still coming down hard, but the spruce's branches mitigated the assault.

I dialed the number for the Bettles Ranger Station. If Brinegar didn't answer, my next call would be to 911, which would activate a chain of communication ending with a MedEvacs. It was something I'd learned at my first day of ISB orientation.

Thankfully, Brinegar did answer. He sounded hugely relieved to hear my voice. "Please tell me you aren't still up there," he said. "The weather's gone to hell."

"We are," I said. "We need a ride out of here ASAP."

"No can do till tomorrow at the earliest," he said. "All air transport is grounded. I couldn't even get a MedEvac up there right now."

I wasn't surprised to hear this. It's what I expected—and in some ways, I was glad Brinegar was taking a hard line on safety. I didn't want anyone else risking their lives to come get us. I wasn't worried about dying anymore. Sharing this tiny tent with Hux was going to be awkward, but awkwardness wasn't lethal.

"I'll get things in motion for tomorrow at first light," Brinegar said. "Did you send me your coordinates?"

"Just did," I said.

There was a pause.

"Are you sure these are correct?" he asked. He read them off to me to confirm.

I cross-checked my GPS with Reynolds's topo map. "Yes, why?"

"You're way off the grid there, Agent Harland," Brinegar said. "Hardly any bush planes fly out that way. Who took you there?"

"That's a long story," I said. "But I'd go ahead and get in touch with the Alaska state troopers. We're going to need their help building a case against Bill and Tess Flint."

Brinegar's silence seemed to stretch on for an eternity, until it was punctuated by a loud exhale. "*Who* again?"

"The Flints. I'll explain when we're back in Bettles."

"There might not be time," he said. "I saw them loading up their Jeep just a little while ago—I could tell something was up but figured that's their business."

"Tess Flint confessed to poisoning Tim and Kelsey Greer. I don't have all the details yet, but she may be a flight risk."

"And Bill? He's involved too?"

I started to say, *He left us here*, but something in me held back. My mental image of their six-year-old son, maybe. Margo's experience with broken families. I just couldn't do it.

"We really just need to focus on locating Tess," I said.

"What about Reynolds? Do we need to mobilize any resources for him?"

"No," I said. "Reynolds is dead."

Brinegar swore under his breath. "Dead? What the hell happened up there, Agent Harland?"

"I'll give you the full report when we get back to Bettles," I said. "I appreciate all your help."

After I'd hung up with Brinegar and sent Ray another update, I gave myself permission to give in to my own exhaustion. Hux laid out Reynolds's sleeping bag, which looked as inviting as any bed I had ever dozed in, despite the nature of the person who had owned it. Hell, it was better than the pillow-top king at the Cabins.

There was one small problem: Hux. I couldn't do that to him.

"We can both fit," I said, avoiding his gaze. "Just get in."

He swatted at what appeared to be a pretend bug on his hand. "Look, um, I can see you're uncomfortable—"

"Of course I'm uncomfortable. I have sleeping-bag-restless-leg syndrome—just warning you." I wasn't sure if he got the joke—not that it was even a joke, not really—but the tentative smile on his face told me he had.

"What the hell is that?"

"I get restless legs in sleeping bags. Sorry."

I pulled the zipper three-quarters of the way down and climbed in, hoping my weak attempt at humor would be enough to make things less awkward. The real problem, though, was that Hux Huxley, for all his modest and chivalrous tendencies, was a very good-looking human being. Hell, he'd just about hit the genetic lottery—the face, the body, the build. He had it all going for him. And I was nervous about sharing a very tight space with someone I was attracted to.

My only consolation was how little effort I put into my appearance out on the trail, which I hoped reinforced the fact that ours was a strictly professional relationship. I spent most hours of the day sweating through my clothes and combing knots out of my hair with my fingers. Sharing a sleeping bag for one frigid night wasn't going to change any of that. Tomorrow, it would be back to business as usual.

"Let's just do this," I said. "I'm your superior. I'm not going to say it again."

He finally relented, scooting sideways as he carefully situated himself next to me in the sleeping bag. His clothes didn't smell like him, but every other part of him did, and I held my breath so he wouldn't know how much I liked it.

He bent forward, grabbed the zipper, and yanked it all the way up. Our shoulders and sides and hips were touching—separated only by Reynolds's thin wool base layers, which did little to blunt the power of Hux's body heat. I supposed that was a good thing. It would make hypothermia a lot less likely, especially with Ollie lying next to us.

Hux took a breath—audible, a little shaky. I did the same. Was he nervous? I couldn't tell. I hoped not. *Should I say something?* I thought. *Or just stay quiet? Is he trying to think of something to say? Was this a terrible idea?*

Before I could spiral into a hundred impossible questions about my relationship with Hux, I heard the satellite phone chime with a new message.

I rolled over to grab it.

"Who is it?" Hux asked.

"Brinegar." I had to squint to read the message. "He drove by the store. There's no sign of Tess and Bill."

"Did he try their house?"

"He's on his way there."

He stared at the top of the tent, as the soothing patter of rain filled the silence. "You know, Cody told me that Tess and Bill were from the same small town in North Dakota. For years, she ran a preschool down in Anchorage. He was a third-grade teacher." He shifted his body a bit, his leg bumping against my knee. He mumbled an apology. "Anyway," he said. "I guess at the time, I wondered why they'd give up a nice life like that for this place. Now I know."

"So what's your final verdict on Reynolds?" I asked.

"I think he had an objective of sorts," he said. "To him, it was business. He wanted to help people, but he also had his business to run—kind of like Tess. The problem was, for her, it was personal. I mean, she had a kid with the guy." Hux turned his head a bit, catching my gaze out of the corner of his eye. "Bill made a bad decision during the worst five minutes of his life. I'm not sure we should punish his kid for that. Hell, I've probably done worse."

"No, you haven't."

The quiet rhythm of his breathing filled the silence. "I was a different person before we met," he said. "I saw things, did things—I can't take them all back, but I can move through the world with a little less judgment." He reached out and ruffled Ollie's damp fur. "God knows I've orphaned kids whose fathers were terrorists and criminals. And maybe it's justified, maybe it's not. But I'm not in that line of work anymore."

Something told me that after a night with Hux, he'd convince me that family was more important than holding flawed human beings accountable for their mistakes. Maybe he was right. Maybe Bill deserved a pass on this one. He loved his son, and wasn't that enough? Wasn't that all Reynolds had been trying to accomplish with his cult in the Alaskan wilderness?

"Harland?"

"Yeah?"

"When is the sleeping-bag-induced, restless-leg disease going to start?"

I laughed. "Any minute now."

"Just so you know, I have a spontaneous bleeding disorder that could get really messy if you kick me all night."

I rolled onto my side to face him, realizing too late that this was the kind of thing you did in bed with a romantic partner, not a professional one. But I couldn't exactly go back to the way we'd been without it being painfully awkward. So I just went with it—my head resting on one hand, my arm propped up by my elbow.

"Seriously?" I asked.

"Nah," he said, laughing. "I think you would've known by now if I had a spontaneous bleeding disorder."

"Well, it's hard to know with you. How's your ankle, by the way?"

"Eh, it feels like a bad sprain. I'll survive."

He looked into my eyes, startling me with the intensity of his gaze. I shivered—not from the cold, but from something else.

My sat phone chimed with a message, ruining the moment.

"Who is it?" Hux asked.

"It's Ray. He said the weather's looking good for the next hour or two, and he found us a chopper." I smiled, but a part of me was strangely sad—like I'd missed an opportunity that probably wasn't ever going to come around again. "Looks like we're getting out of here."

35

Back at the Bettles airstrip, Brinegar was waiting for us in his official NPS vehicle. Emily was in the front seat, watching me and Hux disembark the helicopter. Her face was stoic, her dark eyes reflecting a quiet internal resolve.

"I told her about what happened," Brinegar said. "But she wanted to hear it from you."

I nodded. This was part of the job—a necessary part. These were the moments that fueled my pursuit of justice, even when things seemed hopeless. I was anxious to track down Tess and Bill, but I also knew that Emily deserved to hear how her uncle had died. After all, she had supported our investigation at every step of the way.

Hux and I sat in the vehicle with her and told her what had happened, while Brinegar stood outside in the wind and rain. She didn't ask any questions. For the most part, she just kind of looked off into the distance, at a wilderness that must have felt like home to her.

"I'm very sorry, Emily," I said. "We're going to do everything we can to track down Tess and Bill."

"They're not at the store," she said. "We just drove by there. They're gone."

"All the planes are grounded. They can't go far."

"They could float the river. Or you could take the Dalton Highway down to the Yukon and float it from there." She shook her head. "There are so many ways to disappear."

"We're not inclined to let that happen," Hux said. "You have our word on that."

"Tess is smart." Emily looked down at her hands, which were tanned from the sun. "She knows the area better than anyone."

"But you know it too," I said. "So what would you do? Where would you go?"

She was quiet as she looked out at the fog as it settled on the flatlands surrounding the airstrip. I recognized Bill's Cessna in the hangar along with two other smaller planes. The only reason they'd risked coming back here was to collect their son, but would they take the chance of flying out again? Bettles didn't have a robust police force, and no one was going to be guarding that hangar until word got out that two federal agents had disappeared in the wilderness. For now, Brinegar and Emily were the only two people in Bettles who knew we were alive. I intended to keep it that way until we located Tess and Bill.

"Emily?"

"They've got their boy with them," she said. "I wouldn't go anywhere at all. I'd wait till it was safe to fly out of here." Her expression changed, like a new thought had suddenly occurred to her. "Tess and Bill own some land on the Koyukuk, not far from the store. There's an old hunting cabin down there somewhere. I saw it once when my uncle and I were floating the river, but it's not right on the water. It's in the woods a ways."

Hux and I exchanged a glance.

"Where?"

* * *

We drove to Bettles Outfitters first, but just as Emily had said, the store was shuttered. The small house behind the store was dark too, no lights on inside despite the gloomy weather. There was no sign of Tess's all-terrain orange Jeep.

Dirt roads were better than asphalt when it came to tracking vehicles, but all the tire treads led to the main road. We canvassed it for a couple miles in each direction, searching for dirt roads that led into the woods, or some lucky glimpse of Tess's orange Jeep.

Nothing.

"You said their land is south of here?" I asked Emily.

She nodded. "But I only saw that cabin once, and it was a few summers ago now. I don't know if it's even there anymore."

I turned to Hux. "I'll get out and have a look."

He made a move to join me before I could even open the door. "I'm coming with you," he said.

"No chance." I glanced at the bag of ice duct-taped to his ankle. "You're staying here."

"Not if you plan on paddling the river." Hux pointed at the surging waters of the Koyukuk, swollen from the recent rains. "You'll need a captain."

"Fine," I huffed.

The door to the structure housing the outfitter's watercraft was slightly ajar thanks to the wind. I went inside with Brinegar and Emily and picked out a suitable two-person canoe, based on their recommendation. Together, we carried it to the take-out in the river. The air was raw and wet, the mosquitoes out in full force.

"You won't last long out in this," Brinegar said.

"We won't push it," I said, catching a glimpse of Hux as he extricated himself from Brinegar's vehicle. He hopped on one foot down to the river, Ollie trailing close behind him. "But I think Emily's right—chances are they're close by. They won't be expecting a full-scale search at this point, as long as they think we're missing."

Brinegar and Emily helped us load the last of our gear into the canoe. Ollie bounded in.

"All right," Brinegar said. "Good luck."

Hux tipped his hat to the older man. "Thanks, Chief."

We pushed off with our paddles, but the river did the rest—absorbing our little vessel into its cold, rushing waters. I wasn't the most seaworthy person in the world, but Hux was Navy-bred, which meant he could handle just about anything of a marine nature.

I tried to enjoy the scenery a little bit, but all I could think about was Tim and Kelsey Greer, whose families might never get justice if we couldn't track down Tess and Bill Flint. After all, Reynolds was dead, Vince and Yiyin weren't talking, and Ana and Diego were fugitives. Ray had informed me that the Fairbanks FBI had no clue how to track them down and that we'd probably have to help them out at some point. Secretly, I relished that opportunity. I was still smarting from the way Calvin James had treated me out in the field.

Hux seemed to share this sentiment. He was in his "tracking zone," using his map and compass and his knowledge of the terrain to make an educated guess about where to go and what to look for. While I paddled the canoe, he scanned the forest for signs of human inhabitation.

Hours passed. The wind picked up, making it harder to stay the course on the river. Despite my best efforts to keep my base layers dry, everything touching my body was wet with sweat. Hux noticed my teeth chattering. "Maybe we should call it," he said. "We can lay low and wait for them to go back to the hangar to get Bill's plane."

"We can't lay that low," I said. "Everybody's got a radio up here. I bet they already know we're alive and looking for them."

"Could be," he said. "But that doesn't change the fact that we're in real danger of freezing our asses out here."

I was running out of rebuttals when I spotted something in the woods—a flash of color enmeshed in the browns and greens. It wasn't orange, but gray—*a tent*? "Hold up," I said to Hux. "Pull over here."

"You see something?"

"Maybe."

He paddled into the shallows, and with Hux on one foot and me on both of mine, we lifted the canoe onto the gravel bar. My heart was ramming in my chest, alerting me to a new danger. As we stepped up onto the riverbank, I could see clearly now that the gray color belonged to a tent—a twofer. On the door flap was a familiar logo:

"Bettles Outfitters."

Hux had seen it too. "What's our move here, boss?" he asked, his voice whisper-soft.

I took a breath to settle my nerves. "We go in together—calmly, no sudden movements. We have to assume their son is with them." I suddenly remembered his bum ankle, which still had the ice pack duct-taped to it. "Are you sure you can do this?"

He nodded. "I'm good. You take the lead—I'll back you up."

"Keep your weapon handy."

We approached the tree line, an imposing row of spruce trees that seemed to guard the river. I knew Bill would be armed and that the stakes were high for both of them. I couldn't help but think about Reynolds's sniper rifles too. It was possible that someone was watching us right now, all but ready to take us out.

I gave the nod to Hux to announce our presence but to leave out our names for the time being. I wanted them to know we were here, but not to know who we were.

"Hello!" he called out. "Park Service here. If you're in there, please come out!"

We waited.

Nothing.

"Come on out! Or we're moving in!"

There was movement in the tent, a person getting into position. Voices.

A child.

Hux and I exchanged a glance as we stood there, stiff-armed and ready to pounce, our nerves humming. "We don't want anyone to get hurt," Hux said. "Just come on out."

This time, the tent flap fluttered open, an ominous sound that didn't seem to belong in this natural, wild place. I watched Bill climb out of the tent first, followed by his son, Sean. Bill was holding the boy's hand.

"Place both of your hands on your head, please," Hux said to Bill. "Sean, you're good, buddy. Just come on over here with your dad."

To my surprise, Bill looked distraught—dark circles around his eyes, his hair all askew. Even his flannel jacket looked dirty and unkempt. He kept looking at his son, nudging him along with a gentle hand. Sean was sniffling.

When they got to where we were standing, Hux searched Bill for any weapons on his person and found none. "He's clear," Hux said.

I turned to Bill and said, "Where's Tess?"

"Inside," he said. "Please don't hurt her."

"We're not here to hurt anyone."

"She's Sean's mother."

I moderated my voice without conceding any authority. "I know that."

Bill stepped up to me and said, "Can you go talk to her? Just you? She might listen to you." His shoulders sagged. "I know we put you in danger. I know . . . you must think we're terrible people. I just didn't want Sean to grow up without a mom."

I didn't bother telling him it was too late for that—Tess was directly involved in the deaths of three people, after all, but if he and Tess were cooperative, it would end better for all of them.

"Okay," I said. "I'll go alone, then."

"Hold up a sec," Hux said. "I don't know how I feel about this."

"I'm not going inside," I said. "I'll just go and see if she'll talk to me."

Hux frowned, clearly dissatisfied with this approach, but I felt like this was our best chance at a peaceful resolution. After all, Tess was alone now. She was without her husband, without her son. She had already lost. My sister Margo liked to say that the stakes mattered in these situations; when the accused had nothing to lose, they were more likely to talk.

I walked in the direction of the tent, stopping about ten feet from the Bettles Outfitter logo. The zipper to the door flap was back up again.

"Tess, it's me—Felicity Harland." I kept my voice conversational, hoping it might draw her out. My intention was to sound more like a friend and less like a cop.

She didn't answer.

"Bill and Sean are with Hux. They both want to go home."

Silence.

"Bill wants this to be over, Tess. He was there; he's sorry for what happened. He wants to cooperate." I kept my focus on the tent, trying to detect any movement from the inside. "He's thinking of your son, Tess. I know you want what's best for Sean."

The wind blew, rustling the leaves overhead. A bald eagle soared across the gray skies above, a spectacular display of solitude and strength. It reminded me of where we were—far from home, far from anything. Nature was our witness here.

As I glimpsed the eagle fly over the river and disappear behind the trees, the canvas rustled a bit. Tess was moving. I lifted my Glock into position—arms locked, finger on the trigger.

I heard Bill say something to Hux—"Please, just let me go in there—please!"

Hux's voice was loud, forceful. "Stay back, Bill. Just stay where you are."

"You don't understand—" He sounded frantic.

I remembered the look on Tess's face during her confrontation with Reynolds—the chaotic storm of anger, regret, and betrayal. She was a hard woman, with a curdled edge to her rage. But with her son, those hard edges softened into tenderness and affection. The love she had for Sean had none of that obsessive toxicity.

It was about loss.

I holstered my gun and stepped forward. The zipper was gone, somehow, which made it impossible to access the tent the way it had been designed.

My heart in my throat, I took out my knife and cut it open. The fabric made a loud ripping sound as it tore open. I knew that if Tess was armed and intended to shoot me, she could. I was as vulnerable as a person could be in this situation.

But Tess had been vulnerable too, once. Years ago, when she'd gone to Reynolds for help—the same way *all* these women had been when they ventured into the wilderness in search of something greater than themselves. I couldn't relate to that desire, but I understood what it meant to put it all on the line to get something you wanted.

I tore open the hole in the tent and peered inside. Tess was lying on her side on her sleeping bag, one hand up by her chest, clutching a mug with a white residue lining the rim.

Baneberries.

"Tess." I bent down and shook her by the shoulder. "Tess."

She inhaled—a deep, ragged breath. Her eyes fluttered open. She stared straight ahead, directly into the jagged hole I'd made with my knife. She would have had an unobstructed view of the river, of the trees well beyond it, of the vast expanse of this unforgiving place.

I already had my sat phone out to call for a MedEvac. At this latitude, it could take an hour, or three or four. I didn't know how much time we had to reverse the damage she'd done, but I had faith in the rescue personnel up here. If she survived this, I intended to hear her side of the story—if not today, then some other day. The Greers deserved it, and so did Emily. But there was Sean to think about too.

"I love my son." Her voice was a dry whisper in her throat. "Everything I've ever done—I did for him."

"I know," I said.

"No, you don't." She turned her head slightly to face me head-on. Her skin was ashen. "You *can't* know."

36

Two months later

IT WAS OCTOBER, and my assignment in Denali was officially over, the culmination of six hard months in Alaska's spectacular wilderness. I was ready to get back to the lower forty-eight—Seattle first, to see my sister Margo; and then Reno to clear out my apartment before my lease was up. I hadn't been there in months, and the thought of going back there filled me with dread.

My next assignment was up in the air, but I knew for a fact that I never wanted to spend another night in that apartment. It wasn't home. It wasn't anything, really. I needed something more permanent, something that felt like mine.

Hux, of course, had his cabin in Sequoia. Even though we hadn't actually talked about it, I knew he intended to spend at least a few weeks there before our next assignment came through. I envied him for that, but I didn't dare say so—especially since he was still seeing that archaeologist from Anchorage. I got the feeling they were getting serious.

I was packing up the last of my things in the Anchorage field office when Hux walked in carrying a box of notebooks and photos. He had, in fact, managed to break his ankle during our escapade in the Gates, which had relegated him to a desk for eight weeks. But he was better now, hardly a hitch in his stride. He liked to joke that if rehabbing from an injury were an Olympic event, I'd win gold and he'd take the silver. Neither one of us liked to sit around and feel sorry for ourselves for more than a hot minute.

Hux put the box on the table. The big red letters on its side gave a good clue to its contents: "GOTA/Greer." I had updated it periodically over the last few months, adding layers to it as Tess Flint recovered and provided her account of events. In the end, she took the blame for everything—including abandoning us in the wilderness. Hux and I had decided not to pursue any charges against Bill, which was what Tess wanted. After all, he'd had nothing to do with the Greers' death or my attack outside the campsite. The agreement Hux and I came to with him was a personal one.

"I gotta say, I'm glad Tess took the manslaughter deal," Hux said. "It would've been a painful trial for her kid to sit through."

"Well, she was true to her word—about putting Sean first, I mean."

"It's a shame, though, for their family. I feel for them."

"There were a lot of victims in this case, Hux. But at least we got justice for the Greers and their families. I'm not saying it's a happy ending, but that's how it goes sometimes."

Hux's sat phone chimed with a message.

"You're popular these days," I remarked.

"It's Emily and her mountaineering crew," he said. "They want to have another go at tracking down Ana and Diego before winter rolls in."

"They think they're still out there?"

He nodded. "There was a sighting up near Boreal Mountain just a couple days ago of a man and a woman who fit their description."

"You don't think they're dead? It's been months now."

He shrugged. "Hard to know. It could be they got injured and that slowed them down. Maybe they're in no huge hurry to get to Canada." Hux sat down at the table across from me. "That's the thing about people—they're unpredictable."

"No argument there."

I was having a hard time meeting his eyes for some reason—something about the awkwardness of a goodbye, maybe. I didn't want to tell him that I was giving up my apartment in Reno, because then he'd offer me his cabin in Sequoia out of some combination of guilt and obligation. I knew Hux; he was always trying to help me out. This time, though, I didn't need his help. I needed my own thing. I already had my eye on a couple cabins in California and Nevada, not like my budget could afford them. But it was nice to dream.

"Where do you think we'll land next?" he asked.

"No idea." I took the massive box in his arms and stacked it on top of the others with a grunt. "Anyway, it's late. I'm gonna head back to the hotel—I've got an early morning."

"I can't believe you're driving all the way down to Seattle, boss. Are you sure you don't want company?"

"Nah," I said. "Don't you have plans this weekend anyway?"

He shrugged. "I guess. But I could cancel 'em."

"Don't," I admonished him. "You'll be hearing from me and Ray soon enough. Enjoy the break—you've earned it."

"Putting up with you, you mean?"

I cracked a smile. "You always knew that was going to be part of the deal."

"The very worst part of the deal." He grinned.

"Yes, the kind of deal that permanently affects your mental health and takes years to recover from." I grabbed my jacket off the door. "That is, if you ever recover."

"Maybe I shouldn't have taken this job."

"Maybe you shouldn't have." I was teasing him, but I wondered if he could hear the kernel of truth in it, too—the opening I'd just given him into a deeper, more revealing conversation.

He didn't take it. In his usual chivalrous fashion, Hux opened the door for me and escorted me out.

"Have a good night, Harland," he said.

"You too."

* * *

That night, in the cold comfort of my Hampton Inn, sleep called to me. Ollie was by my side, the window cracked open so I could hear the goings-on of the great outdoors. I went to bed thinking about my first wilderness trip with Kevin—a two-day excursion to Acadia National Park in Maine. Our tent back then was a cheap rental, our campsite a miserable spit of sandy dirt next to a bunch of RVs and a parking lot. It smelled like fish and exhaust.

But those memories faded into something else as sleep came over me, and I dreamed of sequoia trees and California sunshine—

And saw a man—a friend, a lover, maybe a stranger; I couldn't see his face. He was standing with his back turned, oblivious to my presence. Bright sunlight spilled through the trees, and it was warm, the air infused with summer.

Whoever the man was, he stirred in me a deep longing—for friendship, for companionship, for love. As he started to turn around, I heard his voice inside my soul. Had he spoken? I couldn't tell.

Look at me, I told him. *I'm here.*

A gust of wind rustled the trees, blowing a wayward strand of hair across my face. I didn't know where we were—the river, the mountains; they were features of a generic landscape—but I supposed it didn't matter.

When the man turned around, I finally saw his face, and I understood what those feelings were. Every part of me understood.

I wasn't wandering anymore.

I was home.

ACKNOWLEDGMENTS

MY HEARTFELT THANKS to everyone who made this book come together, especially my agent, Beth Miller, and the team at Crooked Lane. Writing a second book in a series was a new endeavor for me, and as fun as it was to venture back into the world of these characters, I couldn't have done so without the support of these thoughtful and talented people.

I'd also like to acknowledge my dad, who can always be counted on for his honest opinion; and Fletcher, my husband, who helps me find the time, space, and confidence to write.